DEVON LIBRARI

Please return/renew this item
Renew on tel. 0345 155
www.devon.gov.uk/li

GW00788560

WITHDRAWN
FROM
DEVON LIBRARY SERVICES

D5656561815086

CHILDREN OF THE SUN

CHILDREN OF THE SUN

The Fall of the Aztecs

Elizabeth Manson Bahr

Book Guild Publishing

Sussex, England

First published in Great Britain in 2009 by
The Book Guild Ltd
Pavilion View
19 New Road
Brighton, BN1 1UF

Copyright © Elizabeth Manson Bahr 2009

The right of Elizabeth Manson Bahr to be identified as the author of
this work has been asserted by her in accordance with the
Copyright, Designs and Patents Act 1988.

All rights reserved. No part of this publication may be reproduced, transmitted,
or stored in a retrieval system, in any form or by any means, without permission
in writing from the publisher, nor be otherwise circulated in any form of binding
or cover other than that in which it is published and without a similar condition
being imposed on the subsequent purchaser.

While some of the characters in this book were real people,
this is a work of fiction.

Typeset in Garamond by
Ellipsis Books Limited, Glasgow

Printed in Great Britain by
CPI Antony Rowe

A catalogue record for this book is available from
The British Library.

ISBN 978 1 84624 310 3

DAWLISH

0 1 NOV 2018

For Terry, who has lived with the Aztecs for so long, and without whose encouragement I would never have finished this journey.

Contents

Acknowledgments

The map on page ix is taken from *The Broken Spears* by Miguel Léon-Portilla © 1962, 1990 by Miguel Léon-Portilla. Expanded and updated Edition © 1992 by Miguel Léon-Portilla. Reprinted by permission of Beacon Press, Boston

The poems, songs and prayers quoted in this novel are taken from the following sources:

In the Language of Kings – An Anthology of Mesoamerican Literature – Pre-Columbian to the Present, Miguel Léon-Portilla and Earl Shorris W.M. Norton, New York 2001

Everyday Life of the Aztecs, Warwick Bray, B.T. Batsford 1968

Daily Life of the Aztecs, Jacques Soustelle, Stanford University Press, 1961

Pre-Columbian Mexico-tenochtitlan

Map of the island city of Tenochtitlan
Taken from *Broken Spears* edited by Miguel Léon-Portilla, published by Beacon Press.

● Otumba

● Teotihuacan

LAKE OF TEXCOCO

● Texcoco

Tacuba ●

● Tepeyac

● Tlatelolco

● Tenochtitlan

Chapultepec

∧ Mt Tlaloc

Tepepolco

Coyoacan ●

Iztapalapa

Xochimilco ⊙

● Chalco

The Valley and Lakes of Mexico in 1519

0   5   10
miles

Iztaccihuatl
Volcano

Popocatepetl
Volcano

x

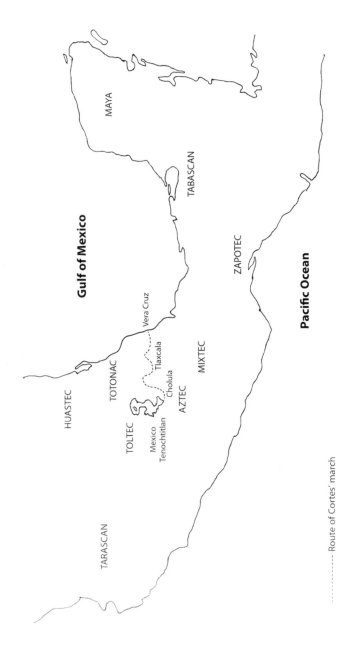

Gulf of Mexico

MAYA

TABASCAN

ZAPOTEC

Pacific Ocean

Vera Cruz

Tlaxcala

Cholula

HUASTEC

TOTONAC

MIXTEC

TOLTEC

Mexico
Tenochtitlan

AZTEC

TARASCAN

--------- Route of Cortes' march

Mexico in 1519 Showing Areas Controlled by Different Tribes

The Legend of Quetzalcoatl

In Mexico in 947, the year One Reed, a priest-king named Quetzalcoatl – the Feathered Serpent – quarrelled with his rival, Tezcatlipoca – Smoking Mirror. He was exiled and left for the east, vowing to return and reclaim his kingdom in the year One Reed.

In March 1519, when the Emperor Montezuma the Second ruled the Mexica, five hundred Spanish adventurers under the command of Hernán Cortés landed at Tabasco on the east coast of Mexico. According to the Mexica cycle of years, 1519 was also the year One Reed.

Oh friends this earth is only lent to us.
We shall have to leave our fine poems,
We shall have to leave our beautiful flowers.
That is why I am sad as I sing for the sun.

Part One

March 1519 – September 1519
The Year One Reed

March 1519

The Month of the Flaying of Men

Montezuma the Great Speaker, ruler of the Mexica, stood on top of the Great Pyramid, his hands outstretched to greet the sun. The warrior's body lay crumpled at his feet. A priest, his black cloak flapping like the wings of a crow, stepped from the shrine and kicked the corpse over the edge, watching it bounce down the steps and splatter onto the earth below.

Around them the island city of Tenochtitlán seemed to float precariously on the misty waters of Lake Texcoco. Montezuma could see the canals and streets, the gardens and palaces, and the green fringe of islands that encircled them. Today the three causeways linking the city to the mainland were jammed with people arriving for the festival. In the distance the hill of the Grasshopper rose from its marshes. On the eastern side of the lake, where a ridge of snow-capped mountains erupted from the earth, he glimpsed the familiar shapes of the Smoking Warrior and the Sleeping Maiden.

Clutching the bowl with the dead man's heart, he moved past the chanting priests, back into the shrine where the god sat upon his wooden bench, his shell eyes glittering beneath a black mask. Montezuma held the bowl to the bloody lips and tipped the still-fluttering heart into the god's open mouth.

He felt exhausted. A man had to steel himself to ignore the look of terror in another man's eyes that even holy drugs could not extinguish. It took years of training and many mistakes to acquire the swift flick of the wrist, that twist and turn under the ribs, that tug, neither too strong nor too weak, to remove a living heart, and with every act a part of himself seemed to die. He told himself that the warrior flew to the sun and joined the souls who lifted it into the sky each morning. Without their blood, the sun would not rise and the world would end. It was a glorious death. His own would not be so glorious. It would come soon. He had lived fifty-two years, a full cycle of time. He prostrated himself on the stone floor in front of the god.

When the priests found him later that night, he knew why they had come. He knew his messengers had arrived from the coast. He knew what news they brought. His heart hammered in his chest. His hands shook. His mouth felt parched. He felt his way down the one hundred and fourteen steps, searching for the pools of light cast by the braziers. In the city below, pine torches flickered in the deserted streets. Faint sounds of music drifted up from the houses where people still feasted after the sacrifice. The walls of his palace – jasper, black stone and alabaster – sparkled in the moonlight. The moon was sister to the sun. The sinister hours of night were her domain. With every dawn came the struggle for control of the world, and with every dawn came the threat of its demise. A conch sounded the midnight hour. He pulled his fur-lined cloak tightly around him.

In the House of Serpents where his councillors gathered, hissing pine torches cast an uncertain light on the walls. The priests warmed their hands over a brazier. The messengers shuffled nervously. They had crossed three mountain ranges and one salt desert to bring this news to their emperor. Terrified by the enormity of their message, they huddled together. They lacked the words for what they had seen. They spoke of houses that travelled on water, of men who rode on giant stags, of slobbering dogs with dangling tongues and machines that spat fire.

'. . . and stones!' said a messenger bolder than the rest who pretended to explode like a fireball machine and fell quivering to the floor.

Once the Emperor would have found this amusing. Now he ignored it.

'How many men are there?' he asked coldly.

The messengers thought about five hundred. There were sixteen stags. They had not counted the dogs. They handed Montezuma a cloth with drawings of the floating houses, the stags and the hounds. He saw the weapons that spat fire and, in the smudges where his artists' hands shook, he read their fear. Then he asked the question which troubled him most.

'Does Quetzalcoatl – the Feathered Serpent – return?'

The brazier spat suddenly. Flares mixed with scented resin wafted their smoke like fog, revealing and concealing the priests. Outside in the hall a musician dropped his drum. The Chief Councillor, Cihuacoatl – the Woman Snake – spoke from behind the curtain of smoke.

'The Mayans from Tabasco who have fought these people do not consider them gods.'

Montezuma looked scornfully at his priests and councillors. In the corner of the room, the Keepers of the Books turned the holy pages with their long-nailed fingers.

'The signs are not clear,' they murmured in unison.

The signs had not been clear for some time, but one thing was certain. These men had arrived on Quetzalcoatl's day of Nine Wind in the year One Reed, just as he had promised. They would expect a cordial welcome. Which of his lords could he entrust with this journey? Apart from the Woman Snake, they were an unimpressive lot. He beckoned to his Chief Councillor.

'Woman Snake. You will go to the coast and see whether these are men or gods. You will take with you the treasures of Quetzalcoatl.'

Woman Snake protested. He considered the lure of gold dangerous. Too much gold and these adventurers would stay. The priests gasped. The Emperor did not like to be challenged, even by the Woman Snake, whose power equalled his own.

'Nonsense!' said Montezuma firmly. 'You will go. You will tell me everything. No detail must escape you.'

The first fingers of light were already slipping through the doorway. The great red ball of the sun swayed in the sky as the warriors lifted it from the underworld. The world would not end yet. Today's dawn brought the promise of life. He saw that Woman Snake stood waiting.

'Go! I am impatient to learn the truth.'

He dared not admit that he feared it.

He was raised to be fearless, a child of the sun born to feed his father with the blood of his enemies. The soothsayers named him Montezuma Xocoyotzin, which meant 'Sun Piercing through Clouds' or, in simple language, 'Angry Young Lord', for they saw in his temper the signs of a warrior who would make his mark. He did not disappoint them. He devoured the holy books. He could recite the histories and read the stars. He was brave, eloquent and wise. He had made his people rich. He had purged his city of corruption and increased sacrifice to the gods.

When he was six years old his mother took him to see the painted books of his people. He had travelled with his fingers from the seven caves, past the place of herons, through forests of ocelots and jaguars, to the lake where the god Huitzilopochtli had directed his people to build their city. His people had been poor, squatting in the marshes eating algae from the lake, and some were enslaved. Then the Mexica were known as 'the people whose face nobody knows'. As he read the books, he became aware of his destiny to lead his people and serve the gods.

This knowledge had changed his life forever. Now all such certainties had vanished. Five years ago the first floating house had appeared. It had not stayed long but he had asked himself where it came from and where it went and whether its passengers were divine or human. Were there countries across the sea unknown to the Mexica, who considered themselves rulers of the known world, a world that extended north and south but not east or west over the seas? Ever since then he had been unable to sleep, to think, to eat, to govern. The omens had long forewarned him but he had not understood their message. The waters of the lake had boiled, a fire in the heavens had set light to the Great Temple and a strange bird had appeared in the city. In the mirrors mysteriously set into its head, he had seen reflections of ghosts riding animals. Or were they mirages of his own mind? For where he saw visions, his magicians saw only emptiness. He had had them starved to death, but, for the first time, he doubted himself. He who had always seen what others could not, now feared the emptiness in his mind.

His servants lifted him gently into his litter for the short journey home. They understood how the Emperor suffered from the burden of his responsibilities.

Woman Snake dreaded this trip. He was forty-eight. His chest troubled him and his war wounds ached. The roads were difficult, the climbs steep. It was a voyage of extremes, of ice and snow, of rain and drought, of swamps and desert. It was a journey to places where the air was too thin to breathe. He rarely travelled outside the city now. He was responsible for the internal administration of the Empire, an immense task, and under Emperor Montezuma, who liked making laws, his burden had grown. What Woman Snake had heard from his own spies did not suggest the sanctity of these strangers. He thought this journey a waste of time.

His servants prepared his steam bath and lifted cloaks from a long wicker chest for his approval. There was a green cloak with an eagle design and a fluffy cloak of white duck feathers with a wolf's-head pattern. There were the usual capes hung with shells, but this occasion called for the severe black and white mantle of his office. Woman Snake was the second most important man in the Empire. He was Commander of the Army, Director of Sacrifices and President of the High Court. His title, the Woman Snake, was the name of the Earth Goddess whom he had served as priest. It represented the duality of life, the light and the dark, the male and female, life and death. This morning he did not feel up to his task.

He sat back in his litter under the tasselled canopy and peered into the houses lining the canals. They were single-storeyed, built of sun-dried brick and thatched with grass. Through open gates he saw women sweeping their courtyards, turkeys scratching in the dust. A paper god, left over from a feast, hung from one of the doorways where a small child tried to spin cotton threads on her toy spindle. He enjoyed these pictures of amiable domesticity; he was a sentimental man at heart.

His litter passed through the crenelated Serpent Wall which surrounded the Sacred Square. He crossed the jagged shadow cast by the pyramid, passing between the carved Stone of War and the racks where skewered skulls bleached in the sun, and out again through the Eagle Gate guarded by its stone menagerie. A road led north over three bridges to Tlatelolco, a small city now incorporated into the larger metropolis of Tenochtitlán. He would take the causeway to the mainland and begin the climb into the mountains where his procession would join him. His cooks, his porters, his bearers, the sages and magicians, and a slave whom he would offer for sacrifice.

Woman Snake reached Tabasco ten days later, relieved to escape the interminable drizzle of the cloud forest and the incessant chanting of the magicians. He stood on the ridge enjoying the warmth of the breeze and the turquoise sea that stretched east to the place of light and life from where these people had come. In the distance frigate birds swooped low over the water searching for fish. With their long necks and clumsy bodies they were as ungainly as he was. The gods had not given him beauty but they had given him something far more precious, a voice as delicate and subtle as a solitaire, a dull bird with a golden voice. He had been chosen for the position of the Woman Snake as much for his tongue as for his lineage.

From this ridge he could see the land curving around a wide bay where eleven floating houses sheltered. He had never seen houses that travelled on water. In his city of Tenochtitlán people lived on floating islands but they did not travel on them. Smoking Eagle, the Governor of this coastal region, told him the strangers who travelled in these houses rode on giant stags. He could not imagine why men wanted to ride stags. Nor was he even sure he believed Smoking Eagle, a man of eager familiarity who sought friendship where it was not offered. He scratched his face, swollen from mosquito bites. This moist land was a very different place from the high dry valley of his home.

He followed a rough path down to the shore where canoes waited to carry him over the water. Behind him snaked a long procession of nobles and porters carrying baskets of gifts and food. Two scribes ran forward clutching their bark paper and charcoal. The porters lifted Woman Snake and Smoking Eagle into the first canoe. Four baskets containing the gods' treasures were loaded in with them. They rowed out to the largest house. It towered above them, a wooden three-storeyed building with windows and a balcony where strange people waited. An Indian girl leant over the side and asked in Nahuatl, his own language, where he came from. He bobbed up and down in his canoe, feeling queasy. He only travelled on the lake at home when the weather was calm. Someone threw a ladder over the side. The canoe paddled closer. Woman Snake clung to the ladder, terrified of the sea waiting to swallow him. The open mouth of a fireball machine greeted him. He smelt sulphur and unwashed people, urine and excrement, women and cooking fires and an unrecognisable animal smell, all struggling to escape from this fetid house. He tried to conceal his disgust, he was a fastidious man. A man in a high-backed chair watched him carefully. The hound by his side stared hungrily. Its long tongue dangled between dagger-like teeth. Mexica dogs were small, hairless and edible. This hound could devour men.

The man, with his white skin, black clothes and red hat, resembled a frigate bird. The dust-coloured hair that hung to his ears and clung to the sides of his face terminated in a neat pointed beard much like the Emperor's. Whiskers of hair framed his full feminine lips. He wore puffed trousers which ended above the knee and a black shiny jacket, edged with gold braid. His cold black eyes stared greedily at the forty-nine gold frogs dangling from Woman Snake's necklace.

As Woman Snake bent down to sweep the ground and offer an

empty welcome – for there was no earth to gather here – he heard the floating house creak and groan as its demons struggled to escape. He raised his hand nervously to his mouth.

'If the god will hear us . . .' He waited nervously for the god's reaction. 'Your deputy Montezuma has sent us to you. He welcomes you home to the land of the Mexica. He knows the god is weary.'

The girl changed his words into Mayan, speaking to another man who changed them into a barbarous tongue. But the frigate man, as Woman Snake now called him, seemed not to understand the words when they reached him.

Men appeared from a hole in the floor, from the poles that rose to the sky, from the front and the back of the house and stared at Woman Snake as curiously as he stared at them. Some had gold hair, some had red, some had none, and there was a man with skin as black as night whose hair, like the fibres of the maguey plant, curled tightly to his head. They covered themselves with so many clothes that the only flesh showing was on their faces. Some wore silver helmets. Others had red scarves or wide-brimmed hats to shade their faded eyes from the sun. They all looked ill.

'Where are these people from?' he asked imperiously.

'Spain,' replied the girl as if he should know where it was. She pointed vaguely to the east. She knew no more than he did.

'Do they ever wash?' He tried not to hold his nose.

She laughed. 'They do not believe in washing but they let women speak.'

Women Snake ignored her. He took out his flint knife and cut his wrists, spilling the blood into a sacred bowl, which he then offered to the frigate man. But the frigate man knocked the bowl onto the floor, spattering blood everywhere. The porters dropped the baskets and scurried back down the ladder.

'I am here to dress the god,' announced Woman Snake nervously.

The dog bared its teeth as Woman Snake laid the god's treasures carefully on the floor: the crown of jaguar hide with a great green stone, the pendants, the collar of jade, the helmet with gold stars and a gold and mother-of-pearl shield with iridescent feathers; a carmine cloak, bracelets of gold bells, a slice of conch shell and a smokey obsidian mirror that reflected the path to the underworld. The frigate man turned the smooth conch shell over in the sun. He did not recognise Quetzalcoat's wind jewel, nor did he seem to understand its meaning.

When Woman Snake tied a serpent mask over the man's face he noticed how his pale skin showed every bite and scratch. His own face revealed its scars of war only on close inspection. Woman Snake was tempted to press the white skin and and see what impression his fingers left. Below the man's waist, a padded pouch covered and at the same time exaggerated his private parts. Woman Snake tried not to stare as he bent down to replace the man's clumsy boots with jewelled sandals. A muffled voice emerged from behind the mask.

'Don Hernán asks if there is more.'

'More?'

'More gold,' repeated the girl.

Big Belly, the slave, climbed the ladder. Only the top of his head and the whites of his eyes showed above the rail.

'We bring you Big Belly to sacrifice,' said Woman Snake quickly.

Don Hernán leapt from his chair, dragged Woman Snake across the floor and shackled him to the fireball machine. And from its mouth came a terrifying noise as a stone exploded on the water. The house rolled again and Woman Snake found himself slipping with the fireball machine down into the depths of the sea.

'Is there any news of Woman Snake?' asked the Emperor plaintively.

It had now been twenty-six days since Woman Snake's departure and nothing had been heard of him since. It took no more than ten days to reach the coast and ten days to return, and even allowing for a day or two's observation this did not add up to twenty-six days. He had sent scouts to wait on the pass but they had not returned. He regretted that he had not sent another of his councillors. He relied too much on Woman Snake, as he had done ever since they were boys at school together, clever boys with clever tongues competing with each other.

His table had been laid for lunch. His councillors stood beyond the gilded wooden screen that gave him privacy. Young women carried in bowls of water and towels, followed by the dishes of the day. He could have anything he wanted – turkey, pheasant, partridge, quail, duck, deer, wild boar, venison, hare and fish – but he did not feel hungry. Even the fish in calabash-seed sauce and fried grasshoppers failed to tempt him. Only when they brought his favourite childhood meal – tamales stuffed with fruit served with clear turkey soup – did he eat anything. As he sipped the soup, he looked back at that nervous child at the Feast of Izcalli whose mother had given him tamales with soup to comfort him. He could not remember whether he had cried and disgraced her when his neck was stretched over the hot brazier.

Montezuma washed his hands in a finger bowl. This was the signal for his singers:

For water, for rain
with which everything flourishes
on earth . . .

The ocarinas sang like birds. The rattles shook like rain. One of the flautists Montezuma noted, was not in tune. He shouted at them all to get out. A girl brought a bowl of warm chocolate but he gave it to the dwarfs larking behind the screen. He looked around the room – at the courtiers, the dwarfs, the hunchbacks, the musicians, the hangers-on. They irritated him. He wanted Woman Snake. He was impatient to know what these people were like.

This afternoon an interminable queue of supplicants waited in the huge reception rooms of his palace. Many of them had come for the feast and took this occasion to petition their emperor. Merchants, lawyers, clerks, captains, tax collectors, local chieftains and ordinary people filled all three courtyards with their noise, drowning out the soothing sound of the fountain. He felt exhausted, worn out by nights of prayer and fasting. Last night blue sparks had escaped from his body, a sign of a holy man, and this had comforted him.

He dressed in a clean white loincloth; he changed four times a day. His chest and arms were covered with gold. Even the soles of his sandals were solid gold. A nose ring of rock crystal with a kingfisher feather filled the septum between his nostrils. His triangular diadem was studded with lumps of turquoise. His cape, made from thousands of blue and green feathers, rustled and shimmered as he moved slowly down the steps, along the corridors, across the first courtyard, into the second courtyard, past the cages of squatting prisoners waiting to feed the gods. He usually looked forward to the merchants' visits for they were his ears and eyes. Through them he could see the invisible, he could hear the unspoken. Today, though, he could hardly concentrate. He wondered what the newcomers would bring. He hoped Woman Snake would bring something back. One of those spotted hounds, perhaps, with burning yellow eyes.

Woman Snake sat glumly on a high-backed chair. All morning he had been forced to watch the stags galloping up and down the beach, stirring up clouds of dust and sand that irritated his chest. These terrifying beasts pawed at the ground and snorted like madmen. They tossed their heads and swished their tails. Giants' teeth poked from their lather-coated lips. Grease oozed from their skin. When Don Hernán made Woman Snake touch one of these creatures, its smell had lingered and it had taken three rubs with sand and repeated washing in the salt sea before his hand felt his own again. He suspected the Spanish mocked him but their faces were impossible to read.

Don Hernán had pulled him back from the sea. There had been much joking and slapping on the back and he had been put into a canoe and with Smoking Eagle sent to the shore, where he was given a sword and told to fight. The Spanish crowded round and roared with laughter when he tried to wield his unfamiliar weapon.

The Spanish ignored the green stones, the feathers and the cotton. When he asked the girl why, she said only gold was important to them. These were sick men who needed gold to cure them. It was not surprising that they looked ill because they ate stale biscuits which tasted like ground maize stalks. They never washed and even slept in their clothes, and they did not sacrifice to their god. He wanted to know more about their god, but before he could speak the wretched girl interrupted his thoughts again. Did she not know that women were admired for the frugality of their words? Such impertinent questions too! Was the Lord Montezuma old or young? Was he vigorous? Did he suffer the ailments of age? Was his hair white? Woman Snake replied tersely that his emperor was mature, slender, handsome and did not limp on crooked legs. This made Don Hernán split his sides and exaggerate his limp like an actor at a feast.

'Don Hernán wants to meet the Lord Montezuma,' said the girl suddenly.

'The Lord Montezuma does not travel.'

'But Don Hernán can travel to him.'

This was unexpected. Tenochtitlán was impregnable. Its two hundred and fifty thousand citizens would not be friendly. All they had to do was to shut the causeways and trap the Spanish. Yet Don Hernán did not *look* foolish.

'We would not counsel such a dangerous journey.'

'Nothing is dangerous for Don Hernán.'

'There are demons and witches on the road.'

The girl laughed scornfully. 'Don Hernán does not fear demons. His god protects him.'

'What is your name, girl?'

'Malinalli,' she said after a long pause.

It was a terrible name. No wonder she hesitated. It was the name for the knotted grass of penance that sinners pulled through their tongues. It meant 'eater of sin' and was the name of a bringer of change. No wonder her parents had sold her.

'Malinalli,' he repeated angrily. 'You should go away and not bring your bad luck here.'

She looked as if she were about to cry.

'The Spanish consider me lucky. Here I am among friends. Look.' She pointed to where the bay widened into an estuary. 'Don Hernán plans a display. He will want you to see this.'

She led him over the sand to where the stags gathered at the end of the bay. Some of Don Hernán's men followed, tugging at Woman Snake's feathers, pulling at his earrings. He noticed that one of the men wore a helmet like the God of War's in the temple. But the man vanished in the throng of people surging up the beach. The stags raced at Woman Snake. The noise deafened him. The earth juddered. Woman Snake peered nervously through his fingers to see the stags and the helmet emerging from clouds of sand.

'That helmet . . .' He could not finish for coughing.

Don Hernán jumped from his stag and pulled the helmet from the man's head.

'Don Hernán says it is old-fashioned, but you can have it. He asks that you return it filled with gold.'

The girl turned it upside down to make a bowl.

A boy appeared carrying Don Hernán's chair and a red hat with a gold badge, necklaces of clear green and yellow stones, a crystal cup with carvings and a basket of the biscuits that tasted like ground maize stalks.

'Gifts,' said the girl, 'gifts for the Lord Montezuma.'

Something hit the water. The air stank of sulphur. Woman Snake felt sick. The porters fled into the trees. The Spanish laughed. The girl spoke again but he could hardly hear her for the drumming in his ears.

'You Mexica. You think you own the world, yet you fear a bit of smoke from a cannon!'

She stood mockingly with her hands on her hips. Smoke still wafted from the floating house. He shook the sand from his cloak. He wondered whether the smell of sulphur would ever leave him.

'Don Hernán fires that cannon to mark his friendship with the Lord Montezuma. You *will* promise to tell him?' urged the girl.

'I will tell him,' said Woman Snake, in a hurry to leave. When he reached the first line of trees, he heard footsteps. The girl came running up the hill. She waved her arms.

'More gold!' she shouted. 'Don Hernán asks you to bring more gold!'

He turned angrily on her.

'Watch your tongue, girl. You may even poison yourself!'

How he enjoyed the glimmer of fear in her eyes.

April 1519

The Month of the Great Vigil

'What is the god like?'

Woman Snake coughed. He took a deep breath.

'These are men like us, and yet they are not like us.'

'You speak in riddles.' Montezuma held up the drawings. 'Their leader looks like Quetzalcoatl. He wears his colours.'

'He has a Mexica girl with him. She has tutored him in our ways.'

'Have these people cast a spell on you, Woman Snake, or have you been drinking pulque in that inn?'

Woman Snake's limbs ached. The journey home had been terrible. Four porters had gone missing in the high passes and the guest house under the Smoking Mountain had run out of logs and pulque. In the scorching salt pans the mirages had tricked them.

'We have never seen people like these. They are so strange they must come from another world, another time.'

The Emperor fingered his beard nervously.

'Are they gods?'

'The girl tells me that there are many countries in this world where men like the Spanish live. Does this make them gods?'

'What does that girl know? The heat has addled your wits. These people arrive in the god's year, on his day.'

'Quetzalcoatl would have recognised his wind jewel. That was the most precious jewel there and yet the Spanish ignored it. The girl says they need gold for some ailment.'

'Are they sick?'

17

'They are pale but they wear so many clothes you cannot see their bodies. They are not handsome. Even gold will not improve them.' Woman Snake beckoned to the porters. 'They send gifts, a chair and a hat, some necklaces, a cup and some mangy food.'

Montezuma thought the carved chair with its high back uncomfortable. He was used to chairs made of reeds. He sniffed the biscuit, then he cracked it on the chair several times before it broke. He nibbled a piece tentatively.

'No wonder they are sick.'

The priests and the dwarfs giggled as they counted the number of times the biscuit bounced before it crumbled.

The red hat reeked of its former owner, but the necklaces and the engraved crystal cup intrigued the Emperor.

'It is a hunting scene,' said Woman Snake. 'It shows how their dogs hunt for them.'

Montezuma did not understand. Dogs were meant to be eaten.

'They send something else.'

When Woman Snake held up the helmet, Montezuma rose from the chair and moved towards him like a sleepwalker, his hands outstretched, his body shaking.

'It is Huitzilopochtli's helmet!'

'It is an old Spanish helmet. It is a coincidence.'

'Nothing is a coincidence, Woman Snake. You of all people should know that.'

'They want it filled with gold.'

Montezuma clutched the helmet. 'Then we must send them all the gold they want.'

'If we ignore them they might die from their sickness.'

'If we give them enough gold, they will leave.'

'They are robbers. We kill robbers.'

'They have not stolen anything.' Montezuma's eyes dilated with fear. 'Quetzalcoatl returns to claim his kingdom. If we fight him it will be the end of our world. This is what the omens warned. If you knew what I have seen in my dreams at night, you would not question my decision.' He rubbed his chest as if it pained him. 'Do you want to know what I have seen?'

Woman Snake sighed. The Emperor's dreams grew more dramatic with every year.

'I held one of those Spanish knives,' he told Montezuma. 'It cuts everything and it never blunts, and the fireball machines destroy anything in their path.'

'They will not bring those machines here, over three passes and one salt desert. Who will carry them? You are deluded, Woman Snake. I regret now that I sent you to the coast since I can no longer rely on your judgement.'

Woman Snake was hungry and thirsty. Once the Emperor would have accepted the truth. Now he wanted consolation. He moved to the window. Despite the heat it was clear today and he could see the mountains, towering above the valley. The rain would not come for a month and only after the Emperor had climbed the Tlaloc mountain and fed the god.

Black Dog, the High Priest of Tlaloc – He Who Brings the Rain, sat in the Emperor's canoe watching him trail his fingers in the water like a schoolboy. The Emperor seemed cheerful today. He enjoyed travelling on the water. He said the water encouraged poems. The Emperor was rather good at poems. He said the words hovered above the surface of the water waiting for the right person to give them birth. But Black Dog could see only flies and midges. He pulled his shabby cloak around him. He was susceptible to bites and swelled up at the slightest nip.

Black Dog observed the Emperor closely. He had become so capricious. His moods changed several times a day and you never knew which man you were speaking to. Last month Black Dog had accompanied the Emperor on a pilgrimage to the Place Where Men Became Gods, and the Emperor's fear had so unmanned him that Black Dog had to guide him up the staircase of the ruined temple in full sunlight. And then the Emperor had said something shocking. He asked whether Quetzalcoatl had been right to say there was only one god. One god! How could there be one god? Where did this leave the others, in the world of make-believe? This insult to the gods from such an unexpected source shocked Black Dog, but all the same he had sat on the top step with his arm around the Emperor as if they were brothers.

The boat rocked suddenly. The golden bells on its fringed canopy tinkled furiously. The gourds of drinking water rolled under the seat. The Emperor gripped the sides and watched the shore approach. Here, on the eastern side where the lake was saline, where mounds of salt dotted the shore, a litter usually awaited him. The only person waiting today was his nephew Cacama – the Lord of the Corn Cobs – the young king of this city, who came rushing out to greet them dragging his precious cloak through the mud. His diadem balanced precariously on his head. What, thought Black Dog, could be so urgent that the youth risked losing his crown? Cacama scrambled clumsily into the boat.

'Uncle, the Totonacs welcome the Spanish into their town! They have let them destroy their gods. They are convinced that Don Hernán is Quetzalcoatl.'

'We can do nothing until Tlaloc sends the rain,' insisted Montezuma, looking anxiously at the cloudless ridge. 'If the rain does not fall, we die with the plants. That is so, is it not?'

'It is so,' agreed Black Dog. He began to intone the prayer to Tlaloc: *'O Lord Tlaloc, water the earth. For the earth, the living creatures, the herbs, the stalks are watching, waiting, trusting . . . they cry out.'*

'*The earth's seeds have withered. Like old men and women they have shrivelled. O our Lord, let it not go on like this,*' prayed Montezuma.

'*Let there be fullness and abundance for all,*' mouthed Cacama.

A litter twisted its way across the salt dunes. Porters waded out through the reeds and carried Montezuma to the shore. Cacama stumbled after him.

'Uncle, wait! There is more bad news!'

The sacred hill loomed above them with its hallowed gardens, its statues and bathing pools, its rare plants and cages of sacred birds. Here Montezuma would start his journey to Tlaloc's shrine, regardless of the news. He would deal with the Spanish after Tlaloc had been fed but the boy would not stop shouting.

'The Totonacs have also seized your tax collectors.'

Montezuma looked up at the mountain where the hungry god waited. He was impatient to get on with the journey.

'Uncle. The Spanish are cunning.'

'What do you know about the Spanish?' shouted Montezuma.

'They encouraged the Totonacs to take hostages, then in the dead of night released them secretly. They trap their allies and secure our friendship. You cannot ignore them, uncle!'

'It must wait until my return.'

'It cannot wait!'

'The god cannot wait!'

Montezuma turned away towards the trail, a perilous climb over bumpy slopes where the mountain had spewed out its ash and where, if a man slipped, he fell into the heart of the earth. He knew every clump of grass, every rock and cliff, for this was a sacred landscape burnt into his mind. He ignored the child, cowering in his litter, shivering with cold and fear and hunger. He had seen so many children. This one was probably an orphan or a child sold by desperate parents. His death would be glorious. He would become a precious turquoise in the House of the Lord of Sustenance where he would sip nectar and his tears would feed the earth – surely a better prospect than years of poverty.

After four hours they reached the shrine high on its summit where the god lived with his thunderbolts. Steam from vents in the earth scorched their feet. Far below, brown fields begged for rain. In the distance gaped the mouth of the Smoking Mountain. At the end of the procession, the flutes played faintly like birds who had forgotten to nest for the night. Black Dog began reciting the prayers on behalf of all the creatures on earth – the flowers, the birds, the beetles, the trees, the serpents – all begging for rain. His voice competed with the snow falling off the thatched roof.

Montezuma dressed the statue in its regalia. The kings laid out the presents – the great green feather headdress, the jade serpent earrings, the mother-of-pearl ornaments that glistened as if newly washed in the sea, and Tlaloc's collar, heavy with green stones and a disc of gold. Black Dog dragged the sobbing boy to the god's statue. Rubber sandals too large for the child's feet tripped him up.

'Make the child cry,' ordered Montezuma.

If the boy did not weep, a year of drought would ensue. The boy whimpered and curled into a ball, tearing the paper wings stuck onto his back, squashing the green feathers in his hair. The blue rubber spots stuck on his skin scattered on the floor. Montezuma hit the boy with his lightning-bolt stick. The boy screamed for his mother. Black Dog pulled him to his feet. With one stroke of the knife, Montezuma slit his neck. The blood spurted up like a spring after the rain. From the boy's throat came a shriek, turning to the gurgle of a dammed river, as he drowned noisily in his own blood. The wind rose suddenly from the north, blowing through the gold needle grass. The wind was the voice of Quetzalcoatl. It always brought change. A wind from the north brought death.

From her roof terrace high above the Sacred Square, concealed by the luxuriant growth of morning glory, Jewel felt the change in the weather. She spent much time up here observing what went on in the city. This was her favourite place. Only the wealthy had houses with roof gardens, although hers was modest compared to her father's.

From here she could see her father, the Emperor, lead his lords into the House of Eagles. She liked to see him display himself to his people. Someone would call 'the Emperor is here' and everyone would drop what they were doing and crowd into the square to throw flowers and cloaks. Even the sun seemed to know when he would emerge because it would catch him in its rays and make his blue cape sparkle. Today there was no sun, only a wind that ruffled the councillors' feathers and swept away an Eagle General's head-dress.

This morning, Jewel watched with dismay as her father rushed down the steps into his litter and moved off across the square without acknowledging the crowds. Woman Snake was standing awkwardly next to her husband, Falling Eagle, who was gesticulating angrily. The two high priests huddled together as they never did. Then all the lords and the generals emerged from the meeting. She spotted her cousin Cacama and the lame old King of Tlatelolco, who used his stick like a weapon. Something was wrong. Perhaps they were discussing the floating houses. She hoped this would not upset her father and prevent him attending the family dinner that night.

Everyone was terrified of the floating houses. It was Ant Flower, her maid, who first told her about them. Ant Flower knew what went on in the city. She had friends everywhere. And although Jewel felt fear, she felt a flutter of excitement which came and went like the flame on the pine torches. The news that reached her daily via Ant Flower told of white-skinned men in silver suits who rode on giant stags. Half of her hoped these creatures would visit Tenochtitlán, but the other half would curl up with fright at the thought of it.

It was becoming too windy to sit on the roof so she moved down to her rooms, adjusting her eyes to the darkness. An ornately carved wooden screen separated the sleeping and living areas. Low chairs, little more than a support for a cushion, and a table completed the furnishings. Her clothes for the evening – an embroidered white cotton skirt and matching shift – were laid out on a long wicker chest. She shouted for Ant Flower. A head peered through the curtain of bells protecting the door.

'Send for the sorcerer to read the grains.'

This was unwise. If anyone found out that a man had visited her rooms she would be punished, as her aunt had been. Oh, but it was boring sitting here waiting for her husband, Falling Eagle, to visit. He rarely visited now and when he did it was only to find fault.

If only she could surprise them all and fly away to the mountains on the other side of the lake where the snow lay all year and where the god blew red flames and smoke from his mouth to show his temper. She, too, had a temper but could not make the earth shake. But now she was fifteen, grown up and twice married, she must forget those childish dreams. Women did not travel. They were rooted in their homes like trees planted in the earth.

Ant Flower said that two men lived inside Falling Eagle, the severe man who visited her lady and the cheerful one who did not visit at all. Sometimes to pass the time, Jewel pretended she was a dancing woman, 'a woman of joy', with her hair loose, her feet bare, dancing until she felt quite dizzy and unbearably happy. It was more fun than prayers or embroidery, even if the happiness did not last long.

Would the sorcerer notice that she had painted her face? Ant Flower said that many women enjoyed the sorcerer's other skills. He was a Huastec, from a coastal people famous for their sexual prowess. The thought of him excited her. Not that she dared to do anything. It was too much of a risk and the Huastecs – well, they were scum with large *tepuli*s, but scum nevertheless.

This Huastec was a scrawny man whose loincloth showed no sign of a bump. At first his skills impressed her. He roasted maize kernels without a fire, willed beans to jump across the room and made fish leap from the pond in the courtyard. But when it came to reading the grains he proved disappointing. Her grains sank to the bottom of the bowl, promising good luck, but when she asked him to read her father's, they floated to the surface – a sign of bad luck. And then, when the man had packed up his bowls and grains, he said something very odd. He told Jewel she would have five children but that none of them would be Mexica.

'If not Mexica,' she taunted, 'what else?'

'They will be strangers, Lady . . . with different fathers.'

She did not want to hear any more. Did the sorcerer think she was a whore? It was so obviously false that she could not believe anything he said, but at least she no longer had to worry about her father's bad luck. The man was not worth the cacao beans he charged.

Ant Flower began scrubbing the yellow ointment from Jewel's face. Only loose women painted their faces. She pulled back Jewel's hair and began twisting it into two tight braids.

'Ouch! You are hurting me.'

Ant Flower ignored her. She wound each braid into a horn of hair and secured one on each side of her face. Jewel was proud of her hair. It flowed to her waist like a black river and was rinsed with indigo to make it shine. When she was twelve, her hair had been bound, its eroticism concealed. Only prostitutes or dancing girls wore long hair in public.

'I want coloured ribbons.'

'Your father prefers white.'

Jewel stamped her feet.

'Coloured or nothing.'

Ant Flower opened a basket full of ribbons, pulled out the brightest and began weaving them through Jewel's braids. Then she jumped up and down enthusiastically. Ant Flower was so excitable.

'You look beautiful, Lady.'

Jewel knew this was a lie and, anyway, if she were pretty, her husband would visit more often. Ant Flower picked up her drum and danced around the room. Then she tripped over a mat on the floor. Despite her size, Ant Flower could be clumsy. Her head and body did not match her limbs. There were many dwarfs like her in Tenochtitlán. They were the first to climb the stairs of sacrifice whenever the moon swallowed the sun. Jewel giggled loudly. Ant Flower had no idea she was so comical.

Jewel sent for her singers. There was a new song doing the rounds. She wanted to learn the words so she could sing it for her father. She rehearsed for hours, and when it was time to leave, she grabbed her posy of flowers and her fan and ran to her litter. The gates opened. The bearers lifted her chair. A servant ran ahead with a flare and her banner of rank. It was not far to her father's home but a lady did not walk through the streets at night. She peered from her litter at the women rushing home with their baskets of produce and the musicians and dancers on their way to a feast in

Tlatelolco where the merchants lived.

A group of elderly men and women danced past in their paper loincloths. They had made their confessions to the goddess Eater of Filth. Jewel tittered. They looked so droll. Would she look as silly when her time came? Only one confession was permitted in life. One of the old women stared angrily, and Jewel hid behind her posy. The bearers crossed the Sacred Square, illuminated by huge braziers. Her father's palace lay on the eastern side. A vast building surrounded by gardens, it housed administrative chambers on the ground floor with the family rooms above. A garden covered the roof. In its grounds were waterfalls and pools and a zoo full of exotic birds and animals.

The litter passed under the row of coloured pennants and through the gateway where a carved rabbit frolicked above the lintel. Her father had built this palace in the Year of the Rabbit, the year of her first marriage. The rabbit was the sign of love but, as she now ruefully reflected, there was little of that in her marriage. Her litter deposited her at the main entrance. She resisted the urge to look at her reflection in the pool and walked down a long corridor into a huge hall whose walls were faced with rare stone and covered with paintings. Beams of carved cedar exhaled the comforting smell of the mountains. She felt the old aunts' eyes boring through her as she walked up to her mother sitting at a table next to her father's second wife. Her mother was the Emperor's first and senior wife. Concubines and princesses from other parts of the empire filled the room with their children, but they were not legal wives. Her mother and father had married young, before her father was elected Emperor. Did her mother mind sharing her husband with all these other women? If so, she concealed it well. She greeted Jewel warmly. The frangipani flowers in her hair exuded a sickly scent. Her mother always wore flowers.

The table was laid with fine red and black Cholula pottery and golden cups. There were bowls of salted gourd seeds and large jugs of frothy chocolate waiting to be drunk. Jewel loved chocolate. It was a treat; she did not drink it every day. Jesters and clowns rehearsed in an alcove off the hall. In a corner, the children sat on mats and drank their juice. Soon they would grow restless. Their nurses escorted them to empty their bladders and wash their hands before the food arrived.

Her father took his time. His litter, carried on the shoulders of his lords, deposited him in the centre of the room. Jewel watched them lower him to the ground. He did not look his age and his movements were still nimble. His fine hair hung to his chin and his small beard was neatly trimmed. His hands and feet were as delicate as a woman's. His large eyes, set wide above a prominent nose, expressed the enthusiasm of youth and the caution of age. They could laugh and they could be terribly severe. Apart from her husband, he was the most handsome man Jewel knew. Today, however, he looked weary. She wanted to run and throw her arms around him but she had to wait. He would pick her out. She was his favourite. She nibbled some seeds. She was starving. She hoped the food would come soon but she could not wolf it down as she usually did. The old aunts watched like eagles. She sat primly on a stool, her hands folded in her lap and waited.

He reached her when the pine flares were burning low, when braziers had been brought in to warm the night air. He touched her cheek and searched hard for signs of make-up. His mood was distant. She spoke first.

'I have a new song for you, father.'

'Not now. There is no time for songs.'

'But I have rehearsed for hours!'

'Not now,' he repeated shortly.

'I shall forget the words, father. You know I do not remember them like you.'

'Don't waste your time on songs. Remember what your teachers told you? To be useful, never idle. You know what they say about idle hands.' He patted her shining plaits fondly, upset by the hurt on her face. 'Is there a gift you would like?'

'A dog, father. I should like a dog.'

He laughed heartily, like his old self. His daughter could have everything she wanted and she asked for a dog. She was born on the Day of the Dog, which bestowed a cheerful disposition. He was still laughing as he moved on to his other children.

As soon as he had passed, Jewel's sister Butterfly rubbed Jewel's face with her fingers.

'Traces of yellow,' she said, 'father must be going blind if he did not notice. His eyes are usually like a hawk's. You know what he thinks of painted women. He will tell you that your husband will prefer you with a clean face. Or does your husband neglect you? You know what mother says. You do not try hard enough and you have no skills to amuse him.'

'I know everything.'

'How can you say that?'

If only Butterfly knew. If only they all knew how she lay awake at night imagining she was one of her husband's fancy women, fondling her secret parts, shuddering and moaning with delight. That was what 'women of joy' did but they did not do it alone.

'You are just jealous, Butterfly. You are not married yet. I know you like Lizard, but he is destined to become a priest and father would never let you marry him anyway.'

Butterfly began to cry.

'You are cruel. Mother always said your tongue was too sharp for a woman. No wonder your husband looks elsewhere.'

May 1519

The Month of Dryness

There was never enough time, thought Woman Snake, who had hoped to see his son Lizard at the family feast. He was not as skilful as the Emperor in juggling work and family, as his wife reminded him constantly.

After the meeting in the House of Eagles when no one could agree on how to deal with the Spanish, several councillors approached Woman Snake and suggested a private meeting. Woman Snake felt uneasy. He knew that among these faces were friends and enemies and some who were neither. It would be a long evening. He made sure that the tables were generously laid with pipes and tobacco.

Most of the council turned up. No one seemed in a hurry to drink or smoke. They sat closely together on their stools staring angrily at Woman Snake as if he were responsible for the Emperor's state of mind. The Emperor's brother, the Lord of the Two Waters, spoke first. He considered the capture of the tax collectors and the desecration of Smoking Mirror's temple reasons enough for war. Woman Snake reminded him that the Emperor was in a difficult position, caught between his people and the gods. A battle with gods had no victors and brought only destruction. The Emperor's dilemma was how to welcome Quetzalcoatl without offending his rival, Smoking Mirror.

The council agreed that this was a delicate matter but they could not sit here and do nothing. These strangers were as human as the Mexica. Woman Snake, who considered them dangerous whoever they were, reminded his fellow councillors how the Spanish, although outnumbered, had defeated thousands of Mayans. The Mayans reported that the Spanish took no captives. They fought to kill and they fought brutally.

'No one defeats the Mexica,' insisted an Eagle Knight.

Woman Snake reminded the Eagle Knight that during last year's war with Tlaxcala, the Mexica had not managed to defeat the Tlaxcalans, only to force sanctions on them.

'What does the High Priest think?'

Everyone stared at Black Dog who sat apart from them. The urine leaking from his pierced *tepuli* made him smell and no one wanted to sit near him. The peeling black soot on his face made him look as if he suffered from some strange disease. His heavy cape exaggerated his hunchback. Today his long matted hair was neatly tied back with a white ribbon. A bright white conch shell hung over his chest.

'Whatever we do will offend the gods.'

'Take the Spanish by surprise,' insisted Falling Eagle. 'There are only five hundred of them.'

Half the councillors agreed that it was important to deal with the Spanish before they could make other allies besides the Totonacs. Woman Snake pointed out that sometimes it was wise to wait and let events take their course.

'You always were too cautious,' sneered Falling Eagle.

'It is the role of the Woman Snake to be cautious,' Black Dog reminded them. 'The Woman Snake is both male and female, human and divine. He sees everything from both points of view. We would not want it otherwise. This will not be war as we know it where everyone knows the rules and the victor is the side with the most captives. The Woman Snake assures me that this war will bring useless deaths that do not feed the gods. He has seen the Spanish weapons and the fireball machines and the stags. What if they use them to fight us?'

Everyone laughed at such a ridiculous suggestion.

'What if the Tlaxcalans give them their support?' asked the Emperor's brother.

The Tlaxcalans had been humiliated for years by the Mexica and their young men and women offered for sacrifice to the Mexica gods. It was one thing for the Totonacs to support the Spanish, but the Tlaxcalans were altogether more dangerous. On the other hand, they did not live near the coast and were only fifty miles from Tenochtitlán – the Spanish were unlikely to reach Tlaxcala unchallenged.

'At the least we must force the Spanish to leave,' said a newly elected lord, nervous of saying too much.

'That is the problem,' said Black Dog. 'All of us here agree that they should leave and yet we cannot agree on how to do it.'

'Perhaps the Spanish will grow tired of the mosquitoes and the flies, the heat and the damp,' said Woman Snake. 'When the Totonacs stop feeding them, the Spanish will starve. There are already shortages and some of them are ill with fever. They may bring about their own downfall. There have been arguments. Unlike the Lord Montezuma, Don Hernán can take no action without his men's approval.'

'Do ordinary men have choice?' drawled the Lord of the Corn Cobs, the Emperor's nephew.

'These do!' Woman Snake puffed his pipe, waiting for his words to take effect.

'Can Don Hernán persuade them to travel here?' asked a shy young lord.

'He is certainly bold enough, but I am not so sure about his men. Although they all have come for our gold, some are keener than others. Many may want to return home with the gold they already have. He blew his smoke into circles. 'The Spanish might even leave of their own accord.'

'What about Don Hernán?' asked the Emperor's brother.

'All men have their weaknesses.'

'What is his?' queried a Jaguar Knight.

'Greed. Greed can cause a man to lose his judgement. The Spanish may even fight among themselves while we wait. Then we shall have victory without pain.'

'There would be no captives for the gods,' interposed Black Dog.

'We should fight now and ask questions later,' shouted Falling Eagle. 'Attack them when they are weak.'

'We should do as the Emperor suggests,' said Woman Snake. 'Contain the Spanish at the coast and send them just enough gold to keep them happy while we wait and see what happens.'

The Emperor's brother banged the table with his fist, angry that he had to shout loudly to make his voice heard.

'Let them eat the gold! Pour it down their throats!'

Councillors leapt up, punching the air.

'Let them swallow it until they vomit!'

'I should like to try once more to persuade the Emperor to change his mind,' persisted Woman Snake, once things had died down. 'He is not a fool. He will see reason.'

'And if he doesn't?' taunted Falling Eagle.

'We fight!'

But Woman Snake did not feel confident. It was not the right time of year and the armoury was only half full. So it was a relief when the councillors voted to give him one last chance to persuade the Emperor. They would meet again after the Feast of Dryness. He hoped the Spanish would spring no surprises on them.

The crowds poured into the city for the feast – merchants and traders, thieves and murderers – all unaware of their rulers' dilemma. They blocked all three causeways and choked the lake with their canoes, hoping to catch a glimpse of the two holy boys before their sacrifice. Extra lavatories had been provided along the causeways and street sweepers and guards had been hired.

This was one of the holiest feasts. The double sacrifice honoured two gods. Tezcatlipoca – Smoking Mirror, the old god of war inherited from the people who had lived in the valley hundreds of years before, and Huitzilopochtli – Hummingbird on the Left, the Mexica god of war who had led them to this place. The two youths were carefully chosen, for they would become the earthly form of the gods for whom they died. Everyone agreed that this year's boys were the most handsome they could remember. They played their flutes exquisitely and performed the sacred dances like professionals and it was hard to believe that they had only trained a year for the performance of their lives.

The coloured paper streamers hanging from the trees and the pots of blood-red flowers that lined the steps of the Great Pyramid added to the festive air. Sellers of food and flowers, jewellery and gifts filled the marketplace for one of their best selling opportunities of the year. A cheerful lady whose reputation for tamales had spread beyond the valley had spoken to both boys and even given them some of her wares. She announced that, despite her girth, she would be among the first to dance with Smoking Mirror's boy to the edge of the lake from where he would depart in a canoe to the holy island of Tepepolco.

Woman Snake observed how everyone, rich or poor, enjoyed these feasts. Not only did they entertain the people, they defined the year. Every month had its feast and its sacrifice. He would celebrate at tonight's dinner given by his friend, the merchant Wandering Coyote. They had been friends since Wandering Coyote had lent Woman Snake a large sum of money at a difficult time. Many lords owed their fortunes to the merchants.

Tlatelolco, where the merchants lived, occupied its own small island separated from the main city by a wide canal. Although a bridge linked them, Tlatelolco retained an air of aloofness and a suspicion of the Mexica, even though they spoke the same language. Not so long ago the two cities had fought each other, a result of a domestic argument. Woman Snake considered wars between allies foolish. And in any case he liked the informality of Tlatelolco. He enjoyed the company of the merchants, and the girls were always beautiful.

Woman Snake had hoped that tonight's dinner would be an intimate affair so when he saw litters blocking the narrow streets near the merchant's home he turned to go home. He almost collided with Wandering Coyote, who insisted on dragging him into the crowded banqueting chamber. The stew was being served. Cheap layers of dog meat covered succulent turkey flesh. Wandering Coyote always pretended poverty, and this usually amused Woman Snake, but today he did not laugh. Above the beat of the drums rose the clear sound of a flute. Wandering Coyote nudged Woman Snake as he helped himself to the stew.

'I have a new girl for you. You will like her. Huastec women are as lustful as their men. First the dog meat then the female meat. Ha, ha!' His belly wobbled when he laughed. 'Before the dancing we should discuss what you wish to invest in our next venture. We travel south. There will be emeralds there. The arrival of the Spanish does not stop trade. It might even improve it.'

Wandering Coyote grinned boyishly. His hair hung loose like a woman's. His teeth, filed in the Mayan fashion, made him look like a coyote. No one knew where he came from. Whatever his origins, he served as a successful agent of the Mexica operating secretly in enemy lands. It was dangerous work but there was nothing Wandering Coyote could not sniff out.

The lights dimmed. The flute ceased. A dancer slipped into the middle of the room. Naked except for her turquoise necklace and her gold bracelets and anklets, her black hair hung below her buttocks. Her pert breasts with their brown aureoles caught the light. Wandering Coyote leant over and whispered.

'I have some news for you. The Spanish are building a town on the coast with stone houses and something that looks like a fort. I have managed to bribe a Totonac who serves them. He tells me there is the threat of mutiny. Don Hernán is supposed to share his gold, but he has not and many of his men now wish to return home.'

Woman Snake gulped his pulque.

'Don Hernán does not wish to return. The Totonac tells us that he has the support of a loyal group. But fights have broken out among the others and now Don Hernán struggles to hold his men together.'

Woman Snake grinned and took another helping of turkey. Wandering Coyote continued.

'I do not think Don Hernán will leave. He paid for most of those boats. He will want a return on his investment. And there is something else. Of course my spies are not always right, but they observe many things. This report comes from one of my boldest men. He pretends to be a carpenter and works for the Spanish, building those houses. He says that we are no match for the Spanish. Compared to them we are mere nothings. Those are his very words.'

Woman Snake almost choked. 'What can he mean? We are the Mexica.'

'He says although they are rowdy and disobedient and argue all the time it only makes them stronger. Every man has his voice and every man expects to be heard. They are quite fearless. And as for this sickness, my spy does not consider them sick at all.'

'And their god?'

'That is a puzzle. They pray to him every day – you could say they are godly people in their own way, although some might consider them neglectful since they do not feed him. My spy says they are men who can drink all night and fight all day. They sleep little but they never tire and they never give up. He is convinced that they plan to travel here to the city for they have heard so much about our wealth that they will risk their lives for it. Don Hernán will never give up.'

'So your spy thinks we should send Don Hernán gifts, as is the Lord Montezuma's wish.'

'Forgive me for saying this, Lord. He thinks as do many of the merchants: that the Lord Montezuma lacks the will to fight. That is why I tell you this rather than the Emperor.'

A guest next to Woman Snake began to scream from the effects of the morning glory seeds. Others shouted. Some sobbed like women and hugged each other. Others fell onto the floor and sprawled there open-mouthed like the dead.

The dancer stepped over the bodies. Now she swayed closer, so close Woman Snake could smell the crushed rose petals on her skin and watch the light run down her body to the faint shadow between her legs that led to the moist place where a man could bury himself. She moved in and out of the light to show her qualities, like a jewel held up to the sky, or a snake wriggling in the sun. Woman Snake drank more pulque. It might make him feel like a Spaniard, able to make love all night and fight all day. Around them other men, still on their feet, left with serving girls. Wandering Coyote looked expectantly at Woman Snake.

'I am tired, friend.'

'You are always tired these days,' scolded Wandering Coyote. 'This girl will invigorate you, make you forget the Spanish.'

He led the way up the stairs to a small room under the roof which looked out over the lake dotted with the flickering lights of the huts on stilts, and left them there. The girl unravelled Woman Snake's loincloth and straddled him. He willed his *tepuli* to swell. She bent over him. As he felt her mouth, as soft as his *tepuli*, there was a sudden commotion outside. Courtiers ran up the stairs to announce that the Emperor had imbibed too many mushrooms and lay in a deep sleep from which no one could wake him.

The Emperor slept for two days. When they woke him, he raved of deserts where spirits rode on stags and men with blemished faces turned into monkeys. He had seen the sun blown away from the world and fire rain down upon the earth. He curled up into a ball and wept.

When he refused to eat or bathe or change his clothes, Woman Snake sent for the healers who purged him and gave him infusions of holy plants and, as a last resort, placed a golden rain stone on his stomach to draw out the sickness. The Emperor confided that, since the arrival of the Spanish, he had lost all confidence. He no longer knew what pleased the gods. He had seen such terrible things in his dreams. When they brought his daughter Jewel to comfort him, some of his old spirit returned. She sat beside him and cooled his head with ice and wiped the dried blood from his ear lobes where he had pierced himself.

'Listen, my daughter. Remember what I used to tell you all those years ago? How I warned you of the difficulties of this world, a place of weeping, a place of pain, full of thirst and hunger. And how you would laugh at me and tell me what a wonderful world this is.'

'It is, father. It is.'

'It *was*! And those difficulties will now come sooner rather than later. That is what my dreams have told me. You must prepare your-self. You will have to be brave.'

'I am brave, father.'

He patted her hand.

'You see, Woman Snake, my daughter should have been a boy.'

Woman Snake knew his own daughters feared him. This girl loved her father. How like him she was with her luminous eyes and expressive hands. She was as shiny and glossy as a bird. His own daughters did not like her and called her a spoilt petulant girl. He sat awkwardly with the two of them until the Emperor fell asleep again. When he rose to leave, Jewel tugged at his cloak.

'Falling Eagle says my father is mad.'

Woman Snake took her hand and held it. Such a dainty hand. She shared her father's elegant fingers.

'Falling Eagle exaggerates. Your father is not mad. He is exhausted. Power is exhausting.'

'My father told me he did not seek power. It was the gods who chose him.'

'That is right. He was elected by his council and chosen by the gods. He follows a difficult path. There is only one road and many false turnings. He is a wise man but even wise men falter. Now, my dear, you must go home. I shall see you to your litter.'

'Is it true what my father says – that difficult times approach? You see he spoke so often of the terrors of this world that I stopped believing him.'

'There are always difficulties. We live in the fifth and last period of time. Like the previous four periods, it will not go on forever, but I am sure it will not end tomorrow.'

She smiled happily.

'My father always said you were wise, Lord Woman Snake.'

It was after sunset when the bead curtain rattled noisily and Ant Flower danced into the room. Ant Flower could hardly conceal her excitement, her feelings were squashed so tightly into her tiny body that they sought every means of escape. Jewel's husband followed her.

He had untied his warrior's knot and his hair hung loose. His skin was pale, his face long, his eyes wide set and grave. He perched proprietarily on a stool and lit his tortoiseshell pipe, the one her father had given him. The smoke smelt pleasantly of charcoal and herbs, dried flowers and bitumen. Which husband was visiting her tonight? The gruff one or the amusing one? She watched him inhale the smoke and then press his nostrils together. She waited for his sneeze.

'How is your father?'

'He is better. He eats and drinks.'

'He will not have heard the rumours.'

'What rumours?'

'Huitzilopochtli's boy struggled up there on the stone. He fought the priests. Some say he suffered a fit. Others say it was a bird that flew across the shrine shrieking fiercely. Whatever the cause, it will not please the god. Yet your father ignores the signs and consoles himself with mushrooms.'

'He eats mushrooms so he can travel to the gods.'

'He spends more time with them than with his people.'

'Why don't you just go away and leave me?' she shrieked angrily. She felt instant regret. How she hated this constant bickering.

Falling Eagle pulled the curtain sharply across the door, setting off the warning bells, and waited for the servants outside to scatter. Then he paced the room.

'We have all warned your father. He will not listen even to his wisest men. He says that Quetzalcoatl returns to claim his kingdom.'

'He does return. He does!'

'You would believe anything. The Spanish are building a town on the coast, yet your father does nothing to stop them.'

'He has his reasons.'

'He cannot make a decision.'

'He is a holy man.'

'His devotion is excessive.'

'The lords chose him for his holiness.'

'Look, I did not come to argue with you. I came to sleep with you.' He sounded weary.

'I sometimes wonder whether we are married,' she said sadly.

'You wanted me.'

It was true. She had begged her father for Falling Eagle and her father could deny her nothing. Many women desired Falling Eagle. How foolish to think that he would desire her, that everything would be perfect after the wedding.

Falling Eagle did not even bother to remove her sleeping shift. He was perfunctory, polite. She knew she wasted her time trying to please him. He did not visit her for pleasure. That was reserved for the other women. Was he polite with them? Ant Flower assured her that these women were no more beautiful than Jewel, only older and more skilful. Ant Flower said that love was a messy business. It was noisy and boisterous. It was not polite. As soon as it was over, he reached for his loincloth and wiped himself.

'There is something you can do.'

She was still sleepy.

'Speak to your father. Persuade him to fight before it is too late.'

'I am a woman. Why would he listen to me?'

'You are his favourite. He denies you nothing.'

His voice was heavy with scorn. He stood there naked in front of her, his wasted *tepuli* drooping like a corn shoot in drought. How she loved his body. She watched him dress and leave the room in such a hurry that the bells on the curtains rattled loudly from the force of his departure.

Ant Flower brought a bowl of fresh rose petals and began to rub Jewel's skin. They felt like thorns.

'Ant Flower. Did something happen at the feast?'

Ant Flower stopped rubbing.

'There were rumours, Lady. There always are. The Priest of Tlaloc addressed the crowds. He assured them that nothing had gone wrong. I saw that boy climb myself. He played his flute. I did not recognise the tune but it was exquisite. At the top he bent and, with one go, broke his flute on the steps. I saw him walk calmly to his death. As the knife plunged, the sun caught its blade. It was beautiful, Lady, beautiful. We all wept.'

June 1519

The Month of the Eating of Maize and Beans

For Black Dog the month of the priests' trials was a time of change and regeneration. He would float in the lake during the ceremonial swims and reflect. He desperately needed a new novice and had set his sights on a boy he taught at school – the son of Woman Snake. He did not ask himself whether the boy in question wanted to become a novice. No one had asked *him* after all. The priests who had arrived in his village long ago had assumed that a poor six-year-old hunchback would be delighted to train as a priest. And they were right. It was an honour to serve the gods, and the city of Tenochtitlán offered chances no village could match. But such chances did not come without their cost. A life without children was one.

Black Dog did not desire women. Nor was he tempted by the men disguised as women who sold their bodies by the roadside. But he loved children. Looking was no sin. Anyone could desire secretly. So he was surprised and shocked when the youth in question tried to run away from him. He had pleaded with him, offering him the chance of scholarship. He could choose anything – astrology, divination, music, poetry or the healing arts. But the boy refused. What madness! How could he hope for better? He was illegitimate, the son of a concubine and his birth sign was not auspicious for a warrior. No one, rich or poor, could rise in Mexica society without success in war.

When Black Dog, called on the boy's father, he did not expect a refusal. The Woman Snake too, had proved resistant, especially when Black Dog dared mention the boy's illegitimacy. Black Dog suspected that Woman Snake did not like priests, although, like all Mexica princes, he had served his apprenticeship in the temple. Woman Snake had even referred to unsavoury practices in the priestly houses, and Black Dog had left in such a hurry that he forgot his conch shell and a slave had to bring it back, by which time he had returned to his swim in the lake.

This holy swim was the first pleasant interlude in the last three difficult months. Since that last council meeting, the Emperor's health had deteriorated, as Black Dog feared it would. At the last meeting the Emperor had seemed more nervous than usual. He had screeched painfully, a sure sign of anxiety, and although a nasal voice was a sign of nobility, the pitch seemed exaggerated. He had even lost his temper, storming out of the meeting, leaving his box of piercing thorns behind. The Emperor *never* forgot his thorns. And there was something else. During this month's purge of the novices, ten, including Black Dog's own, had failed the tests. Never before had such a high number of boys failed. He dreaded telling the Emperor.

He flapped about in the freezing water, washing under his arms and between his legs, and running his fingers through his knotted hair to loosen the grease. A priest was supposed to suffer, but he hated the dirt. He hated the smell and he hated the festering sores on his skin where he pierced himself for the gods.

Around him priests and novices were imitating the cries of herons and ibises so he did not hear the slave shouting from the shore. Somewhere, far off in the reeds, a priest even made a high-pitched squeak like a duck. It made Black Dog laugh so much that he gulped too much water and almost drowned. He, too, had pierced himself in all the right places, but he still did not squeak like a duck, although sometimes his tongue was so swollen that he could not speak and when he passed water it stung like viper's poison. He turned and swam to shore. By the time he reached the fishing nets, the slave had become quite hoarse. Black Dog vowed he would try to persuade

Woman Snake again. He needed a new novice. The Woman Snake would relent once he saw the advantages the High Priest could offer his son.

Cuetzpalin – Lizard dared not leave school. Lizard was not his real name. His name was Eagle, but he was no eagle. He was the lizard his father nicknamed him, darting nervously between cracks in the rocks, flicking his long tongue, observing with his beady eyes.

Today Lizard peered anxiously through the pillars on the porch of his school overlooking the Sacred Square. For some days now the High Priest of Tlaloc had stalked him, accosting him in the most unlikely places. Nowhere seemed safe. Lizard was in no hurry to serve the gods. He enjoyed school. He was fortunate to attend the school for nobles with its wide choice of subjects. But whenever he passed the Houses of the Young Men, the schools for ordinary boys, he would stop and listen enviously to the sounds of singing and dancing and long for such freedom until he remembered that ordinary boys did not learn to write. He could not imagine a world without writing. He loved the smell of paper, a mixture of fig bark, chalk and charcoal. He loved its smoothness, a result of its struggle for perfection. Soaked in lime water and beaten to a pulp, it was then mixed with vegetable gum and dried and coated in chalk. There was nothing more exciting than an empty sheet of paper waiting for his mark. He was a careful writer. There were no charcoal smudges on his work.

Today it was his turn to collect the teachers' food. He peered again through the pillars. The school faced onto the temple plaza and overlooked the ball court. Ever since his first match as a boy, it had been his ambition to compete there. And what a match that first one had been between two rivals, the King of Texcoco and the Lord Montezuma, to settle some argument about the meaning of the constellations. The King had wagered his kingdom, the Lord Montezuma three miserable turkeys. Many fortunes had been lost that day, including the Emperor's turkeys and his pride.

There was no sign of the High Priest, so Lizard ran down the steps, towards the circular temple of Quetzalcoatl. When he reached the skull rack, the High Priest leapt out and grabbed him. Lizard dropped his basket and sprinted out through the gate, towards the lake and over the islands of canoes tied up in the reed beds close to shore. When he reached the outermost canoes he jumped in and paddled quickly out towards the islands, beaching his canoe and sitting under a tree looking towards the mountains. He wanted to see those mountains, visit both seas and learn other languages. The life of a priest was that of a slave, a slave to the gods. He would rather run away. But where could he escape? He could not disgrace his family. His father, the Woman Snake, would send servants to find him. He lay all night staring at the stars, but by morning he had still not decided what to do.

At midday someone arrived, swimming from Tenochtitlán. The island was a long way from shore. Only a good swimmer could reach it. A dot moving on the water turned into a novice priest, as astonished to see Lizard as he was to see the novice. The boy took off his wet clothes, sat on the sand and covered his face with bruised hands. After some time he stood up. He hung his loincloth on a branch to dry then he stared across to the other side of the lake as if estimating its distance.

'You will never swim that far,' pronounced Lizard.

'It is worth a try. I have failed the novices' tests. I tried so hard. Now my family will disown me. I have disgraced them. Better to die than to go home.'

'Do you want to be a priest?'

'What has wanting to do with it? Who among us has choices? I do what I am told.' He stared at Lizard. 'Why are you here?'

'They are forcing me to become a priest and I don't want it.'

'I told you we have no choices. That is your fate. I would be happy with it.'

'Listen,' the novice went on, 'I will tell you something shocking and you will understand why I am escaping. I have not dared tell anyone this until now.'

He told how, when serving at last month's sacrifice, the sacred youth had struggled with the priests, how the heart had leapt from the officiating priest's hands, how he, a novice, had grabbed it before it slipped over the edge of the steps.

'The heart escaped?'

'It was dead when it fed the god.'

'The gods will punish us.'

'I no longer care what happens to the Mexica,' said the boy. 'I shall fight you all one day.'

'You are Mexica.'

'My mother is Tlaxcalan . . .' The boy grinned. 'But I shall spare *you* if we meet in war.'

'We will never meet in war.'

A canoe approached in the distance. The novice grabbed his damp loincloth and tied it around his waist. He looked longingly at Lizard's canoe. The canoe came closer. The boy seemed terrified. Lizard felt sorry and envious at the same time. This boy could run away. His family would not pursue him.

'Take it.'

'You are sure?'

'I am sure. That boat comes for me.'

He helped the novice drag the canoe to the water and held it while the boy stepped in.

'What is your name?'

'Angry Turkey.' The boy paddled east towards Texcoco. 'I shall not forget you,' he shouted.

Woman Snake came straight to the point.

'You will serve the High Priest.'

'You promised I could continue my studies.'

'Priests are learned men. Black Dog is respected for his scholarship.'

'You punish me, father.'

'You run away from school, steal a canoe, and you wonder why you are punished.'

'*Borrowed*, father! I borrowed that canoe.'

'I had to pay for it.'

'I will not serve the High Priest.'

'The High Priest seems much impressed with you. It is a great honour to serve him,' said Woman Snake dryly.

'I want to be a scribe, father. My teachers say I am good at writing and painting.'

'Let the boy become a scholar. In my opinion we have too many priests but we can never have too many scholars.'

The owner of the voice, a large man of Mayan appearance, sat in the corner of the room.

'Your opinion does not matter, Wandering Coyote, since you do not respect the gods. Up there' – Woman Snake pointed at the sky – 'is chaos. Down there – he pointed at the floor – 'is chaos. All that protects us is the gods. They command and we obey. What better honour is there than serving them?'

Woman Snake noticed how thin his son was, how lacerated his legs were from piercing, and although he felt concern, it did not deter him from his fatherly speech. He spoke about respect for the elders, the consolation of the poor, the need for good works. Lizard shuffled nervously.

'If you do not heed my advice, son, you will come to a bad end and it will be your fault.'

The Mayan chuckled.

'*That* old speech' he said. 'Every son must know it by heart.' He rose awkwardly from his seat and crossed the room and put his hand on Lizard's shoulder. He wore a merchant's badge on his chest.

'Boy, I shall give you all the paper you want. Just ask for Wandering Coyote in Tlatelolco. Everyone knows me there.' He bent down and whispered. 'It is not for ever. You have the right to leave the priesthood at twenty.'

'Twenty! That is six years away.'

'It will pass quickly. Learn what you can. It will always stand you in good stead.' He winked. 'Keep writing, boy.'

Woman Snake interrupted angrily.

'You will serve Black Dog. I will listen to no more grumbles.

You will do as you are told.' Woman Snake felt exhausted. None of his other sons were as difficult as this one. 'Your duties begin now.'

It was time for lunch. But the food did not tempt Woman Snake. He suspected he had been too harsh. The boy reminded him of his mother. Perhaps that was the problem. Woman Snake had never recovered from her betrayal. He wondered whether she had returned to her people, or was she now someone else's favourite concubine? Perhaps he would change his mind . . .

There was still the more pressing matter of persuading the Emperor to fight the Spanish before they sprung any more surprises. They were still building their town. It now had a temple, several houses and a harbour. What would they do when it was finished? He summoned his litter.

He would challenge the Emperor over lunch.

Montezuma's voice shrieked painfuly from behind his screen. He had seen visions of hell in the crushed morning glory seeds he smoked in his pipe.

'They were all there, Woman Snake, in my dream. My father and my uncle dressed in their warriors' feathers.' His voice quivered.

'The Emperor does not eat,' whispered an elderly retainer. 'Every morning we send a runner to collect ice from the Smoking Mountain. You know how he likes his ice crushed with honey, but he does not touch it. He has sent to the Oracle of Huemac.' He cleared his throat. 'It is not good news. The Oracle is critical of the Emperor's behaviour. It urges him to repent of his sins, deny himself his luxuries, his flowers, his perfumes and his women. He must eat no more than one tamale a day, but he does not eat even that.'

Woman Snake peered through the latticework. The Emperor sat hunched on his carved stool.

'We must arrange a meeting with the councillors', he told Montezuma. 'They have matters to discuss with you.'

'Can they not wait?' asked the Emperor peevishly. 'There are far more important issues to consider. Their words irritate me. What can they tell me now that they have not already said?'

'They are concerned about the Spanish.'

'They are still at the coast. I send them gold and food. There is no reason for them to move inland, is there? My spies keep watch. I know everything Don Hernán does. I even know the time of day when he voids his bowels.'

'That information does not help us.'

'It shows he is a man of regular habits. Men of regular habits are easier to predict.' He sighed. 'Now leave me, Woman Snake, I am weary. Whatever it is that the councillors wish to discuss it can wait until after the Great Feast of the Lords.'

'That is still a month away.'

An orchestra began to play. A singer rushed past Woman Snake, put her mouth to the screen and sang like a solitaire. The Emperor closed his eyes.

July 1519

The Month of the Great Feast of the Lords

Woman Snake did not look forward to this month's celebrations. His chest felt as if a snake was tightening its coils around him and he whistled with every breath. This weakness had been with him since childhood. The healers had tried everything – sweet chilli water and honey, passion-fruit juice, even the black water at the temple of Ixtilon, which cured all ailments but failed to cure his – and now he had come to terms with his affliction.

This year he expected something to go wrong. It was not the usual concern about the food running out – for the eighth month was a lean month when the granaries always ran low. It was more a feeling of *time* running out. They were living in the fifth and last cycle of time and no one knew when it would end. The only certainty was that it would. The last meeting with the councillors had ended in bitter arguments. Woman Snake felt he was losing his authority but, at the last moment, he had won the argument and gained more time to win the Emperor over. He had agreed to pin him down after this feast. It was something he did not look forward to.

He looked around at the great hall. Its display of power and wealth was an impressive achievement for a people once scorned for their obscure origins. Bowls of small black mushrooms, flesh of the gods, sat on tables with silver and tortoise shell pipes filled with aromatic tobacco. The statue of the God of Feasting, suitably dressed for the occasion, waited at the entrance. The Emperor's new cloak of tiny hummingbird feathers, precious not only for the rich palette of dazzling colours but for the sheer number of feathers that made up its bulk, was finished and ready for him to wear. In the House of Songs the poets and the musicians and the dancers were rehearsing their new pieces. The guest palaces had been prepared and the rooms laid out with clean sleeping mats for the visiting lords. The lavish gifts the Emperor gave away had been gathered in the warehouses. The canoes, full of maize gruel and tamales, were moored ready for the Emperor to distribute to the poor. Woman Snake had hired beautiful young girls, free of disease, to serve the food and satisfy the guests afterwards. Nothing had ever gone wrong with this feast and yet Woman Snake found himself instructing the servants to look in every corner and under every table, to lift all the mats, to peer inside the wicker baskets, and search for evil spirits.

As he watched the lords acknowledge the God of Feasting, he observed how some of them greeted the god with more warmth than they did the Emperor. Did they notice something in Montezuma's smile which demonstrated his weakness, or did they too feel the changes that threatened the Mexica? Woman Snake felt sure he was not the only person here to suffer those unsettling thoughts and dreams that told him that nothing would ever be the same again. Everyone here knew that the Emperor had been ill, that the Spanish had settled at the coast, that Don Hernán was boasting of travelling to Tenochtitlán and that the Mexica seemed unable to make a decision.

Woman Snake kept careful watch. This was not a feast where he could relax. Nor was it a night for drinking too much. He noticed how the councillors kept a wary eye on him as they mingled with the guests. He saw Montezuma greet everyone and observed how the Emperor noticed who was there and who was missing and how the Tlaxcalans who had been invited, had not even bothered turning up. And Woman Snake knew how, even as he smiled graciously, the Emperor planned to teach them a lesson. But there was no sign of his anger as he nibbled salted gourd seeds and signalled for the flutes to sound the first notes.

The pine torches hissed noisily as from the kitchens appeared a procession of young girls with bowls of water and clean napkins. And when hundreds of pairs of hands had been washed and hundreds of pairs of eyes had assessed the girls, the food arrived. There were mushrooms, beeswax, honey, frogs, snails, tadpoles, axolotls and even live insects. There were baskets of multicoloured tortillas, ground so fine they looked like muslin. There were salads of tomatoes with ground squash seeds, sliced avocado and papaya, and roasted peppers with spicy chillies. There were lake fish and sea fish. There were oysters, crabs and shrimps, water flies, cactus grubs, toasted grasshoppers, ants, grilled crayfish, crickets and crunchy maguey worms. There were turkeys, partridges, wild boar, marsh birds, pigeons, rabbits, venison with red chilli and stewed duck. There were roast iguana and stewed armadillo and every kind of sauce, including one made from the precious black fungus that grew on the heads of maize. There were prickly pears with fish eggs, frogs with green chillies, locusts with sage and many kinds of sweet potatoes. There were expensive pineapples from the coast, and pulque and chocolate carried in jugs on the strong shoulders of the pretty girls. One girl caught Woman Snake's eye, but the Huastec girl was waiting at home and he was becoming fond of her. Familiarity had its comforts.

The speeches came with the tobacco. Long praises to the gods, homilies to the warriors. The Emperor loved performing and he did it exceedingly well. Blue smoke rose from the pipes lining the room. Montezuma seemed his old self.

'*Here it is told . . .*'

He raised his hands dramatically. From the flutes came the shrill sounds of chattering voices. Woman Snake knew the story of the founding of Tenochtitlán was about to begin. It was a sign of the Emperor's confidence.

'*. . . how the ancients who were called, who were named.*
Teochichimeca, Azteca, Mexitin, Chicomoztoca, came, arrived,
when they came to seek,
when they came to take again possession of their land here.'

50

The drums beat the sound of marching feet.

'In the great city of Mexico, Tenochtitlán . . .
in the middle of the water where the cactus stands,
where the eagle raises itself up,
where the eagle screeches . . .'

The larger flutes screeched. The dancers spread their arms.

'where the eagle spreads his wings,
where the eagle feeds,
where the serpent is torn apart . . .'

The war drum throbbed, gently at first, then rising to a climax. The dancers linked their hands and broke apart. The Emperor looked around the room to make sure he commanded his guests' full attention.

'Where the fish fly,
where the blue waters and yellow waters join . . .'

The dancers ran in a circle shaking the seeds on their ankles to make the sound of water.

'where the water blazes up,
where feathers came to be known,
among the rushes, among the reeds, where the battle is joined,
where the peoples
from the four directions are awaited . . .'

The rattles ushered in the wind.

there they arrived, there they settled . . .'

51

A sudden commotion at the door stopped him. A messenger forced his way through the guests and threw himself at the Emperor's feet. His hair was matted with dust, his cheap cloak torn and ragged. Some of his toes were missing, a sign of a slanderer.

'The Spanish have destroyed their boats!'

The band stopped playing. The lords fell silent. Woman Snake's stomach churned as if the grasshoppers he had eaten returned to life. The Emperor's hands fluttered nervously.

The messenger explained that when a small group of Spanish had tried to escape on a boat, Don Hernán had destroyed ten boats, sending only the largest east with the treasures of Quetzalcoatl. Now the Spanish could never return home. What a clever move, Woman Snake reflected, to silence your enemies and turn your volunteers into desperate men! This was something no one could have foreseen.

Feet shuffled outside in the corridor. In the great hall many of the lords had collapsed in heaps on their mats, their minds dazed by pulque or mushrooms. Woman Snake slipped quickly away, missing the stilt walkers and the clowns and the hymn for the day. He must prepare for his meeting with the Emperor in the morning.

'Did you have any knowledge of this?' shouted Montezuma accusingly as his servants dressed him for the morning's ceremony. He did not believe Woman Snake's denial.

'What kind of people destroy their homes and deliberately put themselves at the mercy of the unknown?'

'Perhaps Don Hernán is mad,' suggested Woman Snake half-heartedly.

'We will soon find out,' said Montezuma curtly, as he stepped past the musicians and dancers and into his litter.

This morning it was his duty to feed his people, but he was surprised by the sheer size of the crowd waiting in the streets. He was grateful they were kept in check by the whips of the officials. When he reached the distribution point, where islands of canoes full of maize spread out into the lake, a seething twittering mass of humanity surged forward, holding out containers made of anything they could find – leaves, sticks or even their cloaks which they folded into sacks. The officials flicked their whips and the people shrank back into tight groups. When the first canoe was unloaded, there was such a rush that some people were crushed and extra officials had to be brought in to maintain control. Montezuma did not notice how desperate some of the people looked, too poor even to own a bowl for the free maize. He saw only how they prostrated themselves, how they loved him. These were his children and it was his duty to protect them. He vowed to send more gold to the coast immediately.

The councillors met in a building in the Place of the Mosquitoes to discuss the latest developments. They could wait no longer. It was too much of a risk. Even the high priests agreed. They had always thought that the Emperor's closeness to Quetzalcoatl affected his judgement.

'He was dedicated to him at birth,' Woman Snake reminded them.

'Don Hernán is *not* Quetzalcoatl,' insisted Falling Eagle. 'We cannot stand by and watch the Mexica destroy themselves. We are like animals paralysed by the moon.'

Woman Snake knew that he would never convince the Emperor to fight until the end of the unlucky year of One Reed. There was little point in trying and the new year was still seven months away. This morning on his way to the temple, after a sleepless night, he had seen a pair of white cranes flying west towards the sun. They flew so close they seemed joined by the tips of their wings. Then they veered apart as if they could not agree in which direction to fly and he knew that this was a sign.

'We will prepare the warriors and build up the armoury and then, if the Spanish move inland, we attack them.'

It took all of Woman Snake's skill to persuade the councillors not to rush into war. He warned them that this would be a battle without rules. Even the sharpest of weapons would not cut metal. He did not want to start a war before he considered all the options.

Caution was preferable to failure. His spies observed the Spanish constantly. He would know the minute they left the coast.

The councillors left reluctantly, glowering at Woman Snake. Black Dog was the last to leave. He pretended to search for his conch trumpet.

'You are wrong to wait, Lord Woman Snake.'

'*Now* you speak.'

'At first I agreed with you but now I have changed my mind.'

'How I have struggled with this decision! I suppose that is why I am the Woman Snake rather than the Emperor.'

'Some would say it is the more important role.'

'The Emperor deals with gods. I deal with men. Which is the more difficult?'

Black Dog wiped his face with his dirty cape. He sweated profusely.

'That is not a question I can answer, but I believe we should attack the Spanish now when they least expect it. You do not wait for the jaguar to pounce. You do not put your head into the jaws of a coyote.'

'So you too are against me?'

'Not *against* you, Woman Snake. I understand you want to preserve unity in the council, but don't wait for the Spanish to arrive, because by then it will be too late.'

August 1519

The Month When the Fruit Falls

Ant Flower brought news of the boats. She found Jewel whirling around the room in emulation of the women dancing outside for the warriors. Bright yellow spots of colour dotted her cheeks. Ant Flower forgot the boats.

'It is your own husband you should be dancing for,' she scolded.

'He does not notice me.'

'I have heard', said Ant Flower, 'that there are tricks women can use.'

'What would you know about such tricks?'

Ant Flower blushed.

'Nothing, Lady. Men do not look at me and what I have seen of love between men and women makes me glad of my own ugliness, but you, Lady, are as beautiful as the other women Falling Eagle sleeps with.'

'I am plain.'

'That is what your mother tells you so you do not become vain. Your father calls you beautiful. He would not lie.'

Jewel ran from the room and out into the courtyard, and stared at her face in the pool. The face that looked back was disfigured by the movement of the water. She ran back in again.

'The water tells me otherwise.'

'The water lies.'

Ant Flower had an odd way of peering at you as if her eyes did not focus. Jewel felt sure she did not see well.

'So what is your advice?'

'Become the kind of woman Falling Eagle admires. Learn something to please him, play the flute or dabble in poetry. There are many women who do these things. And there is another suggestion . . .' Ant Flower hoped she was right; she knew little of men's appetites. 'Do not be too eager with him, however much you want him. Play games with him as his other women do.'

'Is that all? I thought that a wife did not need to play games.'

'Oh no! A wife needs more skill than a courtesan. But you will have to wait. The Lord Falling Eagle has left the city. Some think he prepares for war.'

Jewel whirled again.

'They say in the city that the Spanish have destroyed their boats. They cannot leave now!'

Jewel stopped in mid-flow.

'You think you know everything, Ant Flower, but I think you make it all up.'

She *hoped* Ant Flower had made it up. What would the Spanish do if they could not go home? Would they come here?

'I do not make it up, Lady. There are too many rumours to be false.'

'And what does my father say?'

'Even I, Lady, do not know what your father says. It is said in the city that some councillors have broken away to form their own group.'

'Falling Eagle!' whispered Jewel.

Ant Flower turned away and busied herself tidying up the clothes and putting them back into the chest.

As Woman Snake watched his clerks climb the ladders checking the tribute in the House of Birds, Black Dog's warning echoed in his mind. Although he thought it unlikely that the Spanish would travel inland, through hostile territory, over three high mountain passes and a salt desert where an army could go mad, the High Priest of Tlaloc understood the gods. His warning should not be ignored.

The Spanish were not like other people. They surprised you. They always did what you least expected. What did Wandering Coyote's spy say? 'Compared to them, the Mexica are mere nothings.' At the time, he had not entirely believed Wandering Coyote, who was prone to exaggeration.

Up and down the administrators bobbed among the shelves of coloured feathers that stretched from floor to ceiling. Legs, arms and heads emerged and disappeared in filaments of parrots and troupials, cotinga, roseate spoonbills, blue herons, hummingbirds and, most precious of all, the purple and green feathers from the tail of the quetzal. These were the shadows of the sacred ones, exquisitely delicate and coloured by the gods. Compared to them, silver and gold were vulgar. There were shelves, too, of green stones and turquoises, corals and little quills of gold dust finer than sand. Woman Snake loved the magic and colour of this place where he used to play hide-and-seek with his brothers.

Some of the treasure stored here came from the Tlaxcalans whose warriors were captured to feed the Mexica gods. For some years now the Mexica had also denied the Tlaxcalans salt and cotton. He checked on the scribes sitting cross-legged on the floor as they painstakingly drew the items and listed the quantities. This year's tribute was good. The demands to the tribute cities had increased despite Woman Snake's arguments against such taxes. At a council meeting not so long ago, he had questioned the use of all this wealth since it only made enemies, but he had been outvoted.

He checked too, on the status of the weapons in the armoury, in preparation for the war that came after the harvest. No one fought *during* the harvest. Wars were ritual affairs fought in the eleventh month of the year after the harvest was gathered. War required preparation. Ambassadors would have to be sent. In Mexica battles both sides understood the rules. Victory went to the side who took the most captives, the side whose gods would be rewarded. A war against the Spanish would be a different kind of war, a war without rules. How easy would it be to capture people wearing silver carapaces? He heard a cough. Wandering Coyote stood on the threshold.

'Terrible news, Lord Woman Snake! The Spanish have left the coast. They march for Tenochtitlán!'

Montezuma searched the holy books and peered into mirrors while diviners argued among themselves as to the meaning of the bundles of knotted ropes thrown around the room. Woman Snake avoided the diviners and stepped over the obsidian mirrors and jars of water. Montezuma's gaze did not wander from his mirror.

'I know what news you bring.' Montezuma turned back to his mirror where he thought he saw the faces of his ancestors. 'What do the knots say?'

The diviners bent over the tangled knots spread over the floor. 'The meaning is not clear, Lord.'

Nothing was clear any more. He told them to keep throwing.

'The Spanish have already crossed the first range of mountains,' Woman Snake reminded him. 'Four hundred of them march for Tenochtitlán. They bring the Totonac army with them, pulling the fireball machines in the chests on wheels. Those wheels move over everything.'

'Did you think I do not know? That my spies have not warned me? They have led the Spanish to the most difficult pass where two of the chests on wheels broke down. There are still two mountain ranges to cross. Anything can happen.'

'What happens when they reach Tlaxcala?'

'There is a wall around Tlaxcala.'

'It will not resist fireball machines.'

Woman Snake thought it more likely that the Tlaxcalans would ally themselves to the Spanish. The Totonacs had already done so. Black Dog's words echoed in his mind. 'It will be too late . . . too late.'

'What can we do?' whined Montezuma. 'It was foretold. There are many questions I ask myself now. I ask why the gods abandon us. I ask why the ancestors are angry.'

'These are no gods. We can stop them.'

'Where? In Tlaxcala? The Tlaxcalans may fight them and do our work for us.'

'The Tlaxcalans may seek allies against us. The Spanish are the obvious choice.'

'Why would they choose strangers?' Montezuma turned back to the holy books. 'What do the gods say? Tell me what they say.'

Ant Flower rushed into the room. The Spanish were marching to Tenochtitlán. She wrung her tiny hands.

'We are doomed, Lady.'

'Don't be so dramatic!' scolded Jewel. 'My father will send warriors to fight them.'

'That is not what they say in the city.'

'What do they say in the city?'

'They say the Emperor will never fight. They say he fears the Spanish, that he hides in the temple and seeks solace from his magicians.'

Jewel threw a stool.

'My father loves his people. He will protect them.'

Ant Flower picked herself up and rubbed her bruise. Then she busied herself folding and unfolding the skirts and blouses and putting them back in the chest. She unfolded the cedar screen and put the stools together next to the mat on the floor. Outside in the city people gathered for the sacrifice of the girl who would become the Earth Goddess, Teteo Inan. The noise of their chatter and music reached Jewel's rooms. She had never experienced this festival. The fear that invaded the city and its palaces made her bold and she felt she could slip out unnoticed. She wanted a dog and the best dog market was in Tlatelolco where the goddess would display herself to the warriors and encourage them to fight.

'I cannot sit here all day and think of the Spanish!'

'We could visit your mother,' suggested Ant Flower.

'We will go to the market.'

Ant Flower looked terrified.

'What if we are seen?'

'I will go alone if you won't come with me.'

'What will your father say?'

'He will never know if what you say is true. He is locked up with his magicians and could be there for months. Come, we must get there before the Spanish.'

She put on a plain cloak and moved towards the door. Ant Flower struggled to keep up.

'Don't jest!'

Jewel laughed as Ant Flower lolloped after her like a clumsy dog, all body and no legs.

They went on foot, crossing the bridge over the wide canal separating Tlatelolco from the main city. It was a struggle to squeeze through the crowds of people pushing and shoving their way over the bridge. Porters with sacks on their backs jostled with housewives haggling for bargains. Dull-eyed slaves shackled by wooden collars shuffled down the backstreets. Jewel stared in horror at the debtors selling themselves into bondage. Some of the people spoke languages she did not recognise. Because she did not come here often, she did not know where the dogs were and pushed her way past stalls piled with jaguar and fox and deer skins. Like millions of small birds, feathers floated through the air from the feather stalls whenever the wind ruffled them. She fingered the shoes and ropes. She inspected the dyes and pots, wooden dishes, firewood, charcoal, torches. She felt the bark paper and blew through a bamboo pipe. There was everything you could want. Glue, paint and lacquered gourds, building wood and such a display of food, it made her hungry. She stopped at a stall selling maize sugar syrup and took out some cacao beans. The stallowner recognised a naive young woman unused to shopping and saw a chance to make a profit. He took several beans from her. Ant Flower grabbed at them.

'Cheat!' she shouted. 'I will report you to the market guardians.'

The stallholder looked down the street fearfully and quickly handed back all the beans. Jewel did not want to draw attention to herself and crossed the street where stalls sold pots of excrement for manure and urine for the tanning of skins. Next to them, impervious to the smell, people queued for a haircut from the barber and women squatted on small stools next to their baskets of finely ground tortillas and spiced maize porridge.

'Come!' urged Ant Flower, looking around to make sure they had not been noticed. Such festivals, with female sacrifices, made her nervous. Whenever the moon swallowed the sun, Ant Flower hid herself in a secret place where no one could find her. She did not want to join the dwarfs who fed the gods.

'Where are the dogs?' asked Ant Flower of a passing merchant.

The merchant, who was shabbily dressed, cast his practised eye over Jewel. He liked what he saw, a respectable girl, up to no good in the market. He was about to flirt with her when Ant Flower interrupted scornfully.

'We search for dogs, not men.'

As the merchant pointed to a maze of streets leading to the dog market, a man ran into them, forcing them roughly against the stalls.

'He is an escaping slave,' said the scruffy merchant as he made a half-hearted attempt to catch the man. 'If he succeeds in reaching the Lord Montezuma's palace, he will be a free man . . .' He looked up the street where the slave had disappeared. 'Here comes the goddess. She, at least, will not escape.'

The goddess came with her escort of midwives and naked guards, muscular Huastecs whose enormous phalluses preceded them like weapons. Jewel giggled nervously.

Ant Flower nudged her. 'Don't stare, Lady.'

The goddess' singing turned to noisy sobs. The midwives blew their whistles and kept a beady eye on the girl. If she stumbled or fell asleep, wars would be lost and children born dead. The girl, half-dazed with exhaustion and weeping, looked ahead blankly. When she reached Jewel, she stopped, still swaying on her sore feet. She could not have been more than thirteen. The merchant stared greedily. But the girl ignored him, looking enviously at Jewel's plain clothes and unpainted face. Jewel knew she was a tribute girl, nobly born, for only the best would do for the Sacred Mother. The girl turned away but not before Jewel saw the tears in her eyes. Then Jewel surprised herself – she put her hand on the girl's shoulder to comfort her.

'Don't cry. You have lived amongst us as a goddess.' The girl had been treated as a princess for a year.

The girl spoke bitterly. 'You Mexica think you own us all!'

Her women dragged her away and forced her to dance up the street, throwing maize seeds into the air. Jewel ran to pick them up, holding them tightly in her hand, trying to imagine herself in this girl's place. Did the girl know she was living the last day of her life? That her skin would be flayed and worn by a priest? That her pert little breasts would adorn his desiccated chest? Did she know that a hole would be cut out for his parts in the delicate place between her legs? What did it feel like to be violated by a holy man, whose seed would die as soon as it was sown in you? And which priest was the holiest, which priest would penetrate the girl for the first time? She shuddered.

At the end of the street the girl looked back at Jewel before vanishing with her women.

'Who sows his seed in the goddess tonight?' asked Jewel.

A toothless old woman grinned maliciously. 'Everyone knows. Where have you been girl? I would not object to his handsome worm in my dry vessel.' The old woman cackled. 'You, by contrast, are as pretty as the goddess.'

Jewel turned away contemptuously. 'Who asked for your opinion, old mother.'

The street was becoming crowded. Prostitutes emerged from the surrounding streets and surrounded them. The crowd smelt hostile, and Ant Flower dragged Jewel quickly away.

'So who is it?' Jewel persisted. 'The old priest of Huitzilopochtli?' She could not even imagine him having a *tepuli*, and even if he had surely it would be full of holes.

The Huastec guards struggled to control the crowd. They stood so close to Jewel that she could have grabbed their *tepuli*s.

'It is the way things are,' said Ant Flower quietly, trying not to attract the attention of the guards. 'The Earth Goddess gives us her seeds. She gives her life to the temple. She gives her skin to the warriors and she gives her virginity to the highest priest. If she did not give herself, there would be no victory in war.'

Ant Flower led the way to the dog market, where the dogs were all fattened like sacrificial victims.

'I want to know who it is! If you don't tell me I shall ask someone else.'

The guards had followed them.

Ant Flower took Jewel by the arm.

'It is only symbolic. He does not do it for pleasure.'

Bundles of small red and white dogs were sniffing each other, mounting each other. Suddenly they revolted Jewel. A terrible suspicion crept into her mind. She grabbed Ant Flower.

'Tell me!'

'Ant Flower shuffled in the dust.

'The holiest priest in the land.'

It couldn't be. It wasn't possible.

'You lie!'

Jewel pushed her way through the guards and ran down the street. Into her mind crept a terrible image of her naked father straddling the goddess.

'Why did you bring me here?' she shouted at Ant Flower, before retching into the gutter.

Her father sent for her the next day to join him in his gardens at Coyoacan – the Place of the Coyotes where he had planted a new grove of trees. She sat glued to her stool. How could she look at her father with that grisly image in her head?

'If you do not go, you will upset him,' said Ant Flower. 'He has little time now for such outings. You must go. I have the litter waiting. Hurry!'

She pushed Jewel through the bell curtain and into the courtyard. She was strong for such a small person.

The banner carrier ran ahead pushing the crowds out of the way.

Jewel held on tightly as the bearers ran across the square and out through the Eagle Gate, past the twin fortresses and along the southern causeway. Up here, twelve feet above the lake, she could see water servers filling pitchers on the aqueducts and, to her left, the great dyke stretching for ten miles that protected Tenochtitlán's fresh water from the salty parts of the lake. She could see, too, the fringe of islands that surrounded the city. These were man-made islands, built of wicker canes and water plants and anchored to the lake bed by willow roots. They yielded several crops a year. Ripe heads of corn sprouted among rows of brightly coloured flowers. Further out in the lake, rocky islands housing sanctuaries and temples dotted the water. The litter turned left and she was on the mainland.

She arrived first and waited by the gates of her father's nursery. Seedlings came here from all over the country to be potted and planted. There were plants from the wetlands, the drylands, from the cloud forest and the mountains. There was always something new to see.

Her father arrived late. She noticed how he waited until his litter was lowered before stepping out. He usually liked to jump out before his litter touched the ground. It always amused Jewel to see the panic of his bearers, fearful lest the Emperor injure himself. He moved slowly, not seeing her until she moved out into the sun. The images churned in her mind. There were so many questions she wanted to ask.

He put his arm around her as they walked together along the paths between the flower beds where he would stop and bend down to check some minute scrap of green poking from the earth.

'You know, if I were not an emperor, I would be a gardener. There is nothing more cheerful than seeing things grow.'

And on they would move to the next bed, past fences of bright red poinsettias. When they reached the tropical section, they sat down on a bench together, overlooking a lake where freshwater birds searched for food

'You had a song for me,' he reminded her.

'I have forgotten it.'

He seemed disappointed. 'I have been preparing poems for the festival.'

He was famous for his poems. He had won at many of the festivals. She had gone once to the hill in Texcoco, where poets gathered under the open sky to recite their works to its ruler who sat in judgement under his green canopy. She remembered how their voices had struggled against the water rushing down from the aqueducts.

'Do you want to hear them?'

He did not wait for her reply. He began with poems of love, moving to war and death. The impermanence of life was a common theme. She changed the subject.

'Father, when will the Spanish leave?'

'I fear they will not.'

'Not leave! What will we do?'

'We will have to accommodate them.'

'That is not what Falling Eagle says.'

'What does Falling Eagle know? He has not met these people. If they are gods and we anger them, then what? Falling Eagle lacks the wisdom of the years.'

'Falling Eagle is not disloyal, father. He tries only to please you.'

She had made this up but she felt sure it was true. It must be true. This was not the first disagreement between her father and her husband. She never knew whose side to take.

'Then he should stick to war and capture warriors to feed the gods. The gods can never have too many hearts.'

'I am sure he will, father. He is brave.'

'One day his turn will come and he will know how difficult power is.'

'What do you mean?'

'It is impossible to please both men and gods. How I have tried! ... I love this place,' he said wistfully. 'There is nothing more peaceful than a garden. I shall leave these to you when I am gone.'

'Not yet, father.'

'No one lives forever.'

A small hairless dog ran towards them. She screamed. She saw the writhing dogs in the market with their glistening pink *tepuli*s. She saw the struggling Earth Goddess. She saw her father with his legs apart.

'This is the dog I promised you.'

'How can you, father?'

He stared at her.

'What is wrong? He is the most delicious shade of gold. You can use him as my funeral dog.'

She leapt up and ran from him. The dog sniffed at her sandals.

'I don't want it, father. Do you hear me, I don't want it.'

He studied her as if he knew another question lurked that could not be spoken.

'I hope there are no secrets between us, my dear.'

He saw her to her litter before climbing sadly into his own. The dog followed him.

September 1519

The Month the Gods Arrive

At last it was the harvest. Woman Snake hated the noise and chaos of the old month of Sweeping when the healers and midwives ran uncontrollably through the streets pelting each other with marigolds and reed balls. He did not approve of boisterousness in women. He had been kept awake all night and the gods knew how he needed his sleep. The Spanish had reached the wall surrounding the Tlaxcalan lands. The thought of an alliance between the Spanish and the Tlacalans was too terrifying to contemplate but when Woman Snake bumped into Montezuma's servant, Deer, on his way to consult the Emperor, he could not believe what he heard.

'You will never believe this, Lord Woman Snake, and I am delighted to be the first to tell you. The Spanish have broken through the wall and reached Tlaxcala . . .' He paused for dramatic effect but was too excited to wait. 'The Tlaxcalans attack them. The Spanish are surrounded. Messengers came early this morning to Lord Montezuma. He is much cheered.'

'It makes no sense,' said Woman Snake. 'Why should the Tlaxcalans attack potential allies?'

He found the Emperor sitting in his rooms, his mouth open like a fish while his doctor nervously mixed salt and charcoal into a paste to scour the tartar from his teeth.

'Why do you question everything? I told you the Tlaxcalans would do our work for us. They have even killed two of those stags. You see they are mortal after all. The Tlaxcalans have sacrificed one of them.'

'Have they sacrificed any of the Spanish?' asked Woman Snake.

The Emperor spat grey plegm into a bowl before licking his polished teeth. He admitted that the Spanish fought like demons. The Tlaxcalans threw thousands of men at them and still they fought back. The Spanish had taken refuge in a temple on the hill outside Tlaxcala where they were surrounded. Now the wrath of the gods would fall upon the Tlaxcalans, absolving the Mexica of all blame. Things could not have worked out better. He ate his food eagerly, enjoying his first bowl of chocolate for two months. The Earth Goddess, Teteo Inan, had mocked him, turning their sacred union into a struggle rather than a merging of earth and sky. She had cried out at the moment of penetration and he had feared the war and death that would follow. Now he felt more cheerful, as if a spell had been broken.

For three weeks the news remained hopeful. The Spanish were sick and starving on their hill. Don Hernán had not been seen for many days. Every morning messengers brought good news to Woman Snake until he almost began to believe that the problem would resolve itself.

This morning he sat listening to the Huastec girl playing her flute. Wandering Coyote had sent her as a gift. Since she had moved into his house, it had become a habit to begin each day with music. The girl played exquisitely. This was a rare moment of peace before the tribulations of the day. The life of a Mexica official became more demanding with every year. He heard shouts. The flute paused. A breathless Falling Eagle pushed through the curtain with five senior councillors.

'The Spanish have defeated the Tlaxcalans! Now they enter the city of Tlaxcala in triumph where the old king welcomes them as gods.'

Woman Snake felt the blood drain from his body. When he spoke, his voice was hoarse.

'How?'

'We do not know how. All we know is that the Spanish survived a night attack by thousands of warriors. They observed no rules of war and they took no captives. Although Don Hernán suffered terrible diarrhoea, he still managed to fight.'

'Have any Spanish been killed or taken prisoner?'

'None of them have been found dead although a stag was buried. The Spanish rampage through the countryside taking their revenge on ordinary people, hacking off noses, ears, arms, feet and testicles.'

Such brutality shocked Woman Snake. Ordinary people did not get tortured in war. War was a formal meeting between warriors who knew the rules. Those who were captured took the honourable path to feed the gods.

'Cholula is next on the route,' Falling Eagle reminded him.

He shifted from foot to foot as he always did when he was nervous. He was young, only twenty-three, a man of promise, although he still had much to learn.

Black Dog's words ran through Woman Snake's mind. 'It will be too late.' It must not be too late.

'Sit!' ordered Woman Snake. 'This will be our council meeting. There are enough of us to take a decision.'

Woman Snake's resolve to fight in Cholula surprised them, but they all agreed to his plan. Ambassadors would be sent to the Spanish, bringing rumours of the reputed riches of the city and encouraging them to pay a visit. At the same time, they voted to send warriors under Falling Eagle to hide in the ravines and hills around the city. When Woman Snake suggested tentatively that the Emperor should not be consulted, there were no arguments, only congratulations all round that a decision had been taken at last.

Woman Snake left for Cholula in the morning. A two-day journey, it wound through the extensive maize fields and pine forests below the Smoking Mountain before crossing Woman Snake's estates where he would spend the night.

The Great Pyramid of Cholula could be seen from a distance, rising from the plain beneath the mountains. It was the holiest city in the Empire, its large temple complex dedicated to Quetzalcoatl. Here Quetzalcoatl had taken human form, and from here he was exiled by Smoking Mirror. The city was prosperous too. Surrounded by fields and orchards, it boasted four hundred and thirty temples and twenty thousand houses and gardens crammed among its narrow streets. Its market was well known for the quality of its feather work, its pottery and its precious stones. Understandably, its joint rulers did not want war – what could Cholula gain from such a confrontation?

'It is the Cholulans' duty to support the Mexica,' Woman Snake reminded them sharply. 'And there would be substantial tax bene-fits.'

'And if we do not accept?' asked the Lord of the World Below the Earth, the older of the two rulers.

Woman Snake responded icily. 'Tlaxcala refused our terms and they have suffered ever since.'

There was a long pause, so long that Woman Snake thought he had been forgotten.

'We have one condition,' said the younger lord at last. 'You must remain with us throughout. We do not want the Mexica to abandon us should things turn nasty.'

'We are giving you thousands of warriors!'

'That may not be enough.'

'Not enough?'

'The Spanish are powerful.'

'Queztalcoatl is powerful.'

'He will not like war in his holy city,' chorused the rulers.

Still, they ordered the Cholulans to dig holes in the city streets and fill them with stakes. They barricaded some of the streets and collected collars and ropes for prisoners. An ambassador arrived from Tlaxcala. A tall dignified man who carried himself proudly, he brought an offer of friendship from the Spanish. The lords bound the ambassador. They flayed his face and his arms to the elbows. Then they cut off his hands and sent him back to the Spanish with his wrists dangling on loose straps of skin.

Falling Eagle always arrived when Jewel least expected him. She had not seen him for several months. She wondered whether to tell him her news. Sometimes she was sick and did not feel like eating. It might not mean a child; there were many false alarms. But she was terrified because when she counted the months on her hands, the ninth month coincided with the five 'empty' days at the end of the year. The Mexica year had eighteen months of twenty days which left five 'empty' days that did not fit in. And days that did not fit in were dangerous days when no child should be born. So she kept her secret, hoping no one would notice. But Ant Flower knew. Ant Flower missed nothing.

Tonight Falling Eagle seemed cheerful. She almost regretted what she had to do. She dismissed her servants. She untied her hair. She brought Falling Eagle's pipe and sat on her stool watching him in the light of the brazier. How she loved it when he shouted and waved his arms around. If only he could be as passionate with her. But she steeled herself. She would try Ant Flower's trick. She would listen, but not too much. She would appear distant. She would not plead. She had been practising for this moment. She popped some chewing gum into her mouth.

'Jewel?'

He looked horrified as she opened and shut her mouth, licking her lips and cracking the chicle between her teeth. It had the desired effect. She clacked her teeth. She pouted her lips. She suggested pleasures he had not associated with her. She opened her mouth again, red, swollen, hot and hungry.

'You behave like a street woman!'

He turned away but she knew he desired her. She draped herself over her chair. She played with her hair. She rolled her chicle into a ball and pushed it to the front of her mouth.

'Jewel, you are not listening.'

'I am listening.'

'You do not want to listen.'

She moved the chicle from cheek to cheek, opening her mouth and pushing the ball out through her lips. The shock made his hands shake and he dropped his pipe.

'What has changed you?'

'It is you who have changed. I am tired. Perhaps you should leave.'

'No doubt you are exhausted from chewing gum all day.'

How she wanted him. She would happily spread her legs for him, there on the floor in the light of the pine torches, as brazenly as any woman of joy. She hoped he would not leave.

'If that is how you feel.'

He made his way to the door.

'Falling Eagle!' she pleaded.

He half turned. Oh it was difficult. Was she doing the right thing? The words were on the tip of her tongue.

'Goodbye.'

'Is that all you can say? I have made a special effort to visit you tonight.'

This infuriated her. She wanted to be a pleasure, not a duty.

'Either you want me or you don't,' she snapped. She found herself stamping her feet like an obstinate child.

'You are my wife.'

'So?'

She enjoyed a brief wonderful feeling of empowerment. It was almost worth sacrificing some pleasure for.

'I go to fight the Spanish in Cholula.'

She stared in horror.

'Why didn't you tell me?'

'Would it have made any difference?'

'You will return?'

He pushed his way through the bell curtain. She screamed with rage and frustration. She screamed at Ant Flower. Then she cried herself to sleep. She did not fancy a lonely life of self-pleasure, and she could never take a lover. Was Don Hernán as insatiable as a Huastec? Was his *tepuli* the same as other men's? Or was it as white as his face and as large as a sea slug? Ant Flower told her that in the city they said that Don Hernán boasted a *tepuli* bigger than a Huastec's and that women clamoured for his attention.

All night Jewel dreamt that giant slugs nibbled at her flesh and sucked at her mouth and the lips between her legs. Now she was the Earth Goddess struggling beneath her father, torn apart as he penetrated her. She woke up screaming.

Don Hernán sat proudly on his stag. He showed no signs of sickness. The sun had darkened his face and hunger exaggerated his bones. The girl stood by his side. The Cholulans swung their braziers of incense to clear the air. Despite their long stay at Tlaxcala, the Spanish still reeked like pirates.

The twin rulers bent and kissed the earth. Woman Snake estimated that five or six thousand Tlaxcalans accompanied the Spanish. He noticed that they all wore strange plaited garlands of feather grass on their heads.

'If the Lord will hear us,' he said. 'The city cannot feed so many. We ask that the Tlaxcalans remain outside the walls.'

To his surprise, Don Hernán agreed. The girl leant forward.

'I recognise you, Lord. Have we met before?'

Woman Snake smiled politely.

'I think not, Lady. I have never left Cholula. Tell Don Hernán he is welcome. We have set aside a palace with food and drink.' Don Hernán's stag pawed at the ground impatiently. 'And grass for the stags.'

Everyone laughed. As they approached the city gate, Woman Snake saw how Don Hernán scanned the houses and roofs for signs of fortification. He hoped that the warriors were safely hidden in the woods and ravines.

'Don Hernán asks why there are no women and children in this town,' said the girl.

'It is late in the afternoon,' replied the twin rulers. They are indoors preparing the meals. We have different customs here in Cholula.'

She whispered something in Spanish to Don Hernán.

'Where does Don Hernán go next after Cholula?' asked Woman Snake.

She stared at him.

'You do not know? You cannot guess?' She laughed loudly like a whore, opening her mouth and exposing her teeth like one of those stags.

At dusk Woman Snake tried to slip out of the city with the traders. They found the gates locked. No one could leave until morning so they returned to the market square and camped on the stones. Woman Snake had forgotten how hard the ground was. He tossed and turned all night.

An explosion woke him at dawn. He heard the distinctive sound of stags' feet and the clatter of armour. He smelt sulphur and pitch. The traders sat up bleary-eyed to see Don Hernán on his stag in the middle of the square. People in the surrounding houses emerged from sleep and crowded onto their roofs and balconies. Don Hernán was making a speech.

Woman Snake heard snatches of disconnected words as the girl translated – accusations of treachery . . . the torture of ambassadors . . . sodomy . . . the eating of flesh with salt and pepper . . . the one true god. Someone fired a smoke stick. That, too, smelt of sulphur and pitch.

The roofs and balconies emptied. Woman Snake pushed his way through the crowd fleeing into the backstreets, trying to avoid the stones and the pits with their sharpened stakes. When he saw the first of the Tlaxcalans surge into the city and block off the narrow streets, he ran back to the temple. There were many hiding places in its depths.

He climbed, stopping frequently to catch his breath and look down on the Tlaxcalans torching and looting the houses. He saw bodies in the streets and from his eagle's-eye view, he saw refugees fleeing to the city gates where they were mown down by Tlaxcalan arrows. There was no sign of Falling Eagle's men. When Woman

Snake saw the Spanish close the gates to the square he knew it meant only one thing. He ran to the top of the shrine.

'Run!' he shouted to the priests and the lords who stood looking helplessly over the edge. 'Hide inside.'

He hid himself in a cave next to the shrine, full of pots and bowls of blood left from a sacrifice earlier that morning. The Spanish would be unlikely to linger here but they stomped into the shrine in their heavy boots and their jangling metal, feeling the walls for gold and silver. Their hands roamed over the god's body searching for jewels. One of them picked up a flare and searched the shrine but they did not venture into the cave.

There Woman Snake huddled in a corner, listening to the fighting and the screams, waiting for the Spanish to leave. He heard the sound of feet running to the edge of the pyramid. A muttering of prayers and someone jumped. He crouched in the corner and, when it was quiet, he emerged gingerly, clutching a pine torch. Below in the square, he saw the faint light of flares as people moved between the dead, removing everything that was precious. Where could he go? He knew that the pyramid was laced with hidden passages. He did not know where they led, only that some of them were traps.

Feet ran up the steps. He fled from the shrine, down the first three flights to a door in the third level. A shout came from below as men rushed up to cut him off but he slipped through the door and down a narrow tunnel. His pursuers followed him. Woman Snake took the first turning right and then left, running down into the depths of the pyramid where it was darker than night and as cold as a tomb. He felt his way along the walls, wet with the moisture from hundreds of years. The tunnel turned into a room. He stumbled on something on the floor, shards perhaps, but when he bent to look he saw bodies scattered in the dust. This was a room of skeletons. The torch went out suddenly, leaving him alone with the dead.

Falling Eagle turned up at Woman Snake's estates outside Cholula, his clothes bloody, his arms bruised. There was a gash on his thigh.

The steward informed him that the Lord Woman Snake had not returned. The steward sat him down and brought refreshments and sent for a healer to stitch the wound.

'The Spanish planned this,' said Falling Eagle. 'They came prepared. The Tlaxcalans wore special headbands of feather grass so they would recognise each other. Now the Spanish celebrate in Cholula. They have released the prisoners and opened the market. They have scrubbed the shrine and put their god in it. Some Cholulans have returned.'

'I hear', said the steward nervously, 'that many warriors have died. We have sent scouts to look for the Lord Woman Snake.'

Now Falling Eagle realised what kind of enemy the Mexica faced, they had no choice but to fight the Spanish in Tenochtitlán. With the causeways lifted, they could not escape. This time it would work. At least something had been learned from Cholula and the Mexica had not lost too many men. When Falling Eagle saw the thousands of Tlaxcalans enter the city, he fled with his warriors and left the fighting to the Cholulans.

'We have heard that the twin rulers are dead, together with all the priests. There are rumours that Don Hernán will appoint the next ruler himself.'

Falling Eagle knew that he must reach Tenochtitlán before the Spanish and warn the Emperor before it was too late. He took some food and water and climbed up into the pine forests, reaching the high pass at sunset where he was surprised to meet a tramp blocking the path. Falling Eagle went to push him out of the way, but the tramp dragged him to the pass, bidding him look down on the valley. And when Falling Eagle looked, instead of the lights of Tenochtitlán, he saw flames and smoke where the city stood. Then the tramp disappeared and Falling Eagle knew that Smoking Mirror had appeared on earth in one of his many disguises. He hobbled over the pass and into the long gorge below. When he arrived in the city, depressed and exhausted, the gash in the leg had opened up and he was bleeding badly.

Jewel's world had shrunk to the routines of pregnancy. There were no more escapes to the market. But she did have a companion now, the golden dog.

Every morning a midwife arrived to palpate Jewel's belly and pronounce on the health of the child. The midwife was a chatterer. She was sure the child was a girl. She could read the signs. A woman could never have too many daughters. Daughters were not lost to war. They were like the embers in the hearth, always comforting, always there. Every afternoon the old aunts and cousins would arrive. Women with shrunken faces and shrunken wombs, living their only moments of glory as the mothers of past warriors.

Jewel listened politely, fondling the dignified little dog who sat on her lap and stared at the endless procession of old ladies. The days stretched on monotonously and without news. She did not even know what was going on outside the walls of her home. Nothing had been heard of Falling Eagle since he left for Cholula.

She was in her steam bath when news of the massacre finally reached her. At first Jewel thought Ant Flower was lying, with her hysterical tales of priests falling from the sky like black rain. Ant Flower told her that even in Tenochtitlán people were in a state of confusion, running wildly here and there, gathering their children, terrified of the horrors that approached. Jewel scolded her for listening to rumours. But when she closed her eyes she could hear the thud of the priests' bodies as they hit the ground.

She stepped from the bath and covered herself with a shawl. At the window overlooking her courtyard, cotton awnings had been pulled down for shade. She would dress and sit there. She had not been there long before she heard cries from the streets and, peering over the edge of the roof, hidden by shrubs, she saw the lake and the canals so clogged with canoes that some of them had over-turned. She felt a terrible dread and then a pain, as if a knife were turning, twisting slowly in her gut. And into her mind flashed an image of the young Earth Goddess, Teteo Inan, violated and bleeding. Something warm and sticky ran down her thighs and, without thinking, she felt with her fingers. They were covered with blood. As the shawl slipped off her, she slid to the floor. She heard herself scream and a voice that sounded like her mother's.

'The girl has holy fits like her father!'

When she woke later she found herself in her room surrounded by fresh fir branches spotted with blood. She had not flown to the sun after all; she was still in the world of people. She smiled with pleasure. Ant Flower brought her a drink of pulque, considered healthy for a pregnant woman. So she was still pregnant.

'We feared you were dead, Lady.'

Jewel felt her stomach. Nothing moved there. Ant Flower shook her head.

'What the gods give, Lady, the gods take away.'

Jewel knew now that the Earth Mother had cried when her father forced her. Now there would be wars and death. She had become used to the child growing inside her. She had even given it a name, which was foolish, because only diviners could name a child. Perhaps it was just as well. Now there was no risk of her child being born during the empty days. She had spurned her husband and resigned herself to abandonment. If only she had not listened to Ant Flower.

'Would you like some music?'

'Go away!'

She climbed the stairs to the roof. The flowers still bloomed. The bees still buzzed. But in the city below the streets were empty. Everyone had disappeared. She cried out for her little dog, who climbed into her arms and together they waited for Quetzalcoatl to arrive.

Lizard carried Black Dog's incense burner, tobacco pouch, his box of cactus spines and a gourd with pellets of snuff to dull their hunger. They were on their way home from visiting the hospital at Chalco. It had been a terrifying experience seeing dribbling people with crooked eyes and boils all over their bodies. Black Dog said it was the result of carnal desire. Unlike the other healers, Black Dog did not like being touched or kissed by his grateful patients, although he had laid his hands on everyone there and had pasted a healing ointment of honey, eggs and ground root juices onto the stump of a man who had lost his leg. But the worst experience had been the stench of that stump as it was plunged into the hot ashes. Lizard had to run out and vomit.

They had just turned off the main road onto a track leading to a small temple in the marshes when they heard the sound of marching men. Black Dog pulled Lizard up the steps into the temple.

'It is Falling Eagle's men,' Lizard said excitedly.

'No, they make too much noise.'

Black Dog forced Lizard to crawl into the gap behind the altar. They felt sure the intruders would hear the thumping of their hearts. Feet climbed the steps. A voice shrieked in a strange language and a beast with yellow eyes stared at them. Something crashed to the ground. A Tlaxcalan shouted. The beast roared.

'Hey, look what's here,' said the Tlaxcalan, pulling the hound away and dragging Lizard and Black Dog out into the temple where the god lay shattered in pieces. Men with white faces and silver suits surrounded them.

'May the gods protect us,' whispered Black Dog. 'They are the demons of the night.'

The Tlaxcalan kicked Black Dog in the ribs. He paused when he saw Lizard. Lizard gaped at the warrior. The last time he had seen him was in a canoe.

'What are you doing here?'

'We stay the night in the Place on the Salt-Coloured Water as guests of the Emperor,' boasted Angry Turkey. 'Can you believe it? Guests of the great Montezuma. And tomorrow we visit Tenochtitlán. You see I have come a long way since I met you.' He kicked Black Dog again. 'Until we meet again!'

The white-faced men clustered around them. Angry Turkey spoke to them haltingly in a strange language. Then he waved and they all left. Black Dog sat down on a stone. His hands were shaking. He looked like an old man.

'We must return to the city before it is too late.'

The Emperor had retreated to the House of Serpents. He did not ask who had started the fighting in Cholula. It would have made no difference. Quetzalcoatl was in a malevolent aspect in his role as the Evening Star. An attack on his holiest city would anger him. He was disappointed there was no news of Woman Snake.

'We could try again,' insisted Falling Eagle.

'What do you mean?'

'Tenochtitlán is an island. If we remove the bridges in the causeways and canals, we will trap the Spanish. There will be no escape but we must not let in the Tlaxcalans.'

'No. It will not work! Do you think I have done nothing all these months? I have tried everything. I have tried diplomacy. I have tried magic. I tried to bribe the Spanish with gold but it was never enough. I even offered to serve their king. You did not know this, did you, Falling Eagle? You think you know everything. Then I considered fighting them, although I did not want to fight Quetzalcoatl. And when I asked myself whether these are humans, as you and the council insist, this gave rise to other questions. Now I ask myself how many boats are out there and how powerful is this place from which the Spanish come? Should I fight them or welcome them?'

He bowed his head and did not speak for some time, and when he did, he sounded like an old man who welcomed death.

'What help is there now? Is there a mountain for us to climb. Should we run away? We are Mexica. Would this bring glory to the Mexica nation? Pity the old men and the old women and the innocent children. How can they save themselves? But there is no help. What can we do?'

Montezuma looked pleadingly at Falling Eagle, who seemed composed and showed no signs of nervousness.

'We will be judged and punished. And however it may be and whenever it may be, we can do nothing but wait.'

Part Two

October 1519 – July 1520
The Year Two Flint

November 1519

The Month of the Precious Feather

The sun wobbled as if it could not make up its mind and for a moment Montezuma held his breath. The quail cowered in their cage. He split their chests and filled a bowl with the tiny hearts. He had prayed all night, moving between his rooms and the temple, staring at the lights burning on the other side of the lake where the Spanish were celebrating. He felt surprisingly calm. This was the day he had dreaded and, now that it had come, he was impatient for it to begin. He could already hear his lords massing in the courtyard below, competing for the honour of carrying his litter.

His servants covered his arms and shins with gold. A heavy gold pectoral hung on his chest. His cloak was made of hummingbird feathers, and this morning he wore the great green headdress of Quetzalcoatl with its four hundred and fifty emerald feathers. Someone handed him his posy. Jasmine, such delicate flowers. They reminded him of Jewel. He moved slowly down the long corridors, past the rows of servants, out into a crisp autumn day, just the day for hunting. It was the day of One Wind in the month of Hunting, the day when Quetzalcoatl would appear as a whirlwind. It was the day when the world would end or begin again.

When he saw the Tlaxcalans, Lizard wished he had obeyed the priests and stayed at school. He had been so impatient to see the stags and the silver suits and the spotted dogs as large as ocelots that he had risen early and run with his friend Brown Fox over the causeway, only to find that the inhabitants of Tenochtitlán and all the other lakeside cities already occupied the best positions. The lake was crowded with families packed tightly into their canoes. The only spot that remained was a narrow space on the rickety wooden bridge connecting the causeways. The boys held tightly to each other to secure their position, which was being eyed by latecomers.

At first it was exciting to discover a world full of strange new creatures. Perhaps the most frightening were the stags who made high-pitched noises when you might have expected them to roar. The silver bells around their necks tinkled like an orchestra. It was a pity they had such ugly teeth and smelt of sweat and oil, sex and manure, and their mouths were big and vulgar like the mouths of prostitutes. And then there were the dogs, not like dogs at all, more like coyotes, who dribbled their saliva on the ground and spread their urine in puddles where it steamed in the heat.

The soldiers who followed walked noisily as if they owned the earth. The pounding of their feet drowned out the drums, flutes and whistles that accompanied them. A giant juggled with a huge banner, tossing it into the air and catching it. The crowd laughed. This was the kind of magic they enjoyed. But their laughter died at the arrival of more soldiers marching sternly in lines. Only their white faces were visible through their layers of clothing. More stags followed, prancing and dancing, displaying themselves to the mob like flirting women at a festival. And then the Tlaxcalans arrived. Thousands poured along the causeway, shouting and jeering at the crowd. Some of them pulled fireball machines in chests on wheels. The Indian women and the porters who marched with them laughed and joked as if on their way to a festival. Lizard stared in horror. The Tlaxcalans should not be here. Why were they not stopped outside the city?

'Vipers!' he shouted.

As the Tlaxcalans pushed the crowd back, the bridge shook and they all fell into the lake. A Tlaxcalan peed into the water. The boys swam to the reeds and climbed out near the fortress and ran to warn the Emperor that the whole of Tlaxcala seemed to be following the Spanish, but the crowds were so thick they could not force their way through.

'I wish we hadn't gone,' whispered Brown Fox. 'I wish we'd stuck to lessons.'

'It was all right until the Tlaxcalans arrived,' muttered Lizard.

The Emperor waited at Xoloc in the south of the city where two causeways met and twin shrines jutted out over the water. The musicians played the small drums they carried around their necks. Warmed in the morning braziers, they gave a mellow sound. Dust swirled into the instruments, into the musicians' eyes, over the magnificent mantles of the nobles fussing noisily around Montezuma. They carried posies of flowers and their feather headdresses competed with each other in height, magnificence and colour.

From the Iztapalapa causeway, five miles to the east, came the rumble of feet. Montezuma moved out into the sun and towards the bridge, stepping on his nobles' cloaks spread over the dust. Falling Eagle supported his right arm and his brother his left. Three stags approached. It did not seem possible that humans could remain attached to such monsters, but their riders showed no sign of nervousness.

A girl stood in front of him. An ordinary girl dressed like a Tlaxcalan princess but speaking like a man.

'Are you Montezuma?'

The Emperor drew himself to his full height. His green feathers waved like ferns in the wind.

'I am he,' he replied meekly as if his voice had been taken hostage. He could not tell which rider was the leader. They all looked alike. A man slid off his stag. He was not glued to it at all. He ran forward, clinking and clanking from the metal that covered his body, and hugged Montezuma. Montezuma recoiled in horror. His lords rushed to separate them. Once on the ground, the man looked quite ordinary – small, not a giant at all. No doubt if you removed the silver suit, there would be nothing left of him. When he grinned his teeth were crooked. Montezuma wondered whether he slept in his silver suit? He began his speech.

'O Lord, our Lord, you are weary. The journey has tired you, but now you have arrived on earth. You have come to your city Mexico. You have come here to sit on your throne, to sit under its canopy. Welcome to your land, my lords!'

The girl translated, but Montezuma doubted whether a village girl could understand the language of gods. In the language of the Mexica, each word was a jewel, to be treasured and displayed.

Don Hernán listened carefully, nodding as if he understood. And when Montezuma welcomed the god from the clouds and the mist to sit on his throne, Don Hernán had to be restrained from hugging him again.

Montezuma could hear, through the snorting of the stags and the roaring of the dogs, the chants of the Tlaxcalans. He had never expected to hear those war chants in his city. He wondered how many Tlaxcalans there were. From here he could see people stretching along the causeway all the way to the mainland.

He climbed into his litter. Dust coated the emerald-green canopy and the gold tassels. The Spanish leapt back onto their stags. The litter bearers took their places. The canopy bearers took theirs. The procession struggled through the crowded streets. People hung from the balconies and rooftops. They perched in the branches of the trees and even sat on the temple steps. Girls ran out to scatter petals in the dust and rush back to the safety of the crowd. A long black line of priests blew welcoming conches from the top of the temple. A drum began its slow beat.

In the Old Palace on the edge of the square, servants waited to greet their new masters. This rambling palace was large enough to house an army and it still concealed the treasures of Montezuma's father behind a false wall. New awnings and wall hangings decorated the rooms. There were scented braziers, new reed mats, and leather pillows, quilts and rabbit-fur robes, and, for the stags, grass to eat and rose petals for their beds. In the great hall a banquet had been prepared. The Spanish gawped at the girls with their bowls of water and their napkins. They did not remove their weapons or their metal suits. Nor did they wash their hands and they looked suspiciously at the salted gourd seeds and the roasted grasshoppers, but they enjoyed the fish and sweet stuffed tamales, laughing when the hot crust crumbled in their mouths. Some of them sucked at the pipes but did not know how to smoke them. Soon it was time for the speeches. Montezuma hoped his voice would not screech nervously like an old crone's as it had during rehearsals.

'Some people may have told you I am a god.' What a relief, he sounded normal. 'Do not believe them. Believe only what you see with your own eyes.'

He lifted his loincloth to show his *tepuli* with its dusting of hair, nestling between his thighs, as delicate and refined as its owner.

'You can see I am no god.'

Everyone gasped. Some stared. Some tittered. This was certainly no god's *tepuli*. Don Hernán smiled, patting the leather pouch over his own parts, as if it were perfectly normal to compare parts. Montezuma turned to display himself to everyone in the room.

When his turn came to speak, Don Hernán did not remove his pouch or expose his *tepuli*. He spoke of his god who sacrificed himself like the gods of the Mexica. But this god, like Quetzal-coatl, did not demand sacrifice. Don Hernán spoke of the first man and woman from whom all men, including the Spanish and the Mexica, were descended. He said it was sinful to sacrifice brothers. The lords made themselves comfortable. Long speeches were common at receptions and it was impolite to contradict the speaker, but this speech ended as soon as it had begun. The lords shuffled nervously on their seats. Then another Spaniard, with gold hair and beard, jumped exuberantly to his feet, and they settled again in anticipation, although they doubted the girl repeated everything that was said.

'This is a magnificent city. We have seen nothing like this.'

The golden Spaniard sat down again. The lords puffed their pipes and waited but no one else rose to speak. Montezuma smiled proudly. Of course it was a magnificent city. It was the centre of the world, the home of gods. He told Don Hernán that this was Quetzalcoatl's day of One Wind in the year One Reed. He did not tell him it was a day when Quetzalcoatl returned as a whirlwind blowing brigands and thieves into the city.

Don Hernán replied that it was November the eighth, in the year of our Lord 1519. It was a day they would both remember.

Don Hernán wanted to see everything. The tour started with the aviary which contained every bird in the world. Montezuma could recognise them all. He showed the Spanish the precious quetzals, farmed for their tails and the sharp-beaked hummingbirds, so small and fast that if you blinked you missed them. Past the parrots, there was a small cage containing a pair of solitaires. Don Hernán stopped to look.

'These seem dull birds compared to the others.'

'They have beautiful voices,' said Montezuma.

By the time the gods created the solitaires, they had run out of colours and had compensated the birds by giving them heavenly voices. The Spanish waited by the cages, but the solitaires refused to sing. They continued around the lake to the zoo where jaguars and ocelots prowled restlessly. Don Hernán stared at a limb on the floor.

'Don Hernán asks what the animals eat,' said the girl. 'I have told him that the limb is human. He does not believe me.'

'They eat the corpses of the sacrificed,' replied Montezuma.

Don Hernán crossed himself. Montezuma led the way into the monkey house where the howlers shrieked and tried to entice the visitors through the bars of their cage. The three-toed sloths amused Don Hernán, but he did not like the rattlesnakes. Montezuma observed how many of these creatures were new to these people. At the end of the animal house, in a separate cage, white-skinned people with pink eyes were sitting disconsolately.

'Don Hernán finds this abhorrent.' The girl pointed to the white-skinned people. 'He says these albino people have souls like us. They should not be caged like animals.'

'Nonsense, they are fed and cared for.'

Montezuma led the way out of the zoo back into the Sacred Square. Don Hernán looked up at the temple and asked to visit it. Montezuma quickly pointed out that the steps were dangerous. Don Hernán asked whether the Mexica were ashamed of their gods.

'Absolutely not!' said Montezuma. 'Our gods give us everything.'

The gods of the Mexica had sacrificed themselves for humans. They had died to bring the sun to life, to bring light out of darkness. This debt could only be repaid with human blood. Montezuma decided to show Don Hernán how the Mexica honoured their gods. He led them to the green frogs at the bottom of the steps and began to explain the history of the gods' abode.

'This pyramid recreates the sacred Serpent Hill.' He pointed to the pyramid from which the braziers blew out their smoke and incense. 'This mountain was the birthplace of our god. It is built on four platforms. We call these steps the Jade Steps.'

He pointed to a carved stone set at the bottom of the steps. A woman's face and limbs framed a torso compressed in the middle of the stone. Her breasts with their swollen nipples hung over her waist. Don Hernán grimaced. Montezuma continued, although he wondered if he was wasting his words.

'This goddess is the sister of Huitzilopochtli. She is the moon. He is the sun. They fight every morning for control of the earth. It is here on this spot that the bodies of the sacrificed land after they are thrown down the steps.'

The strangers looked in horror at the relief of the butchered goddess. It was hot. They began to sweat in their metal suits. They started their journey. From the top they could see the whole city spread out below. The Spanish were so entranced by the view that they stumbled over a reclining polychrome chacmool – the divine messenger – knocking over the container that was used to hold hearts. Behind him, in front of the twin shrines, the green stone of sacrifice glistened with fresh blood from the morning offering. The shrines with their stuccoed frames were newly painted – red and white for Huitzilopochtli, blue and white for Tlaloc. The Spanish clung tightly together.

In front of the curtained sanctuaries, two stone figures, covered with turquoise and mother of pearl, guarded the way. Gold masks concealed their faces. Belts of snakes embraced their waists. Gold heads hung around their necks. Montezuma pointed to one of the figures.

'This is the Earth Goddess, mother of Huitzilopochtli. His name means Hummingbird on the Left. She was decapitated by her four hundred children and her head replaced by a serpent's.'

The goddess towered above them. Her small mean eyes stared down at them. Four fangs protruded from her mouth. Her pendulous breasts were covered with a necklace of severed hearts and hands. Two pairs of hands cradled a skull. A skirt of interlaced snakes reached to her toes, half human, half claw. Don Hernán studied the statue from all angles.

Black Dog, the High Priest, emerged from the shrine. Don Hernán looked at the blood dripping from his hands and at his stained robes, and began to kiss his medallion vigorously. His men crossed themselves. Montezuma led the visitors to the stone of sacrifice but they did not even look at its carving.

'What about inside the sanctuary?' asked Don Hernán.

Montezuma hesitated. He consulted with the rows of black-robed priests, lined up in front of the shrines, beating a mournful dirge on their wooden drums. The curtains were lifted and the visitors entered. Two altars emerged from the gloom. One was dedicated to Smoking Mirror, the other to Huitzilopochtli. A wooden Huitzilopochtli sat on his bench. He clutched his golden bow and arrows. He wore his headdress of hummingbird feathers and a golden crown and where the face showed beneath a black mask, it was striped blue and yellow

'He is the God of War.' Montezuma pointed to the god's necklace of skulls and hearts.

Behind the god crouched a jewelled granite creature, half man, half lizard, covered with a cloak. This was the God of the Harvest.

His body contained all the seeds of the world. The visitors stared at the blood-coated walls, at the god's open mouth stuffed with fresh hearts. This was the holiest of shrines. No ordinary Mexica came here. So Montezuma was surprised and irritated to see some of the strangers retch and run out to vomit on the holy platform. Even Don Hernán lost his composure.

'These are not gods. These are devils. I hope you will allow us to place our cross here. It will terrify them.'

The priests struggled to contain their anger. Even Montezuma replied with some of his old force.

'I would not have shown you my gods had I known you would say such dishonourable things. We are proud of them. I beg you not to insult them.'

He moved quickly back into the shrine to atone for his sin in bringing such disrespectful visitors to the temple.

The Spanish priest in his woman's skirts ushered the men towards the stairs, trying not to slip in the blood, their pace quickening as soon as the stairs widened. Black Dog took the Emperor's place. He noticed how the Spanish avoided him, how they wrinkled their noses at his smell. He grinned. The tour was not yet over. The Spanish wanted to see everything; he would show them everything.

Black Dog led them to the room where the bodies of the sacrificed were butchered and cooked. He showed them the cell where Tlaloc's children were kept. He showed them the cooking pots and the containers of flayed skins, carved to represent the globules of fat from the flesh they contained. He even lifted a lid to expose the rotting contents. He had to agree that the stench was vile, but how he enjoyed the visitors' reaction! They followed him through the rock garden, inhabited by the spirit of the god Mixcoatl – Cloud Serpent – to the ball court in front of the pyramid. He saw how impressed they were by its size, how they examined the stone rings on the side walls and almost slipped on the smooth plaster floor. Don Hernán smiled nervously.

'A game!' he said with relief.

'This is no game,' admonished Black Dog. 'This court represents the universe. The ball is the sun and the moon. This game, as you call it, is sacred to the gods. Nothing,' he stared sternly at Don Hernán, 'in the city of the Mexica is a game.'

The visitors were silent as he showed them the wall of skulls in the Sacred Square. The Spanish crossed themselves several times and hurried across the square, past the schools and the House of Flutes where the sacred music was taught. Don Hernán muttered to himself.

These people were becoming tedious. Black Dog wished he could sacrifice them all. In his mind he imagined them climbing the steps, naked, shivering. They would not be so bold then.

The girl pointed to the skull rack and continued to translate Black Dog's words.

'These people died to feed the gods and to keep our world alive. You should know that. Where you come from, do they sacrifice?'

'Not on the scale of the Mexica,' said the girl, becoming more confident. 'Don Hernán observes how this city is both beautiful and hideous at the same time. Everywhere there is the smell of flowers mixed with the stench of death.'

'That is life!' said Black Dog, angry now. 'It is both beautiful and ugly. Life and death are two sides of the same. We are all part of the same cycle.'

'Don Hernán sees life differently.'

'It is the same life,' replied Black Dog tartly. 'How many Tlax-calans accompany you?'

'Thousands!' said the girl. 'We could not stop them. They have been so kind to us.'

December 1519

The Month of the Descent of Water

The world did not come to an end. The sun rose, the sun set. The gods were fed and the Spanish made themselves at home. They had an impressive appetite for gold, food and women. Even the Tlax-calans behaved well but the main concern was how long they would stay and whether the food would run out. And then everything changed when a gift arrived from Smoking Eagle, the Governor at the coast.

The gift stank. Bulbous eyes stared from its bloody wrapping. The corpulent head was covered with greasy black hair, its fleshy lips frozen in a scream of terror. The long beard showed that this was a Spaniard. The Emperor buried the head and filled the Great Hall with lilies to drown the lingering stench. He had almost forgotten the incident when Don Hernán turned up unexpectedly with thirty of his men. It was unusual for him to bring so many companions. Montezuma nervously picked a fruit from a bowl and handed it to Don Hernán with a flourish.

'It is sweet, is it not? As sweet as my daughters, but not as deli-cious. I offer you one of my own sweetest fruits. There is nothing as succulent as a beautiful woman.'

Don Hernán laughed but refused the fruit.

Montezuma picked another. 'There are many beautiful women among the Mexica.'

The girl interrupted. He had not noticed her presence.

'Don Hernán says he can no longer trust you. You honour him with your daughter and yet you betray him behind his back.'

At first Montezuma did not understand. Don Hernán did not have messengers running between Tenochtitlán and the coast. Surely he could not know about the head. The girl did not mince her words.

'You have murdered his friend.'

She sounded as indignant as if the head had been her father's.

'I know nothing of his death. Why should I kill friends? It does not make sense. Perhaps the Totonacs at the coast killed one of your men. I am not responsible for what they do.'

'You are the ruler. You must know everything.'

Don Hernán's men surrounded him. What a hairy smelly rabble they were. Perhaps they were pirates after all, as Falling Eagle insisted. Don Hernán braced his legs and thrust his pouch forward. The girl cast him an admiring glance.

'Don Hernán thinks you are responsible.'

'Me? I have welcomed Don Hernán to my city and given him everything. Why would I insult him?'

'Don Hernán asks the same question. He doubts you are responsible but his men are angry. He fears he cannot control them.'

'He is their leader.'

'Only as long as they choose. Unlike you, he is not appointed by God.'

The men guffawed. What a cacophony they made with their big mouths and protruding teeth. He had not noticed how like their stags they were.

'I too am answerable to my council.'

Montezuma's lords massed protectively behind him. Outside in the hall, his servants and guards waited. One shout and they would be here. And yet he felt helpless. His tongue was frozen. He noticed now that all the Spanish carried weapons. None of his councillors carried weapons in his presence. He fumbled with the seal from his bracelet and handed it to a councillor.

'I will find the person who has done this terrible deed,' he announced loudly.

'Don Hernán's men are angry,' repeated the girl. 'They suggest that you live with them until this matter is cleared up.'

Was the girl mad or had she changed the words to suit herself? Who knew whether she spoke the truth? He tried to speak as calmly as if he were in the council chamber. He was not used to defending himself to a slave.

'I cannot be a hostage. But I can offer a son and two daughters until this matter is settled.'

'The fact is, Lord Montezuma, you are at risk from Don Hernán's men.'

The men stood in front of him. Tall and short, dark and pale, stocky, skinny, with missing teeth and crooked eyes and shabby, all of them shabby.

'Don Hernán is their leader!'

'Only as long as they want. They could choose another who might not be so well disposed towards you.'

'Do men have choice?'

'These do.'

Montezuma noticed one of the men had the same lips and bulbous eyes as the head. Had the dead man's ghost returned? He tried to sound confident.

'I cannot be made a hostage, even if I would like it. My people will not suffer it.'

'Don Hernán says you will be his *guest*. He does not want to force you,' wheedled the girl.

Montezuma stood up.

'No one can force me. I am the ruler of the Mexica.'

'It would better if you came willingly,' implored the girl. 'It will give Don Hernán a chance to get to know you. He would so like to be friends . . .' She hesitated, unsure whether she had overstepped the mark of familiarity. 'This death will be forgotten, provided you come quietly. You can bring whoever you like, your lords, your women, your council. You can select your rooms. It will only be for a few days.'

'I have to officiate at the temples. I speak to the gods.'

'You are not a prisoner! Don Hernán will not stop you speaking to your gods. You can tell your people that your gods have commanded you to live with us.'

One of the Spanish rushed up to Montezuma and screamed in a piercing ear-splitting voice. A gob of spittle landed on Montezuma's chest. Even the girl seemed shocked.

'I hope you don't mind my speaking out of turn, Lord Montezuma. These are my own words. I know these men. And if I were you, I would go with them.' She leant closer. 'If you do not do as they say, I feel sure that they will kill you. I would not like to see the great Montezuma die in such a way.'

What if she spoke the truth? What would happen to the city, to the Empire, to the gods? He tried one last time.

'You can tell Don Hernán that he can have all the treasure in my father's house.'

'We have already found that.'

'There is more. Don Hernán can take whatever he wants.' He hesitated. He did not want to sound desperate. He would offer his Jewel. It would only be for a short time. It would save him and the Mexica.

'I offer something far more precious.'

His voice sounded as if it too had been taken hostage.

'More precious, Lord Montezuma?'

'My daughter.'

He regretted the words as soon as he had spoken them.

'Don Hernán says you have already offered your daughter.'

'This is my youngest daughter.'

'Don Hernán says he will take the treasure and both girls.'

Montezuma gripped the stone arms of his throne. This was like one of his dreams. Yet his lords stood there in their usual order of rank and his servants waited outside the door. His musicians and dancers rehearsed in the next room. In the kitchens his cooks would be preparing his meal. Don Hernán gripped the handle of his knife. Those knives could slice off a man's head with a single swipe. Montezuma did not fear death but he feared the chaos that would follow.

'You must come with us,' entreated the girl.

He rose as if hypnotised and stumbled out into the courtyard and into the blinding sun. Two of his councillors followed, running alongside his litter as it covered the fifty yards to his father's palace. Now Tlaxcalans occupied its courtyards. He chose his father's rooms on the first floor. From here he could see the mountains. Here he could speak to the gods. Some of his furniture was brought from his palace, a low table for eating, a comfortable chair, his sleeping mat with a fresh cover and a statue of Quetzalcoatl. He would live here like a hermit serving the gods in the same rooms where his father had been found dead with the crown of the Mexica clinging tenaciously to his head. He noticed that armed men guarded the entrance to his rooms.

'For your protection,' Don Hernán assured him pleasantly. He fussed over Montezuma, making sure his chair was placed in the right position and chasing away some of the courtiers who were plaguing the Emperor with their requests. He smiled pleasantly.

'At least we know that you are safe.'

Woman Snake crept back into the city. His feet were lacerated, his arms cut and he stank of the corpses who had shared his cell in Cholula. His servants, visibly shocked by his appearance, asked no questions but they reported that Don Hernán had taken the Emperor hostage and that the Spanish seemed to be in control of the city.

This was no surprise to Woman Snake. On his journey home he had seen torn paper streamers hanging in the trees, and he had foolishly stepped in stag manure. But it was a surprise to smell the Tlaxcalans. He wondered how many had entered the city. That steam bath would have to wait. First he would inspect the armoury and make sure the weapons were still in place.

At first the guardians did not recognise him. He found the shelves neatly stacked with weapons. Lances and bows, shields, javelins, cotton slings and bags of stones, wooden clubs, arrows and obsidian blades so sharp they could cut off a head with one blow. Then he counted the wooden helmets and harnesses, padded cotton armour and shields waiting to be customised with the crests of their owners.

When he had satisfied himself that the armoury was full, he

slipped out through the back door onto another path that led along a canal. He did not take this path often. He had almost reached the end of the towpath when two men stepped from the shadows and blocked his way. One twisted Woman Snake's hands behind his back, while the other held a pine flare up to his face.

'Where have you been at this hour?'

Woman Snake hoped they had not seen him emerge from the armoury. He mumbled some story about an aged uncle, slurring his words as if he were drunk. The men let him go. He had almost reached the gate to the square when the men caught up.

'Make it look like a robbery.'

The other man, a Tlaxcalan who smelt strongly of pulque, held a knife.

'So where is the armoury?'

'Armoury? How should I, a humble peasant, know?'

The first man grabbed Woman Snake's hands.

'Clean and smooth like a lord's!'

'I am a scribe.'

'A peasant or a scribe?'

The knife pressed into Woman Snake's back. The men pushed him along the towpath.

'Lead us there.'

Woman Snake searched desperately for other people but no one was out in this part of the city at such a late hour. Beyond the reeds, the lake beckoned. He hated the water. When one of the men stumbled over a tree root, Woman Snake jumped into the reeds thrashing his way through the water out towards the fishing nets. He saw the glint of the knife and he heard arguments. When the two men ran in the direction of the armoury, he climbed out and stumbled home in his wet clothes and bare feet. He heard the conches sound midnight.

His bath restored him. The luxury of hot water on a cold night was one of the joys of the civilised world that the Mexica had created. He sent for the girl to play her flute. Music, warmth and food were all a man required. If he were to die, he would die clean, with a full stomach, in a haze of pulque and serenaded by music. It would be better than dying alone in that terrible tomb in the centre of the pyramid, forgotten by the world. Had it not been for the youth being fattened for the gods, who showed him the way out, he would never have survived, and it was a shame that he had had to push the boy to his death.

He climbed up to his roof. Pine flares outlined the city streets and canals. Up on the shrines he saw the priests lighting the braziers. There was no sign of the Spanish. Here nothing seemed to have changed.

He could not sleep. He dozed, rising hourly to pee in his bowl. But no sooner had he emptied his bladder than the urge returned. And then, just before dawn, Falling Eagle arrived with terrible news. The Spanish had raided the armoury during the night. They had taken all the wooden weapons and were building a giant pyre in front of the temple.

'Who will they burn?' asked Woman Snake.

'No one knows.'

'Why did no one challenge the Spanish?' asked Woman Snake. 'After all most of the lords were there with the Emperor.'

'The Spanish were armed. I was not there, but I am told that the Emperor followed Don Hernán like a child. His mind has been taken hostage with his body. No doubt he will give you his reasons, if he has any. The lords I spoke to were convinced that Don Hernán had put a spell on him, but there is no doubt that the Spanish would have killed him if he had resisted. He knew that.'

'How did you know I had returned?'

'You were seen at the Eagle Gate. Not much goes on around here without someone knowing. I am glad you survived Cholula. We had given you up for dead. It is not the same without you in charge.'

'There is not much I can do to resolve this without arms.'

'I do not care about the Emperor,' said Falling Eagle, 'but I do care about our reputation. This makes a mockery of the Mexica.'

Since dawn people had been gathering to claim the best positions. The pyre was large enough to burn them all. A few sparks already teased the wood. It cracked and spat for the wood was dry. The smoke turned the rich colour of flames, leaping like dancers, wrapping themselves around the weapons, sending fingers of heat out towards the crowd, warming them in the chilly dawn. Woman Snake stared at the ground where the dust crystallised in the heat. A voice shouted.

'May the gods preserve us. The Emperor is chained like a prisoner.'

The Emperor emerged from his palace, accompanied by his two high priests and the Spanish priest in his woman's skirts. The crowd parted to let them through. Don Hernán and his soldiers followed with bands of drummers and flautists. The Emperor stumbled and would have fallen, had not Don Hernán rushed to support him. Whispers floated through the crowd like the wind in the rushes. 'They will burn him!' The councillors and the Eagle and Jaguar knights clustered helplessly together. The fire hissed like a snake. A Spanish drum rolled. Someone played a whistle. A man in opulent robes emerged from the room beneath the temple.

'It is the Governor, Smoking Eagle!' gasped Woman Snake. He watched Spanish soldiers drag Smoking Eagle towards the flames and kick him into the fire where red tongues devoured him.

A voice yelled from the crowd. 'A curse on the Spanish!'

The girl called nervously. 'Don Hernán warns this is what happens to those who murder his men.'

A corpulent man from Smoking Eagle's retinue struggled with his captors as he too was pushed into the flames.

'Fight, or you will be next, Mexica!' came another cry.

The flames snapped hungrily. The lords watched in horror as Smoking Eagle's sons followed him into the inferno. The Emperor showed no emotion. He did not even wipe the sweat from his face. Woman Snake spat out the bitter bile rising in his throat. His lips were blistered, his hair smelt scorched. The crowd did not move until a woman collapsed and sobs broke out among the girls.

A soldier bent and unlocked the Emperor's chains. Montezuma rubbed his ankles, looked up at the sky, then turned and, shielding himself with his cloak, followed the Spanish back across the square.

'He fears us more than the Spanish!' spat Falling Eagle.

'Don Hernán has stolen his soul!' gasped Woman Snake.

'I shall leave the city,' declared Falling Eagle. 'I cannot stay here a moment longer. There are many who will come with me.'

Montezuma sat in his chair smoking his pipe. Lords, courtiers and councillors fussed around him. He smiled feebly when he saw Woman Snake.

'At last you return! I had thought you quite dead. I had almost chosen your successor. Some good news at least.'

He saw Woman Snake glance at the remains of a meal scattered on a table and at the four Spanish soldiers lounging in a corner.

'This is not what you think. It is only temporary. I am still the ruler of my people. You will see how the Spanish respect me.'

'The armoury is empty. We have no weapons.'

Montezuma took a puff of his pipe, pinched his nostrils and coughed vigorously.

'We do not need them at present. My relationship with Don Hernán is cordial.'

'So Don Hernán rules us now?'

'You do not understand.'

'Smoking Eagle was one of your most loyal governors.'

'If he had not sent that head, I would not be here now.'

'Don Hernán planned this. That head was only an excuse.'

'The Spanish were armed. I had no alternative. It is important that we remain on good terms. I am an ambassador for my people. I must convince Don Hernán that I still rule the Mexica.'

'Here as a prisoner in this room?'

'Don Hernán assures me this is not forever. The Spanish will will release me. The girl assures me they are honourable men. They cannot stay here without my permission, and you are still my Chief Councillor. I insist on daily meetings, here in this room and sometimes Don Hernán will join us.'

'So you are not concerned by the Tlaxcalans. There are thousands here.'

For a moment Montezuma looked frightened. 'Thousands?'

'Thousands. How will you control them?'

'Don Hernán assures me he has the situation in hand.'

Woman Snake turned and left, pushing his way through the curious Spanish clustering around the doorway, past the hordes of Tlaxcalans blocking the corridors and stairs. Once outside, he ordered his bearers to run across the square past the smouldering pyre, through the narrow streets. He did not feel safe until his gates slammed behind him.

Montezuma watched Woman Snake leave, without the usual polite farewell. Diplomacy was the only way to proceed now. Don Hernán had proved most cooperative once Montezuma had agreed to the public burning. Don Hernán visited every day, sitting on a stool, discussing matters of state. He even accompained Montezuma to the temple, although he used the time to speak of his god. These arguments about their gods did not end amicably.

Don Hernán admired the Mexica and wanted to know their history. The only problem was that all their conversation passed through that girl and she was no friend of the Mexica. But Don Hernán's enthusiasm was infectious. His latest idea was to build boats with sails that could travel on the lake and impress all the other cities. Montezuma was so intoxicated with this idea that he agreed to provide the wood and carpenters and the work had already begun. He had not dared tell Woman Snake. Woman Snake was so gloomy these days, seeing problems where there were none. In fact, all the councillors were gloomy. None of them appreciated what their emperor was doing. A good relationship with the Spanish was better than war and there was little the Mexica could do until the unlucky year of One Reed ended.

And were it not for the uncertainty, this would be a pleasant interlude.

'A game, Lord Montezuma?'

Don Alvarado stood in the doorway. His nickname was 'Tonatiuh' – the Sun. Montezuma did not trust or like this handsome man. There was a cruel curve to his mouth and he was, unlike Don Hernán, a man of rough temper, although he played a good game of *patolli*.

'Bring the counters!' ordered Montezuma.

The guards moved into the room. The Emperor was generous with his winnings. His pockets were always full of jewels. The truth was that he was terrified of being alone, terrified of the demons that threatened him at night, terrified of the hostility of his people and was prepared to pay for company.

January 1520

The Month of Growth

Jewel huddled disconsolately in her chair, clutching her rabbit-fur blanket. She could smell the burning flesh and taste the ash that settled on the air. If her father could not save Smoking Eagle, how could he protect her? What would happen to them all now? In the city people went about with their heads bowed.

She was still huddled in her chair when Falling Eagle peered through the bead curtain in the doorway laughing at her. She would not have been so embarrassed had he found her naked. Her flute with its bird's head lay on the floor where she had thrown it. It was such a struggle to learn the flute. Even her little dog left the room when she practised.

She wondered what had brought him here. He had not visited for four months. And now he found her half dressed with her hair hanging loose, her feet bare and with yellow ointment smeared on her cheeks.

He let the curtain fall, then he checked to make sure the servants had gone. It was not unusual for them to squat outside and eavesdrop. He perched awkwardly on a wicker stool next to the open window while Jewel ran to find his pipe, which he had left in her rooms. She wondered how many pipes he had in other women's rooms around the city.

'I leave tonight,' he told her. He peered warily at the yellow spots, as if she suffered some terrible disease. 'I cannot say where I am going. Otherwise, your father, that traitor,' – he spat out the words – 'will find out. I cannot risk it.'

'Alone?'

He hesitated as if he did not trust her.

'There are many who think like me.'

'My father listens to the gods,' she said defensively.

'So the gods tell him to burn his most loyal governor?'

'I do not know what they tell him.'

She wanted to enjoy Falling Eagle, not argue with him.

'My spies assure me that Don Hernán is as human as we are.'

'He had divine help at Cholula.'

'He had warning of our plans. Either the Tlaxcalans heard something and warned them. Or . . .'

'Or?'

'Some say that girl, Malinalli, warned him. She made friends with some foolish woman in the city who told her to escape while she could. And, of course, she told Don Hernán.'

'She betrayed her people.'

'She is not a Mexica.'

'Is she as beautiful as they say?'

'Not as beautiful as you.'

'Me, beautiful?'

'I have always thought so.'

'Why didn't you tell me?'

'You think beauty makes such a difference?'

She knew it did. None of his other women were plain.

'I am sorry if I disappoint you.'

She kept her eyes demurely at the floor. Men liked women who were demure.

'On the contrary. You do not disappoint me at all.'

He stared hungrily at her. Did he notice that she had reddened her lips just a little?

She lowered her voice. 'Do you have to leave now?'

'Not right now.'

He unfolded the carved screen and divided the room, and placed two sleeping mats on the floor. Light from the braziers flickered through the holes in the screen like stars. She no longer had any appetite for games. She wanted Falling Eagle too much. He seemed clumsy as if he had forgotten her. Perhaps this was a good thing. Perhaps they could start again without the shadow of her father hanging over them. He untied her hair and ran his hands roughly through it, pulling on her scalp. The pain was exquisite. He had never noticed her hair or any other part of her. She untied his loincloth. He stood there with the light from the brazier playing on that secret part of him, where his legs met his body, where his 'worm' nestled.

He pulled her to the floor. The folds of her shawl mixed its colours into her hair. His hands travelled roughly over her body. When she felt his fingers touch her place of joy, she moaned and opened her legs until she could stretch them no further, like the warm earth opening its pores to the seed corn. He sat up and held a taper over her body.

'I thought you did not like me.'

'That was only a game.'

He blew her hair off her face. 'You don't need to play games with me and you don't need to paint your face.' He rubbed the yellow spots. 'I am sorry my visit has to be so brief.'

She laughed again with happiness.

'You will return?'

'I certainly intend to.' He stretched out for his loincloth. 'We leave tonight.'

His grave eyes belied his cheerfulness. They had no right to be so happy. Her father was a prisoner. Tlaxcalans roamed the city. She watched him dress.

'They have humiliated my father.'

'He does not see how Don Hernán manipulates him. The Spanish are building new boats. Do you think they will use them for pleasure? No. They will explore our lake and make new allies. Yet your father provides the wood and the carpenters. He does anything Don Hernán asks. He has even agreed to go sailing in them. Those boats must be destroyed.'

Ant Flower appeared coquettishly with Falling Eagle's cloak. Ant Flower always flirted with Falling Eagle. Apart from the Lord Montezuma, he was the only man she admired.

'Can I come with you?' begged Jewel.

Falling Eagle seemed surprised.

'There is no place for a woman.' At the door he looked back. 'There is something else. I almost hesitate to tell you.'

'You can tell me anything.'

'I would rather you did not visit your father.'

'He is my father.'

'The Spanish have put a spell on him. Your father is so in thrall to Don Hernán that he would give him anything he wants, even his own daughter.'

She did not believe him. It was impossible. Her father would never give her away. When she was young, he would not even consider her marriage to anyone beyond the valley.

'He offered you as hostage to save himself. All his lords heard him.'

'No! It is not true.'

'He would do anything to save himself. I do not want you in danger. I shall not be here to protect you.'

He took his cape from Ant Flower and was gone, leaving Jewel alone with her fear. How fragile love was! One minute exhilaration, the next weeping. Her father would never give her away like a sack of maize. But what if he had changed, as Falling Eagle said? A man whose soul was stolen by demons might give everything away, even his daughter. She pulled her fur coverlets around her and called for her braziers. The nights were cold in December. There would be a frost tonight.

In the morning her father's servant Deer turned up pleading for her to visit. Her father suffered terrible dreams; he shouted in his sleep. He was a man who loved his family. He asked why his daughter did not visit.

'No!' she said.

She turned her face to the wall. But Deer came the next day and the next, and the next.

'No,' she repeated.

'The Emperor begs you to come, Lady.'

Ant Flower offered to go with her. She did not believe that the Lord Montezuma would give his favourite daughter away.

Jewel dressed plainly. She wore no jewellery. But she did carry a posy of her father's favourite flowers. When she had suffered her first bleed, he had given her a posy of jasmine. 'Such a cheeful little flower,' he used to say.

She walked boldly across the square with Ant Flower tagging behind and Deer beside her. It was an ordeal. They almost gave up. Tlaxcalans were everywhere, pushing themselves in front of her, taunting her, pinching her, mocking Ant Flower. Jewel had not realised how many Tlaxcalans occupied the Old Palace or that she had to pass through them to cross the courtyards. She refused to let herself be frightened and walked proudly, ignoring the men who crowded around her. One of the Tlaxcalans thrust himself in front of her, pressing his body against her so that she could feel his *tepuli*. Hands crawled up her skirt.

'Lady, you will soon feel many of these in your vessel.'

Fingers probed roughly. A soldier held her from behind. She could feel his *tepuli* pressing between her buttocks. She saw Ant Flower struggling. She saw Deer pushed to the ground. She screamed. But she was surrounded by Tlaxcalans. She slipped to the floor and tried to crawl away from the dirty hands that prodded in all her secret places. She closed her eyes. Then the Tlaxcalans backed away as a pale-skinned Spanish boy rushed forward with his sword. For a moment Jewel thought he too would join in, but he beckoned her to follow him up the stairs. Ant Flower clutched Jewel's hand.

On the staircase, two Spanish skirmished with their swords. The Spanish boy escorted her to her grandfather's old rooms. She saw the serpents' eyes in the murals had been gouged out and the cross of the Spanish god drawn over the fang teeth. At the end of the corridor, at the entrance to the old apartments, a girl waited. This must be the traitor Falling Eagle had spoken of. It was foolish to come, but the thought of running the Tlaxcalan gauntlet again terrified her. She bit her tongue. The girl was lovely. Then Jewel remembered Falling Eagle had said she was even more beautiful. This knowledge gave her confidence. The girl spoke first.

'So you are his daughter?'

'I am.'

The girl smirked.

'You'd be surprised how many wives and daughters he has.'

'That is true. He does.'

'These are not wives or daughters.'

The girl pointed through a half-open door where Montezuma sat with two councillors in a small room full of Spanish soldiers. He looked like a seedling blighted by huge conifers. Jewel ran and threw herself into his arms.

'Father!'

He sniffed her posy.

'Such cheerful little flowers.'

She began to cry. She dared not tell him about the Tlaxcalans.

'Do not cry for me. This will not last.'

'Falling Eagle makes plans. I know he does. He will rescue you.'

She had gabbled indiscreetly. She had not meant to say anything.

'Rescue me? I am here of my own free will. I do not need rescuing. Do not allow resistance on my behalf.' He paused a moment. 'You know where Falling Eagle is?'

He saw a chance to redeem himself. It was Don Hernán who had brought the humiliating news of the deserters. How could he admit that he had not known, that his visitors no longer confided in him?

His guile shocked her.

'I have no idea,' she said quickly.

How glad she was that Falling Eagle had not confided in her. Such a chatterbox as she could not be relied upon. She changed the subject.

'You will find release in poems. You have always complained of a lack of time. Now there is much of it.'

'Maybe too much,' he said sadly. 'Poems are particular. They will come only if they want. What news?' he asked suddenly.

She could think of nothing to say. She spoke of her mother, of her dog who was becoming fat, of her clothes and her sister, of her struggle to learn the flute. Her father interrupted.

'I was foolish to marry you to Falling Eagle. He is a traitor.'

'I love him, father.'

'He is unlucky. Look at his name, "the eagle that falls". The sun that drops from the sky brings death and destruction.'

Now she felt terrified. Her father had given her away after all.

'He has atoned for his name, father. You know that.'

'It has not changed anything.'

They sat awkwardly next to each other, looking out at the sky where wispy clouds chased each other like naughty children. This was something she had not expected: that her father, whose oratory was lauded throughout the empire, had been abandoned by his words. When she was a child her father had told her that the air was full of words searching for suitable tongues to give them life. And she would run out into the garden looking for those elusive words. How her father used to laugh.

'I have discovered just how perfidious words are,' he said sadly. Some days they do not visit at all.'

Were the words that passed between himself and Don Hernán perfidious?

Jewel heard the rattle of metal. Don Hernán walked in. He stared boldly at at her.

'Is this your delicious fruit? How many fruits are there in this orchard of yours, Lord Montezuma?

Jewel clung to her father. Guards blocked the doorway. No one could escape from this room. Don Hernán stepped closer. She saw the hair clinging to his face and the voluptuous lips. She smelt his stale breath. As his body brushed against her, she felt the heat of his *tepuli*.

The girl laughed. 'You needn't worry. Don Hernán does not force himself on women.'

'No doubt you are one of them.'

'One of your sisters and two of your cousins are,' replied the girl quickly. 'Your father is generous with his women. You will be next. He has already offered you.'

'Whore!' shouted Jewel.

'So would you be in my position.'

Jewel glared at the girl.

'My name is Malinalli,' said the girl.

'What kind of name is that?' shrieked Jewel. She knew she sounded like one of the witches of the night. 'You should stay at home and not spread your bad luck among us.'

'I tried to,' said the girl sadly.

'Daughter, daughter' said Montezuma sadly. 'Go quickly. Juan will escort you.'

The boy took her arm roughly. She tried to shake him off and ran out onto the stairs, past the Spanish men still practising with their arms and the Tlaxcalans who were blocking the doors. Now she clung to Juan. In the courtyard the Spanish were preparing a feast on an open fire. Jewel hid her face in her shawl and followed the boy across the square. When they were safely across, Jewel shook the boy off and ran with Ant Flower through the gates to the gardens bordering the canal. She would have run all the way to Coyoacan if she could. She ran past the statues and the empty benches and the sad ahuehuete trees whose mossy hair hung like abandoned maidens'. She had lost Ant Flower! She turned right onto a wide path guarded by a coiled serpent, past the stone seat with its carved water dog, and nearly tripped over the poinsettia roots wrapped in damp bark ready for planting to flower at Huitzilopochtli's birth feast at the end of the year. Out across the withered grass, past the cages of animals and the pink-eyed, white-skinned creatures who poked their fingers through the bars as she rushed past, out along the canal and to her father's palace where her mother and sister lived.

When she reached the women's rooms, she was trembling. The aunts and the cousins ceased their chattering and stared with their eagle eyes. Jewel felt sure they could see the finger marks all over her.

'What is it, daughter?'

'Father . . .' she stuttered, 'father has given me to Don Hernán.'

Her mother put her arms around her. Jewel saw that her mother had been crying.

'It is not you he has given away. Your sister Butterfly moves today to live with Don Hernán. She will be his whore.'

The aunts and the cousins muttered that if the girl had been found a husband none of this would have happened.

'Nonsense' said the Lady Tecalco briskly. 'Even a husband could not save her.'

'My father says my marriage to Falling Eagle is a mistake. What can I do, mother?'

The Lady Tecalco sighed.

'There is nothing we can do. Demons have stolen your father's mind. There is no knowing what he will do next.'

February 1520

The Month of the Ceasing of Water

The four Spanish boats were completed at the beginning of the new month. Each carried seventy-five men and four cannon. On one an awning had been erected and here Montezuma sat dressed in his ceremonial cloak, comforted by this proof of his importance. The sun caught one of the brass cannons, making it reflect like a mirror, and Montezuma could not resist snatching a glimpse of himself. The cavernous hollow-eyed ghost who stared back shocked him. Either this mirror lied or magic had changed him into a person whom his own gods could not have recognised.

The boat moved from its mooring and started to bob up and down, as if uncertain where on the water to settle. Montezuma sat down quickly. How could anyone trust the wind? But the Spanish seemed unconcerned. They tied cotton sheets onto the poles, where they flapped like the wings of a giant crane, and the boats began to slice through the water, like knives through flesh. The wind grabbed Montezuma's headdress and blew his hair into his eyes. And for a moment he felt his head detach itself from his body, as if it wanted to be left behind. It was a most curious sensation. How the wind played tricks with men.

As the first island approached, he watched as the cotton sheets were lowered and tied around the poles. The boats anchored in the water. His servants carried Montezuma and the lords ashore. Everyone fanned out for the hunt. The beaters blew their whistles. And when everything on that island had been hunted down and left for the slower canoes to collect, the lords and the Spanish returned to their boats and scudded on to the next island and the next and the next, reaching islands on the far side of the lake which it would have taken a day to reach in a canoe. As Montezuma became used to the motion of the water, he began to enjoy the speed and the movement of the boat. He watched the sails engage with the wind. He watched the cannon being lit and the stones explode on the water like rocks dropped from the sky. He smelt the familiar odour of pitch and sulphur. And then he felt fear. What if the wind should drop and leave them stranded out here in the middle of the lake? Would the oarsmen be able to row back before the emergence of the twilight monsters? Don Hernán seemed relaxed. Did he fear any demons? Even Quetzalcoatl had been defeated by his enemies. Montezuma beckoned to Malinalli who seemed at home on the water. He asked whether Don Hernán feared demons.

'His god protects him from demons.'

How this girl seized every chance to speak about the new god. People who changed their gods always were the most persistent. It seemed a good time to converse, sitting here under his awning watching the light on the water. It would soon be time to feed Tlaloc at his shrine in the mountains. Perhaps Don Hernán would permit the procession to travel in one of these boats.

'You know,' he said to Don Hernán, who shared the awning with him, 'this is a marvellous way to travel. I wonder why we did not think of it ourselves.' He knew perfectly well why the Mexica had not thought of it. Quetzalcoatl might have been offended by such frivolous use of the wind. Men could not presume on the gods. Only Quetzalcoatl himself could use the wind.

'Where we come from,' replied Don Hernán pleasantly, 'men have sailed like this for thousands of years.'

Thousands of years! No doubt Don Hernán would blame the Mexica gods for this lapse. If only he would forget his god. The Mexica did not force people to adopt their gods. Rather, they absorbed the conquered gods into their own pantheon. You could never have too many gods. He had offered the Spanish god a home in the dark temple which the foreign gods shared with the old Earth Goddess, whose feast fell during this month. But the gummy toothless goddess had revolted Don Hernán.

'Woman Snake!' called Montezuma.

Woman Snake was leaning over the end of the boat.

'This is a wonderful invention. There is just one problem. The boats travel too quickly for poems. The words would never find us. They would never catch up.'

He wanted to share his excitement with Woman Snake, but he was leaning over the end of the boat vomiting. He felt the frost on the air. This was the most dangerous hour and he was relieved when the boats turned for home where, despite the demons, large crowds still lined the shore. The lords, now huddled in their cloaks, watched the city rush at them and some of them clung to the edge of the boat, terrified it would not stop in time. The cannons fired their sulphur balls. The sails were miraculously lowered and the boats manoeuvred gently back into place. Montezuma could not hide his excitement. It was a wonderful thing to combine wind and oars. Such a miracle had never been seen before in Tenochtitlan. Now he was safely back on land, he could not wait to go sailing again.

He felt elated. Don Hernán had made a fuss of him. He had even shown him how to use a smoke stick. But it made too much noise and mess for hunting. It had blown his hare to pieces. It was heavy to carry and difficult to light. It was not a useful weapon. Don Hernán had been more attentive than the Mexica lords. The Spanish had treated him regally, as he deserved. That night he slept like a baby.

Woman Snake did not enjoy the boat trip. Apart from the sickness he worried constantly that some kind of accident might be engineered by the Spanish to rid themselves of the lords who opposed them. He had observed how Don Hernán placed himself in Woman Snake's place next to Montezuma. It was clear Don Hernán planned to usurp Woman Snake's role as advisor. He watched Don Hernán charm and flatter Montezuma. Nor was Woman Snake fooled by the purpose of the trip. Those boats went out frequently now and not always for hunting. They explored the lakes, discovering there were five of them, how they ran together in the wet season, how their levels varied, how some were fresh and others saline. They measured the depths and discovered the sources of the springs. And as he observed them out on the lake Woman Snake had a terrifying thought. These boats were an ideal weapon for war, capable of carrying many people and the cannons, which could be used, he noted, even when the boats were moving. And that was not all. With these boats, the Spanish could escape quickly even if the causeways were lifted. This realisation focused his mind as nothing had done before. It was not enough to store stones and replace the wooden arms burnt by the Spanish. He would have to search again for allies. It would not be easy. What could the Mexica offer now?

But the next morning a canoe paddled over from Texcoco with the news that the Emperor's hot-headed nephew Cacama was assembling an army. Although it was not certain whether Cacama planned to rescue his uncle or seize the throne, the Mexica were not ready for war. There were not enough weapons to replace those that had been burnt and the time was not auspicious. Nor was Cacama the man to lead a rebellion.

Woman Snake dared not summon the council for there were some who would side with Cacama. He sent for his fellow chief councillors and the rulers of Tacuba and Texcoco and, because he was a wise ruler who had lived through difficult times, the old Governor of Tlatelolco. No one could believe what he told them, but they all agreed on Cacama's bad timing, although none of them wanted to betray the young king. If the youth led his army to confront the Spanish in Tenochtitlán, it would look as if the Emperor had colluded in the plan and this could result in another Cholula. The plot would have to be revealed to the Spanish in such a way that they would not suspect Montezuma or anyone connected with him, and so it would have to be the Emperor himself who did the deed. It would relieve him of all suspicion. The councillors argued as to who should inform the Emperor. They all, without prompting, looked at Woman Snake.

The Governor of Tlatelolco agreed to accompany him. They crossed the square together, Woman Snake helping the Governor, who limped badly.

'He will be pleased to see us,' said the Governor.

Montezuma was so engrossed in a game of *patolli* with Don Hernán and Don Alvarado that he did not notice them at first. When it was his turn to shuffle the counters, he called out.

'Alvarado cannot add up properly. He gives Don Hernán too high a score.' They all doubled up laughing. Then they divided jewels into little piles on the floor.

'But this time I win.'

Montezuma handed his winnings to the soldiers guarding him. He has become one of them, thought Woman Snake. He curries favour with his guards.

'I do not think he lacks for company,' he whispered to the Governor. He had not seen Montezuma so animated for years. He knew the names of all the men and introduced them to Woman Snake.

'This is Juan,' he pointed to the boy, 'and here are Pedro, Trujillo and Bernal Díaz, all valiant fellows when you get to know them, although they have terrible table manners.'

The Spanish laughed. Even their laughter sounded coarse.

'They have cast a spell on him,' whispered the Governor. 'How will we speak to him privately?'

'Speak up' said Montezuma. 'There are no secrets here.'

'I wish, Lord, that I had practised more at *patolli* so that I could match these valiant fellows.'

When the boy translated, the Spanish smiled broadly. The boy divided the red and blue counters among the players. Montezuma had first throw of the black beans. He prayed to the god Five Flower and then threw a perfect ten. He grinned like a schoolboy.

'See, Woman Snake, how the gods favour me! Come and join us.'

Woman Snake perched stiffly on his haunches and took up the black beans and threw.

'A poor throw. The gods do not favour you at all, Woman Snake. They never did.'

Montezuma threw another perfect ten.

'I was always lucky.'

He turned to give his winnings to a rough-looking soldier who guarded the door. Woman Snake watched the man's face break into a smile. He realised the Spanish loved the Emperor more than his own people did. Don Hernán left. But the guards and Don Alvarado lingered. The girl was not here. There was no one who spoke Nahuatl. Montezuma shook the counters again. Woman Snake leant forward and whispered.

'Cacama has raised an army against you.'

The counters clattered onto the floor. Montezuma looked around to see if anyone had heard.

'You lie!'

'He does not come to rescue you.'

'What are you suggesting? He is my sister's son. He has not fled like the others.'

'For good reason!' Woman Snake retorted. 'Someone will have to warn Don Hernán.'

'I do not understand you. You dislike Don Hernán and yet you wish to warn him. What is your aim here? Do you plot against me as you did at Cholula? Did you think I did not know?'

'We do not need war now.'

'I thought you wanted war.'

'Not now, with no weapons. If you warn Don Hernán, you will gain his trust and save thousands of Mexica lives. If anyone else speaks up, Don Hernán will assume you deliberately concealed this information. He will associate you with the plot.'

Montezuma hung his head in his hands.

'Why did you not hide this from me? Cacama is no traitor. What are you trying to do? Betray our family? How can I trust you now? I know you wish to destroy Don Hernán, yet you betray Cacama who has the same desire for war as you do. Do you think me blind? What is your plan?' He hesitated. 'No, do not tell me, for then I am placed in an impossible position. I know the council consider me a traitor, but everything I do is to protect the Mexica.'

'If you will not tell Don Hernán, I will do it. But this will only demean you in his eyes.'

'Is there someone else who could be blamed?' Montezuma looked desperately at Woman Snake. 'You do not understand my struggle. Nothing will convince me that my nephew plots against me.'

'Your nephew brags that he will kill the Spanish in four days. He calls you feeble-hearted. Are these the words of a rescuer?'

Montezuma hid his face in his hands. The guards looked up and one of them sidled over.

'Whatever I do will be wrong,' whined Montezuma. 'I wish I could retire to the cave of Huemac. Perhaps when this is all over, I shall do so. I shall be the first ruler of the Mexica who has willingly relinquished his power. How will the histories judge me, as hero or coward?'

Woman Snake turned to leave. At the door he threw the last of his jewels and watched the Spanish scrabble for them.

'Nothing but pirates all of them,' he muttered. The Governor of Tlatelolco, who was fond of Montezuma, volunteered to stay and keep him company.

It was at night that Montezuma felt his isolation most keenly. It was not the comforting isolation of the hermit when the gods are close; it was the desolation of exile. The days promised by Don Hernán had turned into months. Don Hernán assured him it was for his own protection and that he was not a prisoner, although guards sat outside his door and he had to ask permission to travel and never went anywhere without an escort. He felt like a tree struggling against the wind, blowing daily in a different direction. When the wind blew him north towards the region of the dead, his depression returned. Some days when the wind turned him west towards the setting sun, he felt like an old man. But most days the wind blew him south into the direction of uncertainty.

Sometimes, in his more desperate moments, he wondered what would happen if he escaped from his daily procession to the temple and disappeared into the crowd. But what would it achieve? No, this was neither the right time nor the right year. The time would come when he would know what the gods advised, but for now there was the problem of Cacama.

He loved the youth like his own son. He remembered the family feasts, the picnics and the hunting trips. Five years ago he had sent his warriors to make sure Cacama inherited the Texcoco throne, for there were other heirs. Now the boy had raised an army to rescue *him*. There could be no other explanation. The boy was ambitious. They had often laughed about this, but he would never betray his uncle.

But when Don Hernán arrived the next morning, Montezuma did not feel so confident. Don Hernán perched on a stool, as if he expected it to collapse beneath him.

Montezuma cracked his knuckles nervously.

'News has reached me of a plot.'

Don Hernán peeled his gloves from his fingers and placed them on a table.

'Do you know who is responsible?'

Perhaps, thought Montezuma, he could implicate someone else. But Don Hernán said nothing and Montezuma realised that somehow Don Hernán knew everything. He found himself babbling nervously.

'Cacama is young and foolish. He does not mean what he says. I ask that you treat him mercifully.'

Don Hernán stared at the bowl of butchered quail.

'Mercy, Lord Montezuma? The boy would kill us all. Even you! He tries to seize your throne.'

'It is a harmless escapade.'

'Then your warriors must take action. It is better if we keep out of your domestic affairs.'

He could not fight his nephew. He could not fight a member of the Triple Alliance. Tenochtitlán, Texcoco and Tacuba were allies. They never fought each other, whatever the circumstances. But Don Hernán would not understand this.

'Very well,' said Don Hernán after a long pause.

'You will be kind to the boy?'

Don Hernán did not reply. Outside in the streets Montezuma could hear the sweepers cleaning in preparation for a new day.

Don Hernán seemed quite at home in the Old Palace. He sprawled comfortably in one of the Emperor's wicker chairs.

'I will come straight to the point.' Don Hernán fingered his beard and waited for Malinalli to translate. 'Were you aware of this plot?'

This was difficult. If Woman Snake professed to know nothing, it would demonstrate his lack of power. On the other hand he must distance himself from the Emperor.

'I never trusted the boy,' he said slowly. 'He takes advantage of his uncle. You see, his mother was the Emperor's favourite sister. She died in unpleasant circumstances and the Emperor raised him as one of his own sons. I doubt this was anything more than the foolish dreams of youth. The boy wants to save his uncle. He acts impetuously as you or I might have done once.'

Don Hernán listened coldly.

'I was never so foolish and I suspect that neither were you.'

'The Emperor did warn you as soon as he heard rumours.'

'So you knew nothing?'

'Cacama does not confide in me.'

'It surprises me that none of the Emperor's councillors have attempted to rescue him.'

Woman Snake knew that Don Hernán did not trust or like him. Did Don Hernán know more about him that he himself knew? Don Hernán was the kind of man to find out everything about a man and use this information to destroy him. This was how he won wars.

Woman Snake smiled graciously.

'The Emperor enjoys your company. You yourself say he is no captive. He assures me he is no captive. There is no need for rescue. I have a question for you. I am curious to know how you discovered our lands.'

'Ships have been sailing these waters for some years now. The Pope . . .'

'Pope?' interrupted Woman Snake.

'He is like your high priest, only more powerful. He has given your lands to us.'

'Does he know our lands?'

'No.'

'How can this priest give away lands he neither knows nor owns?'

'He has the right to give away lands whose people believe in false gods. He sends us to bring you the true faith. That is the reason for our visit.'

'Visit?'

Malinalli seemed embarrassed.

'So you will return home some day?'

Malinalli interrupted.

'All these questions, Lord Woman Snake, serve no purpose. You should be pleased that this holy man wishes to save us all.'

'No wonder you praise his virtues since he has saved you from slavery.'

He knew he had angered her. No doubt she played her own game. Or did she do this out of love for Don Hernán? He laughed loudly.

'You find scorn amusing?'

'No, Doña Marina.' He used her Spanish name to flatter her. 'I admire you for your courage. You are wise beyond your years.'

'The Spanish' – she looked fondly at Don Hernán – 'allow women to speak. I am not subject to men's orders.'

'Not even to Don Hernán's?'

'What I do for Don Hernán I do of my own free will.'

'How long will you stay free, Doña Marina. How long will your tongue remain useful?'

He noticed a flicker of fear in her eyes.

'I see no end to it.'

For a moment Woman Snake felt sorry for her. Still, life was as uncertain for women as for men, even if their voices were louder. He rose to leave. He had found out nothing about the lands of the Spanish. He would ask again next time.

'I am sure we can find you friends among the Mexica.'

The girl's mood changed.

'Never, Lord Woman Snake. Never.'

March 1520

The Month of the Flaying of Men

Cacama hobbled painfully on bare feet. The chains had cut into his flesh.

'Here,' jeered a Spanish soldier, 'is the King of Texcoco.'

Nephew!' Montezuma moved to welcome him.

Cacama's eyes were dull from torture and lack of sleep.

'You have made a mistake, Uncle. The real traitor is my brother Vanilla Flower. He has sided with the Spanish, yet you ignore him. These people bewitch you. They steal your soul. Your body has been usurped by a coward. You could have fought, yet you lack the will. We could have killed these barbarians in an hour. Out there' – he pointed to the lake – 'warriors are waiting.'

'You mean Falling Eagle waits out there?'

'You are shameless, Uncle. I know nothing of Falling Eagle's whereabouts. And if I did I would not tell you.'

'You betray me, after all I have done for you.'

'You did it for yourself, Uncle. You wanted me safely on the throne of Texcoco so you could rule through me. I cannot stand by and watch you give everything away. These people are thieves and how do we deal with thieves? We strangle them. These people will destroy Texcoco and use it as a base against you. I tried to prevent this. Now you have no allies there.'

He collapsed into a heap in the corner exposing feet that were raw and bleeding.

'Boy, what have they done to you?'

'Burnt me. Burnt my feet until I told them where the treasures of Texcoco were hidden. There are few treasures left. But they did not believe me and burnt me again. These are your new friends, Uncle. No, do not touch me. I cannot bear your smell. I cannot avoid my fate, unlike you, Uncle, who do everything to defer the day when the gods must decide. No one can trust you.'

The Spanish priest, Father Olmedo, appeared with a bowl of water. He bent to wipe Cacama's feet. The youth did not resist.

'Did you plan to kill me?' pleaded Montezuma.

Cacama did not bother to look up. Now Montezuma would never know.

The Emperor sagged back into his chair. He wanted to win back Don Hernán's respect. Treasure seemed the easiest and quickest way to ingratiate himself and so he decided to open up his personal treasury.

It astonished him that the Spanish had not yet found it. But the building was concealed in a watery side street. Deep shelves lined the walls of its huge rooms. Every shelf was stacked with gold and feathers, shells and stones. Yet the Spanish emptied it in a day. Montezuma watched them throw themselves upon the shelves, climbing like monkeys searching for food. At first their exuberance amused him until he noticed it was not the beauty of the treasure that excited them. For where the gold was attached to feathers or shells or stones, the Spanish tore the gold from them. Nor did they bother with the fans or shields or headdresses and they left the green stones for the Tlaxcalans, who slunk after them like scavenging dogs.

After the treasury had been emptied so that barely a feather remained, Don Hernán brought Montezuma a lump of gold, made of melted jewels, which he seemed to value more than the precious objects that had created it. Montezuma examined it carefully, seeing only a lump of excrement. And far from showing gratitude, Don Hernán asked whether there was any more gold hidden in the city, which he, Montezuma, might have *forgotten*?

Now Montezuma sat curled up in his wicker chair in the small room where he slept alone. He felt as dry and as cold as the weather. Yesterday his wife had visited and had been subjected to Malinalli's taunts. His wife, who never raised her voice, had shouted so everyone could hear – 'Liar, whore!' Montezuma hated anger in women. Only the Cihuateteo, the witches of the night, could shout like that and they had reason, having lost their lives in child-birth. It was his fault that his gentle wife should behave like a witch. He stared down at the empty courtyard until it grew completely dark. As his body chilled, he realised that his brazier had been forgotten just as he himself was slowly being forgotten. Suddenly the courtyard filled with the sound of drums and rattles; tambourines they called them. Spanish soldiers were dancing. A Mexica woman's voice rose high above the drums, creating a fusion of old and new sound.

At last someone came to light his brazier. It was not his servant Deer who prepared him for sleep. Don Hernán's page, Juan, stood at the door holding a beeswax candle. He brought terrible news. Deer had been murdered on his way to the Old Palace.

'You have killed him.'

'Oh no, Lord Montezuma, it is your people who have killed him. Anyone who serves you is deemed a traitor. Don Hernán sends me to wait on you now.'

Since the Emperor's captivity Black Dog had slept in the shrine, stretched out in front of the god. Who knew what the Spanish might do next? They had destroyed their allies' gods. Nothing was safe. Every day for the last week a man with a coyote's face and a black beard had climbed the steps and sniffed around like one of the Spaniards' dogs. Now Black Dog examined the statues every morning to see whether they had been profaned during the rare moments when he dozed.

Black Dog was by no means the only priest to spend his nights up on the Great Pyramid. Many now joined him, so the gods were never left alone. Black Dog knew that Montezuma had refused permission for the Spanish god to occupy these shrines. But how long could the Emperor hold out?

He stood at the top of the steps and looked down to see if Lizard was on his way with food. He worried about the boy. It was not safe now with all those Tlaxcalans causing trouble. He saw someone approach the steps. He thought he recognised the coyote man. This time he brought a companion. He recognised Don Hernán's walk, for he swayed as if his legs were different lengths. Men were not designed to ride on the backs of animals. Neither man saw Black Dog watching them. They climbed quickly as if they had urgent business.

'Sound the drums!' shouted Black Dog.

The priests stood in a line to protect the shrines. From behind them came the beat of the hollow wooden drum whose sound could carry for six miles. The carved eagle on its sides, the symbol of the city it protected, vibrated angrily with each beat. A light gong joined the drums. And then another and another, and a chorus of smaller drums reverberated from the top of the pyramid.

The two men pushed the priests aside. As they entered the shrines, they released the warning bells lining the hemp curtain. Black Dog wished he were a warrior with an axe lined with vicious flints, until he realised that even an axe would barely leave a dent on a silver suit.

Don Hernán made a speech. He liked making speeches but no one could understand what he said for this time the girl had not come with them. Black Dog answered back, although he knew the Spanish could not understand him. Words could be powerful weapons, even if they only comforted the speaker. He swallowed. His tongue was swollen from piercing and his words struggled to emerge.

'In this land we all hold these gods dear. We are all here through the power of Huitzilopochtli, whose creatures we are. We hold our families, our children as nothing compared to this god, and would rather die than see you here.' He swallowed again. 'We are willing to die for our gods.'

Don Hernán did not listen. He pulled his knife from its sheath and swung it at Tlaloc. It caught the edge of one eye. Black Dog threw himself in front of the god. The coyote man picked up a stone and threw it at the statue. The two men began hacking at Tlaloc's face. Don Hernán, elated by his success, splintered a goggle eye. Several priests tried to drag him away, but the coyote man pulled out his own knife and thrust it into the flesh of one of the priests, whose blood spurted over the floor. Don Hernán ran to the shrine of Hummingbird Wizard next door and slashed at the wooden figure, pulling the gold mask from his face. The priests began to wail and drool and tear out their hair. Don Hernán waved his sword at them. By now forty armed Spaniards had arrived and there was a struggle for space on the platform. In the city below people ran out of their houses and gathered helplessly in the Sacred Square. Black Dog bent down and scooped pieces of the god from the floor of the shrine and placed them gently in a bowl.

The bells on the curtain rang again. Lizard appeared carrying warm tamales in a basket. Black Dog looked up from the floor. He held a fractured stone limb.

'Go back to school, boy. There is nothing left for you to do here.'

Lizard fought his way through the soldiers cluttering the pyramid and slid down the steps. Still clutching his basket, he ran across the square and along the canal to his father's palace. He ran up the steps, along the endless corridor, up to the second floor where he found his father preparing for a session in the law courts.

'Father! The Spanish destroy the gods!'

'Don Hernán does not listen to me.'

'You are the Woman Snake!'

'Don Hernán is the new Woman Snake.'

Lizard stared aghast. He ran down the steps, back along the canal, across the square, dodging the crowds, and through the great gates of the Old Palace. He found the Emperor's rooms crowded with Mexica and Spanish, with soldiers and serving women. He saw Cacama and some lords he did not recognise chained in a corner. Montezuma sat dejectedly on a stool.

'Uncle! The Spanish are destroying the gods.'

Montezuma looked up. His eyes seemed vacant.

'Do something!' begged Lizard. 'You are their protector.'

The room smelt of despair, of sweat and death and dead flowers. The old Governor of Tlatelolco pulled him to one side.

'Boy, the Emperor does his best. It is a juggling act which requires great skill. He stands on the edge of a precipice. One false move and we all fall with him. His endurance is to be admired.'

'You mean his weakness.'

'No, not weakness, boy. One day you will understand.'

'Tell him we have to save the gods.'

The Governor whispered in the Emperor's ear, then shuffled back to Lizard.

'The Emperor says that he will ask Don Hernán's permission to remove the gods to a safer home. You are to tell the high priests.'

Lizard was in such a hurry to leave that he tripped over Cacama's chains. Cacama did not even stir. He seemed half dead. Lizard slipped down the stairs, back across the square, and up the steps of the pyramid. He had never run so fast.

'Black Dog!' he shouted as he struggled for breath. 'You must remove the gods quickly.'

Black Dog stared, uncomprehending.

'How can we remove them? This is their home. They cannot be dismantled and carted away like old stones.'

'You must do it!'

Lizard threw down the basket and leapt down the steps. He did not care if he fell. That evening, after the Spanish had left, he returned with boys and priests from his school, and from the other schools in the city. Each carried their sleeping mat. They joined the priests from other temples in the city who brought rollers, ropes and mattresses. Many citizens, some of them old, who had sat all day in the square to protect the temple, joined them. It was dark that night, as if the stars did not want to witness the shameful task of evacuating the gods. Down in the square the Spanish cannons pointed up at the temple. The schoolboys covered the steps with their mats. Then the priests organised a pulley system with ropes and mattresses. Slowly and painstakingly, the gods were lifted from their shrines and lowered over the edge. The man-lizard, whose body contained all the seeds of the world, seemed in such a hurry to leave that he almost fell off the platform. Blinded Tlaloc offered no resistance. But Huitzilopochtli would only leave after his mother, the Earth Goddess. Each of them was wrapped carefully in mats and eased slowly with pulleys, down the one hundred and fourteen steps where they were placed on mattresses and carried away in litters.

When the gods had gone, the priests swept the floor for any broken parts, wrapped them carefully in their cloaks and spirited them away. Only the divine messenger, the chacmool, remained to guard the approach to the shrines and, within, the maize effigy of Huitzilpochtli, due to be replaced at the next feast. The priests huddled disconsolately in their room next to the temple, waiting for the conches that never sounded. Without the gods, the shrines were meaningless. Some of the priests dispersed to other temples on the mainland. Black Dog and the High Priest of Huitzilopochtli remained to keep an eye on the shrines until the gods returned. And when they did, the Spanish would be dragged up the steps of the temple to feed them.

'I for one will have great pleasure in ripping out their hearts,' said Black Dog. Just before dawn the sacred Bundle of Years was found to be missing. A young priest was sent to retrieve it. It would soon be a new year, time to add another reed to the precious bundle.

'We have chased out the devils,' reported a cheerful Don Hernán. He ignored Montezuma's protests. He scoffed at his warnings that the city would rise to defend their gods. But his men slept in their armour and he kept the horses saddled.

The Spanish cleaned the temple. They washed the jade steps and scrubbed the shrines. Carpenters pulled down the partition walls in the sanctuaries. They smashed the maize effigy of the god. They kicked the chacmool over the side and removed the ashes of the ancestors stored in carved boxes hidden in crevices in the walls.

They stole every jewel and lump of gold. They left the temple to dry for two days and then they returned with lime wash and painted the walls, the shrines, the platform, the steps, brilliant blinding white. They lit beeswax candles and decorated the altars with flowers. And when they had finished, a holy procession crossed the square and climbed the steps to place their cross in Huitzilopochtli's shrine. Because their goddess wore blue, Tlaloc's colour, the colour of water, they placed her image in his shrine. They prayed and sang as they processed around the platform. And when the ceremony was over, and only soldiers remained to guard the shrines, a group of Mexica climbed up to where no ordinary Mexica had ever been permitted before. They timidly placed wilted stalks of maize in front of the goddess.

'The rain will never come now,' pronounced Black Dog.

'The rain will never come now,' echoed the people.

They retreated to their homes, bolted their doors and waited for the gods to punish them. The next day the city woke to rain, pouring down the gutters and flooding the streets.

April 1520

The Month of the Little Vigil

Montezuma found comfort in the past. He liked to reminisce. It was something old men did, like those ancient relatives whose memories went back into the mists of time. As a child he had lived for their stories. Even though he found some of Don Hernán's questions offensive, and his attacks on the gods unpardonable, he enjoyed telling the old stories, although he never knew whether they impressed or shocked Don Hernán.

One day Don Hernán asked whether he had chosen to be ruler of the Mexica, as if it were something shameful. So Montezuma started at the beginning with his name, for a name given by holy men defined the way you led your life. Don Hernán found his name poetic, although when Montezuma explained that it also meant 'Angry Young Lord' in ordinary language, Don Hernán laughed because Montezuma denied his temper, whereas Don Hernán, who concealed his, confessed to a terrible one. There was nothing poetic in Don Hernán's name. It did not even have a meaning. Don Hernán's parents had been neglectful. A name was important. It travelled with you through life.

'How did you know that the gods chose you?' asked Don Hernán.

'When the scorpions did not sting me, I knew the gods had spoken.'

He remembered that night when he had crept out into the desert with the other boys to search for scorpions to crush for the priests' holy paste. A giant moon had hung in the sky. Coyotes' eyes circled him in the dark and he had been just a little frightened but you could never confess to fear. When a scorpion had struck him on the leg, he had brushed it off in horror for a boy stung by scorpions was rejected by the gods, but it left no trace and he knew that the gods had chosen him.

'You see,' he told Don Hernán, 'the gods became my companions. They swam with me in the lake. They sat on my shoulder during lessons. They told me that I would rule my people.'

Don Hernán wanted to know more about the Mexica. So Montezuma described, in the words of the ancestors, the early days of his people – a time of wandering, starvation and famine. He told how the Mexica had been mercenaries and had ended up dominating the societies around the lake, adopting the practices of the great Toltec civilisation that preceded them. Then he stopped in mid-flow, wondering whether he had revealed too much. What he did not tell Don Hernán was that his priests were advising him that Huitzilopochtli was now favourable to war.

He thought it odd that Don Hernán did not mention *his* ancestors. All men had ancestors; perhaps the Spanish did not honour theirs. But when Don Hernán spoke of his bare brown country with few men and many sheep, an animal Montezuma could not imagine, it did not surprise him that Don Hernán had left it. What did surprise him was the discovery that Don Hernán was a common man. Somehow Montezuma expected such an eloquent dandy to be noble and for a moment he wondered whether Falling Eagle had been right when he had called the Spanish 'second-rate men', for only second-rate men would leave their homes. In spite of these doubts, Montezuma's admiration for Don Hernán grew with every visit. It was not only that he was a willing listener, and a poet, but that they agreed on everything, except for their gods.

Don Hernán was a man who gave life to dreams. He spoke of countries and people beyond both seas of whose existence the Mexica were unaware. Speaking to Don Hernán was like travelling through a painted book full of unknown places and people. The land which most appealed to Montezuma was a fabled kingdom called China, far away in the west, which Don Hernán hoped to conquer with the help of the Mexica and which they might rule together as the greatest rulers in Christendom. And Don Hernán's face would light up because there was even more gold in China than in the lands of the Mexica.

'We shall rule as brothers,' he declared dramatically.

And despite the terrible destruction of the gods and the warnings of his priests, Montezuma found himself tempted by Don Hernán's promises, although he was not sure he wanted to sail the ocean for months. Perhaps the people in China would respect him more than his own.

'Are the people there like the Mexica?' he asked.

'They have cities and emperors like the Mexica and they too worship false gods. But we shall soon change that.'

Sometimes Montezuma found himself confiding in Don Hernán, as he would never have confided in his councillors. When, in an unguarded moment, he admitted how he would like to rule without the restrictions of his lords, Don Hernán confessed he too had problems with his men.

'We could rule together without the council,' he suggested. 'The Mexica and the Spanish together could conquer all the lands to the south.'

'As well as China?'

'As well as China.'

Don Hernán was a man for whom anything was possible. He was everything Montezuma admired. So he ignored his priests', his councillors' and generals' advice to fight now – *before it was too late*, they said. The gods demanded revenge. He wished they had told him this before he had grown fond of Don Hernán.

One day Don Hernán made a proposition – that Montezuma should swear an oath to the King of Spain. At first this made Montezuma feel important, as if he were being recognised as an equal of those rulers of the unknown countries across the sea. Such an oath was a small price to pay for membership of such an exclusive society. Moreover, if Montezuma were to give the lands of the Mexica to this king, it would convince him of his loyalty and bring huge benefits to the Mexica. The oath was to be written down, though Don Hernán assured him this document was only a formality. It would be the first step in their joint plan – it would seal their relationship and make them equal partners and allies. Don Hernán was particular about legalities. This would be a proper agreement, drawn up amicably between friends, a confirmation of the trust between two rulers. He suggested that Montezuma consult his chief councillors. He would bring four of his own advisors.

The councillors protested fiercely.

'It will make us more powerful,' insisted Montezuma. He wished they would all go away and leave him to negotiate the deal.

Woman Snake banged the small table, where the scribes scribbled furiously, making their hands shake and smudging the ink.

'Out there are the Tlaxcalans waiting to seize our land and eat our corpses. Do you not think Don Hernán will reward them? This will give Don Hernán legitimacy to rule us in the name of his king? He will do what he wants and he will say that you gave him permission.'

'Quetzalcoatl demands this,' argued Montezuma obstinately. 'Don Hernán offers us an honourable alliance. Together, we shall be stronger.'

'Nothing about Don Hernán is honourable,' insisted Woman Snake. 'Do you think this king across the sea will care about us? No. He will leave everything to Don Hernán. And what will he do? He will rob us and ruin us. We will be nothing more than slaves.'

'That is not the agreement.'

'That is not how you see the agreement. If you sign this paper, you will fall into a trap.'

'I shall still be ruler of the Mexica.'

'You will be a vassal of the King of Spain.'

'It might be better to ally ourselves with the Spanish. Who knows what other people are out there?'

'You are blinded by your admiration of Don Hernán. He is nothing more than a brigand. None of us will give our agreement.'

'I do not need your agreement!'

'Then why do you ask us? You must have known we would never agree.'

'Have you replaced me?' shouted Montezuma. 'Have you elected Falling Eagle? He is not the right man. He will bring death and destruction.'

His eyes showed that he knew what his councillors would do.

When Woman Snake and the three councillors returned to the Old Palace the next day, they found the great hall decorated for a festival. Spanish musicians played in a corner. Don Hernán greeted them enthusiastically.

'This is a momentous day!'

Woman Snake said nothing. He had prepared his arguments well, although he wondered whether his words would be wasted. He had dressed to impress. He wore his most expensive cloak and several necklaces. He carried his butterfly fan. Among the soberly dressed Spanish, the councillors stood out like a flock of tropical birds. They listened stony-faced as Malinalli struggled to explain the implications of the oath.

'How can we believe this girl? She has the tongue of a viper,' said Woman Snake. He remembered their earlier conversation about the Pope. 'Why does Don Hernán require our signatures since the Pope has already given him our lands?'

The priest, Father Olmedo, interrupted nervously.

'Don Hernán and his king wish to legitimise this treaty. Popes change as do kings. Don Hernán does not wish to force you. He is not a thief. He does not steal people's lands.'

'Not a thief!' echoed the councillors, clutching their sides and stifling their laughter. Don Hernán did not smile. The Emperor stared at the floor.

'Don Hernán asks again whether the Emperor Montezuma agrees

to swear on oath that he makes a gift of the Mexica lands to the King of Spain?'

'No!' said Woman Snake.

'No!' repeated the councillors.

Don Hernán put his arm around the Emperor.

'It is as I thought, Lord Montezuma. Your councillors do not appreciate this generous offer. They lack imagination. They cannot see that the world is changing and that we must change with it. The King of Spain is the most powerful monarch in the world. Most countries would welcome an alliance with him. Perhaps I should explain again.'

He asked Malinalli to explain the oath a second time.

'We do not need this agreement,' insisted Woman Snake.

'Don Hernán is reasonable,' pleaded the girl.

'Then Don Hernán does not explain it properly,' said Woman Snake. 'Or else you hide something from us. You know we will not like what Don Hernán says so you change it. These are your words, not his. They are false words from a false woman.'

Malinalli hid behind Don Hernán. Montezuma began to weep. He was prone to weeping on emotional occasions, and sometimes for effect, but these were the genuine sobs of a man unsure where his loyalties lay.

The musicians stopped playing. And then some of Don Hernán's men began to argue with him. The guards rushed to console the Emperor and joined him in an orgy of weeping. Don Hernán suspended the meeting.

When the meeting resumed a couple of hours later, Don Hernán seemed in a hurry and did not want to waste time with further explanations, and a dry-eyed Montezuma, ashamed of his lack of control, found himself agreeing to words he did not understand, while one of the Spanish wrote his promise down in that clumsy writing of theirs. When Don Hernán saw his words recorded he smiled.

'Now all that remains is to seal our agreement with hostages.'

'Hostages?' queried Montezuma. 'We have made an agreement.'

'Since you are not Christian men, Don Hernán cannot be sure you mean what you promise,' said Malinalli. 'He suggests your youngest daughter, Lord Montezuma, the one you gave to him before.'

'He has my older daughter.'

'So why not the younger? Don Hernán knows she is more beautiful.'

'We can all offer hostages instead,' said Woman Snake quickly.

'I am prepared to wait for her,' said Don Hernán as he placed his document on a table in front of Montezuma.

The councillors urged him not to sign. But he lifted his hand and made his mark shakily, black ink on white paper, a record of shame that would outlive the man who made it. Then he changed his mind and tried to rub the mark away but it blurred on the paper with his tears.

Every morning, as Lizard went to collect the priests' food, he watched the horses clip-clop across the causeway to exercise on the mainland. A week ago black columns of smoke had risen from the city's courtyards. The fires had burned for several days and nights. It was rumoured that the new people were melting down the gold they had found. No one knew what they did with it. Some said they ate it to cure some strange sickness.

Lizard kept a wary eye out for Tlaxcalans. Only last week, as he walked with his friend Brown Fox, a gang had attacked them. Had it not been for the Spanish, they would both have been killed. He hated the Tlaxcalans even more than the Spanish. The Tlaxcalans could never resist humiliating the boys at school. They would line up on the steps and taunt them. Sometimes they hurled stones.

'Young Lord . . . ?'

One of his father's servants had followed him so quietly that Lizard had heard nothing. This man would be a good scout.

'You father sends for you.'

Lizard wondered why. His father rarely sent for him now. His father greeted him curtly, although he did offer him chocolate, a luxury unknown at school.

'I have offered you as a hostage to Don Hernán. You will live among the Spanish in the Old Palace.'

'No, father! I have work to do. You know what work.'

Last night the priests had ordered the boys to start making weapons. The instructions came from the Lord Woman Snake. The whole city would make weapons. Every house and palace and temple would become an armoury. People would collect rocks and stones at night and store them on their roofs. Lizard noticed two Spanish soldiers waiting in the hall. Both carried swords. Woman Snake barely acknowledged them, although he kept his voice low, in case they understood Nahuatl.

'Why me? Is it because I am unimportant?'

'On the contrary, it is because I can trust you. I know you will observe everything. You can tell me what you see there in the Old Palace, however unimportant it might seem. That is your work. If you do it well, I might even release you from serving the priests. I will arrange for you to go to the best teachers in the arts of writing and painting. Does that encourage you?'

Lizard grinned.

'Of course, father. Am I on my own with the Spanish?'

'You are not alone.'

'What are we hostages for?'

'You are there to ensure that the Emperor keeps his word. He has given away the lands of the Mexica to the King of Spain. He says it is better to share the world than destroy it. Listen! The Lord Montezuma is as much a prisoner of his own people. He fears them now. They killed Deer as they kill any servant who brings him his food. You must be careful. It is your own people you should fear now. These soldiers are not here to guard you. They are here to protect you.'

Lizard found the Old Palace turned into a workshop. Cauldrons of bubbling gold hung over a huge fire in the centre of the courtyard. Gold bars were stacked against the walls. Horses tied to pillars stamped their feet impatiently. Chained dogs howled like coyotes. The pool in the middle of the courtyard had dried out, its fountain stilled, its fish long gone. Now it was filled with gold and silver objects waiting to be melted down. An encampment of Tlaxcalans had taken up residence in shabby thatched huts. The smell of their fires mingled with the stench from the latrines.

People rushed up and down the great staircase with baskets of food. In a corner of the great hall two Spanish skirmished with their swords. The soldiers led the hostages up the stairs, past jeering Tlaxcalans and red-faced Spanish. On the steps a fair-haired boy cleaned armour and weapons. He jumped up and led Lizard to a small room where Don Hernán sat writing. He wrote a word, then he lifted his pen, dipped it into black paint and began another. The writing intrigued Lizard. Mexica words took hours of painstaking work whereas Spanish writing had only black lines and no pictures. Lizard craned his neck to see more. He wondered how lines could speak. To his surprise, the boy spoke in Nahuatl.

'Don Hernán says you are not prisoners.'

'Then why are we here?'

'A hostage is not a prisoner,' insisted the boy. My name is Juan. I am to take care of you. The boy stumbled over his words. 'Don Hernán asks if any of you can write.'

'Of course we can write,' said Lizard proudly.

'Don Hernán asks whether you would like to learn our writing.' Don Hernán held up the page with its black marks and no pictures. 'He says that if you accept our god, he will teach you to write our way.'

Lizard wondered how long it would take to learn to speak and write Spanish.

'How long will Don Hernán stay in the lands of the Mexica?'

Juan seemed to consider this a stupid question.

'As long as it takes to bring the true God to your people.'

'Our gods have given us everything. Why would we abandon them for an unknown god?'

'It is our god who gives you all those things. Your gods are false.' When the boy spoke of his god, his eyes sparkled like stars. 'But your lessons will have to wait. I am to go with Don Hernán to the coast. We shall be away three to four weeks. I go everywhere with Don Hernán.' He smiled proudly. 'But I am sad to leave the Lord Montezuma. He is lonely. He is more of a father to me than my own. He is a good man. Perhaps you could keep him company. Few of his family come now. His daughter used to visit and his Chief Councillor, that awkward man with the scarred face.'

'My father.'

'Your father? Mind you, the Emperor does not look forward to their meetings. I hear them arguing the whole time. None of you realise how the Emperor makes sacrifices for his people.'

'He has given away his country,' said Lizard tartly. 'Why do you go to the coast?'

Juan seemed nervous.

'Don Hernán has business there. It will soon be over and we will return. Come, I will show you your room.'

As they walked through the courtyard, a dog bounded after them, sniffing and peeing. Those dogs peed all the time. The smell of urine would soon replace the smell of blood. Lizard laughed loudly.

'You find the dog amusing?' asked Juan.

'Hilarious,' said Lizard.

He wished he could take the boy and the dog back to school and introduce them to everyone.

'How you do speak my language?' he asked Juan.

'Malinalli taught me first. Now the Lord Montezuma instructs me. He is a excellent teacher. He promises that I can be his scribe when things return to normal.'

At the beginning of the Mexica New Year, Montezuma felt a change in himself. It was as if he had gone to sleep and woken up reborn. The terrible year of One Reed had reached its end and he was still alive. The five 'empty days' had passed and the world had not been destroyed as the priests had predicted. Don Hernán did not understand the 'empty days'. Montezuma explained that as the Mexica year consisted of eighteen months of twenty days, this left five days that did not belong. Don Hernán found this amusing. There were no 'empty' days in the Spanish calendar. The Spanish counted time differently. Their new year came in the seventeenth month of the Mexica year, the month of Stretching. Don Hernán called it January.

The new year, Two Flint, was auspicious. Flint was associated with beginnings. A flint knife had fallen from the sky onto the Hill of the Seven Caves, the birthplace of the Mexica and had given life to sixteen gods. Flint was associated with Huitzilopochtli, and the Flint years were kind to rulers. With the passing of the old year, Quetzalcoatl's influence diminished and Montezuma heard the voice of Huitzilopochtli as God of War, urging him to fight the Spanish.

When messengers from the coast brought a painted cloth in their food basket, Montezuma knew this was the sign he had been waiting for. The cloth showed two boats with sails. The messengers reported that the new arrivals, although Spanish, were no friends of Don Hernán's. There had been fights between the two groups. If Montezuma supported Don Panfilio who led the new group, he promised to destroy Don Hernán and restore the Mexica empire.

These men would be his allies. He would use them as Don Hernán used the Tlaxcalans. He felt sad this would bring an end to those interesting conversations and he would even miss the arguments about their respective gods. But Huitzilopochtli whispered in his ear and he knew he had no choice.

He studied the painted cloth carefully. Yet he felt uneasy. Whom could he trust? Don Hernán too had professed friendship. But the gods had spoken. Don Panfilio would not know of the agreement with the King of Spain. He would not see those words on white paper. Montezuma removed his gold armband and gave it to the messengers.

'Tell Don Panfilio his enemies are my enemies.'

He folded up the cloth and hid it in his chest.

A reply came in eight days. Don Panfilio confided to Montezuma that Don Hernán did not have the backing of the King of Spain. He was nothing but a common thief. Montezuma sent more gold and confirmed his support.

Woman Snake did not share his optimism. Lizard had reported frenetic activity in the Old Palace. This was an experienced army returning to the coast, an army led by Don Hernán who had killed thousands of Cholulans. Woman Snake studied the cloth carefully. These Spanish might be enemies of Don Hernán's but that did not make them friends of the Mexica. They might even prove worse than Don Hernán. It would be wise to be cautious. Besides these new arrivals did not have Don Hernán's knowledge of the country. Nor did they have Malinalli to speak for them. And as for the Totonocs who now supported Don Panfilio, they changed sides whenever someone offered a better deal.

Montezuma sighed.

'You have criticised me for months for appeasing the Spanish. And now I take a firm decision, you disagree. You are contrary.'

'This is not the time for action.'

'Huitzilopochtli does not agree.'

'Don Hernán will punish us all.'

Woman Snake rushed home and tried to recall the Emperor's messengers. But it was too late. They had left for the coast. He sent a fast runner to catch them up.

Lizard helped pack the food and the stores for the expedition to the coast. He washed and groomed the horses. He had overcome his fear of the beasts. He had learnt how to understand their moods, although he was not yet brave enough to sit on their backs.

The Spanish fascinated him. They were such noisy boisterous people with little sense of rank or manners. The Mexica considered such familiarity impolite and at first such intimacy shocked him, but now he had become used to it. Here inside the walls of the Old Palace another world existed, a world seemingly oblivious to the hostility beyond its gates, just as it ignored the missiles that landed every night. No one spoke of the Mexica waiting outside or of the sacrificial stones that awaited them. They escaped into music. The Spanish had brought magical instruments with strings that made even the strongest man weep. Lizard would listen for hours and forget that he was a hostage in his own city.

This morning he counted the soldiers who were to leave with Don Hernán – there were some two hundred of them. One hundred and sixty would remain in Tenochtitlán under the command of Don Alvarado. Lizard feared Don Alvarado with his quick and cruel temper. Because he was beautiful, with his gold hair and his magic power over the horses, everyone admired him and no one, other than Don Hernán, dared cross him. Don Alvarado was capricious and dangerous and it astonished Lizard that Don Hernán could even consider leaving him in charge of such a volatile city. As he watched the soldiers leave and listened to the flutes and the drums playing their victory airs, he planned to escape as soon as Don Hernán had left.

He did not want to remain here with Don Alvarado in charge.

Don Hernán called to say goodbye. He explained that two new boats had arrived at the coast and he was curious to see what they wanted.

'It must be a relief to see these boats,' said Montezuma jovially. He was sad to see Don Hernán leave but concerned about Don Alvarado. He wondered what Don Panfilio was like. 'At last you know that your country has not forgotten you. You can all go home.'

'Not at all!' said Don Hernán. 'These men are brigands who threaten our existence. I shall challenge them for both our sakes.'

Montezuma's heart missed a beat. This was not what he expected to hear. What if the messengers were wrong? What if these new Spanish were even worse, as Woman Snake suggested? He no longer had Smoking Eagle on whose opinion he could rely.

'Any enemies of yours are enemies of mine,' he said weakly.

The crystal on Don Hernán's finger flashed vulgarly as it caught the sun. Sometimes Montezuma thought of himself and Don Hernán as the light and the dark. He was the light, Don Hernán the dark. Together they could be formidable. Other times he thought of Don Hernán as Smoking Mirror who brought only death and destruction. This was Smoking Mirror who stood in front of him. It was Smoking Mirror's feast next month. He could hardly believe a year had passed since the last one. He hoped this year would prove more auspicious.

'It is our Feast of Dryness next month. We seek your permission to celebrate it.'

Don Hernán hovered in the doorway.

'On one condition,' he insisted. 'There must be no sacrifice.'

No sacrifice. There could be no feast without its sacrifice and this was one of the most important celebrations in the calendar.

'No sacrifice!' insisted Don Hernán.

'There will be no sacrifice,' echoed Montezuma.

He offered Don Hernán the assistance of his army. But Don Hernán declined politely. He promised, on his return, to resume those interesting conversations which he had so much enjoyed.

May 1520

The Month of Dryness

Woman Snake proceeded cautiously with preparations for the feast. A hot wind from the mountains spun the soil into clouds of dust, irritating his lungs as well as Don Alvarado's temper. An uneasy mood settled over the city. A life-size effigy of Huitzilopochtli, made of cornmeal and amaranth paste, dressed in the sacred clothes, now took the place of the banished statue. It seemed more elaborate than last year's, as if people were determined to make up for the gods' absence. Or perhaps there was a deliberate intention to shock the Spanish, who were so sensitive that even the sacred dances upset them.

But the Spanish seemed in jovial mood as they wandered around the square waiting for the ceremony to begin. So far, so good, thought Woman Snake, watching with concern as young Mexica warriors displayed their war captives, whom they hoped to sacrifice. He had tried, without success, to stop this display for he knew it would anger Don Alvarado. And there had been disturbing rumours that three Mexica captives had been seized by the Spanish and who knew what they might have revealed under torture? Although Woman Snake questioned the provenance of these rumours, there was no doubt that the Spanish had thrown a warrior off the roof of the Old Palace and that his feet had shown signs of burning.

The three gates to the square opened and the boy-god entered in his litter. All the lords, the priests, the captains and the warriors were there, and as many spectators as could squeeze in. Four hundred dancers, waiting to perform the sacred routines, formed themselves into an orderly line and in the right order of precedence, for such positions had to be earned. The crowds clapped their encouragement. The drumming began. The dancers linked hands. Those who had forgotten to urinate, opened their feathers and pissed on the stones. Once in line, total concentration was demanded. Any lapse or mistake risked a beating by the festival guardians.

The boy-god led the dancers, emulating the serpent whose dance this was. Woman Snake took his place behind the boy. The dancers followed in a long swaying line of feathers, gold, jewels, crystals, amber, jade and tassels. The ancient steps comforted Woman Snake. Their movements were so ingrained in his mind that he could dance them even if he were blind. He closed his eyes to let the rhythm lead him to the secret world of the ancients.

He did not notice the closing of the three gates to the precinct, or the men guarding them, or the Spanish and the Tlaxcalans mingling with the dancers, for there were many fools and jokers in odd clothes who joined in the festivals. No one heard the shout above the noise. And if they had, they would not have understood, for Don Alvarado shouted in his own language. The dancers swayed. Someone cried out. Woman Snake felt the line jerk. He opened his eyes, furious at such carelessness in the middle of a sacred dance. He saw the flash of knives moving among the crowd. The boy-god's head rolled under Woman Snake's feet, his eyes still open. A silver suit moved towards him.

'Run!' he screamed.

Everyone tried to flee at the same time. Some hid behind the canopies shading the square. Others ran up to the shrines. Some fled into the priests' quarters and others into the House of Eagles. A man with one leg hobbled, with the aid of a friend, towards the Gate of the Reed, where both were hacked to pieces. Some people held onto their entrails, trying not to trip over them. Others struggled to contain gaping holes where their stomachs had been. All the exits from the square were blocked with soldiers. Woman Snake looked at the mounds of mutilated Mexica and the pools of blood now covering the stones. There was only one place where he could hide. He threw his cloak over a dying drummer and burrowed under a pile of bodies. Others thought as he did, two dancers already hid there. His chest tightened and he struggled to coordinate his coughs with the groans of the dying and control his bowels which threatened to erupt over those hiding below. He saw the ancestors beckoning. Then the smell of blood and faeces overwhelmed him.

Black Dog too had taken every precaution to avoid a repetition of last year's disaster. This time his hands would not shake and the heart would go straight into the god's mouth. Then he remembered there was no god's mouth. The heart would go into a bowl to be carried to the god in his hiding place in the mountains. It would be a problem sacrificing the boy without the Spanish seeing. But none of them were up here in the shrine and the guardians were Mexica who would keep their mouths shut. As Black Dog selected the required pots and pans and bowls, he showed Lizard how such things were done, saddened that this year there were no gods in the shrines, even if their effigies guarded the steps. How empty the shrines seemed, with no statues, no decoration, nothing to remind him of the past.

Black Dog should have seen the gates being closed. His eyes were sharp. He could see everything from the top of the pyramid. But he was too busy organising the other priests and the acolytes and showing Lizard how to hold the bowl to collect the blood. He had not known until the last minute whether the boy would come now he was a hostage. But Lizard had managed to escape at the last minute.

When Black Dog heard the screams he thought someone had fallen down the staircase. It had happened before. He ran to the edge of the shrine and saw the Spanish moving among the crowds. He thought it odd that they carried their shields. There were few of them – he guessed no more than sixty – probably there as observers, although they did not normally join in the ceremonies. When he saw people desperately climbing the walls of the precinct he still did not understand. Lizard moved beside him. He clutched the cross of the new god, taken from the shrine.

'What do you plan to do with that?'

'Kill them.'

Black Dog saw the temple guardians below bravely hitting out with their wooden sticks. Both sticks and men were sliced into pieces. Now he realised what was happening; his first thought was to protect the boy.

'Quickly, hide in the shrine.'

The other novices ran into the shrines but Lizard did not move. He still clutched the image.

'We must fight them.'

He ran towards the top step.

'No!' cried Black Dog.

He grabbed Lizard. They would be safe up here for the Spanish would not dare climb the steps.

'Into the shrine!' he ordered, pulling the boy with him.

The shrine was crowded as everyone hid inside, listening to the sounds of massacre below. Black Dog heard the distinctive clang of armour as someone climbed the steps. Four men appeared, their silver suits flashing in the sun.

'You must get away, boy!' He pushed Lizard behind him. 'I will distract them and when they are not looking, you slip past them and down the staircase.'

But Lizard would not leave. He brandished the god's image at the phalanx of men blocking their way. The boy hit out but the cross was knocked from his hands.

'Your knife!' he screamed.

What knife? Black Dog looked down. There in his right hand was his knife. The coral eyes of the carved human figure peering from a serpent's mouth urged Black Dog to kill. As the Spaniard came towards him, Black Dog pounced like a jaguar thrusting his knife into the gap between the silver suit and the helmet. This time there were no doubts, no shaking of hands. His aim was sure. The rough blade plunged into the man's neck. And there it lodged and would not move.

'I am sorry,' Black Dog murmured to the knife, like an old man who had lost his wits. This was Tlaloc's knife. He did not want to leave it behind in barbarian flesh. Soldiers surrounded him.

'Leave me, boy! Go quickly. Remember to serve the gods.'

He felt himself lifted and carried to the edge of the pyramid and dangled there in the air. Far below, he saw the dying and the fleeing. He looked up into the sky where vultures circled. Perhaps they waited for his death. Hopelessly, he thought, for his scrawny tortured body would not even feed a crow. His long black hair blew into his eyes, his black cloak flapped like wings. The hands let him go. For a moment he hovered as the wind unravelled his cloak, before plunging faster and faster until the earth rose to meet him. He saw his life rush before him. He saw the neat little house surrounded by fields of red volcanic soil. He saw his mother throwing her tortillas on the hot hearth stone. As a child he would count the number of times she hit the stone and know that there would be plenty to eat that day. On other days, the stone was silent. How pleased he was to be chosen as the priest of Tlaloc. Now Tlaloc demanded he die a warrior and feed the sun with his blood.

In the chaos on top of the pyramid, no one noticed Lizard slide down the steps, searching anxiously to find somewhere to hide. He ran behind the temple into a small alleyway and threw himself under a pile of bodies, listening to the sounds of fighting intensifying around him. He heard the running of feet and the ping of arrows on metal. A voice shouted.

'Mexica! What are you waiting for? Fight with your bare hands.'

The war drum sounded but he dared not emerge from his hiding place. He hardly dared breathe. Footsteps ran down the alleyway and someone climbed over his pile of bodies, burying Lizard deeper under the corpses. One of the bodies took its time to die, jerking and twitching like the sacrificed who continued to move even after their hearts had been removed. Lizard dared not stir even when one of the men pissed all over him. And it must have been several hours later, for the body had grown heavy and cold, when Lizard heard the light steps of his people and the hissing of torches as they searched for their dead, but he was still too frightened to move. Even when women's voices echoed over the square and the sound of weeping filled the night, he did not stir. By now the smell, magnified by thousands of bodies, was worse than any sacrifice. He gagged.

He must have dozed for the women's weeping had gone. Someone approached the alleyway. The distinctive voice of the High Priest of Huitzilopochtli echoed over the square.

'Here is Black Dog's cloak. He must be here somewhere.'

Lizard heard the rustle of the priests' cloaks as they searched the bodies.

'Are they all dead?' asked the High Priest.

It was impossible for Lizard to move under the weight of bodies. Nor could he speak for his head was buried in a warrior's wet groin. He felt searching hands and saw a faint light as his dead companion was lifted from him. The High Priest held up his flare.

'It is Lizard.'

The priests untangled the mound of bodies and helped Lizard out.

'Where is Black Dog?' he asked.

'Dead!' replied the High Priest.

Lizard remembered Tlaloc's knife.

'The sacred knife lodges in a Spanish throat. We should search for it.'

'It has found its target,' pronounced the High Priest.

Lizard could not control his shaking.

'Black Dog saved me.'

'For a purpose, boy,' consoled the High Priest. 'To become a holy warrior and fight, as he would were he still alive.'

Lizard followed the priests to the school. Even there bodies blocked the doorway, for no place was sacred to the attackers. He washed himself in the sacred pool. This day was his initiation as a warrior. He would destroy every Spaniard and Tlaxcalan until the city was cleansed, until every Spaniard had been thrown down the temple steps with a hole where his heart should be. That would be his debt to Black Dog. He would serve his gods. He would not abandon them now.

Woman Snake waited until the heavy footsteps vanished, before he emerged from his hiding place. Although covered in blood and bruises, he was not hurt. But as he staggered to his feet and saw the desolation, he felt a terrible rage. He climbed up the temple steps and called for war. Some of the wounded who had lost one or both legs dragged themselves on their stomachs towards the gates. Others, blinded, stumbled over obstacles in their way. But he could not help them now. There was little time. Although the Spanish had retreated behind the walls of the Old Palace, Don Hernán would soon return with extra men and horses. And when he did, the Mexica had to be prepared.

He ran to the priests' quarters where he found bodies lying in the corridors. The High Priest of Huitzilopochtli greeted him enthusiastically. They had feared him dead. The High Priest confirmed that many had died. Already some priests were out there treating the wounded, although their wounds were so terrible that few would survive. But the High Priest was able to pass on some cheerful information. Lizard was alive and someone had seen Falling Eagle handing out weapons and encouraging the people to fight. Barricades were being placed in the canals, roads were blocked, and bridges had been pulled up. Now the Spanish had retreated with their allies to the Old Palace, it was time to starve them. The High Priest looked forward to offering so many Spaniards to the gods. But there was sad news. Black Dog had been killed.

Woman Snake made his way to the school. The only light now came from the many torches as relatives searched for their dead. Even in the dark, Woman Snake knew the way for this was his old school. Down the corridors into the hall, he found a gloomy group of pupils sitting on their mats. One of them jumped up and ran to him.

'Father. Are you hurt?'

'Only stains.' Tears welled up in his eyes. He was a man who rarely showed his feelings. He clung to his son. Then he remembered there was still another task to perform.

'Are any boys willing to help me?'

Every boy jumped up. They ignored his smell and his blood-soaked garments and followed him out of the school, weaving their way between the corpses, down to the Eagle Gate where the Spanish boats were moored. Woman Snake watched them rocking gently in the water.

'Sink every one,' he said bitterly. 'Use anything, stones, rocks.'

As the rocks smashed against the wood, making the sound of breaking bones, Woman Snake imagined another Spaniard killed. But as he crept home that night, like a smelly old idiot, two Spanish soldiers seized him.

Until he heard the drums Montezuma remained cheerful, waiting for news from the coast, hoping that his new allies would defeat Don Hernán. Right up to the morning of the feast, he remained hopeful that he would take part in the ceremonies. He had even dressed for it. But Don Alvarado was capricious. With Juan and Malinalli at the coast with Don Hernán, there was no one to change the words between Don Alvarado and himself. It made for awkward conversation. And then, just before the feast, Don Alvarado had thrown him into chains.

With only one hundred and sixty soldiers left to patrol the city, Montezuma had felt falsely reassured. How foolish he had been! A week ago his generals had asked for permission to hide weapons in the temple. Fearing another Cholula, he had chided them and they had not broached the subject again. Then one of his nephews brought a club and concealed it in Montezuma's clothes basket. He had laughed. What use was one club against Don Alvarado's men?

He strained to listen for sounds from outside. But the only sound he heard was the clanking of metal as someone ran up the stairs. A breathless Alvarado rushed into the room. He wore his armour. His helmet was missing. Blood poured from a gash in his head.

'See what the Mexica have done to me!'

Montezuma stared in horror.

'You have ruined us both, Alvarado.'

'You have ruined yourself, *Lord* Montezuma.'

Alvarado lunged with his sword. Montezuma was prepared to die. It would be quick. One of the men whispered in Alvarado's ear. They all laughed. They pulled Montezuma to his feet and dragged him to the room next door where Cacama sat in his chains. The youth raised his bloodshot eyes. Alvarado lifted his sword. It sliced Cacama's head in two. His shocked eyes squinted at them. Alvarado turned his attention to the old Governor of Tlatelolco.

'Nah. Not worth it.' He turned to Montezuma. 'This one is still useful.'

He pushed Montezuma to the bottom of the stairs and shoved the old Governor after him. Both men limped up the steps to the roof. Montezuma in his chains and the old Governor with his bad leg. Below them, in the square, people struggled to move through a sea of bodies.

'You must speak to the people, Lord!' urged the old Governor, looking anxiously down the stairs where Spanish soldiers blocked the way. He eased Montezuma towards the edge. But Montezuma's words, if not his tears, deserted him. He stood beside the parapet, looking down at the mass of people and corpses in the square below. What could he say? Only prayers for the dead were required now. But he must try even if he knew his words sounded feeble.

'My people, there is no future in battle. Put your weapons down.'

A voice shouted from the square.

'What says the fool, Montezuma?'

Montezuma stepped back from the parapet.

'I do not have the words.'

The old Governor pushed his way to the roof's edge. When the people saw him they fell silent.

'Hear me, Mexica.' His voice faltered. 'We are not the equal of the Spanish. Abandon battle. Let the arrow and shield be stilled. Consider the elderly and the young. For this reason, your leader says, let battle cease.'

People began to move away. The old Governor took Montezuma's hand and helped him down the stairs.

'I am dead to my people,' said Montezuma sadly.

Not even a victory by his new ally, Don Panfilio, could change things now. He found Don Alvarado at the bottom of the stairs, grinning maliciously. Blood from his wounds dripped onto his armour.

'You have served your purpose, Lord Montezuma. You might as well be dead.'

He lifted his sword.

Montezuma bowed his head. This was the message of the Feast of Dryness. Everything, however glorious, ended in death as drought destroyed the rain's bounty. A brief moment of beauty was followed by an eternity of torment. No one, not even the ruler of the Mexica, could escape his destiny. Alvarado began to laugh. 'That scared you! I'll let Don Hernán deal with you.'

The Spanish dragged Woman Snake through the streets of the city. If they were going to kill him, it would be better to do it now when he could die publicly as a symbol for his country. He tried to push the Spanish away so that he could look his people in the eye, showing them that he shared their pain. But every time he tried to stand the Spanish hit him. They dragged him over the stained stones in the square, through the dust in the streets, through the gates of the Old Palace where the Tlaxcalans spat at him. They pushed him up the stairs and into a room where he found the Lord of the Two Waters and the old Governor.

'At least you are not dead,' said the Lord of the Two Waters wryly.

'Not yet,' replied Woman Snake, 'but thousands are. We did not stand a chance. Don Alvarado planned this. He knew he could trap us in the square. With weapons we might have defeated them. Thousands of us against sixty Spanish and some Tlaxcalans. What has happened to Montezuma?'

'I do not know and I do not care,' said the Lord of the Two Waters. 'We suggested storing weapons in the temple and he refused.'

They heard a scuffle outside. Two soldiers rushed in and dragged the Governor along the floor towards the door. It took one movement to slice off the old man's head. Woman Snake shuffled towards the quivering bleeding body and cradled it gently. The soldier kicked the head into a corner.

'He was a cripple!' cried Woman Snake.

The soldier kicked Woman Snake.

'What about him?'

Don Alvarado held his nose.

'Nah. Not worth the bother. He smells of shit. Let him stink out the others. Anyway he bleeds to death.'

'One less to feed then,' said the soldier.

The disappointed guard pointed to the Lord of the Two Waters.

'That one is the Emperor's brother.'

Don Alvarado considered for a moment.

'We had better wait for the return of Don Hernán before we deal with him. He is on his way home now. He brings Don Panfilio as a prisoner. That should teach anyone who threatens Don Hernán.'

Jewel heard the great drum six miles away in the palace on the Salt-Coloured Water and knew something terrible had happened. No war drum ever disturbed the ceremony of Dryness. Since Don Hernán had left for the coast, the mood in the city had grown volatile. The women of Montezuma's household had crossed the causeway to the mainland. And although Jewel loved this summer palace with its lakeside gardens, it had been contaminated by the Spanish who had slept here before their arrival in the city. Their mess had been cleared up but their smell remained, despite the flowers and the incense.

She longed to be back in the city. It was the story of her life, always wanting to be somewhere else. During her first unhappy marriage to her uncle, she had spent her days here moping in these orchards and gardens, watching the birds come down to drink, proud when she had learned to identify them and could impress her father with her knowledge. If only she could go and fight with the warriors, do something useful. Even if she only killed one Spanish soldier it would help.

As the great drum sounded, she felt sure that Falling Eagle was there, speaking to her across the water. She feared for him, and for her sister Butterfly in the Old Palace. The drum kept on beating. She heard the desperation in its voice and went down to the lake edge for a better view. Smoke rose above the Old Palace. Oh why didn't someone come to tell them what was happening?

At dusk, her half-brother, Handful of Reeds, rode in his litter over the causeway. The family, the servants, the musicians and dancers, all desperate for news, assembled in the big hall. They could not believe what they heard. Thousands of Mexica had been slaughtered by their guests. The servants wept.

'How is the Lord Montezuma?' begged his wife, trying to keep calm.

'Imprisoned in the Old Palace,' said Handful of Reeds.

'Imprisoned?' gasped the Lady Tecalco, who had always insisted that Montezuma had offered himself as a hostage.

'How is Falling Eagle?' asked Jewel.

Handful of Reeds confirmed that Falling Eagle had not been seen since the massacre. He thought that now the Mexica were fighting back at last, it was better for the ladies to remain here. The Spanish and the Tlaxcalans were besieged in the Old Palace and denied food and water. There would be four days allowed for the collection of the corpses, followed by eighty days of mourning. The cremation of so many bodies would take a long time.

'Did none of the Spanish die?' asked Jewel.

'No more than five.'

'What about Butterfly?'

'Don Alvarado has no fight with women.'

The Lady Tecalco begged him to stay with them and enjoy a meal. He felt ravenous. He had spent all day helping the wounded and searching for relatives. Because he had arrived late in the square, he had escaped the massacre. He watched Jewel pick up her little dog.

'I would take good care of that little dog of yours. The people search for dogs to accompany the dead on their final journey. There are not enough dogs in the city.'

'You tease, brother.'

She knew her brother rarely teased.

'I do not. And your dog is a handsome shade of gold, just the right colour to lead a funeral procession.'

Jewel glared at him. From now on her dog would share her sleeping mat.

June 1520

The Month of the Little Feast of the Lords

Montezuma sat chained in a small cheerless chamber. He was hungry and thirsty and his clothes had not been changed for days. He entertained himself with poems. He had moved away from those long war epics, all of which he could recite by heart, although some of them lasted for hours.

> *It is not true, it is not true*
> *that we come on this earth to live.*
> *We come only to sleep, only to dream.*
> *Our body is a flower.*
> *As grass becomes green in the springtime,*
> *so our hearts will open and give forth buds*
> *and then they wither.*

This morning he heard sounds of fighting as the Mexica besieged the palace, throwing rocks and stones into the courtyards and setting fire to the Tlaxcalan huts. Last night they unleashed a parade of ghosts. A head attached to a foot, jumping heads, and corpses rolled around in the courtyard. The tricks amused him but terrified the Tlaxcalans. The news from the coast was that Tlaloc had sent thunder and rain to help Don Hernán defeat his enemies. Montezuma still hoped that he could count on Don Hernán's friendship. They had parted on good terms. Don Hernán could not have known of his support for his enemies. He needed Montezuma for their joint dreams of conquest. He could not control the Mexica without him.

But when Don Hernán returned and did not bother to call, Montezuma knew that he had been cast aside by everyone, by the gods, by his people, by his family, and now by Don Hernán. He felt betrayed. He had bared his soul to Don Hernán. He had shared the histories with him. Those words had been meaningless, spoken to fill up time. He had been tricked, just as Woman Snake insisted. The dreams of conquest vanished. There was no role for him now. He curled up into a ball and waited for time to pass.

The food ran out and the market closed down, forcing Don Hernán to visit the Emperor. He wasted no time on civilities. He demanded food and water.

'You have it all,' said Montezuma sadly. 'The granaries have run out. The Mexica starve so that you can eat.'

'Liar!' shouted Don Hernán. 'You speak nothing but lies.'

Montezuma sighed.

'I can do nothing. I am an emperor who no longer exists.' He had an idea. He hoped it was not too late. 'But there are two councillors who could help you.'

Who would best serve the Mexica – Woman Snake, or his belligerent younger brother, who would be firm but might bring conflict and war?

Don Hernán hesitated. He ordered the guards to release Montezuma's chains and escort him back to the large room where his brother and Woman Snake sat.

'Well, here is Montezuma risen from the dead,' drawled Woman Snake.

'Like the Spanish god,' mocked the Lord of the Two Waters.

Montezuma watched as Don Hernán released his brother.

'Starve the Spanish,' he whispered. 'Prepare the warriors to fight. Guard the causeways.' He was not sure whether his brother heard him, he left in such a hurry.

'You and I are the only ones left here, together like the old days,' he said genially to Woman Snake. 'How we used to argue! What shall we argue about now?'

'You are mad!' said Woman Snake. 'How can you speak as if nothing has changed?'

'I know how you despise me, Woman Snake,' said Montezuma sadly. 'You see me as a traitor. I did what I thought was best. I did everything to avoid a confrontation in the year One Reed, the year that destroys rulers, or have you forgotten?'

He tried not to hold his nose. How terribly Woman Snake smelt. Did he smell as badly? One of the Spanish guards bared his backside and farted loudly. Another relieved himself in front of them. At first Montezuma pretended not to notice. But when another man pissed and the smell became unbearable, he took a small jewel that his wife had given him and handed it to the guard to discourage him. But two more soldiers opened their pouches and sprayed the floor.

'Is there a new emperor?' Montezuma asked.

He dragged himself away from the urine that flowed chaotically over the stones. When Woman Snake did not reply, he leant against the wall, shut his eyes, and tried to remember happier times. He started with his wedding. He saw Tecalco, her ears weighed down by jewellery, her small feet painted with copal and with so many flowers she seemed like a walking garden. He had written a poem for her. He remembered the birth of his Jewel during that feverish year when the corn shrivelled and they ate locusts. He had returned early from hunting. She should have been a boy but when he saw the tiny creature with the bright birdlike eyes, he knew the gods had sent him a jewel. He looked at Woman Snake, curled in a heap on the floor. Had Woman Snake ever loved anyone?

'Did you love my sister?' he asked suddenly.

'What does it matter now?' mumbled Woman Snake.

'We have nothing to do but talk. I feel like turning back the years and discovering the truth. I live much in the past now. I sometimes thought you feared women, although you were never one for men.'

Imprisonment had certainly changed the Emperor. He did not usually speak so frankly. It was true that somewhere in Woman Snake's mind lurked a fear that would not go away. Every time he looked at a woman's body, he saw the dark place between a woman's legs which led to the void in the centre of the earth.

'I did not fear my wife,' he replied laconically. 'After all, we have several children.'

His wife was a homely woman who never stopped chattering even during the act. Perhaps he only feared beauty, associating it forever with the Salt Goddess.

'You were sick at our first sacrifice of the Salt Goddess. After that you changed.'

'I had no idea you were so observant,' spluttered Woman Snake.

It had been his first proper sacrifice. He was fourteen at the time. He remembered his horror as he watched the girl chosen for the goddess, spreadeagled over the sacred stone. The wind had caught her skirts, exposing the mysterious parts between her legs. He had watched her body twist and jerk as her neck was slowly sawed by the serrated edge of a swordfish beak. Even now he could still hear the bloodcurdling noise of her feet drumming on their padded sandals and remember how his *tepuli* had exploded as blood and urine erupted from the girl's body like a holy spring. He still felt the shame and the exhilaration of that moment, and something else he did not recognise, a mixture of pain and pleasure.

'I always enjoyed women,' boasted Montezuma. 'They are there like flowers in a garden for us to enjoy. Few visit me now. Anyway my inclination is more for poems:

> *"How will you make love to me,*
> *my companion of pleasure?*
> *Let us do it this way together,*
> *are you not a woman?"*

And she replies:

"What is it that confuses you?
You circle my heart with flowers,
they are your word.
I will show you the place where I weave,
the place where I spin."

'Do you have any poems about love, Woman Snake, or are your words as lean as your women?'

Woman Snake turned his back to the Emperor. It was surprising how words had the power to hurt so. He feared that the Emperor was going mad.

One noisy afternoon during a day when no food or water had been served, when the room stank from the pots of excrement piled against the wall, Don Hernán paid an unexpected visit. He held a piece of white cotton in front of his nose. The Mexica had breached a wall of the palace. Missiles had landed on the roof and a tunnel had been discovered leading into the palace. He ordered Montezuma to speak to his people massing in the square.

'My words carry no authority,' said Montezuma sadly. 'Why should my people listen to me? They did not listen last time.'

'Tell them they destroy themselves.'

'They will not listen.'

'Is there a new emperor?'

'I do not know what happens outside these walls.'

'You will speak to your people.'

Montezuma sighed. 'What more do you want from me? I have given you everything – my lands, my soul, my people. You have taken my gods. I neither wish to live nor to listen to you.'

'You have no one to blame but yourself.'

'There is no point in my speaking.'

Malinalli spoke quietly.

'I am sorry, Lord Montezuma. I did not think it would end like this. But if you could help us, it might save you.'

'You should have thought where your words would lead,' spat Woman Snake. 'You always spoke too many; some were bound to land in the wrong places. Do you think these men will honour you forever? Don Hernán will find another woman if he has not already. Your moment of power will soon be gone and then what will you be, a slave again?'

'What choice did I have, Lord Woman Snake? It was my fate. They told my parents at my birth that I would bring change.'

'That is why they sold you.'

She turned and left the room.

In the afternoon the Spanish priest, Father Olmedo, paid a visit.

'For God's sake, I beg you, Lord Montezuma, speak to your people.'

'Whose god?'

'All our gods, Lord Montezuma. Listen, if any of us are to survive, it must be through your intercession.'

'I do not care whether I live or die. As for your people I care even less.'

'What about your family? Your daughter who is here with Don Hernán. What about your other daughter who visits and your wife? What about your people?'

'I can do nothing,' repeated Montezuma. 'We all live and we all die. What does it matter? My people will have elected another ruler. None of you will leave the city alive.'

'We can try!' exclaimed the priest. 'Our God will protect us.'

'Then you do not need my voice.'

'There you are mistaken, Lord Montezuma. I plead for your people. I plead for mine. There has been enough death.'

Montezuma felt weary. He did not dislike this priest, although he disliked his message. Had Don Hernán been more accepting of the gods of the Mexica, Montezuma would have given him his own temple and appointed this man as its high priest. Outside the crowd shouted and jeered. A stone landed on the roof. Montezuma's hair hung limply. His loincloth was stained. He wore no sandals. He could not appear before his people like this. He told the priest to send for his clothes.

'One of us will die here,' he said, looking around at the dirty walls, at the soiled floor. 'I hope it will be me. And in which case,' – he turned to Woman Snake – 'I leave the care of the Mexica to you. You have been a wise councillor and I have neglected to praise you. Do one last thing. Dress me.'

Woman Snake ignored him.

'I will dress you, Lord,' offered Juan, hovering by the door.

The clothes arrived in their wicker basket. Juan washed the dirt from Montezuma's feet and tied on the golden-soled sandals with their tufts of jaguar fur. The ceremonial loincloth was missing and the Emperor had to wear his dirty one but the ornaments were all there. The triple gold necklace, turquoise earplugs, a jade nose ring and his favourite crystal plug with its kingfisher feather. With shaking hands Juan painted Montezuma's face but the Emperor's tears washed away the pigment. The sacred cloak of hummingbird feathers proved too heavy for Juan to lift.

'Please, Lord Woman Snake.'

Woman Snake looked up at the Emperor. The runny paint on his face made him look like a clown.

'Please!' pleaded Montezuma.

They were boys again together, praying, arguing, fighting, confiding in each other. Friends and cousins, clever boys with clever tongues. Woman Snake struggled to his feet and helped Juan lift the sacred cloak. It was the colour of that ocean where all this began only a year ago. He held up the crown with the turquoise and placed it carefully on Montezuma's head. The sound of celebration rose from the square. Woman Snake knew what his people celebrated and that it would be too late to change their mind.

'What shall I say?' asked Montezuma. 'I do not have the words. Give me the words, Woman Snake.'

'Don't go!'

A Spanish soldier pushed Montezuma roughly up the steps. He shuffled uncertainly to the edge of the roof. Two Spanish guards moved behind him. Montezuma was unsure whether they protected him or whether they would cut him down if his words failed. He gazed down at his people crammed into the square where their relatives had been murdered. Some of them began to weep when they saw him. Someone called for forgiveness.

Montezuma stepped closer to the edge of the roof. His two nervous guards raised their shields to protect him. He noticed how their hands trembled. But he felt no fear. He leant over the parapet. He begged the words to come to him. They came with the shrill piercing voice of the eagle. They echoed over the square. A voice shouted from below.

'We pray every day for you, Lord Montezuma.'

The guards dropped their shields. Another voice screamed.

'The Spaniards' whore is no longer our ruler!'

The crowd's mood changed. Darts and arrows flew through the air like angry birds. The stone came straight at him. It knocked the crown from his head. He saw his people gape in horror. Then everything went into slow motion. Darkness wrapped itself around him. He felt someone catch him as he slipped to the floor.

The next morning Juan appeared with a soldier at the palace on the Salt-Coloured Water. He stood awkwardly in the great hall, holding his hat in his hand. looking around as if making a note of everything he saw. Don Hernán had sent him to bring the Emperor's wife and daughter back to Tenochtitlán. The Emperor had been hit by a stone and seemed to have lost the will to live. He asked for his family.

'Is he dying?' whispered the Lady Tecalco.

Juan smiled tentatively at the ladies clustering around. One of them fingered his hair, admiring the streaks of gold.

'He will not eat or drink.'

'He is moody,' said the lady, who had nursed the Emperor through such spells before. But this time she feared they would all be taken hostage. She put her arms protectively around Jewel.

'I cannot spare you. Your father can do without you.'

'I know this boy. Let me go first and then I will send for you,' volunteered Jewel. Here was a chance to do something. 'I go to visit our father and Butterfly. Is that so terrible? I will return. Don Hernán has not attacked women. Now he is back we shall be safe from Don Alvarado. Butterfly has not been held prisoner. She speaks well of Don Hernán.'

But her mother would not stop crying.

'Look at me,' she scolded herself, 'weeping like a street woman!'

Jewel comforted her mother, then she bent down and picked up her little dog. She remembered her brother's warning and handed her dog to her mother.

'I leave him to keep you company.'

It was a beautiful day. She left with Ant Flower. She noticed Juan and the soldier take out their swords and hold them ready. Both looked around constantly, like animals covering their tracks. They had barely walked half way when five Mexica leapt from a canoe hidden beneath a folding bridge and pulled Jewel and Ant Flower into the boat. Jewel held tightly to Ant Flower. Had these Mexica come to kill her? She looked fearfully into the water. Should she try to escape? Neither she nor Ant Flower could swim.

She was relieved when they turned in the direction of Tacuba, a modest city on the western side of the lake, responsible for provisioning Tenochtitlán. Its wide unswept streets were lined with small low houses where people tended their gardens. Stones now covered the roofs. There were no signs of any Spanish here.

The men pulled her roughly out of the canoe and escorted her down a small alleyway in the lee of the temple. On one side a wall concealed doors leading to small gardens. Her escorts stopped at the only house with two storeys. They opened the door and pushed her inside. In the small garden women prepared tamales. They blew on the embers, singing to encourage the flames. Jewel felt hungry. One of the men propelled her quickly through the door as if he did not want to be seen. Jewel expected enemies, but there in the small room sat Falling Eagle.

It was an ordinary little house. It was noisy, it was dirty, it was crowded, but for two days it seemed like a palace. One small room up on the roof was set aside for Jewel and despite the lack of privacy and the constant comings and goings, this became her home. She forgot her father. She forgot the Spanish. She thought only of herself and Falling Eagle, but it did not last long. Falling Eagle had sent for her for a reason, not for love. He insisted she visit her father. She would be their spy. She could tell them what she saw there in the Old Palace, how the Spanish defended the place, and whether they planned to escape. Don Hernán would not suspect a woman. She could observe everything.

'What if Don Hernán takes me hostage?'

'He has far too much on his mind for women.'

'I have heard that nothing curbs his appetite.' Her voice trembled.

'Mexica warriors will soon curb his appetite. You must go before the Spanish kill your father.'

'No!' she screamed, disturbing the people in the next room. 'No! We must rescue him.'

'Are you mad? Your father's time has come. Let's hope he dies with dignity.'

She sobbed. She did not care if the people next door could not sleep. Why should they have a peaceful night if she could not?

The next day Handful of Reeds arrived to escort her to her father. She felt terrified. Afraid to see her father and afraid of capture. Handful of Reeds insisted that some of the Spanish were genuinely upset to see the Emperor so ill. Her father took only water and refused all medicine and food.

She felt torn between her father and her husband. She pleaded to stay but Falling Eagle insisted she go. Falling Eagle seemed to have forgotten last night. Men forgot love so quickly.

'You would risk me?'

She hoped he would say no.

'We are at war.'

'I am frightened.'

'A Mexica woman is never frightened,' he told her curtly.

July 1520

The Month of the Offering of Flowers

In the city smouldering funeral pyres filled the air with ash and fat vultures strutted boldly through the streets. Unwashed widows wandered aimlessly. They would do this for eighty days and then they would scrape the dirt from their skin, wrap it in paper, and give it to the priests. That was what widows did. Would she too mourn like this one day? She pitied these women who had lost their husbands and sons. Their Emperor could not help them now.

Inside the palace Tlaxcalans still hovered restlessly. Some stared greedily at her but did not confront her brother who seemed quite at home here. In the courtyard she saw the smouldering remains of the Tlaxcalan huts. She noticed that the horses were saddled ready to leave. She saw large baskets on wheels, with slits for windows. Along the corridor again, past the murals to her father's room, where she smelt urine and death. Her father lay on his mat, supported against a pillar. His eyes were half closed. On one side sat the priest Olmedo, his white robes the only splash of brightness in the room. On the other side Juan cradled a bowl of water. She saw how gently he comforted her father.

'Lord Montezuma, here is your daughter.'

Her father turned to look at her. Juan left the room. Now they were alone. They could say whatever they wanted. She saw a thin shell of a man, his arms scarred by penance, his face marked by pain. His cheeks were sunken, his skin yellow. A large bruise covered the side of his face and there was a wound on his head. She ran to him and stroked his cheek.

'Father, I beg you, do not die. Do not leave us. We need you. Mother, Butterfly and I and all the others . . .'

Her father smiled weakly.

'Don't cry for me, my beautiful Jewel. My time has come. My people do not need me. You must be brave. You will have to take care of yourself.'

'I will be all right, father. I will make my own life with Falling Eagle.'

He struggled to sit up. She put her hands under his arms and lifted him, surprised at how light he was.

'No! Falling Eagle is not the future for you. His signs are not good. I will make provision for you and Butterfly. Don Hernán . . .'

'I do not like Don Hernán.'

'Only Don Hernán can help you now. I have given you your own estates, the lands of Tacuba and the gardens at Coyoacan. Whatever you think of Don Hernán, I am confident he will look after you.'

'Father, you will give me to Don Hernán as you have given him Butterfly!'

'Nonsense. I speak only of the estates I leave for you. Don Hernán will see that they are well managed.'

'Father, how can you trust him?'

She wiped his face with her shawl. He was feverish. She saw that she exhausted him. He fumbled for her hands.

'Remember what I do is for the best. I wish to rest. But do not leave, stay with me.'

She sobbed floods, as if Tlaloc had invaded her mind. She could not stop. She loved her father. She loved his words, his wisdom, his gentleness. And now he was leaving her before she could tell him how she felt. She whispered.

'I have always loved you, father.'

A hint of a smile touched his lips.

'I am not worthy, my dear. I shall be remembered as the Emperor who gave away his country.'

'No, father! You did what you thought was best at the time.'

He patted her hand gently.

'I had no choice. Men do not have choice. It is our misfortune to be alive at such a time.'

Someone entered the room. Montezuma held up his hand.

'Stay. I wish to speak of my daughters' future. I want you to swear that you will honour what I propose.'

Don Hernán kissed his medallion. 'I swear on the image of my god.'

'For Jewel I leave the lands of Tacuba and the gardens at Coyoacan. And for my wife and daughter Butterfly I leave my other estates. I leave the care of my people in your hands.'

'I will swear to that,' said Don Hernán.

'You are to baptise my daughter.'

'No!' cried Jewel.

'Listen, child. I know what is good for you.'

'And you, Lord Montezuma. Can we baptise you at the same time?'

Montezuma collapsed exhausted onto his pillows. Don Hernán bowed and left.

'Father, how can you trust that man?'

'I have to. I want him to honour the bequests of a dying man.'

'Please don't die!'

Her father smiled.

'Death comes to us all. Tell me, has Falling Eagle been elected the new Emperor?' He seemed relieved when she shook her head. 'He will not make a good ruler. Who have they elected to replace me?'

'I do not know, father. Why should they replace you? You are alive.'

'If they have elected anyone, it must be a secret.'

She had heard nothing. Even Ant Flower had heard no rumours.

'Father, what is wrong with Falling Eagle?'

'He brings death and destruction. He is the sun that dies.'

He stopped, too exhausted to continue. He begged for water.

She held the bowl to his lips and curled up close to him, trying to warm him with her body. Now he felt cold. His skin was clammy. She put her arms tightly around him to keep him here in the world of men. He dozed a while and then he spoke again slowly, as if the words were an effort.

'You must survive, whatever you have to do.'

'Father!'

'No, listen! My words will not last for long. You must take care of our people. I shall no longer be here to protect them.'

'Please don't speak like this.'

He smiled weakly.

'You must be strong. See that our language lives on, that the people remain true to their gods, even if secretly. See that their lands are not stolen from them. Protect your mother and sister.'

'I am only a woman.'

'Don Hernán may listen to you whereas he will see Falling Eagle as a threat. These times call for a different wisdom. I misunderstood the signs.'

'Perhaps there was nothing you could do.'

'It was foretold. But I will redeem myself and save my people by sacrificing myself for them. I will never accept the new god. For you, the new god will come with your new life. There is no escape and you must submit to it. But there will still be room for other gods in your heart. What you say and what you think need not be the same. But for me, I shall never abandon our gods.'

Jewel sobbed. She wanted to stay with him but when she saw how her tears disturbed him she rose and went outside to weep in the corridor. She did not hear her father whisper.

'May the old gods watch over you, my little bird.'

Her sister Butterfly waited in the corridor.

'Stay here with us, Jewel. You will be safe. Don Hernán plans to escape. He will take us with him.'

'You betray your own people.'

'No. I can do more for my people if the Spanish listen to me. They treat me well. I am free to do what I want.'

'They force you to accept their god.'

'No! You do not understand. I chose to accept the new God. He is kind. He does not sacrifice people. He is like Quetzalcoatl. He loves us all, even sinners, even people who believe in false gods like you.'

'You are Don Hernán's concubine. You are a woman of joy. How can you bear it?'

'I like it,' she said shyly. 'Don Hernán knows how to please me.'

'As he does many other women.'

Butterfly smiled. 'I do not mind.'

'He is hairy and smelly!'

'I am used to it.'

Four soldiers passed in the corridor. They lifted their hats. 'Doña Anna,' they chorused.

'That is my new name,' said Butterfly. 'The Spanish will give you a new name.'

Jewel peered over the balcony into the courtyard below where people were packing baskets. She saw that one of the beams from the great hall lay on the ground. A fire burned in the middle of the courtyard, surrounded by blocks of gold.

'Some of the Spanish are so greedy,' said Butterfly. 'You can never imagine what they plan to do with that gold.'

'I cannot.'

'They will melt those blocks and make them into belts which they will wear under their clothes. Have you ever heard of anything so stupid? And men will hide in those baskets on wheels.'

'When will you go?'

'Soon,' said Butterfly. Don Hernán insists that we all sleep dressed to leave. The Spanish sleep in their armour and their shoes.' She began to cry. 'I have heard that they wait for our father's death. Please say you will come with us. You will not regret it. The Spanish will treat you as one of them.'

A Spanish woman swept past in the corridor. She stopped when she saw Butterfly, who spoke to her in Spanish. The woman smiled and greeted Jewel.

'This is Doña María. She came with Don Panfilio. She rides and fights like a man. You see, the Spanish let their women live like men. Come with us or you will be killed.'

Montezuma waited for death. He knew it would not be long. And although it was comforting to see how his guards wept for him, their concern had come too late. At least he would try to leave everything in order. It was his role to bring order to his people, to his world. He juggled the conflicting interests of the universe. Harmony was never achieved without a struggle. Despite his efforts, he had not achieved it. That was the major regret of his life. When he was young he had wanted to be remembered as the greatest ruler of the Mexica, a torch that did not smoke, the Nahuatl expression for a wise man. Few men deserved such praise.

At his inauguration the world had been full of promise. His lords had elected him unanimously, all thirty of them. They had called him 'valiant, temperate and wise'. He was thirty-four years old. He smiled at the memory.

'Woman Snake! There is something I wish to ask you.'

Woman Snake stirred in the corner.

'Tell me,' – his voice sounded hoarse – 'who threw the stone that hit me?'

Woman Snake dragged himself across the stained floor, avoiding the rotting food and faeces. He leant down and whispered in the Emperor's ear.

'It is as I suspected.'

As he lay there many things became clear. Although he would die and some of the Mexica with him, it was possible that the world itself would not end yet. As long as he honoured his gods, there was a chance that the world would continue. It would not be the same world, but it would not be destroyed. He saw now how Don Hernán had played his part. Like Quetzalcoatl, he was the bringer of change.

The priest Olmedo hovered in the doorway clutching an image of his god, and even Juan begged relentlessly for him to accept the new God, but although he loved the boy, he turned his face to the wall and refused to listen. Now he found himself drifting between light and dark, hearing snippets of conversations which floated on the air like the homeless words he plucked for his poems. He told Juan about the invisible words that searched for homes. But Juan thought his mind was wandering and wiped his head with a cool cloth, and tried to persuade him to eat and take his medicine.

Montezuma watched the sun fade as the eagle dropped below the horizon and the moon goddess rose, a slip of a girl, a half-moon, to enjoy her moment of glory. He remembered how Woman Snake had said it was his duty to remain in the shadow of his emperor. Where was Woman Snake? Was he next door with the other lords waiting for his death? Montezuma regretted it was too late to finish those unresolved conversations.

'Water!' he begged again, from the boy crouching beside him.

Juan sobbed as he held the bowl to Montezuma's lips.

'Now, Juan, do not weep for me. I am not worth it.'

'I weep, Lord, to see you die unshriven, to know that you will burn in hell.'

Montezuma smiled weakly. Had the boy been a spy for Don Hernán, as Woman Snake insisted? He did not want to know. He saw that Juan sobbed uncontrollably.

'I shall tell you about the butterflies,' he said.

'The butterflies?'

'There are millions of them.' He saw them again in his mind. 'They come every year in great clouds of orange, smothering the trees with their wings. Like us, the butterflies live only a short time before they flutter to the ground and die.' He remembered the crunch of their bodies under his feet. 'Such is a man's life. A flash of beauty before sorrow and death.'

'Lord Montezuma,' begged the boy, 'if you believe in the true God, you will find eternal life. Embrace Him before it is too late. Confess to Him now and He will save you.'

'Nobody truly lives on earth. We pursue only a dream.'

He had once composed a poem on the meaning of life. It had won first prize at the festival. He repeated the words slowly so Juan could understand:

> *'Is it true we have roots in the earth?*
> *Surely we are not forever here?*
> *Only for a time we are here!'*

'That is a sad poem, Lord Montezuma.'

'That is life, Juan, sadness and joy, ugliness and beauty. It all ends in death.'

Now he drifted between the worlds of men and gods. He saw his daughter slip back into the room and fling herself down beside him. He felt the cross of the Spanish god brush his face. He felt cold, as if he were walking naked in the snow up to Tlaloc's shrine. He could no longer feel his limbs or his fingers. In his mind, butterflies flew and words tried to escape, searching for new homes. He heard his mother calling but could not move to greet her. As the cross loomed again in front of his face, he whispered his favourite prayer to Smoking Mirror. Jewel repeated the words with him.

> *'O Master, O our lord,*
> *O lord of the near, of the nigh,*
> *O night, O wind,*
> *now in truth I appear before you . . .'*

'Confess, Lord Montezuma, before it is too late.'

Montezuma saw the priest bend over him and felt the cross scratch his skin. What had he to confess now? He saw a shadow push the priest aside. He heard the image crash onto the floor and then Woman Snake's distinctive rasping voice.

'Let the Emperor die in peace!'

Montezuma smiled. He had outwitted them all. He would die with his prayers on his lips, loyal to his gods.

'I leave the Mexica in your able hands, Woman Snake.'

He heard Jewel's birdlike voice fade as if the wind separated them. He waited for the ancestors to beckon but there was only darkness as if the moon had swallowed the sun. He did not hear the explosion of weeping from the guards blocking the doorway.

Someone helped Jewel to her feet. She heard shouts, cries, muffled screams as soldiers ran up and down the corridor. Her father was still warm. How peaceful he looked. She did not want to leave him.

'Lady,' Juan pleaded, 'you must leave now.'

He pulled her to the stairs. He stood between her and the rooms next door as if he were hiding something. She pushed him aside and ran into the grand reception room. There on the floor lay the bodies of the lords who had accompanied her father in his captivity.

'No!' she cried. She had known all these men. She vomited over the floor. She could not stop.

'Lady, go now.' Juan looked around. 'Or you will be trapped here with us.'

'Why do you help me?' she asked angrily.

'Because I loved your father and . . .' he hesitated, 'I know how Don Hernán will use you.'

She feared she would never escape. So many Tlaxcalans spilled into the stairways and the corridors. But she followed Juan. At the bottom of the stairs, her sister Butterfly stood in front of her.

'Stay here with us. You will be safe!' she shouted, but Jewel ignored her, stepping over the bodies blocking the corridor. Jewel started to cry again but Juan pulled her on, through the courtyard past the grinning Tlaxcalans, exhilarated by the massacre upstairs. One of them grabbed her jade necklace, spilling the precious beads onto the floor.

'No!' she cried, fighting to pick up the stones. It was all she had left from her father. But Juan dragged her to the entrance where they found the great gates locked. He looked around in desperation, then pulled her into the shadows of the porch next to the gate.

'When it is dark, they will throw out your father's body. Wait until then and slip out. No one will see you in the chaos.' He turned back 'Consider the true God. How he loves you. How you could be saved. Your father agreed that you should be baptised.'

She stared at him. How she hated them all.

'You will never escape from here.'

'Maybe not,' said Juan sadly.

She hid in the shadows listening to the weeping on the other side of the gate. And just as Juan promised, when it was dark a group of soldiers approached the gate carrying her father's body. Behind them came a procession with the bodies of the other lords. The great doors swung open. Hands stretched inside. One by one the bodies were passed through. As she slipped out with two dead lords, one of the soldiers grabbed at her, tearing her skirt. She ran, holding her skirt, dodging the crowds, out along the causeway to Tacuba where she found a gap where the first bridge should have been. She stared into the black water. From the city behind her came the wailing of the mourners. Someone ran along the causeway. The water terrified her but she feared the Spanish even more. The feet grew closer. She turned and saw the white teeth of a Tlaxcalan bearing down on her.

She jumped. The water was freezing. She struggled to stay afloat but the weeds pulled her down. Water purified. It cleansed. It gave life and it took away life. Death by drowning guaranteed a place in the eternal spring of Tlaloc's heaven. She sank deeper. A canoe paddled above her. Hands plunged down into the water and lifted her to the surface.

'You are lucky, Lady. There are thousands of us waiting here for the Spanish to leave. Otherwise no one would have seen you.'

The body of her pursuer floated on the surface. Two arrows protruded from his back. Now she saw the canoes, twenty deep, nuzzling the causeway. Mexica warriors helped her up the bank.

She ran along the path. Her skirt was ripped. The smell of death clung to her. Her father's blood stained her blouse. She was desperate to wash. But she had to tell Falling Eagle what she had seen.

She stood there in front of him, her hair hanging like the moss in the ahuehuete trees. She told him about the baskets on wheels. She told him about the gold belts and how Don Hernán's men slept in their clothes and shoes. She told him that the horses were saddled ready to go. She did not know why the Spanish had taken down the great ceiling beam. She told him about the woman who behaved like a man. She told him how friendly Handful of Reeds seemed with the Spanish.

'You have done well,' said Falling Eagle. 'Don Hernán does not know that we have thousands of canoes and warriors waiting by the causeways. And if he tries to cross the Tacuba causeway, which he will because it is the shortest, he will fall into the water where I have removed the bridges.'

'The gold will weigh them down, make them slow travellers,' said her uncle, the Lord of the Two Waters. 'They will sink in the mud.'

Falling Eagle thought the Spanish would leave in the morning. It would not be tonight for it had started to rain and a low mist hung over the lake.

The Lord of the Two Waters peered through the door.

'Mist and rain muffle sound.'

'No sane men would leave on such a night,' said Falling Eagle.

'These are not sane men,' her uncle reminded him. 'They sleep in their armour and their shoes.'

They all laughed.

'My father is dead, Falling Eagle.'

'It had to happen. Now we can make our own plans.'

'He was my father!'

She began to tremble.

'He betrayed the Mexica.'

Now she blubbered and could not stop.

Falling Eagle looked at her scornfully.

'We are at war. We cannot afford to mourn.'

It was Ant Flower who helped Jewel from the room, who washed her and prepared her for sleep.

'Men!' she exclaimed. 'All they know about is fighting.'

Ant Flower loosened Jewel's hair and let it hang loose as a sign of mourning. When Falling Eagle crept onto her mat later in the night, he was gentle with her.

'There are only the two of us now,' he told her. 'I cannot replace your father but I can love you as he did.'

She disgraced herself by crying loudly and waking the couple in the next room.

When Woman Snake saw the dead lords, he knew he would have to escape. He hid himself in a steam room. He considered disguising himself as a Tlaxcalan and leaving with the Spanish. But as the fighting intensified he felt sure all the Spanish and Tlaxcalans would be massacred and he did not want to join them. There was no food or water in the Old Palace. The waste mounted daily from the horses, the humans and the dogs. The stench was terrible. He waited until the sounds of killing subsided and then he crept out of his room. On the stairs, he bumped into a group of Tlaxcalans and tried to hide himself among them. Fortunately they were so drunk on pulque and death that they did not notice him.

Down in the courtyard where the Spanish packed their baskets on wheels Father Olmedo was celebrating Mass. The cries and howls of the men and the shrieks of their horses sounded like the keening of dying animals. Heads bobbed up and down in prayer. Hands repeatedly made the sign of their cross. Woman Snake sneaked past the courtyard and out into the great hall. The gates in the outer courtyard were ajar to let out the bodies of the dead. He decided to slip out with the porters and walked unchallenged through the first set of gates. In the outer courtyard he bumped into Handful of Reeds. He started to run, but his sandals were loose and he almost tripped over the flagstones. As he reached the main gate Handful of Reeds caught up.

'You cannot leave!'

Woman Snake struggled but Handful of Reeds was young and strong. Around them swarmed Tlaxcalans and soldiers, porters with litters, men struggling to lift gold bars into baskets. The noise frightened the horses. One of them bolted across the courtyard and made straight for them. Handful of Reeds lost his hold. Woman Snake sprinted towards the gate and slipped out just as the doors were closing. He concealed himself among the porters carrying bodies. When he reached the Sacred Square, although he felt exhausted and was coughing, he ran to check the causeways. He found the first bridge had been removed. He stood on the edge staring at the water. No horses could cross the gaps now and, for men in armour, it would be difficult to swim. Then he saw the thousands of canoes waiting in the shadows. He returned home and collapsed exhausted. He knew the Spanish would leave soon but he was confident that the city was prepared, its warriors ready.

At midnight he heard the drums. At first he thought he was dreaming. Then a woman's voice echoed over the square. He leapt from his mat, shouting for his servants to bring his clothes and weapons. Then he ran out into the city. The rain fell in a steady drizzle. People emerged from their houses in their nightclothes. Some grabbed weapons. Children screamed. Gobbling turkeys ran around in circles. Dogs escaped out into the crowds, dodging in between the running feet.

Despite the lifting of the bridges, the Spanish had already crossed three canals and now they were trapped on the fourth by the warriors in their canoes. By the time Woman Snake reached the fourth canal, half the Spanish had managed to cross on a portable bridge made of the ceiling beam and planks from the Old Palace. The rest were trapped on the city side of the causeway where they struggled under a barrage of arrows from the canoes surrounding them and from the warriors who blocked their escape on either side of the gap. Woman Snake joined the warriors attacking the Spanish from the rear, but when he saw a canoe he jumped into it and ordered the warrior to paddle towards the gap in the canal. The Spanish were more vulnerable from the water.

Heads popped up around him. Limbs thrashed desperately. His canoe sliced its way through drowning men and women who clung to it, threatening to capsize him. Woman Snake slashed at their hands with his axe. Its double-edged blades sliced through the bone and broken limbs, spreading pools of red on the surface of the water. A basket on wheels toppled over into the canal and narrowly missed him. The Spanish were so desperate to escape that they hurled themselves into the gap where the portable bridge had been, on top of men, horses, women and Tlaxcalans. And such was their fear that they did not care whether the bodies on which they landed were dead or alive, only that there was a sufficiency to support them. The bodies were now level with the causeway, twelve feet above the water. Horses and men charged across but sometimes the bodies gave way and they fell, swallowed up by the water.

In the darkness and confusion it was impossible to see who was Mexica and who was not. Woman Snake aimed his arrows wherever he saw the gleam of armour or a white face, ducking the arrows that flew around him, and the silver knives that slashed out blindly. A Mexica warrior in a canoe next to him took aim, sending a Spanish soldier into the water. As he fell, he exposed the gold bars tied around his waist. The warrior lowered his bow in amazement. On the causeway above them a group of women protected by the Tlax-calans waited to cross the gap. They were trapped between Mexica warriors and the human bridge where people still struggled across. Woman Snake felt sure that Malinalli was among them. He took aim. A woman screamed in Nahuatl and a body splashed into lake.

His canoe wobbled precariously. A terrified horse paddled past. A helmet bobbed on the water. A cannon rammed into Woman Snake and holed his canoe. Heads emerged in the darkness as people swam for shore. On the causeway some of the terrified Spanish turned and ran back towards the city. Woman Snake paddled desper-ately to the shore where he abandoned his canoe and ran with the warriors to cut off any retreat.

At dawn a watery sun revealed the chaos of the night. The Mexica pulled the bodies from the canals and stripped them. They loaded the dead Tlaxcalans onto canoes and threw them into the rushes with their painted dancing girls. They laid the waxy Spanish corpses in rows in front of the temple. Seven horses' heads were spiked onto the skull rack. In the lake they found bows, lances, muskets, chain mail, silver suits, shields, saddles and drinking horns. They found gold bars and green stone collars stuck in the reeds. They found knives and daggers and one stringed instrument and the body of the Lady Butterfly with a Mexica arrow in her chest. There was no sign of Don Hernán or Don Alvarado.

And when they had dealt with the dead and swept away the dust and rubble, they decorated the city for the Great Feast of the Lords, filling the streets with lights, illuminating the temples. They hung paper streamers in the trees. Two hundred and forty Spanish prisoners waited in cages to feed the gods.

After the celebrations the new Emperor, the Lord of the Two Waters, promised to begin his reign with a war against the surviving Spanish. He chose the town of Otumba in a dusty valley under the hills of Tlaxcala where it would be easy to surround the enemy and destroy them.

Part Three

August 1520 – August 1521
The Year Three House

Tenochtitlan

August – September 1520

It was a day without wind. Scorching on the ridge, but cold in the valley where the shade brought frost. The warriors lined up along the crest. The Jaguar Knights, sweating in their skin-tight fur suits, crouched in the gullies, while on the crags the Eagle Knights peered menacingly through the gaping beaks of their helmets. Behind them mingled the ordinary men smelling of the brine that coated their cotton armour, and the veterans whose dangling lip plugs danced as impatiently as their owners.

There was no sign of the Spanish. The scouts had reported the slow progress of wounded and sick men with only twelve archers and twenty horses. Woman Snake took a deep breath. His chest felt clear. Up here, among the haunts of eagles, he felt rejuvenated. He had become the eagle, the hunter, the symbol of the sun with its ability to fall and rise again. His angular face peered from his helmet of wood and paper and eagle feathers. An eagle feather cloak shaped like two wings hung over his shoulders. Talons protruded from his sleeves and his tufted leggings. His crested banner frame towered above his head, visible to his men even in the confusion of war. He called out exuberantly.

'Make resound your trumpet of the tigers. The eagle screams upon the circular stone.'

The words made the hairs rise on the back of his neck. Everything the Mexica had came from war – their gods, their city, their wealth, their honour. This day would bring an end to the uncertainties of the last year. It would destroy their enemies for ever. In the distance he saw a wisp of dust spiralling slowly over the plain. The warriors fidgeted impatiently. Falling Eagle looked at him expectantly. He could see the impatience in his commanders' eyes.

'Not yet,' he murmured. 'Not yet.'

He willed the warriors to hold their positions.

Below on the plain the Spanish stumbled through clumps of cactus, mesquite and chaparral. He waited until they reached the first rocky outcrop before he gave the command.

'We will sacrifice your hearts and blood to our gods. There will be such a glut of food. We will feast on your arms and legs and throw your bodies to the animals in the zoo.'

'Zoo, zoo . . .' echoed the hills until there were thousands of Woman Snakes. The conches howled like hungry coyotes. The whistles shrieked. The Mexica roared. They screamed. They yelled. They rattled their weapons. They stamped their feet making the seed pods on their legs hiss like millions of snakes. Down on the plain the Spanish looked up and huddled together, a tiny pimple on the earth, a few hundred men surrounded by thousands of warriors.

Woman Snake led the advance down from the ridge, avoiding the rocks and the jagged mesquite. He kept running, propelled by the momentum of his banner frame. He thought it odd that the Spanish did not move and the five horses and the dogs that came snapping at his heels were a surprise. The demon horses towered above him. Their smell made him queasy. He slashed out blindly with his spear thrower. The rope carriers barged in, throwing their ropes in a vain attempt to hobble the horses. Woman Snake banged his drum frantically. The horses retreated leaving the ground littered with headdresses, shields, weapons. The dust whirled and settled but the Spanish still clung together.

Woman Snake ran towards them, trying not to trip over the bodies on the ground. Five fresh horses broke out. Woman Snake lifted his spear but one horse jumped like an acrobat. Woman Snake's banner frame worked loose and hung lopsidedly on his shoulders. His helmet slipped over his left eye. A dog with a bloody muzzle brought him down in the melee of legs, ropes and animals. The lance that pierced his ribs skewered him to the ground. He heard shouting and running feet and the rustle of feathers and shields. He felt the earth shake and knew that the Mexica fled.

His mouth filled with grit. Piss trickled down his legs, stinging his skin and staining the eagle suit. As he coughed his blood into the thirsty earth, he saw the sun, the eagle who died and rose again, embrace the mountains, a round red ball spreading its light over the bloodied plains. He was surprised it was midday already.

Lizard had marched in the vanguard of scouts, priests and porters. He spent most of the battle sitting with the gods' statues on a ridge above the valley listening to the horns and the barking dogs the drums and the screams, frustrated he could see nothing. It was only when the dust settled that he had been able to run down from the ridge to find a scene of desolation. So many had died, pierced by swords, mauled by dogs or crushed by horses.

It was Lizard who found Woman Snake lying in a ditch. His eyes were open. All his gold had been stripped from him. What remained of the eagle suit could not be separated from his flesh. His split septum showed where his nose ring had been torn from him. Lizard and Falling Eagle had lifted Woman Snake into a litter for the journey home. Lizard would never forget the black clouds of crows and vultures flying in the opposite direction back to Otumba.

His father's friends brought some comfort. Through them he came to know Woman Snake better in death than in life. After the funeral, old friends would call at his father's home, drink pitchers of pulque and reminisce fondly about the man they had known. Even the merchants sent a delegation. They told how the Woman Snake they knew proved a shrewd investor, trading only in the best slaves, the rarest jewels, the finest furs. Others spoke of a brave warrior without a dishonourable bone in his body.

'There were not many bones left in his body,' quipped Wandering Coyote.

They ignored him. Wandering Coyote was considered an outsider. No one was sure where his loyalties lay.

'A man of integrity, a wise man, "a torch that does not smoke",' said a cousin.

'A diplomat!' shouted one. 'No ear for a song,' said another, but they all agreed he had a tongue as sharp as a swordfish beak.

They smoked their pipes, consoling each other, hankering for the times of their youth when the Mexica produced men of Woman Snake's calibre. Otumba was a shock to them all. No one knew why the gods had abandoned them. The priests searched vainly for answers. And now the Spanish, who had recovered from their wounds, had attacked the hilltop fortress of Tepeyac which supplied the Mexica with food. Terrible things had happened there – its citizens ravaged by dogs, its women and children enslaved. The mourners asked why no one had challenged the Spanish. Wandering Coyote thought it was the fault of the Tlaxcalans. He felt sure they would use the Spanish to avenge themselves against the Mexica. Woman Snake's friends considered the idea of a Tlaxcalan army invading the city ridiculous. There were many warriors left to fight. They still had weapons. The Spanish were much reduced in number and those who were left were badly wounded. The very absurdity of it led to jokes that lasted all evening.

The recriminations came after Woman Snake's funeral. The councillors shouted at once. The new Emperor, the Lord of the Two Waters, struggled to hold the meeting together.

'We must ask ourselves why,' shouted the new Woman Snake.

'The old Woman Snake was too cautious,' replied an Eagle Knight.

'He was too close to Montezuma!' screamed another.

'That traitor!' hissed a junior councillor.

'They are all traitors in that family,' shrieked a Jaguar Knight. 'We should kill them all! They have given our country away.'

The High Priest of Huitzilopochtli tried to bring order. 'The question is, why did our gods abandon us?'

Falling Eagle, who had remained seated until then, rose to his feet.

'This has nothing to do with the gods.'

'Blasphemy!' shouted the High Priest.

'The truth is,' continued Falling Eagle, struggling to speak over the noise, 'that this was a different kind of battle. It tells us that we can defeat the Spanish only if we fight like them.'

'Nonsense!' shrieked one of Montezuma's sons. He had his father's high-pitched voice. 'We have hamstrung the Spanish. They will not survive long. They are alone, wounded and sick.'

'You do not know then,' taunted Falling Eagle. How he disliked this man. He knew he had made overtures to the Spanish. He dealt in gold and had changed his gods.

'Know what?'

'The Spanish have managed to reach Tlaxcala.'

'The Tlaxcalans will not welcome them,' insisted Montezuma's son.

'Oh but they have,' said Falling Eagle. 'They have welcomed them as gods. Now they will join forces against us.'

Falling Eagle did not linger after the meeting. Normally everyone would gather on the steps of the House of Eagles and chat. The council had been split even before Montezuma's death. The old loyalties had been sorely tested. Now more and more councillors wanted to make agreements with the Spanish. He did not trust the Spanish – they were dogs scrabbling for gold in the name of their god.

The carnage at Otumba had been terrible. All of Tlaloc's rain would not wash away the stains. The Mexica had so nearly won. It was not cowardice that made them flee. They would have fought to the bitter end had not Don Hernán held up Woman Snake's feathers. Falling Eagle had tried to rally the regiments but there was too much noise and confusion for anyone to hear.

In the Sacred Square, smoke still rose from Woman Snake's pyre, now a pile of grey ashes. Was this all that remained of a man's life? Unlike Montezuma, Woman Snake had been given a civic funeral.

Thousands had lined the streets. How thin the old man had been when they wrapped him in his blankets. Not enough flesh to contain the blood that soiled him. He had gone honourably to the next world with jade in his mouth. The city had mourned as it had not for the Emperor Montezuma. There were no slaves, jesters, dwarfs and hunchbacks at the Emperor's funeral, only a small family group who gasped when the body released a foul odour and exploded into dense clouds of smoke. The Emperor's first wife had screamed that the Emperor had been murdered. 'Who threw the stone?' she shrieked. 'It was not a Spaniard.' As her eyes followed the mourners, did Falling Eagle imagine that they lingered on *him*?

Jewel could not believe that so many warriors had been killed. It was one shock after another. What had her father said before he died? That the good times would come to an end and that she must be brave. She had shown no emotion at his funeral. At least her little dog had proudly led the procession so her father would not travel to Mictlan alone, just as he had foreseen in his garden in Coyoacan before the Spanish arrived. Her father had had the gift of seeing into the future but had rarely spoken of what he saw. Her mother said that some of his dreams were truly terrible. If only they could turn time back. But time did not go back. It went round in circles until it ran out.

Now she was back in the old palace on the Salt-Coloured Water, comforting her mother and the old aunts, running here and there searching for their cactus spine needles which they lost every five minutes. Old people's lives seemed to run in straight lines. And such repetition too. And how could they still ask her about children *now*, when it did not matter. At least Falling Eagle had not died in Otumba. She had chewed her nails down to nothing waiting for news. And when, at last, the messenger had run panting through the city gates, she was ashamedly and ecstatically happy that it was Woman Snake who had been taken. She sat down on a seat on the edge of the lake. It looked as if she would be here for some time. It seemed that some in the city wanted to kill all of her family. It must be true because they had left the city secretly at night, with Falling Eagle's soldiers to protect them.

She knew, although Falling Eagle had not told her, that he had gone to Tlaxcala to persuade them to change sides and fight with the Mexica. She knew too that the last Mexica ambassadors to Tlaxcala had all been sacrificed. Ant Flower had told her that Spanish ships had landed at the coast with more men, horses and guns. And that was not all. Rumours had reached even here on the Salt-Coloured Water of a terrible disease which brought blisters and death. No one knew where it came from. She chewed her fingers again, watching the blood spurt from her flesh like a priest's mortification.

Tenochtitlan

October – November 1520

When Lizard woke one morning with a heavy head and a fever, he thought at first he had purged himself too much. He mortified his flesh twice daily. It helped his grief and brought him closer to his father. He noticed how his legs ached. When he went out to collect his teachers' food, his nose bled so badly he had to lie down on the temple steps where he gathered a curious crowd of onlookers, all with their own ideas as to the causes of his bleeding. Back in the dining hall he vomited over the food and had to escape to the dormitory where he threw himself down onto his mat. He felt as if he were burning.

The priests brought him black water from the temple of Ixtilon and carried him to the baths, making him sweat to bring down his fever. When ulcers erupted in his mouth, a red rash covered his arms, and pimples broke out on his stomach, he remembered the man he had tripped over on the towpath two weeks ago, on the unlucky day of Two Rabbit. He too had a rash and pimples. At first he had thought the man drunk. Bruises and blisters were signs of sexual excess. Then he remembered that bloated corpse in the lake and how the scouts had joked as they kicked the body back and forth in the reeds like a rubber ball.

The priests tried their magic. They scattered grains of maize on a white cotton cloak. But their magic provided no answers. The doctors shook their heads disapprovingly. There was only one reason for such an illness. Lizard told them he had yet to know sexual pleasure. Now he felt so ill, he wondered whether he ever would. He lay alone in his room.

Then two other pupils joined him, and then three more, and five more, until the dormitory was full. And every day the faithful priests came with food to tempt them. But Lizard could not stop retching and could not control his bowels, shaming himself with the mess he made for the women who cleared up. An opossum's tail sacrificed for him made no difference. His blisters swelled and filled with pus until the pain became unbearable. He lay paralysed, unable even to scratch himself and he itched as if ants devoured him.

The only healer who called now rubbed bitumen on the sores and poured pulque on them. Although the pulque stung, Lizard bore his pain like a warrior. Even when the doctor punctured his blisters, replacing the pus with squashed black beetles, he made no sound. And, then, neither the doctor nor the faithful priest turned up. There was no food or water, no one to remove the bodies of those who had died in the night. Lizard floated between the worlds of spirits and men, as if he could not decide where to live. And every day he expected to make his confession to the goddess who would eat his filth.

Then one day he woke to bright sunlight, a parched mouth and the terrible smell of rotting flesh. He pulled away his blanket. His blisters had begun to dry. Scabs flaked off as he sloughed his skin like a snake. Buzzing clouds of flies attacked his eyes and nostrils. He stumbled unsteadily out through the portico. Even the fresh wind off the lake could not disguise the stench. In the square bloated vultures, too fat to fly, gorged on flesh. A dog gnawed at a child's body. People covered with sores dragged themselves to shelter from the remorseless sun. The steps leading up to the shrines were empty. Out on the lake abandoned canoes waited forlornly for their dead owners.

Lizard staggered to the well. He heard demons follow him but when he turned there was only the echo of his sandals on the stones. He felt like the last human in the world. He drank thirstily, then filled a bowl. As he made his way back across the square, he bumped into a woman who dropped her jug and ran away. He put his hands up to his face to feel the pitted scars which covered him. No doubt, with time, they would disappear. He returned with his bowl of water. He hesitated outside his dormitory, climbing instead up the stairs, pushing aside the curtain to the priests' quarters.

Several bodies lay there on the floor. He recognised a teacher, the doctor and the principal, all covered in weeping blisters. He stared, then ran back into the square where he collapsed on the steps. His eyes closed. His head fell back. He felt a sudden pain. Someone shook him. He sat up.

'That was a vulture poking at your eyelids,' said a rough-looking man.

A fat bird with a bloody beak stood watching them, dancing on its feet. The man chased it away. As he sat down beside Lizard, another vulture approached.

'Do you have any food?' the man asked.

Lizard saw how his face was red and scarred.

'Only water,' said Lizard. 'I am glad to see you. I felt like the only man alive. It was a horrible feeling.' He stared at the vultures squabbling over the freshest corpses. A woman twitched. She was still alive.

'What month is it?' he asked.

'It is the month when the gods arrive,' replied the man. 'This is the month for feasting yet the maize rots on its stalk. There is no one to pick it. The Goddess of the Harvest is not only the giver of food but is also the curer of skin diseases. Now she withholds her cure and her food. I ask myself whether it is better to die of this disease than of hunger.' He swallowed. 'Everyone has died. The Emperor and his son are dead. The disease even reaches Tlaxcala where they too die. It is said that even the Mayans suffer from it. The gods do not only punish the Mexica.'

The man scratched his face. 'I do not know why the gods spare me. All my family have gone.'

Lizard rubbed his scars.

'Those scars are the sign of a survivor,' said the man. 'They will not fade. The disease leaves its mark and not only on the skin. It also damages the sight.'

'I am a scribe. My sight is my life.'

The man shrugged. Lizard wobbled as he stood up. He covered his eyes with his hands. He felt as if he had lost his soul. As soon as he felt stronger, he would make a pilgrimage to the shrine on Zincantecatl – the Naked Man Mountain. He would carry a hot brazier on his head and ask for the gods' mercy. He wondered who would succeed as emperor now.

Tenochtitlan

December 1520

It was terrible after the sickness. There were dead bodies everywhere and more vultures than humans. Over half the city had died. Widows and orphans wandered the rubble-filled streets begging for food or a place to live. Many had lost their homes. The city officials pulled down all the houses of the dead on top of their corpses but sometimes a ghost would crawl out of the rubble and terrify the passers-by. No street escaped the purge of its buildings or the mass pyres of its dead. Layers of smoke and ashes covered the city as if the Smoking Mountain had blown all his breath over them. And there were the blind, feeling their way across the city. Few priests or healers could help them now. Up on the shrines, the sacrificial stones were empty, the flowers dead, the braziers unlit. In the fields the maize went to seed. Now and then a lonely conch would confuse everyone by sounding the hour. And people would call to each other 'what time of day is it?' And some even forgot the day.

Even the council were reduced. Ten turned up to elect a new emperor. Nine of them voted for Falling Eagle. The tenth, Montezuma's son, voted for himself.

Falling Eagle regretted he lacked the eloquence of his father-in-law, but he made his speech earnestly, promising to carry the weight and burden of his people. He vowed to be mild in his use of power, showing neither teeth nor claws. He would keep watch on the morning star and serve the gods. But the gods were a problem. How could he feed them without war and how could he fight without warriors? There was only one way. He must rid his land of the Spanish and feed their hearts to the gods. Otumba was a lesson. It had taught him that a great army could be defeated by tactics and cunning.

The messenger came running along the causeway, carrying the new Emperor's banner. Everyone gathered in the courtyard, with clean clothes and combed hair. The litter bearers' sandals clattered on the stones as they searched for a suitable place to deposit the Emperor.

As Falling Eagle stepped from the litter, Jewel saw how thin he was. He seemed older too, weighed down by his duties. He was only twenty-four. He has changed, thought Jewel, and I have not; he has grown up. She noticed the bruises on his arms. This was a holy Falling Eagle. She imagined him, stripped of his finery and emblems of rank, naked in front of the god. Should she look him in the eye? She was his wife, yet there were rules. She kept her eyes on the ground.

'Jewel.' He stood in front of her. His sandals were gold. Little tufts of ocelot fur peeked between his toes. Did they tickle? she wondered. Her feet were brown, burnt by the sun. Her fingernails were dirty. He took her hands gently.

'So now my wife works on the land.'

She pulled her hands from him. Here in the palace on the Salt-Coloured Water, where the gates were kept firmly closed, the family had picked their fruit and drank their own spring water. And some of them had tended the soil. He seemed amused.

'Gardening is nothing to be ashamed of.'

The aunts clustered round; some of them were still holding their embroidery. Did they never stop sewing? And why couldn't she be alone with Falling Eagle? But there was the dinner to be endured and the speeches which would go on for hours. All she wanted was her husband. She wanted to see him as naked as the gods had done. He read her mind. He bent down and whispered.

'Be patient, Jewel.'

Now the aunts were clamouring for attention. The oldest were the worst. Congratulating him, touching him for his holiness. Only her mother stood apart.

Jewel sighed as she followed them into dinner. There was still food here and servants to serve them. There were even some dancers and musicians. Everything seemed quite normal. But it wasn't. She was married to an emperor. Now she would have to share him again with other women.

Her reward came later in their beautiful room overlooking the lake. Here, where the palace was built on stilts, she loved to lie listening to the water lapping below. Tonight she was in no mood to listen to the water. She pulled his face down to hers. This was a man who spoke with gods. Would he kiss her differently now?

Afterwards they talked as they always did. He warned her of the desolation in the city. She wondered what had happened to her school friends. How many of them had died?

'Do the Spanish suffer too?' she asked.

He told her that the Spanish did not suffer although the Tlax-calans did.'

'Why do our gods hate us?'

He could not answer. He ran a strand of her hair through his fingers. It had lost its shine. He promised that, when life returned to normal, her indigo hair rinse would be one of the first luxuries into the city.

'Will life return to normal?' she asked.

He thought so, although it might take a long time. Nothing would be quite the same. The Mexica had been humiliated and it would take many years to change that. He did not tell her that his visit to Tlaxcala had been unsuccessful or that he had had to flee to avoid capture. Nor did he mention how the Spanish had destroyed several Mexica garrisons and cut the supply lines to the coast. He told her how many people in the city were blind or scarred.

'I am glad you were spared,' he told her. 'I could not have borne your scars.'

'Nor I yours.' She laughed. 'Beauty is not supposed to matter.'

'You have never seen such scars. They cover their whole faces and their noses and are even in their eyes. It is hard to care for them.'

She begged him to leave the pine torches burning. She did not tell him how she feared the dark now. He pulled her down onto the mat and covered her with his body.

Later as the sky glowed with the dawn he said. 'There is something else.'

She was in no mood to listen.

'I want you to move back into the city.'

Now she sat up.

'Why? We are safe here.'

He touched her face gently. He looked around at the elegant room with its carved beams and its view. It saddened him that he would have to destroy it.

'You are vulnerable out here on the water. Now I am Emperor, the city offers some protection, and the sickness has gone.'

'I do not want to leave.'

'I can no longer spare men to guard you here. The sickness has taken many men. You are to shut up this place and leave. There are rumours that Don Hernán may come here. Prince Vanilla Flower has taken his army and joined Don Hernán. They are on their way to Texcoco. Don't worry! We watch his every step but I cannot leave you here.'

'Vanilla Flower is a traitor.'

'He is not the only one. The merchants have also sided with Don Hernán.'

'The merchants!'

'Many of them are not Mexica. They have sent a delegation to Don Hernán to offer their support.'

'We should sacrifice them all.'

He laughed. He always did when she pretended to be fierce. 'I plan to destroy this place.'

'No!'

'If the Spanish come here, I have no choice. I plan to open the dike and flood the palace while they sleep.'

'No. Please no!'

He put his arms around her.

'In war much is destroyed. We can rebuild later when we repair the dike. You can design the new house yourself.'

The sun had turned the lake as red as the earth of Otumba. He rose and stood on the jetty where the ducks gathered for feeding. He looked back into the room where she still lay, her body curled up like a child's.

'You will take your mother and your aunts back to the city with you.'

'None of us want to leave.'

'None of you want to fall into Spanish hands.'

She shivered. She put her shawl around her shoulders and joined him on the jetty.

'Once I was unhappy here. Now I love the place. My father planted much of this garden. He chose the carvings for the cedar beams.'

'I know,' Falling Eagle replied gently. 'Nothing stays the same.'

'No.'

They gathered again in the courtyard with their servants, musicians, dancers and cooks. And after Falling Eagle had gone, they all assembled on the jetty, with their clothes and their jewels and their baskets of food. Some of them wept. The oldest had to be lifted into the canoes. The ducks followed them, fighting for the food that Jewel threw. She held back her tears and watched the palace recede into the mist.

The city was a shock. Rubbish littered the Sacred Square and a raw smell of sewage clung to the air. There were beggars everywhere. She was ashamed to feel such disgust at their scars. It seemed as if everyone had died. The streets were quiet. The market was empty. No sound of music escaped from the boys' schools.

When they reached home on the eastern side of the square they found it intact, though most of the servants had gone. But two maids still remained in the women's rooms. Miraculously they had been spared the sickness. They sobbed to see Jewel. They told her there were shortages of food in the city.

'The canoes passed floating gardens that were ripe with corn. Why does no one pick it?'

The maid wept as she told how few men were left to tend the maize, and how few women to cook it.

'Then we will pick it and cook it ourselves,' she told them firmly. She did not feel so optimistic. How would they live without food and servants? But she brushed her mother's pleas aside and ran back down to the canoes moored beneath the palace. She ordered the terrified boatmen to row her out to the fringe of islands beyond the fishing nets. As she set off she looked across to the other side of the lake where Texcoco's glazed bitumen walls glistened in the sun. It was the most beautiful city on the lake, finer even, than Tenochtitlan. Its gardens sheltered all the plants in the world. It boasted lavish palaces and libraries. It housed the archives and books, maps and codices of the Mexica. She had nearly married one of its princes. When she was ten, she had accompanied her father on a visit there. Its old ruler had examined her with his calculating eyes and offered one of his sons as a husband. Her father had refused. And now that son, Vanilla Flower, had sided with the enemies of the Mexica. The boatmen stopped paddling.

'Lady! There are canoes approaching from Texcoco.'

A flotilla approached in the distance.

Jewel ordered the boat to turn for home.

Tenochtitian

January – March 1521

A schoolboy first noticed that the canoes flew the flag of Texcoco. These were Texcocoans fleeing the Spanish. They threw themselves into the water and embraced the Mexica. They spoke of rape, looting and massacre, and wept as they described the destruction of their libraries and palaces. Even the sacred gardens had been destroyed. Don Hernán was building boats, using wood from the nearby forests. The Tlaxcalans carried them in pieces from the Smoking Mountain down to the lake where carpenters had begun to assemble them. They feared that Tenochtitlan would be next.

The Mexica were jubilant. They welcomed the extra warriors and canoes. So far the Spanish had limited their fighting to the small market towns in the valley. Texcoco was right there on the other side of the lake. It was one of the cities in the Triple Alliance. It was part of the family and yet Don Hernán had managed to divide it.

Lizard helped beach the canoes. Then he made his way over the square with five Texcocoans, three of them cousins, to his brother's house. He loathed his brother, the new Woman Snake, but did his best to conceal it. When they reached a junction of two paths, a roughly dressed man bumped into him. Lizard looked up angrily but when he saw the merchant, Wandering Coyote, he greeted him like a long-lost friend, throwing his arms exuberantly around the old man until he noticed Wandering Coyote flinch. Lizard had become used to people, even priests, who were not supposed to mind such things, turning away as he approached, and yet it still surprised him, for there were many scarred faces wandering around the city. Wandering Coyote's face showed no signs of sickness.

'Well, if it isn't the storyteller himself!' exclaimed Wandering Coyote after he had recovered from the shock. There is some comfort to know that our stories will still be told, even if they are sad ones. Come home with me, boy, and I will tell you everything. You see, I am lonely. I was fond of your father. At least he has gone honourably in battle.'

'I suppose so,' said Lizard, seeing again in his mind his father's battered body with its canine teeth marks. Was it an honourable death to be mauled by dogs?

'I am expected at my brother's.'

Wandering Coyote looked the Texcocoans over.

'Come after dinner. He will not miss you, but I will.'

He swept up the side of the canal and was gone.

In his father's palace, the new Woman Snake held sway. He strutted in his black and white official cloak as he proudly showed the cousins such a spread of food that it was easy to forget the Spanish existed. One of the cousins whispered to Lizard.

'We hear your brother has a fondness for the Spanish.'

'He plays games,' replied Lizard, in a hurry to leave and not wanting to be drawn into a discussion. How brightly the Spanish candles shone here. How rich their light. What had his brother done to earn these? He looked around at the puffed-up lords who had sold themselves to the Spanish, all here to enjoy the luxury.

In Tlatelolco, Wandering Coyote welcomed him more warmly than his brother. He had been drinking pulque and was in a mellow mood. He spoke wistfully of the old Woman Snake.

'I used to spy for your father, you know. I am sorry he has gone. I did not respect many of the nobles. He was an exception.'

Rich tapestries covered the walls of this house. Precious pottery filled every alcove and Spanish candles burned in abundance. Lizard remembered Woman Snake describing the sumptuousness of the merchants' homes.

'Nothing has been looted here.'

'I should hope not. People look at my modest home and think there is nothing inside. We merchants do not display our wealth like you nobles. Sit down.'

A girl carried in two bowls of juice.

'This is Marsh Lily. She gave your father much pleasure.'

'So you are still travelling,' said Lizard, trying to take his eyes off Marsh Lily. 'You must see what is going on.'

'I know everything.'

Wandering Coyote knew before anyone else how Falling Eagle planned to requisition all the canoes in city. He had already been out there paddling in his own decrepit craft together with the fishermen and the market traders, the bird catchers, the farmers and the shit collectors. He enjoyed being on the water again, although he would rather not meet a Spanish boat.

'The Spanish and the Tlaxcalans do not fight honourably. They massacre women and children . . .'

'They are elusive fighters,' interrupted Lizard. On a wild-goose chase in maize fields near Chalco, Lizard and the warriors had failed to engage with the enemy and had lost their way. He had staggered home, lucky to avoid capture, his skin scratched and bitten by insects, never wanting to see a cornfield again. Now he found himself training to use a war canoe, which was more to his taste.

Wandering Coyote was not interested in minor skirmishes in cornfields.

'Now they threaten to explore our lake,' he continued, 'and they set fire to any town that is against them. They will turn every town in the valley against us. If anyone can stop them, it will be Falling Eagle. At last we have a proper leader. But there is something else. I have heard rumours that some of Don Hernán's own men planned to kill him. Unfortunately they were discovered, but where they plot, others follow. So you see, even without the Mexica, Don Hernán has his problems.'

He spoke too of the huge tree trunks being carried down from the forests of Tlaxcala and turned into boats, and how a wide canal had been dug to float them to the lake. He feared that the Spanish would attack Tenochtitlan from the water.

'That cannot be true,' said Lizard. 'You did not see that yourself.'

'Merchants are never wrong. If they tell me such stories, I believe them.' He spoke too of the magic things brought by the Spanish. He described an instrument that showed the four directions without the sun or stars and a box that ticked like a rattlesnake and counted time and candles that were made of beeswax and burned so silently you did not notice them.

Wandering Coyote said he was trading these things for gold. They were proving very popular. War brought opportunity. There was much wealth in trade. He looked earnestly at Lizard. 'I could do with an assistant. If you felt you wanted to join me, I would welcome it. I realise a prince like you would never have considered trade before. But as times change, so do men.'

Wandering Coyote did not mention how many merchants in the conquered cities welcomed Don Hernán who offered them free trade throughout the Empire. The Mexica had operated a monopoly over the trade routes, regardless of the merchants' simmering discontent.

'I will think about it,' Lizard replied politely, although he had no wish to become a merchant any more than he wanted to be a priest.

'Trade is safe, boy. Better a live coward than a dead hero. At least you have escaped the priests, although I hear that the High Priest of Huitzilopochtli is on the lookout for likely novices. He is a tyrant, boy. I would not serve him. You will come again? If you need any paper or brushes, let me know. You see I do not forget a promise.'

Lizard felt the urge to paint again. He had a small supply of paper in his room, but it would soon run out. And he would like to see that girl again. He thought of her all night as he tossed and turned on his mat, his hands straying down to that part of his body which grew with his thoughts. He saw the girl's face as she served his juice. He was only a student. He could not ask for her with the paper and brushes. He retreated to his brother's home and waited for the year to end, huddling with his family around their cold hearth. Nothing would happen for five days, unless the world imploded before then.

As soon as the dangerous days had passed, the High Priest of Huitzilopochtli recruited novices to replace those who had died of the sickness. He lectured the boys on their duty, his head rotating like a jaguar assessing its prey.

Lizard protested that he was scarred. The High Priest fingered his conch shell. He reminded the boys that the gods did not require beauty in their servants. The gods had saved them all for a purpose. His hands delved into his capacious pockets and produced boxes of piercing thorns. He called out names. One by one crestfallen boys rose and took their thorns. They collected their mats and moved to the novices' house in the lee of the temple. Lizard missed the luxury of his brother's house. This was even more uncomfortable than school. Open windows without blinds let in every wind that blew over the city and sometimes the rain, too, forced its way in and flooded the worn sleeping mats spread over the floor. The rooms smelt of blood, for everyone pierced their ear lobes, their lips and tongues, their thighs, their fingers, and sometimes their *tepuli*s. Lizard dreamt of escape.

It came sooner than expected, when the call came to fight in Oaxtepec whose leaders surrendered to Don Hernán without a fight. Lizard took his padded cotton armour, his sleeping mat, his sling, his bag of stones and his bow and arrow and marched with the regiments. Many warriors died in Oaxtepec. The Spanish moved to seize the cotton town of Cuauhnahuac. Heavily fortified and built over ravines, Cuauhnahuac was considered impregnable, but the Spanish placed tree trunks over the ravines and a traitor led them into the city through a secret passage. Lizard fled with the warriors and moved back into the grim House of the Novices.

Tenochtitlan

April 1521

If only we could get rid of the Spanish, thought Jewel, perhaps things might return to normal. Falling Eagle had told her that the Spanish did not rush unthinkingly into battle. He thought they were waiting like hungry coyotes, building up their army of allies before they pounced. When she had asked nervously where they might land first, he told her they would probably attack from the lake. She had laughed. Such a ridiculous suggestion! All those canoes waiting out there. Nothing was as fast as a fighting canoe. But what had frightened her most was that Falling Eagle had not agreed with her, or joked as he usually did. He had stared across the lake as if to measure its distances and assess its hiding places. When she had pointed to the giant stakes he had erected to protect the city, he still said nothing.

She saw little of Falling Eagle now and when he called he never stayed long. He told her that the Spanish were winning new allies daily. Don Hernán pardoned those who had sided with the Mexica and released them from paying their taxes, and now he was slowly isolating Tenochtitlan from its sources of supply. When he saw the horror on her face, he reassured her that they could still count on the loyalty of Tacuba and the refugees from Texcoco had included ten thousand warriors with their canoes. Most of the lakeside towns were still loyal.

'Will we beat them?' She hardly dared whisper the words.

'Of course,' he had replied, 'but it might take a long time.'

And then she had giggled like a silly schoolgirl when he told her how Don Hernán had offered to pardon him, Falling Eagle, for defending his own city. And this was not the first time. He told her that he never knew what the Spanish would do next. They had no rules. They fought at night. They fought during the harvest and even during their holy festivals.

'Perhaps they are gods after all,' she had said.

He told her that Don Hernán was nothing more than an opportunist who adopted people's histories to steal their souls. He asked what she thought of his plan to ask the people whether they wanted peace or war. His father had always listened to the people and had never made a wrong decision. She said that she would vote for war.

The people poured into the square, young and old, crippled, scarred, women and children, warriors, beggars, prostitutes, priests and slaves. So many had scarred faces and broken bodies. An old woman cried out from the school arches. 'Tlatoani – Emperor, use your voice to save us!'

Falling Eagle held up his hands to the sun. He had scrubbed away the blood from this morning's sacrifice, but his knuckles were stained where the blood collected in the folds of flesh. He remembered the ancestors who had also spoken here, and how the first Montezuma had wept as he told his people he could not save them from famine. They must sell themselves as slaves. Whole families had left and even the nobles had sold their children for few maize cakes. It must not happen again, he thought. His voice shook as he asked his people whether they wanted peace or war.

'Will we be slaves?' shouted an old man.

'They will destroy our gods,' insisted a priest.

'The Spanish offer peace,' he told them.

'They will steal our women!' shouted a merchant.

'We can negotiate terms.'

'The Spanish cannot be trusted,' called a local clan leader.

'If we do not accept, we will have to fight.'

'Fight!' repeated the crowd.

The roar that came from the crowd sounded as if all the coyotes in the valley howled together. It echoed over the square and the canals and into the streets, so loudly it might even reach Don Hernán in Texcoco. Falling Eagle felt pride in his people and honoured that the gods had chosen him to lead them.

'I will need all your canoes, and all your men, young and old. We will have to fight as never before. We will fight on the water. We will fight at night. We will fight during the festivals.'

The crowd dispersed laughing and joking but when they reached the south gate they were stopped by a ghost in the middle of the causeway. Don Hernán sat calmly on his horse, as if he had heard the cheers and galloped all the way from Texcoco. A nervous page walked beside him.

'Don Hernán wishes to speak to the Lord Falling Eagle,' called the page.

The Mexica stared in horror, astonished by the boldness of their enemy. They clutched their bows and slings. A large Otomi warrior with a head full of plumes shouted, 'Make yourself at home! Come in and take your pleasure!'

Lizard pushed his way to the front of the crowd. He recognised Juan, Don Hernán's page. This was the boy who had befriended him. Now he wanted to kill him.

'Do you think there is another Montezuma here to let you do what you please?' he shouted.

The people around him stared admiringly. An old man patted him approvingly on the shoulder. Don Hernán held up his hand for silence. The taunts abated.

'Are you mad? Is there no lord to whom I can speak? Do you wish to be destroyed?'

An old crone cackled. 'We are all lords here, so you can say what you want!'

'You will die of hunger,' cautioned Don Hernán.

'We will eat you,' bellowed an old man.

A pregnant woman threw a tamale at Don Hernán.

'Eat this if you are hungry. We have no need of it.'

The crowd cheered. Lizard picked up a stone and threw it at Juan. The horse panicked. Don Hernán turned and galloped towards the mainland leaving Juan to run behind. Lizard grabbed the hands of the boy next to him and began dancing. Someone played a flute and the drums began.

'They will not return now,' declared Lizard.

Wandering Coyote had his own opinions, although he too had shouted for war.

'When I was a young warrior . . .' He saw the look on Lizard's face. 'I was a warrior once. I can prove it. Look.' He picked up a small reed basket and opened the lid. 'This was my first sacrifice.' He displayed a piece of scalp with hair. 'He was a bold warrior. I had a real struggle to capture him. I fattened him for the gods. He became like a son to me. I was sad when I walked him to the temple. I keep a piece of him always with me.' He put the scalp back into its basket. 'Falling Eagle is bold but Don Hernán collects friends like a gambler collects patolli counters. The Spanish are sacking all the towns into submission. Mark my words, they will make for us next. We must be prepared.'

He picked up a pipe and offered it to Lizard.

Lizard refused. He did not like the taste.

'Falling Eagle is brave.'

'I do not doubt his bravery. But has he enough warriors to fight? Many have died of the sickness.'

'We have the Texcocoans on our side.'

'Only some. Many have sided with the Spanish.'

'Why do the gods abandon us?' asked Lizard plaintively.

Wandering Coyote blew out his smoke in little puffs.

'They are powerless. Even the priests agree, although they dare not say it.'

Lizard thought of all the time spent purging, the mortification, the flagellation, the long nights of prayer and the terrified faces of those about to die.

'Why do we bother then?'

'Now you talk like a Spaniard, boy. You know what is said about the Mexica?'

'No.'

'They have so many gods that they forget how many they worship. In my opinion, the Mexica honour their gods excessively.'

'How can you have an opinion? You are not Mexica.'

'I have lived here many years. My opinion counts and I will give it to you whether you want it or not. In my opinion . . .' he let his words hang on the air to give them importance, '. . . the Lord Montezuma filled his mind with false omens, so he could no longer make decisions without consulting those useless magicians.'

'You should not speak of holy men with such disrespect.'

'You are a novice. Of course you cannot agree. But these are the words of your father. The Lord Woman Snake thought as I do, that it was time for change. He did not surround himself with magicians like the Lord Montezuma.'

'The Lord Montezuma did his duty. Anyway, how would we feed the gods if we did not sacrifice?'

'The Spanish do not feed their god. At the battle of Otumba, not only were they sick and wounded and outnumbered, they defeated thousands of Mexica. Did their god not help them then?'

'At Otumba the Spanish outwitted us.'

'Everyone says different things about Otumba. But the truth is that Smoking Mirror played tricks on us. Listen, boy! Would you like to live here with me? No, that is silly. You have your brother.' He looked wistfully at his empty dining hall where wicker stools were piled high against the walls. 'We have no banquets now.'

Marsh Lily appeared. Wandering Coyote watched the boy. He saw the desire and the fear. When the time was right, he would give the girl to Lizard. He wondered whether she would mind the youth's terrible scars.

'There is something else you should know. Your brother, the new Woman Snake, much favours the Spanish. I would not trust him.'

'How do you know?'

'I know everything,' confided Wandering Coyote. 'I can name all the enemies of the Mexica and I am sad to say that many of them are to be found in your family.'

He saw suddenly, through the open blinds, a spiral of smoke rising from the mainland.

'Something is burning!'

Lizard ran all the way back over the canal bridge and into the main city.

'Fire!' screamed Ant Flower. She jumped from foot to foot. 'It is the Spanish, Lady. They burn the towns on the mainland!'

Jewel sat up suddenly. She had terrible dreams. Sometimes she could not tell whether it was Falling Eagle or her father who suffered the tortures that interrupted her sleep. She pulled her shawl around her and rushed up to the roof. A few fishermen were out on the lake, tossing their nets into the water. So many fishermen had died, it was difficult to get fish now. Ant Flower pulled her to the other side of the roof.

'Not there, Lady! It is Tacuba that burns.'

My lands, thought Jewel. The lands my father gave me. Ant Flower climbed onto a stool. Jewel felt helpless. She wanted to go and fight to help the loyal citizens of Tacuba. How much could change in a single day. Yesterday people in Tacuba went about their business as normal. Yesterday Falling Eagle had stayed all night. They had burnt many pine torches, not wanting to waste a single moment. He too had smelt of pine and cedar. How sweet love was with him. Her first act of love had not been sweet at all. Before her first marriage when she had been fresh as a turquoise, her father had told her that the gods sent gifts of laughter, sleep, food, vigour and love to sweeten life. Love, he said, not only filled the world with people, it consoled them. Now she knew what he meant. She was too happy to sleep. Then, just before Falling Eagle left, when she felt happy and secure, he threatened to send her to the Mayan lands where he had friends. Of course they had argued, even though he warned she might become Don Hernán's whore.

214

And now, Don Hernán was there just over the water, in her city of Tacuba.

Where was Falling Eagle now? He was supposed to be in Pantitlan throwing all that was left of her father's gold into the springs to appease the goddess. But there was no sign of the golden barque with its green feathers. She watched with Ant Flower while the flames and smoke engulfed Tacuba and people escaped up the causeway to Tenochtitlan. Men ran through the streets below clutching spears and bows. She noticed that heavy stones covered the roofs of the houses and some of the narrow streets had been blocked off. A guard leapt up the stairs panting.

'The Spanish are moving from Tacuba to Xochimilco! They use their cannon, muskets and bows. They use their horses and dogs. The Xochimilcans are putting up a fight. Falling Eagle is on his way to relieve them.'

Jewel gripped the parapet. If the Spanish occupied Texcoco to the east, Tacuba to the west, and Xochimilco in the south, they would surround Tenochtitlan. Was this their plan? Yet here, apart from the odd fisherman, the lake was empty. Even the birds had flown. Did they know something that she did not?

Tenochtitlan

April – May 1521

On the sixth day of the new month of Toxcatl – Dryness, boats with sails were spotted approaching from Texcoco. The crowds in the streets who were waiting to greet the boy-god rushed in panic to the shore. From here the boats seemed to move effortlessly on the shallow lake, as if blown by Quetzalcoatl's breath. But the Tlatelolcans, in the north of the city, were ready and waiting. They had practised for this. They paddled out from the reeds like shoals of fighting fish, zigzagging through the water, taunting and tantalising the enemy, sending them scuttling back to Texcoco. But even as the crowds cheered their victory, and the boy-god played and danced for his admirers, and the hungry god waited on top of the temple, everyone knew that it was only a matter of time before the Spanish tried again.

Falling Eagle summoned his councillors, nine now, since one had died of complications following the sickness. Many men had been lost in the struggle in Xochimilco. The Spanish had sacked Tacuba. His latest diplomatic offensive had failed to persuade the other valley people to join the Mexica. Nor could the priests offer any hope. The High Priest suggested that the arrival of the Spanish had sapped the gods' strength. He could not predict when it might return. Nor could the Keepers of the Books find comfort in the holy words. The new Woman Snake spoke first in the council meeting.

'I have heard that Don Hernán offers peace. Where is our reply?'

'How can we believe Don Hernán?' interrupted the exiled King of Tacuba.

'The people want war,' insisted Falling Eagle. 'They want revenge for Tacuba and Xochimilco.'

He felt nervous. He watched the new Woman Snake play with one of the balls of twisted grass hanging around his waist. He pulled out a cactus spine and pricked his finger. He pretended to be a holy man, although it was rumoured he now served the Spanish god.

'Since when does the ruler of the Mexica consult his people?'

'My father consulted them,' said Falling Eagle, irked by this brazen display of false holiness. 'And he was a strong ruler whom the people still remember fondly. We shall need the support of all our people.'

'Since when do cripples and whores make decisions?' shouted the new Woman Snake.

Falling Eagle ignored his jibes and the tittering of the councillors who supported the Woman Snake.

'Since Tacuba I have removed all the bridges in the causeways. Men with horses and cannon will not be able to cross. Only the Tepeyac causeway remains open and that is carefully guarded.'

'We were unable to defend the towns on our doorstep,' said one of Montezuma's sons, who harboured ambitions.

'We have resisted the first marine advance.'

'By opening the dike you have made the lake level. It is easier for the boats to invade now,' shouted the new Woman Snake.

'There are rows of stakes protecting the city, or have you not noticed?' shouted Falling Eagle.

'By opening the dike you have polluted our water with salt,' said an Eagle Knight.

'We have also destroyed their gunpowder.'

Falling Eagle regretted that none of the Spanish had been killed in the palace on the Salt-Coloured Water. Nor had they retreated; they had stayed and fought in the floodwater. Their actions were never what you might expect.

'I have heard that the Spanish send men to climb down into the Smoking Mountain,' a young lord said hesitantly. He was newly elected, replacing his father who had died of the blistering sickness. 'They use the yellow powder for their cannon. There is much of it in the Smoking Mountain.'

The lords began to mutter. The new Woman Snake looked pleased with himself.

'If we wait too long our allies will abandon us!' shouted another of Montezuma's sons. 'I demand negotiation.'

Falling Eagle stared at Montezuma's sons huddled together at the back of the chamber. How dare they argue with him. He raised his voice. He wished he felt more confident.

'There is a season to fight as there is a season to talk. Now it is time to fight. There will be no negotiation. I am convinced that the Spanish will make further assaults by boats. We are ready for them. Remember how our ancestors, although few in number, conquered this land. Do not lose faith in me because of my youth. Remember the bold hearts!'

'Our former allies are now our enemies!'

No one heard the new Woman Snake. They rose to their feet shouting. 'Remember the bold hearts!' They looked forward to the dancing and singing and the white truffle cactus that would prepare them for battle.

On his way home Falling Eagle made his plans. He knew that although he had won this argument, there would be others. He decided to divide his army into four divisions. One would guard the Tepeyac causeway to the north. Another would protect the Tacuba causeway. The remaining two divisions he would keep in the city. He had left his litter outside the council chamber. It was his habit to walk among the people now. He saw that the square was almost back to normal, apart from some stained stones and broken torch holders. Blood-red pots of flowers lined the temple steps ready for the sacrifice of Toxcatl. Last year this square had flowed with blood as if it had rained blood for days. Among the bodies lying there on the temple steps, and here where he put his feet, were those of his friends. People begin to gather, to prostrate themselves and some of them threw flowers. He smiled gently. He wanted to look at their faces and not at the backs of their heads. When all this was over he would try to be more like his father, who had made his city great by choosing advisers from among the people. And, as he smiled in greeting, he knew his guards were, at this moment, arresting two of Montezuma's sons. He could not allow anyone to challenge his authority. He went out to join his people in the streets celebrating the feast of Dryness. The boy played his flute divinely. It almost seemed like the old days before the Spanish, before the sickness. And if the Sacred Square was not as full as it might have been, those who were there tried to make up for it by singing extra loudly. This year the only death was the boy's, and his the only blood, holy blood, smeared over the god's swollen lips.

The Spanish returned during preparations for the feast of the Eating of Beans and Maize. Although the fishermen had reported an increase in activity in Texcoco, it was still a shock when the sails were spotted a second time. And that was not all. What looked like shadows cast by the clouds turned out to be thousands of Tlaxcalan canoes.

The drums sounded the warning from all the temples in the city. The Mexica hid in the reeds. Although this was the moment they had trained for, the sight of so many canoes made them nervous.

When the horn sounded the advance, they slalomed the wicker fences that protected the fishing beds. After the fences came rows of stakes like giants' teeth, stretching out into the deeper water where the Spanish and their allies waited. A biting wind gusted and howled. It blew into their eyes and blinded them. It snapped the reeds. It bent the stakes and tossed and whirled the canoes. Wandering Coyote was uneasy. He had practised for this but always in clement weather. Lizard, too, was apprehensive. He had capsized during the last offensive. His hair had been caught in the reeds. He would have drowned had not Wandering Coyote come promptly to his rescue.

He kept close to Wandering Coyote. He felt weak from fasting in preparation for the feast.

'Come, boy,' said Wandering Coyote, visibly paler than when he set out this morning. 'What are a few miserable Tlaxcalans? They never were good canoeists.'

They moved out, filling the lake between the city and the island of Tepepolco which the Spanish occupied. They poured from the city canals through the gaps in the causeways where the bridges had been lifted. But when they reached the fishing beds, the wind spun them round. Lizard and Wandering Coyote struggled to negotiate the stakes but when they made it to the middle of the lake, they hit the full force of the storm. It gusted from the east, filling the Spanish sails and blowing the boats effortlessly towards the Mexica, opening the way for the flotilla of allied canoes that followed. Faint sounds of drums and flutes wafted on the wind. Don Hernán brought an orchestra with him.

Wandering Coyote and Lizard managed to paddle towards the Spanish, until a boat separated them. The speed of the boat took them both by surprise. It churned the water in front of it and formed currents behind it and carried soldiers who fired from its decks.

Now Lizard was fighting both the wind and the Spanish. He saw Wandering Coyote's overturned canoe spinning in the current. The open mouth of a cannon bore down on him. He did not wait for the explosion but threw himself into the water, sinking beneath the surface and swimming back towards the reeds.

When he came up for air he found himself surrounded by enemies. A body crashed into the water next to him, its eyes still open. Its face bore the scars of sickness. Lizard used the corpse as a shield, trying to evade the arrows that fell around him. He dared not abandon his dead friend, for the Tlaxcalans scoured the water searching for any Mexica still alive.

A canoe flying the white-heron banner of Tlaxcala paddled furiously towards him. It circled, then stopped and poked at the body, trying to remove its feathers. When the Tlaxcalan saw Lizard he lifted his spear, but the wind toppled him from his canoe and they fell together down into the blackness of the water. Hands gripped Lizard's neck, cracking his bones, forcing his eyes from their sockets. Suddenly the Tlaxcalan let go. His body floated to the surface, an arrow in his back.

Lizard picked out a canoe that had become separated from the others, its occupant slumped motionless in his seat. The white-heron banner flew on its stern. Lizard pulled himself into the canoe. He propped up its dead owner, put the heron feathers on his own head, and paddled through the enemy and back to the city, avoiding the capsized and holed Mexica canoes. Now the stakes were crushed and broken, it was easier to find a way through. The wind, behind him now, blew him back into the familiar reeds. When he looked back over the water he saw the Spanish boats making their way towards the south of city. He dragged his canoe to the shore and ran towards the Eagle Gate.

Wandering Coyote had an equally lucky escape, although his best canoe was destroyed. He, too, ran to the Eagle Gate where the fight against the Spanish lasted all night. The Spanish had hoisted their flag on the city gates. They had landed a cannon and blown a hole in the city wall, from where they destroyed several houses, using the rubble to fill in the gaps in the causeway where the Mexica had removed the bridges.

'It was a terrible defeat,' said Wandering Coyote. He could not see what the Mexica could do now. He coughed. The water still irritated his lungs. 'Now the Spanish see that they can defeat us in our own city, they will get bolder. Things can only get worse. Still I have pulque and mushrooms here to fill your mind with pleasant dreams. The city runs out of such things. I have heard that the warriors no longer sing or dance before battle. Nor do they consume mushrooms.'

'There is no time for such luxuries,' said Lizard primly. 'The Spanish never rest. I saw them last night, fighting like madmen.'

'Perhaps they have their own mushrooms?'

Wandering Coyote opened a basket and took out a handful of

the peyote cactus buds known as 'flesh of the gods'. He felt in need of escape. He would have bet hundreds of patolli counters that the Mexica would win this battle. Their canoes were fast and nimble but the Spanish boats, with their flat bottoms, proved more stable in the wind. He thought it a terrible omen that Quetzalcoatl had sent his breath to destroy his own people. He saw how dejected Lizard looked.

'You must not believe everything I say, boy. Despite my face, I am not of a cheerful disposition. I have seen too much in my lifetime. I do not love the Mexica. But I would be sad to see you defeated. After all, I have spent all my life among you. You have made me rich. Well, boy, if you will not join me in "flesh of the gods", you must join me in food.'

Marsh Lily appeared with bowls and a jug of precious chocolate which she laid on a low table. Lizard watched her hungrily.

'I have not eaten for some time. Perhaps the mushrooms will give me the courage to fight.'

They heard the sound of feet running past the courtyard wall. Wandering Coyote went out to investigate. When he opened the gate he saw people rushing past with torches. He grabbed one by the arm.

'Falling Eagle asks for volunteers to remove the Spanish rubble from the lake,' gasped the man.

'Where are the Spanish now?'

'They have retreated to the mainland for the night. Falling Eagle says they will return tomorrow. We must remove the rubble so they cannot.'

'Wait for me!' shouted Wandering Coyote. He ran back inside the house and grabbed Lizard and they tagged onto the long line of volunteers, many of them women, some even grandmothers.

The Spanish returned in the morning. They stood on the causeway looking down at the water where their rubble bridge had been removed during the night. Don Hernán scratched his head. Don Alvarado jumped down from his horse. They stood there for some time. Falling Eagle's spies reported that there were arguments. He said they had turned around and marched back to the mainland with their Tlaxcalan scouts following at their heels.

Three days later the Spanish attacked from the mainland. They used their boats as bridges and took control of the Tacuba and Coyoacan causeways. But even the golden-haired Don Alvarado could not take the well-defended northern causeway to Tepeyac.

'Now is the time to make peace!' shouted the new Woman Snake at the next council meeting.

'Nonsense,' said the High Priest of Huitzilopochtli. 'We are entering a lucky cycle in the stars. Next time we will win.'

'We still have the Tepeyac causeway,' said Falling Eagle firmly.

'They will soon get round to that!' shrieked the new Woman Snake.

'Is that what your new friends tell you,' screamed an Eagle Knight.

'We all want peace,' repeated the new Woman Snake. 'How much longer can we continue this pretence? The Spanish fill the holes in during the day and then we creep out like moles at night and dig them out again.'

'As long as it takes!' replied Falling Eagle.

'What does that mean?' asked a local governor. 'What if the Spanish besiege the city? After all, the removal of the bridges has not stopped them.'

'They use their boats,' reported the new Woman Snake, rather pleased with himself.

'I have two regiments on the Tepeyac causeway. Food still enters the city,' replied Falling Eagle. 'We can hold out for some time.'

'The city is filling with refugees. Can we feed them too?'

Falling Eagle ignored him. It was a question he dared not ask himself.

'The refugees are useful. We need every person now. And there is good news. We have captured many Spanish in Tepeyac for the gods.'

'You did not get Alvarado!' shouted the new Woman Snake. 'You have a motley collection of terrified men who cannot stop peeing.'

The meeting adjourned to laughter. No one noticed the new Woman Snake slip away with a cousin of Montezuma's.

'There are many forms of war,' Falling Eagle told Jewel when he called on her again. Just seeing him made her cheerful. She knew there were other women willing to comfort the young Emperor of the Mexica but he had chosen his wife. Tonight he seemed weary. She knew the council did not agree with him, although the people were on his side. She watched him eat. There was still chocolate to drink.

'The Spanish make bridges of rubble in our causeways and call it war. Now I am removing the rubble and calling that war. At least I do not need warriors for that.'

'Ant Flower says they use their boats. So why do we bother?'

'Their boats are precious. They use them as a last resort. Anything that makes it more difficult for them gives us time.'

'Time for what?'

'Time for the gods to listen. Time for the allies to return. Time to hope that the Spanish get tired of fighting and leave.'

'Is that likely?'

'Who knows? They did not expect us to fight like this. They thought we would give in like your father did. So the longer we hold out, the more chance we have of repelling them. Some of them want to go home. It is Don Hernán who will not give up.'

'My father once said that it was better to stay friends with the Spanish. He liked Don Hernán and thought he could work with him.'

'Don Hernán is not someone who will share power.'

'Do you think it is all too late?'

He thought a moment.

'I fight as if I believe in a future. What else can I do?'

'Why is Quetzalcoatl on their side?'

'There are many storms on the lake at this time of year.'

'Yes! But the wind came from the east. It came from Quetzalcoatl.'

He sipped his chocolate. The froth clung to his lips.

'I have driven the Spanish back from the causeways. They will not find it so easy to cross now. But whatever happens you are to remain here until I tell you otherwise. There are traitors everywhere, including your own half-brothers.'

'My brothers! What have you done with them?'

'I had no choice.'

'You have killed them!'

She stared in horror. Then she asked, 'Are we in danger too?'

'Not now.'

'I did not like my brothers either.'

He untied her hair, letting his fingers run through the silken threads. He did not mention the latest attempt on his life. He patted the mat beside them. 'Come. We don't have much time.'

His lips tasted gloriously of chocolate.

Tlatelolco

June 1521

Every night Wandering Coyote and Lizard joined the working parties removing the rubble bridges from the causeways. They crossed by canoe to the main city, travelling through the smaller canals where they would not be noticed. Tonight Lizard could see in the stars the shapes of the Tiger, the Scorpion and the Loaf of Bread. The canoes clug together for safety. The Spanish did not know all these waterways and had not used their boats at night, but no one knew what they might do next. And there were always Tlaxcalans milling around looking for loot and women.

Wandering Coyote and Lizard paddled into the city and hid their canoe under a bridge in a small side canal. They made their way through the streets, checking that stones were piled in readiness on the roofs and that the barricades were in place. Every night Wandering Coyote found evidence of the Spanish advance. They had not yet occupied the Sacred Square, but every day brought more destruction, houses burnt, another street occupied, more bodies among the ruins. Last week he had rescued a child and brought it to Tlatelolco. He had not known what to do with it and had given it to a distraught woman whose own child had been killed.

Tonight there was no sign of the Spanish. Wandering Coyote knew that they were celebrating, enjoying food that should have reached the Mexica. He knew that with every victory more allies joined the Spanish. We need a big victory, he thought, before the allies return to us. He remembered that the boy accompanied him tonight.

'We shall finish early. I will take the canoe the long way round north to the Tepeyac causeway.'

'Is that wise?'

'Well, it is not foolish, boy. It is protected by Falling Eagle's men. It should be safe. A merchant friend of mine helps guard it. I learn from him what food enters the city.'

They made their way back to their canoe. They did not use their paddles until they had negotiated the mounds of rubble protruding from the water. It was increasingly difficult to navigate these waters now. Once past the rubble, they picked up their paddles.

'It breaks my heart to see the destruction of these gardens,' said Wandering Coyote as they passed one of the islands surrounding the city. He always hugged these islands for they provided hiding places among tree roots and branches. Sometimes, when he was too exhausted to continue, he slept in the abandoned homes and scrounged for rotten maize cobs or axolotls lurking in the reeds. They were especially good roasted with yellow peppers.

They reached the causeway to Tepeyac, reassured to hear the Mexica guards on the city gate. Wandering Coyote paddled to the end of the causeway where it joined the mainland. A body bumped into their canoe. They withdrew quickly into the reeds. When they heard horses, they held onto a root to stop themselves floating out into the lake. The horses retreated. Lizard picked up his paddle, but it slipped from his hands and smashed onto the water. The horses stopped. A man jumped down and peered over the causeway. The Spanish lined up behind him with their torches.

'Let me do the talking!' barked Wandering Coyote. 'Friends, you are out late!' he called jovially.

One of the Spanish tittered.

'It's that bloody merchant!'

'Working late as usual to provide your luxuries.'

Lizard could not believe what he heard. He opened his mouth.

'Quiet, boy. Do you want to get us killed?'

A Tlaxcalan laughed coarsely.

'That merchant is everywhere.'

'Doing your bidding, lords.'

The horse snorted and pawed the ground. The Spanish rode away. Wandering Coyote saw how the boy stared at him with hate.

'Don't ask questions. I am a merchant. I trade with anyone. I am friend to everyone. Trade is useful. I find out things that no one else knows. I know the Spanish plan to seize this causeway and blockade us. I know also that we will be unable to prevent it.'

'Falling Eagle does his best.'

'He cannot be everywhere at once, which is where I come in useful.'

'Fighting would be more useful.'

'That is where I disagree, boy. Now paddle us home quickly. I need something to comfort me.' In the sky the stars had disappeared. He could smell the seeds of a storm. 'Faster, boy. I do not want to be out on the lake in another tempest.'

Jewel called for a brazier to take the chill from the room. The storm had gathered force. Storms always made her restless. The bell curtain rattled furiously. Ant Flower and two maids rushed in.

'Terrible news, Lady. The Spanish have used the acqueduct to enter the city! They have put one of their cannon on top of the Stone of Sacrifice and thrown the priests from the temple!'

One of the maids began to shriek.

'And that is not all! They have blocked the springs at Chapultepec! We have no water!'

Servants ran past in the corridors. A musician pushed her head through the bells.

'People are leaving the city before the Spanish arrive!'

Ant Flower ran around like a mad dog opening the baskets and pulling out clothes and jewellery.

'No!' said Jewel. 'We will wait for Falling Eagle.'

The maids stared in horror and escaped down the corridor. Ant Flower put the jewellery in a small basket.

'If Falling Eagle is out there fighting, he will forget us.' Her voice trembled.

'He will never forget us,' said Jewel, sitting down firmly on a stool. 'He told me not to leave without his permission.'

Footsteps ran past in the corridor. Now they could hear the desperate sound of the war drums. Outside the storm gathered force as Huitzilopochtli battled with Quetzalcoatl for control of the world.

'At least we could join your mother next door,' suggested Ant Flower. 'Then we would not be alone.'

'No,' said Jewel obstinately.

Everyone left. There was no sound at all in the corridor. They waited but Falling Eagle did not come. He sent four captains. Jewel was to dress plainly and leave with the rest of the family. Jewel grabbed her rabbit-fur blanket and a basket of jewellery and ran down the stairs with Ant Flower. A quick sprint across the court-yard and over a bridge to her father's home where the family had gathered in the council chamber. Her mother, her half-sisters, aunts, cousins and all their servants. Some of the old aunts refused to move. They would die in the place of their birth. Litters were brought for those who needed them. Jewel and her mother moved, with the maids and the cousins and their children, along the canal path out into the main road to Tlatelolco. The rain poured down. Above them Tlaloc banged his pots and sent lightning to terrify them. The momentum of the crowds carried them forward to the Tlatelolco bridge. Sometimes Jewel saw a face she knew. An old priestess who had taught her poetry and the High Priest of Huitzilopochtli cradling the statue of the god. The crowds parted to let him through, staying close, seeking the god's protection.

Jewel was horrified to see the poverty and distress of her people. So many had scarred faces. They carried what they could on their backs, their turkeys, their rabbits, their children, their food tied in their shawls. Some pulled the blind on cords. Others carried their elderly parents. Everyone pushed and shoved in their haste to reach Tlatelolco. Some fell into the lake weighed down by the babies or belongings on their backs. A woman slipped and was trampled. It was like a mad stampede of deer. Ant Flower clung tightly to Jewel's skirt.

'Push!' screamed Jewel. 'We must get there before they lift the bridge!'

Everyone was doing the same. The crowds surged forward. Children screamed. At the other end of the bridge the Tlatelolcans barred the way.

'Go home, Mexica,' they shouted. 'There is nothing for you here!'

They were still a long way from the bridge. The people ahead fought to cross. Some fell into the canal. Others leapt into canoes and capsized. A few tried to swim over but the water was too deep. A man threw his child into the lake and jumped in afterwards. Both sank quickly.

'Please,' begged Jewel. 'We are Falling Eagle's family. Let us through.'

Ant Flower burrowed through the crowd, now pulling Jewel by her skirt. She reached the bridge just as it was being lifted. When the Tlatelolcans saw Jewel, they pulled her over but pushed the servants back. Jewel grabbed Ant Flower and the other maids just as the bridge cut them off from the main city.

Although the palace in Tlatelolco was already full of relatives, space was found for Jewel. Falling Eagle's mother was a princess of Tlatelolco. This had been her home and, although the Tlatelolcans resented the refugees who arrived daily, they could not refuse the Lord Falling Eagle's family. Jewel and her mother were given a small room on the first floor overlooking the crowded market where Mexica camped among the columns and market stalls.

'It will only be for a short time,' comforted Lady Tecalco. 'We will soon return home.'

Ant Flower busied herself laying the sleeping mats in neat rows. An old servant took their wet clothes. She pointed towards Tenochtitlan.

'The Spanish are burning the temple. We are destroyed, Lady.'

'Silence your tongue, woman! Bring us water and food!'

'There is little food, Lady, but I will bring what I can.'

Even in the good times, the food reserves ran low during this month. Now Tlatelolco bulged with refugees and soldiers. They could hear the sound of fighting over the canal in the main city.

Jewel covered herself with her blanket. An old aunt croaked from the corner of the room.

'We are doomed! Did not Quetzalcoatl send his wind to defeat us?'

'Be quiet, old hag,' screeched Jewel.

Her mother called out wearily.

'Go to sleep. Such talk will not help any of us.'

Falling Eagle turned up the next day exhausted. Mercifully, the bruises on his face turned out to be ash stains. He confirmed what they all feared. The Spanish had successfully advanced into the main city and now occupied the Sacred Square. He did not tell her it was becoming increasingly difficult to defend the Tepeyac causeway. If that fell, food would no longer enter the city. His spies had reported something else. Don Hernán was searching for the Lord Montezuma's younger daughter.

'Why?' asked Jewel.

'He promised your father he would take care of you.'

'As he took care of my sister Butterfly?'

He warned her that Tlaxcalans, disguised as Mexica, would find a way here to his childhood home. He had found another house in Tlatelolco, a house where no one would think to look for her.

'It is a merchant's house,' he told her. 'It is modest but comfortable.'

'A merchant?'

'It is discreet and has food, although the merchant is an odd fellow. No one will think of looking for you there. The shortage of food in Tlatelolco will get worse. Don Alvarado is still trying to block our causeway. He uses boats to attack us. We have managed to keep them at bay. But, if they can, the Spanish will try to starve us.'

'So there is no escape?'

'We are not finished yet. But for a time food will be scarce and people will kill for it. The Tlatelolcans do not want the Mexica here at all.'

He told her something shocking. The Tlatelolcans had struck a bargain with the Mexica. When the Spanish were defeated, the Tlatelolcans would lead the Triple Alliance in place of the Mexica. Whatever the outcome of these battles, the Mexica's power would be reduced. When she protested, he told her the Mexica had no choice. They could not fight without the Tlatelolcans. And where would they all live if not here? Don Hernán had tried to persuade the Tlatelolcans to abandon the Mexica and ally themselves with him.

'And do you know, they refused. Only the lure of power keeps them loyal.'

'They are traitors!'

'They do what the Mexica would have done in similar circumstances.'

Falling Eagle had arranged for her and her mother to move tonight. His guards would escort her. He ordered her not to go out of the house. And then he was gone. He had barely stayed an hour.

Wandering Coyote felt some compassion for the refugees who poured into Tlatelolco, but, like the rest of his fellow citizens, he did not welcome them. He had expected this ever since the Spanish had invaded Tacuba.

From his first-floor window he had watched the endless procession pouring over the bridge from Tenochtitlan. Unwilling to share his house, he had resisted the pressure of the Mexica lords who requisitioned empty rooms in the district. Now he was overcome by the grandness of his guests and welcomed Jewel and her mother warmly. He did not greet the dwarf and the maidservants with the same enthusiasm. They were extra mouths for whom food and water would have to be found. He regretted he could not show off his treasures, which he had hidden. Nevertheless, as he took his guests on a tour of the house, he pointed at the empty shelves. He could never resist an opportunity to brag. He showed them the statue of Xipe Totec, the flayed god, perfect except for a slight chip on his headdress. He pointed to the alcove that had housed a granite mask from Teotihuacan. If only he could show the ladies his fine collection.

'From Teotihuacan?' asked the Lady Tecalco. Such treasures usually remained in the royal treasury.

'I paid good gold for that,' boasted Wandering Coyote. He was enjoying himself. He could see that the ladies were impressed.

'I would willingly exchange such treasures for food,' murmured the Lady Tecalco.

Wandering Coyote whispered that he had some stores of food in the house and they were all welcome to share. He surprised himself with his generosity. He led the Lady and her daughter up to a room on the roof. He did not tell them this was the room used by the old Woman Snake when he enjoyed his women.

Jewel looked out through the window and over the crowded streets to the makeshift shacks on stilts stretching out into the lake. Tlatelolco was a dismal place on the bleak northern tip of the island. She knew her mother did not like the room. It faced north towards the region of death. It smelt of dirty water and rotting animals.

'We do not like this room,' she said. 'It is unlucky.'

Her mother interrupted. 'It will do us very well.'

Wandering Coyote smiled unctuously. When the war was over, the Lady would surely remember him. Then he pulled himself together. Such thoughts were foolish. When the war was over, the old rules would return. He hoped that his stores of food would last.

Tlatelolco

July 1521

When Falling Eagle moved his headquarters to Tlatelolco, more refugees followed. They came in leaking canoes or swam over the canal in the dark. In the morning, once the mist had cleared, their bodies floated into the city. The refugees camped in the market square and some squatted in the houses of local people. Others made nests in the reeds or shared the shacks that rose overnight in the shallow water. Only the canal separated them from the main city. They could see Don Hernán's banner taunting them from the top of the temple and wondered how long it would take him to cross the canal into Tlatelolco. Although the city, with its narrow streets, was impassable for horses or cannon, they took every precaution. They blockaded the alleys. They set traps and covered the roofs with stones. And then the moment came when an elderly woman who had risen early saw Don Hernán sitting on his horse staring into the canal.

Falling Eagle seized his opportunity. He knew that Don Hernán planned to cross into Tlatelolco. It would easy to ambush him here where the water was eight feet deep. The plan was to let the Spanish make a bridge and then, after they had crossed, the Mexica would remove everything and trap them on their return as they fell into the deep water.

Lizard lay concealed in his canoe in the reeds beside the canal. Wandering Coyote waited in the line behind. The Spanish approached.

The discussion seemed to go on for ever. Then they left and returned with bundles of reeds, maize stalks and wood, which they threw into the water. Don Alvarado tried the bridge first, balancing and wobbling on the branches. More wood was brought to stabilise it and the Spanish began to cross, slowly, precariously. The few Tlaxcalans who followed had to be stopped from pounding their breasts and chanting their war songs.

Pray to the gods that none of us sneezes, thought Lizard. At times like this sneezes and coughs swarmed like flies. How tempting it would be to attack now. But Falling Eagle had been most insistent. The right moment to attack would come when the Spanish returned, when they least expected it. He listened to Don Alvarado – he would recognise his voice anywhere – coaxing his horse over the floating bridge. It took some time and, when the Spanish had crossed, the canoes moved silently out into the water and removed the floating bridges before returning to their hides.

It seemed hours, although it was still light, before Lizard heard somone run noisily to the gap and fall into the canal. He heard a Spaniard swear. This was the moment at last. The canoes moved out. Warriors fired their arrows from the roofs above. The horses panicked. The Spanish grabbed whatever they could, pieces of wood, parcels of maize leaves and floated on them but many disappeared under the debris.

A man struggled in the middle of the canal. Black eyes stared from under his silver helmet. His hand had three fingers. Lizard hit out with his paddle. The helmet fell off leaving the head exposed. A youth paddled towards Lizard. Together they grabbed Don Hernán's hair and dragged him towards the canoe but a Spaniard, balancing precariously on an island of twigs, lifted his sword and left a bloody stump where the youth's elbow had been. Then he lost his balance and toppled into the water. His sword floated away with the logs. As Lizard heaved Don Hernán into his canoe, two Spaniards jumped into the canal and dragged him to safety.

From the market square came the boom of the drums and the triumphant moans of trumpets and horns as the first Spanish captives were led to sacrifice. On the other side of the canal, Don Hernán stared in horror as his naked comrades climbed the temple steps. Falling Eagle appeared on the Tlatelolco side. He held up a bearded head. A horse floated below in the crimson canal. A body entangled with a bundle of sticks pumped its blood into the water.

'We shall kill you all!'

From the roofs behind him three Spanish heads were thrown into the water.

Everyone crammed into the temple square to watch the Spanish prisoners climb the holy steps. Naked, white and shivering, the prisoners shuffled across the stones. They hung their heads and prayed and some of them bawled like babies.

'You are not so brave now,' shouted an old crone.

The old women were the worst, always lusting for blood and death. A gaggle of them had gathered at the foot of the pyramid, cackling like turkeys, making fun of the flimsy white Spanish *tepuli*s.

The Spanish whimpered and prayed to their god and had to be prodded up the staircase, some of them peeing with fear. When they saw Falling Eagle on top of the pyramid holding the sacred knife, some of them ran to the edge and jumped off. Those that did not escape were dragged up the steps, kicking and screaming. It took many priests to hold them down on the sacred stone and a constant supply of bowls to carry their hearts to a ravenous Huitzilopochtli waiting inside the shrine.

Jewel could not control her laughter. She ridiculed the naked white bodies with their feeble *tepuli*s flapping like old men's stomachs. And the more the Spanish railed at their fate, the louder the crowd laughed. They roared as the bodies rolled down the steps to the butchers waiting below. They cheered when they saw the mounting piles of hands and feet, guts and heads. Afterwards they walked around the poles in the square and counted the human and horses' heads. And some people even danced, just like in the old days. But when the festivities were over, when they made their way home, stepping carefully to avoid the spreading pools of blood trickling down the temple staircase, they couldn't help noticing that it was not a bit like the old days. The paper streamers in the trees were faded and torn, the streets were unswept. Bodies lay abandoned in the gutters. The proud Mexica begged where market stalls once boasted the produce of their empire. Jewel saw children selling themselves for a head of corn. Her mother, a pious lady, told her that honest families who had worked hard in Tenochtitlan were now forced to beg for food and some even sold their daughters. A virgin could be bought for a dog or a handful of lizards. But most terrifying of all was that someone had followed them home. Someone knew where they lived.

They kept the gates locked and took turns to stay up all night to keep watch. Jewel complained that she felt like a prisoner.

'At least you are alive,' her mother replied tartly.

'I bet those white-skinned people in father's zoo were better fed than us.'

Her mother did not reply. What had happened to them? Jewel wondered. Had they been eaten like the animals? It was too noisy and smelly sitting in the courtyard, and anyway there were no plants to look at now. They had either been eaten or died for lack of water. So she stayed inside with the blinds down. No one else complained. Hunger made you such an old grump. It made your stomach ache. It turned you into a bald old hag with rotten teeth. It made you faint and it blurred your eyesight. It made you spy on your own mother to see if she ate more than you and it made you tremble with excitement when you found a worm or a beetle. It made you eat your snot. It tempted you to pick at the rotting corpses piled outside the courtyard. It made you catch whole maggots and stuff them still wriggling into your mouth.

This morning, as Jewel wandered through the empty dining hall, foraging under the stools and the tables for ants, beetles, flies or maggots, for anything that lived, she found a basket stuck high on a shelf. She stood on a stool and lifted it down. Inside there was a piece of skin sparsely covered with hair. She picked it up. It was shrivelled and discoloured but it was skin. People ate leather, so why not eat skin. She took a bite. It tasted horrible but it made her mouth moist chewing it. She sat down on the floor and chewed and chewed. She had just swallowed it when Wandering Coyote entered the room. He saw her, he saw the basket and he ran over. She had never seen him run so fast. He picked up the basket. A few shreds of skin and hair clung to the edges.

'You have eaten the warrior!'

'There was only dried skin and hair.'

Now she felt sick. She vomited over Wandering Coyote's feet. Wandering Coyote bent down and extricated the bits of skin and hair from her vomit.

'You have eaten my brother! I captured him for sacrifice. I keep his scalp with me always. And you have eaten him.'

She wiped her lips with her blouse. The taste would not go away. 'Your brother?'

'My brother in sacrifice. Captives must be treated at all times with respect, even when they are dead. I captured him for the gods. He died with dignity and now you have eaten him!'

Wandering Coyote turned into a monster. He threw the basket at her. He dragged her out into the courtyard shouting so loudly that everyone came running. Her mother stared in horror. Ant Flower and Marsh Lily tried to pull him away.

'Do you think I want you here? Do you think I even like you? I rue the day I ever supported the Mexica. If only the Tlatelocans had had the sense to side with the Spanish.'

And then he told her something terrible. The food she ate came from the Spanish with whom he traded. And when she had accused him of everything she could think of, he pushed her back into the house to his empty shelves.

'What good is your status when you cannot even feed yourself? You have not gone out looking for food like Ant Flower or Marsh Lily. No, you sit here expecting us all to wait on you!' He pointed to his empty alcoves and shelves. 'Where do you think my treasures have gone? They go to buy you food.'

That was what merchants did. They traded with everyone. It did not matter whether they were Spanish, Tlaxcalan or Mayan. His words scalded her like boiling water. Her mother ignored her and put her arms around Wandering Coyote. Jewel noticed how frail she looked.

'It would be better to die with honour!' she screamed.

'Honour! Was it honour that made your father give away his country and his people!'

And then Wandering Coyote did something shocking. He fell onto his knees. He banged his head on the ground and howled like a coyote. His whole body shook. Jewel had never seen a man cry. Men did not howl like coyotes.

She ran upstairs and shut herself in that horrible little room over-looking the lake where more houses rose daily on their flimsy stilts. She blocked her ears to drown the noise. She stayed up there watching the sun set over the lake, as if nothing had changed, as if her father were there on the temple, praying for a safe end to the day.

It was Marsh Lily who brought a precious bowl of water and wiped Jewel's swollen face.

'Wandering Coyote does not mean it, Lady. He is upset because he cannot feed us all as he would like.'

'I have become a witch,' sobbed Jewel.

'We all feel like that. I hate myself because whenever I go out for food, I ignore all the crying children and search only for food for myself.'

'Do you think someone watches us?' asked Jewel.

'Wandering Coyote thinks so. He has placed guards by the gate.'

'They too have to be fed. I am so ashamed.'

They went downstairs together. Wandering Coyote did not speak of the incident again.

The celebrations turned out to be premature. The Spanish did not flee. They retreated to Coyoacan on the mainland, from where they continued to burn and loot and where they built a shanty town to house the thousands of allies who turned up daily to fight with them. Wandering Coyote said that Falling Eagle had failed to take advantage of his victory at the canal. His despair returned but this time he did not crawl on the floor howling like a coyote. He disappeared and did not come back for two days.

The Spanish limbs and heads, hands and feet, skin and toes, and horses' heads were collected and dispatched to the towns around the lake to show how the Mexica were winning the war. But this did not buy them friends. The Mexica stood alone. There were no friends left. Falling Eagle addressed his people in the market square. Now everyone would have to fight, even the old men and young boys, old and young women. This would not be war as they knew it. It would be a game of deceit and trickery. They would fight like their enemy, using their minds as well as their bodies. If they wanted to whistle and shriek, stamp their feet and sing their songs it would do no harm and it would mock the Tlaxcalans. Everyone laughed. They hated the Tlaxcalans who slipped into Tlatelolco at night and kidnapped and raped their women. From now, women would dress as men and men as Tlaxcalans. From now they would fight invisibly. They would slither and slide on the ground like snakes. They would listen and wait to hear where the cannon fired from so they could estimate its distance. He had broken holes in the walls in the houses in Tlatelolco so that, when the enemy entered the streets, the Mexica could escape, using these holes as secret passages. There was no shame in this. Although death in war was glorious, he could not afford to lose any more people.

'So we fight like mice now,' shouted a middle-aged man.

'Mice who survive,' said Falling Eagle.

He ordered the people of Tlatelolco to make as much noise as they could. They were to scream and shout and yell, beat their drums and blow their conches and whistles, day and night, until they drove the Spanish mad. Wars could be won in different ways. Noise could be as powerful a weapon as swords and horses.

When he was not fighting, Lizard spent hours searching for food among the ruins, but no lizard dared sun itself in Tlatelolco now.

No swallow nested anywhere near the city. Every snake had vanished and even the mice had fled. As for dogs, he could hardly remember what they looked like. The only creatures here were humans.

He usually took something with him to Wandering Coyote's house. He had not visited since the canoe battle. Wandering Coyote had criticised him for not killing Don Hernán. Not killing him! A man was captured for the gods. A captive of Don Hernán's status would be worth many hearts. Wandering Coyote insisted that the Spanish would never leave now, not with Don Hernán alive.

Lizard felt ashamed that today he brought only stories to the house. But what a story! The Spanish had made fools of themselves. They had built a giant catapult and carried it up the steps to the top of the temple platform in Tenochtitlan. From here they had propelled stones over the wall into the market square of Tlatelolco. But the stones had had minds of their own and refused to land where they were aimed. The Spanish had argued among themselves so noisily they could be heard on the other side of the canal. Lizard knew this would make them all laugh. But they did not laugh when he told them how someone had followed him to Wandering Coyote's home.

Everyone sat inside with the blinds drawn. Today there was a meal laid out on a plank. A medium-sized lizard, two water-lily bulbs and three snails to be divided between seven of them. One small Spanish candle flickered on the remaining table. It was the last candle left.

Lizard watched the Lady Tecalco divide the spoils, consoling himself that the lizard would be raw and the bulbs bitter and slimy. As they sat down on the floor, they heard the sounds of fighting. The guards quickly barred the gate. Lizard peered through a crack in the wall. He saw people running madly through the streets. Wandering Coyote insisted Lizard stay the night. He offered the white truffle cactus. It dulled hunger and fatigue and its effects could last for three days.

Lizard took it eagerly. It certainly brought dreams. And what dreams! Memories of smooth skin and a smell like no other and fingers that caressed even his scars. It was this knowledge that she did not mind his scars that put strength into his *tepuli*. Or was it the truffle cactus? Whatever it was turned his inexperienced *tepuli* into a giant's, so huge it had struggled to enter the place of warmth, of comfort she offered him. And somehow, with the help of the darkness of the night and the white truffle cactus, he felt close to his father, as if some of his father's essence remained. He had enjoyed her four times, each better than the last. Did his father give her pleasure? He wanted to ask so many questions, but it seemed disloyal, and in the morning Marsh Lily had gone. He rubbed his hands over his scars. He would never feel self-conscious again.

Falling Eagle never visited the house. At night warriors would escort Jewel to him. They covered her with a frayed cactus cape and told her to walk like a man. Every night more bodies filled the streets, for the people were too weak to bury them and there was no wood for pyres. The groans of the dying could be heard beneath the constant din, like the murmur of thousands of wounded animals. She covered her ears with her cape and wondered what present Falling Eagle would bring her this time. Once he had brought her a dainty pink rose, the last flower in Tlatelolco and she had eaten it, nibbling each petal slowly as if it were the most precious of delicacies. A small hand tugged at her skirt. A child, no more than seven, with huge eyes in a skeletal face, pleaded with her.

'Food, Lady. Please, food.'

'Where is your mother?' Jewel asked, although she knew the answer.

'Dead, Lady. They are all dead.'

Jewel felt guilty. She had been dreaming of delicacies.

'I have no food,' she said harshly, shrugging off the child and following the warriors, walking quickly to elude her pursuer. But the girl was suprisingly quick and kept up with them, following them to an old storehouse next to the city wall, where they lost her.

When Jewel saw today's treat, she knew she would share it with no one. It was more precious than gold or feathers. It was the red fruit of the nopal cactus which ripened at this time of year. She watched Falling Eagle cut off the spines carefully, for they were as sharp as obsidian.

'I hear rumours that Don Hernán offers peace,' she said when she had licked every finger, trying to ignore the stinging ulcers in her mouth. Wandering Coyote – they understood each other very well now – spoke wistfully of peace. Athough he admired Falling Eagle, he thought that he fought too defensive a battle. He had not pursued the Spanish after his canal victory. Some of the merchants thought that Don Hernán had decided to destroy the Mexica, here in Tlatelolco. The Mexica under Falling Eagle had put up such a good fight that Don Hernán despaired of taking the city and Don Hernán wanted Tenochtitlan, ruined or not.

'Who tells you that?' asked Falling Eagle angrily.

'Someone in the town. You know how rumours spread.'

'The rumours of merchants are not worth listening to. What do they know of war? Would you accept peace?'

She sucked the cactus stone until there was nothing left. At this moment she would give anything to eat and sleep somewhere comfortable, to wash and wear clean clothes, to sit in her garden smelling the jasmine and never to feel hungry again.

'It is tempting.'

'It is not an option,' he snapped, 'and it never will be. I shall tell you what I think of Don Hernán's offers. I pretend I am considering peace and I send messengers to parley with him, to gain time for my next move. I have no intention ever of meeting him. The priests now promise victory. It will soon be the time of year when Quetzalcoatl, in the form of the Evening Star, disappears from view. For eight days the star will be invisible, at its weakest point. This is the moment to attack. And I plan to do so. But whatever happens I do not want to see Don Hernán take you. I would rather give you to a Mayan lord.'

'Ugh. All those jagged teeth embedded with stones.'

He laughed.

'There are no shortages of food in the Mayan lands. Tomorrow morning my canoe leaves and you will be on it.'

'I can live without food if that is the price.'

'No one can live without food.'

He popped a paste of tobacco mixed with lime into his mouth. He would chew it for hours.

'The Mexica have starved before,' she reminded him.

Her grandmother had told her that during a famine she had smelt flowers to dull her hunger but here even the flowers had been eaten.

'I would eat anything,' said Falling Eagle chewing vigourously. 'However, there is one pleasure still left to us.'

'I feel so dirty.'

She knew she was scraggy. Her hair was coarse and its colour had faded and sometimes great clumps fell out in her fingers. Soon she would be bald.

'Do you think I have washed?' he said. 'At least we can still comfort each other.' He rummaged in a small bag and brought out rose water and chicle. 'Now you can chew like a whore to dull your hunger and we can both smell like the Spanish.'

She splashed them both with rose water. 'Now we do not.'

In the dark she forgot his smell. She whispered like a whore, shameful words, of her soft parts, her place of joy and how she would make her womb move for him. Her words spilled out like her father's words searching for homes. She begged him to knead her like dough, to come into the place where she wove and spun. At first she shocked him with her bawdy language. He asked where she had learnt such things.

'At school. It was not all prayers and holy songs you know. Some of the girls knew more than I did.'

'What else did you learn at school?' he whispered in her ear. How his hot breath tickled.

'Embroidery. I am terrible with a needle.'

His whole body laughed. She felt sure the city would hear them.

In the morning, when she woke, she heard the sound of rain. Water, precious water. She jumped up from the mat and ran naked into the courtyard, holding her arms up to the sky. She swallowed the drops and let the rain pummel her body until her lips and skin felt smooth again.

'What are you doing?'

'I am bathing.'

'We are not alone here.'

She had forgotten she slept in a military headquarters.

Although the rain brought a respite to the burning and replenished the springs, no canoe could go out in such weather. Falling Eagle sent an old man to sit on the side of the canal in the rain and, in full view of the Spanish, eat a huge meal. Everyone watched him jealously, conscious of the hunger that gnawed at their own stomachs.

Wandering Coyote felt such despair. He was so emaciated now, like a slave who worked in the fields, not a rich merchant used to eating two large meals a day. He had grown fond of his belly, an affectionate companion who accompanied him everywhere. He was tired of sharing his house and his food. Two of his friends had been killed under falling masonry. Yesterday he had worked for hours to free a woman and her child from the rubble of their house. And gossip among his fellow merchants only added to his depression. Every night he still went out to help the women remove debris from the canals put there during the day by the Spanish. This had been the pattern of his life for two months now and he felt exhausted. He never returned before dawn. It was a kind of fighting but it never produced results. It would not bring the victory promised by the priests.

He wandered out into his courtyard. All his plants had died. The ferns from the cloud forest were as brown as the earth. His favourite tiny pink orchids had shrivelled. Even the strange plants – he had never known their names – had turned into old vine rope. They sent their roots from great heights to tap into the earth's floor and could survive with little moisture. Even for them the rain had come too late. The stench and noise outside were terrible. He ignored the bodies piling up on the other side of the wall, so high they almost reached the top. Today a small hand slid over the wall, stretching down to the overflowing pots. He pushed the hand back down and made sure the lids were secured on all the pots. It was too dangerous to go out and empty them now.

A child slipped through the gate. A child with hungry eyes and a swollen belly. He chased her out.

'I followed the lady,' she said. She held out her hands. 'Food, please.'

'There is no food here,' said Wandering Coyote as he shoved her back into the street. He retreated inside to avoid the child's cries. Everyone sat huddled on the floor, their shifts tied over their noses.

'There should be less shit now since we do not eat.'

At once he regretted his coarseness. He did not know why he said it. Perhaps just for something to say, to take everyone's mind off the lack of food. There was nothing left to trade.

He watched the Lady Tecalco rise and climb the stairs. He liked the Lady and did not wish to upset her. He dared not tell her the terrible news that the High Priest of Huitzilopochtli had been murdered by unknown assailants. Now the gods would surely abandon the Mexica to their fate.

246

Tlatelolco

August 1521

They sat in circles on the stone floor telling stories to pass the time. Jewel's favourite was the jewel story. And no wonder her father had called her his 'precious jewel', for she was descended from one.

'Once upon a time there was a beautiful princess whose father so feared for her safety that he imprisoned her in a walled garden guarded by spiders and centipedes and armies of bats and scorpions.'

'Ugh!' shuddered Marsh Lily who hated scorpions.

'Her father rejected every suitor for his daughter's hand. But one day a beautiful painted arrow came over the wall and landed in the garden at the maiden's feet. The shaft split open to reveal a jewel. The girl picked it up, tested it between her teeth, swallowed it and conceived my great-grandfather, the first Montezuma. You see, I owe my existence to that jewel.'

She wondered what kind of jewel it might have been – coral, jade or turquoise, or perhaps a sea pearl from the coast? None of them would be much use to her now. Even a jewel could not buy food. The others dreamt of what they would eat when all this was over.

'Fish,' said Lizard, 'baked with herbs.'

'Sweet tamales with a crust,' said Marsh Lily.

'A roasted corn cob,' said Ant Flower.

Wandering Coyote remembered seafood and pineapples and spiced chocolate with chilli – luxuries from the coast. The Lady Tecalco smiled stoically. She had blocked all thoughts of food from her mind, giving her own rations to her daughter. She had passed the point of hunger. Now she felt as holy and as wasted as a hermit.

Sometimes they all sang together and at night, when it was completely black, for there were no more candles, they passed the time speaking riddles. Marsh Lily was rather good at riddles. And sometimes she would play her flute, although you could not hear much above the din.

It was on such a day when they were repeating their stories that a man jumped over the wall, running into the house and making straight for Jewel. She had just reached the bit about spiders and centipedes when the man grabbed her. He dragged her across the yard, over the stones and dust and crockery, over the dead plants and pots. He put his hands under her skirt and began to push her over the wall to his accomplice on the other side. She smashed into the pots lined up so neatly, smearing her hands and body with shit. But this did not deter the man, who pushed with one hand and tried to force the door in the outer wall with the other.

A madman flew from the house with an axe. A madman who looked like a huge scrawny bird, his unbound hair flowing out behind him. There was a terrible scream and a noise like breaking wood. The Tlaxcalan fell to the ground clutching his shoulder.

'The door!' shrieked Ant Flower. 'They are breaking the door!'

Wandering Coyote stood there, his axe ready.

'There are many warriors here,' he shouted. 'We will kill you all.' He turned to Jewel. 'Shout! Pretend you are warriors.'

They shouted. They banged pots and stones. They tried to sound like an army. The voices behind the gate argued and then faded away. Wandering Coyote turned to the man convulsing on the ground watching his blood gush from him and turn his white feathers tomato-red. Wandering Coyote lifted his axe again. The Tlaxcalan crawled along the ground leaving a red trail. Wandering Coyote hit him again and again until pieces of flesh splattered the courtyard and the walls. Then he fell to the ground, hugging his axe. Blood dripped from his chest hands and face like a warrior on the sacrificial stone. Jewel knelt down in front of him.

'We will die here together!'

He put his filthy hands around her.

'No, we will live, Lady. We have lasted this long and we will go on until the end.' She noticed how thin and stooped he had become. 'Someone bribed the guards.' He kicked the body against the wall. 'We could eat him.'

The Lady Tecalco grimaced. She had suffered a bloody flux for two weeks and was so weak she could hardly move.

Wandering Coyote despaired to see her so frail. He knew she left her food for her daughter. Perhaps he could find food in the town. He put on his sandals until he remembered that ordinary men did not wear sandals. He hated going without sandals but he must not draw attention to himself. He removed his shoes and slipped out, still bleeding, still bloody, groaning as he slipped in the oily mud that was part blood, part shit, part flesh. But he persisted, returning victoriously clutching a bat.

But the Lady Tecalco did not come down from her room. She had slipped quietly away to the place of the fleshless, her hand held tightly by her daughter. Her family threw her body into the lake with all those who had died on the same night. For the virtuous Lady there were no marigolds, no pyre, no golden dog and few mourners. At least she was not left to rot for the vultures or, worse, for the scavenging humans.

That night Tlaloc sent more rain to wash away the blood and the dirt and refresh the desperate humans. Jewel found a piece of pumice in one of the flower pots and scrubbed herself. The rain fell continuously for three days and unleashed plagues of mosquitoes. The body lay rotting by the gate. The holes that appeared in the flesh showed human teeth marks.

Wandering Coyote was away much of the time. Lizard had left to fight. Marsh Lily slipped out for food. When she did not return by midday, Jewel decided to search for her. She darkened her face with mud, covered her hair with ashes and her body with a rough cloak. She rubbed her feet and toes in the dust to disguise their softness. It was terrible walking barefooted. Ant Flower blocked the gate with her body and tried to stop her.

In the streets corpses were piled thirty-high against the ruined walls where people squatted, despite the death surrounding them. Jewel's feet sank into their rotting flesh. Sometimes a corpse would come to life and grab her ankles and the fingers of dead hands would rise to plead for help. Sightless eyes witnessed her passing. Children with pot bellies scavenged for maggots burrowing in the bodies.

Jewel held her cloak over her nose and forced her way through the mud, over the bodies, whose fluids leaked into the saturated earth. She continued out towards the shore opposite the spot where a captured cannon sat half submerged in the lake. Here too people squatted in their thousands in makeshift shacks of reeds, watching like eagles for anything that moved. She pushed her way through them to the filthy water. Despite its smell, people were washing in it. She had not expected so many people. She felt her bowels stir as the flux took hold. She had suffered for some weeks now. Where should she go? The reeds were blocked with people searching desperately for food. She crouched in the pouring rain and voided her insides. Oh, the shame of emptying onés bowels in public, even if disguised. She pulled down her skirts and wiped her hands on the reeds. As she moved out of the marsh, two ducks landed on the water near by. Hundreds of people lunged and fought furiously with each other for a piece of those ducks. Jewel threw herself into the melee, pushing an old woman aside, squashing a child, as she scrabbled for a slice of raw duck. But the ducks were torn to shreds and washed away into the lake. Jewel stood there shrieking. She could not believe that such a noise came from her and she looked around to see people staring. She hid her face and staggered home anxious to escape the place of her disgrace and rid herself of the oleaginous mud sticking to her clothes.

This time she took a different route back through the street of the Lime Vendors, looking behind her often, fearful of Spanish or Tlaxcalans. Her feet were torn to shreds. She could not run.

The street she chose was so narrow, she had to squeeze herself against the wall as people bumped into her, She hoped that none of them would see or feel, beneath the mud and the ashes and the heavy cloak, the body of a girl. She had reached the only building left in the street when she stumbled over legs protruding from a doorway, legs spread-eagled like a woman of joy. But there were no signs of joy here. Flies settled on the girl's thighs. The slit between her legs oozed with the emissions of many men. Jewel put her hand over her mouth to stop retching and stepped over the legs. She did not know why she bent down. She wasn't even curious to see the face of the unfortunate girl. She didn't want to know. She didn't want to feel. For a moment she was reminded of the sacrifice of the Earth Mother whose body fulfilled many purposes. But this body had satisfied only lust. An old woman nudged Jewel.

'The Tlaxcalans raid us at night. This is how they use our women. I never thought I would welcome the ugliness of age.'

Jewel pushed the women away. She stared down at a face she knew. The woman grabbed her arm.

'Slow down, girl. Shuffle as the old do. That girl', she pointed to Marsh Lily's body, 'took no care of herself. With a face like that, she asked for it.'

Jewel shook the old lady off and shuffled home. She dared not look over her shoulders. When she reached the walls of the house, she had to climb over four corpses before she could force the gate into the courtyard. The stench clung to her hair and her clothes. She ran into the house, slumped onto a stool and sobbed. Two small hands pulled at her cloak.

'You could sell me, Lady.'

Ant Flower stood there on her stumpy legs.

'Who would want a dwarf now?'

'There are still people with money, Lady. Some of the merchants hoard it. I know who eats in this town. I beg you, Lady, sell me. I should fetch two handfuls of maize.'

Two handfuls, one meal for two of them.

'No! I cannot bear to lose you. You are all I have left. I don't even know if Falling Eagle is alive.'

No one was more loyal than Ant Flower. After her father's death, Ant Flower had been there, day and night, more faithful than any husband.

'No,' repeated Jewel. 'No.'

How many times had she saved her dwarf from climbing the steps of the temple? She tried to remember.

'Lady, I do not like to see you so weak.'

'If we all go in search of food, one of us must find something.'

Jewel was terrified to go out again. Ant Flower wrung her hands nervously.

'Everyone is doing the same, Lady. They are even searching for salt grass in the lake. They eat the weeds. They eat dirt and bricks, and some eat their sandals.'

Jewel held up one of her sandals, repaired in several places. She would have thrown them away but now they were all she had. Perhaps the Mexica were returning to their roots as Falling Eagle believed. But even then, when they were poor and starving, when they too ate anything that moved, the stories did not say that they had eaten their sandals.

She climbed up the stairs to the room she shared with Ant Flower now. Seventy pebbles covered the floor by her sleeping mat. They had been seventy days in this hell. This was where they would die. There was nothing more she could do. She would have to sell Ant Flower.

Wandering Coyote accused her of caring only for herself. A woman who let her mother starve would sell her own children. Jewel shut herself in her horrible room and did not see Wandering Coyote lead Ant Flower away.

It was Lizard who suggested she fight. After Marsh Lily's death, he had disappeared for three days. She knew he suffered Marsh Lily's loss terribly but he never spoke of her.

He warned Jewel that it was terrible out there. Women died every night fighting on the roofs. He carried messages regularly for Falling Eagle and fought feverishly day and night, sleeping where he could on the roofs he defended, or in an abandoned ruin. But he would lie awake in despair, seeing only Marsh Lily's ravaged body. He took her old woman's hands. They smelt of rose water and sweat.

'I doubt Falling Eagle would approve,' he said.

'He will never know.'

'I hope not. Just don't tell anyone who you are. They all hate our family.'

He took her in the morning to a market building next to the canal where captains handed out clothes and weapons and marshalled volunteers into groups. Some were sent into the murky water to remove the rubble from the lake, others to dig deep holes where the bridges had been removed.

She found herself forming part of a human chain to carry rocks and rubble onto the roofs for use as weapons. Most of the group were old women, although there were boys as young as six and two old priests. They carried out their tasks uncomplainingly. They were all thin. Most had lost their teeth. Some of the women had cut their hair to look like men. Jewel noticed how often the elderly warrior in charge counted them. One bent old women explained that every night left fewer women to fight. She took Jewel's hand.

'Here is a pretty hand that has not worked.'

Other women crowded round and stared. Jewel snatched her hand away.

'You are not one of *them*, are you?'

The woman had a weasel's face. The other women laughed kindly.

'Don't mind her. We are all equal here. We are all warriors.'

When they had collected the stones and piled them on the roofs overlooking the street, they climbed up, took their positions and waited. One held out chunks of meat, magically grilled. Was there really any wood left in the city? Was this animal or human? No one refused.

'The Tlaxcalans come at night,' explained Jewel's protector.

'In canoes,' said a boy.

They sat chewing the meat, waiting for footsteps on the street below before they launched their stones. They heard screams and the whistle of arrows. They smelt sulphur and a whiff of horse. One of the women pulled Jewel down beneath the parapet as an arrow flew past. The woman grinned a toothless smile.

'No deaths tonight.'

Everyone laughed.

The next night Wandering Coyote tried to stop Jewel, but she went out dressed as a boy, clinging to Lizard for she feared the streets of Tlatelolco even more than the Spanish. But when the beggars and the thieves and the starving saw two warriors, they smiled and let them pass. The blood in the streets turned the dust to mud. Jewel struggled not to hold her nose. A warrior would not hold his nose.

The women climbed onto the roofs and took up their positions. The boys – there were seven tonight – hid under the parapet with stones.

'When we hear them we fire together,' instructed the warrior in charge.

Below them they heard the rustle of feathers and the clatter of armour. Jewel drew back her bow.

'Fire!'

The volley of arrows arced and fell. Men screamed.

'Stones!' ordered the old woman.

The boys threw the rocks. Jewel ran to help them. When she heard the screams from below, she threw and threw and threw. She could not stop. She wanted to kill the whole of Tlaxcala and all the Spanish. The old woman pulled her back.

'They are dead or they have fled. This is one of the few fights we have won.'

They scrambled down to the street and dumped the bodies in the canal. One old woman gazed wistfully at the corpses.

'We should eat them. Some do.'

Jewel felt sick. She would rather starve than eat a Tlaxcalan. But when someone offered her a chunk of roasted flesh, she swallowed it whole and did not ask where it came from.

They fought for the next five days and nights, using their tricks

254

and disguises, but every day brought the Spanish closer. On the sixth day their commander told them that the gods had spoken. They advised Falling Eagle to send in the Quetzal Owl. This was the ultimate weapon. The Quetzal Owl was an ordinary man, a captain in war, a dyer by trade who would dress himself in the hallowed feathers and sacrifice himself for his people. The very sight of him in his feathers, clasping the sacred arrow, the 'Serpent of Fire', struck terror into every heart. Tomorrow they would accompany the Quetzal Owl. Whatever the outcome, they would all be there.

No one wanted to buy Ant Flower.

'It is you we should sell,' insisted Wandering Coyote, as Ant Flower returned forlornly, limping with a thorn in her foot and lice in her hair. 'We could raise a few handfuls of maize even with your scrawny body.'

Jewel ignored his insults and trained to fight with the Quetzal Owl, but Ant Flower and Wandering Coyote barricaded the gate. Even Lizard said she must not go.

'If you can go, why not me?' asked Jewel.

'It is not certain that the Quetzal Owl will work,' Lizard told her.

'It is magic! How can it not work?'

Lizard said nothing. He made sure his quiver was full of arrows and his sling bag full of stones. 'We can only hope the gods do not abandon us this time,' he said sadly. 'The priests assure us this is the time to strike.'

'You will return Lizard, won't you?' she begged.

He shrugged his shoulders. 'Does it matter if I don't? At least I will die honourably.'

'What about those of us who are left behind?'

'Wandering Coyote has one canoe left. You must go with him. He is a good man with friends in many places.

'I cannot leave Falling Eagle!'

'If the Quetzal Owl fails, he fails too. He will want you to go with Wandering Coyote.'

'Why doesn't Falling Eagle come to say goodbye?' cried Jewel. Wandering Coyote took her arm.

'Be thankful you travel with a merchant. I can pass you off as slaves.'

'Slaves?'

'That is what you will be if you stay here. In fact, I am disposed to leave now, before the Quetzal Owl fights.'

'No! I will not!'

'What choice do you have?'

The yelling, the drums and the shouting grew louder. Sometimes it faded and then rose to a crescendo, but it never stopped.

'If the Quetzal Owl fails, I will come with you.'

Wandering Coyote sighed.

'That may be too late.'

They huddled together and listened to the cries and moans from beyond the wall. For the last two nights someone had knocked desperately on the door. Tonight the sound had stopped.

Lizard dressed in his padded armour. He carried his spear thrower, his bow, arrows and sling. His fellow warriors were scrawny youths, old men and women and children. Some of them limped. Some used sticks. Anyone who could walk was there. They massed in the square to greet the Quetzal Owl.

He came with a great fanfare of trumpets, escorted by his captains. He stood in the centre of the market square, cleared now of bodies, while Falling Eagle dressed him in a cloak of brilliant quetzal feathers. He solemnly took his holy weapons, an arrow tipped with obsidian set on a long shaft. This was the the 'Serpent of Fire'. It would unleash all the power of Huitzilopochtli, but if it touched the earth its magic would die.

The whole of Tlatelolco followed the Quetzal Owl to the edge of the canal. The beggars, the blind, the deaf, the dying, the orphans. They hobbled. They pushed, they shoved, but none of them spoke. They prayed in silence that this desperate attempt would at last bring them the victory they deserved. They watched the Quetzal

Owl climb onto a roof overlooking Tenochtitlan. He perched there, a giant bird, a divine creature. The Tlaxcalans scattered. The Spanish gawped. Falling Eagle blew his sacred horn. The crowd held its breath. A wind off the lake ruffled the divine feathers. The Quetzal Owl lifted his wings and jumped. The sacred arrow rose and fell, rose and fell, and then it rose in one last arc and plunged to the ground.

The silence was shocking. Everything stopped. Even the dying stifled their cries. Huitzilopochtli had spoken. The 'Serpent of Fire' was gone for ever. Lizard climbed the ladder and jumped with the warriors.

That night, at midnight, a ball of flame whirled through the sky before it circled the dike and dropped into the lake. It was a sign the world would end. Those who could walk escaped in the dark, wading through the water with their children on their shoulders. Others threw themselves and their families into the lake. Some left in canoes.

In Wandering Coyote's house, only three of them were left to watch the fearful omen, aware that the Tlaxcalans were waiting like hungry coyotes outside the walls. There was no news of Falling Eagle. Nothing had been heard of Lizard. Wandering Coyote wanted to leave before the Tlaxcalans arrived. He insisted Falling Eagle was dead.

Jewel hovered uselessly, watching Ant Flower pick up her baskets. She felt dead inside. She imagined Falling Eagle's body lying on the other side of the wall . . . The gate crashed open. One of Falling Eagle's lords stood on the threshold. Jewel and Wandering Coyote clung together, laughing with relief. The lord held out a ragged rain cloak. Jewel was to disguise herself as an old woman. There was no room in the canoes for Wandering Coyote but the lord reluctantly agreed to take Ant Flower. Wandering Coyote hugged Jewel. Now he felt sorry to see her go. He would be alone. He would miss them all. He would miss their arguments.

Outside the rain had turned the streets into a quagmire. Jewel and Ant Flower held hands and followed their guide, weaving their way through the ruins of the houses, in and out of the short cuts in the walls, holding their noses, ignoring the beggars who pursued them, who pulled at their clothes, undeceived by their disguise.

When they reached a modest one-storey house in a side street, the guide quickly ushered them inside. Part of the roof had fallen in. One wall was pockmarked with holes. In the courtyard an open hearth showed signs of recent use. Falling Eagle emerged to greet them. Jewel gasped. His face was gaunt but his bloodshot eyes lit up when they saw her. With him were several officials and women and children who greeted Jewel warmly, their voices oscillating over the mud floors. Falling Eagle took Jewel's hand and led her to a room at the back of the house where they would spend the night. A battered carved screen divided the room into two. Canoes were ready and would leave at first light.

'So we all flee,' she said sadly. It was not how she expected it to end.

'We don't flee,' said Falling Eagle. 'We will regroup and return to fight the Spanish. I offered Don Hernán tribute but he refused it. The priests still promise victory. But we are not here to talk about war.'

She untied her skirt quickly. How desperately she wanted him. She itched like a harlot, as if she had rubbed her parts with chillies. She tried not to make a noise. She could hear snoring behind the screen.

'So little of you to love now,' murmured Falling Eagle.

He put his cloak onto the damp ground and lowered her onto it. It was pitch dark. There were no torches to light their journey. She wanted to look at him.

'It is better this way,' he murmured. 'In the dark we can imagine each other as we used to be.'

They were impatient to seek comfort in each other. Her hands slid round over his shoulders, down to his back to cup his buttocks and fit herself around him. At least Falling Eagle's *tepuli* was still plump, unlike the rest of him. They could still pleasure each other. And what better pleasure was there? Although at this moment she might have chosen food.

'I know what you are thinking,' chuckled Falling Eagle. 'I can read your mind.'

'In the dark?'

'It is clearer in the dark.'

'I did not speak.'

'You do not need to.' He laughed. 'I too might prefer food.'

They lay comfortably together despite the rain leaking through the roof. Neither of them could sleep. Tomorrow was the day they would flee their city and leave their lives behind.

'Who will shelter us now?' she whispered.

'We go beyond the hills of Tepeyac. There we will cross the lake where it is narrow. If necessary we go south.'

He knew that, even if they managed to escape, they would have to travel far to escape the Spanish. And it was uncertain whether any of the other people would welcome them.

'Look. We have fought bravely for eighty days. Eighty days with little food or water and yet some of us survive. Like our ancestors, we endure. The histories will speak well of us. We did not give in. We fought to the end. Were it not for my people, I would fight to the death, but when I see how they suffer, it is best we give in now.'

'But we are escaping. They are not.'

'Some of them have left already. It is me Don Hernán wants. He will spare our people.'

'The Tlaxcalans won't.'

'I have sent messengers to plead with Don Hernán. Only he can control them now.'

The rain fell heavily. Puddles of water covered the floor of their shelter.

'There is something missing,' she said. 'The frogs. The frogs have gone. They have all been eaten.'

She tried to make herself comfortable on the rough ground but the stones and rubble clashed with her bones. She tried to sleep but her mind raced. Her life passed before her. There were things that had to be said.

'Are you awake?' she whispered.

The snoring on the other side of the screen ceased.

'Yes.'

'I have fought like a warrior.'

He did not speak.

'Are you cross?'

'No, I am proud, although I would certainly have forbidden it.'

'I liked being a warrior. I enjoyed killing.'

'We are at war,' he reminded her. 'People kill in war.'

'But I have changed for ever.'

'You will change back when this is over.' He squeezed her fondly. 'You are the chief wife of the ruler of the Mexica. You must be the mother of warriors.'

She knew she could never be the same person again. She was someone else now, part boy, part woman, no longer the favourite daughter of an emperor.

'I too have a secret,' he said. 'I have kept it from you far too long.'

'Tell me.'

'I will tell you when we are safely in Tepeyac.'

She heard scratching in the thatched roof and held his hand tightly. She was sure it was demons. He turned desperately to her. He covered her body, crushing her so hard that her bones cracked. He drunk thirstily from her mouth. He devoured her. He took every bit of her, as if this were the last time he would ever see her, as if death waited for them out there on the lake. He did not want to separate himself from her. From the other side of the screen, it sounded as if the other couple were doing the same.

'Whatever happens to us,' he whispered into her hair. 'Even if we are separated, you must survive. You must help your people. Don Hernán has no fight with you.'

'I cannot live without you. I would rather die!'

'Hush,' he murmured. He held her close and stroked her face like her father did when she had childish tantrums.

They rose while it was still dark. She tied back her hair. He hung her rain cloak over her. She stood a moment, looking around the shack, a strange kind of love nest. Now it smelt of them. She took his hand.

'You see. We leave something of us behind.'

He did not see anything.

'Our smell,' she said.

He laughed. They made their way to a cove where her father's mahogany barque was moored. Now the brilliant green feathers were tattered and faded and the some of the golden bells were missing. Around them people were loading their treasures into canoes. A lord she did not recognise helped Jewel into the barge where she squeezed onto the polished seats with Ant Flower, waiting while the boat filled with women and children and various lords. The rowers pushed the boat through the reeds. Past the reeds, they dipped the paddles easing their passage out into the lake. They saw, through the rain, the welcoming shapes of the hills of Tepeyac. They were on their way. Jewel smiled and put her arm around Ant Flower. She stared back at the whitewashed city. It seemed to float above the mist. Would the Spanish destroy it?

They turned north towards the mountains. The golden bells on the canopy tinkled louder and louder. Jewel stood up and tried to silence them. But they rang furiously, echoing through the mist. Suddenly, in the reeds behind them, flashed the white of sails.

'Faster!' urged Falling Eagle.

The barge shot forward. The bells protested. A cannon opened its mouth. The stone that landed next to the barge turned the water into a whirlpool. The boatmen smashed the water with their paddles in their rush to escape. Falling Eagle drummed his hands impatiently against the side of the barge to encourage the struggling paddles. The children began to cry. The women held them tightly and willed the mountains to come closer. Two Spanish boats raced at them. Falling Eagle grabbed his shield and his spear and ordered an attack. The Spanish drew alongside. Another manoeuvred in behind, trapping them. Jewel leapt from her seat, but one of the women pulled her down.

'Lady, do not draw attention to yourself or they will take you too.'

The soldiers dragged Falling Eagle onto the shore. Falling Eagle lunged at Don Hernán. He pulled the dagger from Don Hernán's belt and held it out to him.

'Go on, kill me.'

'No!'

No one heard Jewel for the clap of thunder which exploded above them. Lightning forked the sky as Tlaloc showed his anger. She broke away from the women, jumped onto the jetty and ran through the cordon of surprised Spanish soldiers.

'Falling Eagle!' she shouted. She threw herself into his arms.

He smiled and stroked her face with his hands.

'Don't worry about me, Jewel.'

A Spanish soldier tried to push her away. She saw Don Hernán out of the corner of her eye. She saw the dagger back in his belt.

'No,' whispered Falling Eagle, 'it will only make things worse. Take care of the people. Do your best for them.'

'No!'

The soldiers chained his hands and dragged him away.

'No!' she screamed again. How she hated all these people. She screamed in Nahuatl. She invoked the curses of the gods. Ant Flower's small hand pulled at her skirt.

'It will do no good, Lady. It will only make them want you more.'

They held hands and, prodded by soldiers, stumbled past women sprawled in the mud where impatient Tlaxcalans awaited their turn. A soldier pushed her into the direction of the Spanish camp. He pushed Ant Flower away. One of the soldiers hit her with his musket. The little dwarf stumbled and fell to the ground.

'Ant Flower!' cried Jewel, struggling to escape the hands that held her. But Ant Flower did not rise. She lay in a crumpled heap in the dirt.

Don Hernán sat in his chair under a crimson canopy, an emperor on his throne. He showed no signs of suffering. He stared at the bedraggled girl standing in front of him.

'So,' he said, speaking through Malinalli, 'we have found you. Your father gave you into my care. I would be negligent if I did not honour my promise.'

The thunder still echoed over the city. Jewel could hardly hear herself speak. She held herself erect and looked beyond Don Hernán through a small gap in the canopy to the great temple.

'Don Hernán speaks to you.'

Jewell ignored the girl. What was there to say? She had lost everything, her husband, her sister, her dwarf, her mother, her father, her people, her home.

'The little lady has lost her voice then?' inquired Don Hernán. 'It must be from all that terrible yelling.' He beckoned to a soldier. 'You are too thin. Perhaps some food will revive you.'

The food appeared steaming in a dish, enough to feed four of them in Tlatelolco. Don Hernán stepped from his throne and held the bowl in front of her. The smell made her hungry and nauseous at the same time. She tried to ignore the food, to show Don Hernán that she was not starving.

'Eat!' commanded Don Hernán. He brought a stool and pushed her onto it. She noticed two fingers were missing from his right hand. She took the bowl and ate slowly, to show him that she was not hungry at all. Don Hernán watched her.

'Is there anything else we can do for you, apart from offering you a wash?'

He held a white cotton cloth over his nose, for he seemed to find her smell offensive. She knew she must stink, for the Spanish were not usually fussy about body odours.

'Perhaps you know where your father's treasure is hidden?'

How she hated the Spanish. She took a bite and chewed slowly.

She saw his fingers, five on the left hand, drumming on the side of his chair.

'How should I know?'

She took another bite. His fingers continued impatiently. He seemed annoyed.

'There was treasure in the canoes. Don Hernán asks if that was all,' prompted Malinalli.

Jewel swallowed her mouthful.

'Pantitlan swallowed the treasure.'

'Pantitlan?'

'The whirlpool.'

'You speak in riddles,' complained Malinalli.

'Not at all. If you were a true Mexica,' she noticed the girl flinch, 'you would know that Pantitlan is a whirlpool. The treasures were all thrown into the whirlpool.' She pointed towards the lake. 'Out there in the lake. No doubt someone could dive into the whirlpool and retrieve it.'

After all, people who had descended into a volcano for sulphur would not be deterred by a whirlpool. She saw how she infuriated the girl. Did Don Hernán not know that gold was useless, that you could not eat it, that it could not even buy food in Tlatelolco? Gods' shit, that's what it was. Shit. She took off her bangles and threw them onto the ground watching them roll towards the girl but the girl ignored them.

'No doubt some woman has hidden the treasure in her skirt.'

She did not have to look at Malinalli to feel her anger at this insult. She had called the girl a whore. She felt rather pleased with herself. Her only weapon now was her tongue. Inside she smiled. But outside her face was expressionless. Again Don Hernán asked if there were anything she wanted. Of course she wanted her husband. Where had they hidden him?

'I want my dwarf.'

'Your dwarf?' echoed Don Hernán. 'What odd playmates you keep.'

He turned towards two soldiers and said something. Both men bowed and left. Perhaps she should ask for more.

'Since you ask,' she said, 'I want my husband. I want my home. I want my people. I want my country.'

She stared boldly at Don Hernán. She saw, too late, how this attracted him.

'These are unreasonable requests,' said Malinalli.

'I don't think so. They are all within Don Hernán's power.'

'Don't be foolish,' said Malinalli.

Don Hernán stood in front of Jewel. His eyes bored through her sodden cloak to the bones beneath. What a relief she was no longer attractive. But she seemed to amuse Don Hernán whereas it had been her intention to annoy him. Only the girl seemed angry.

'You try Don Hernán's patience.'

'There is something else I want. I want my people to be allowed to leave Tlatelolco. Only Don Hernán can permit this.'

'Your husband has already made this request. The causeways have been opened.'

'What has happened to my husband?'

Malinalli thought for a moment as if deciding how to reply.

'He is alive. He is a coward who abandons his people.'

'Liar!'

How she wanted to wipe the smile from that confident face, to knock out those perfect teeth.

'Traitor!' she shouted again.

Don Hernán rose from his chair and called two women to show Jewel to a small room. There they removed her wet clothes, bathed her and made her comfortable. Another woman brought fresh clothes. With her clean hair, her scrubbed body and her full stomach, Jewel felt almost normal.

And yet nothing was normal, nor would it ever be again. She was utterly alone, one of a small number of Mexica who had survived to witness their defeat. There would be no return to the past. She curled up on her mat listening to the strange sounds – the Spanish were such noisy people – and the pleasant melody of their music which drifted up from the floor below. She could not sleep. If she closed her eyes she saw visions that terrified her. She saw Marsh Lily bleeding between her legs. She saw women crawling from their captors and children's' bodies floating in the lake. She lay with her eyes open to avoid the visions and to be ready should Don Hernán surprise her.

In the morning the maids woke her without any of Ant Flower's gentleness. They dressed her and took her again to Don Hernán. She saw that her brother Handful of Reeds stood beside him. Don Hernán offered food and took her hand and pleaded to know where Falling Eagle's gold was hidden. She said nothing. She knew nothing. Don Hernán considered her for a moment. Then he told her she would be moving to live with her brother.

'What will you do with our city?'

'Burn it. Burn the houses, the bodies, the disease. And then we will start again. We will get rid of every stain, every spot of blood, every odour of sacrifice and then we will rebuild it as a Christian city.'

He held his white cloth in front of his nose. He did not notice when she left the room.

Part Four

Aftermath 1523–1527

Coyoacan, Mexico – 1523

The table in front of Jewel groaned with turkey and bread and some strange meat called pork. She had been surprised to find this house still standing. Once it would have been a modest house. Now it seemed the most luxurious palace in the world. She knew the owner, a Mexica lord who had 'stepped on his face', the Nahuatl expression for a man who had disgraced himself. Like many others here at this dinner this man seemed ill at ease, as if his loyalty to the Spanish had extracted its price.

Don Hernán fed her titbits. Tonight he was all over her, brushing her sleeve, peering down her bodice, making sure her glass was full. And yet she felt desperate. She did not know how to fend off her elderly suitor, more than twice her age. She saw how Malinalli pretended not to notice, although her eyes never left Don Hernán. She can have him, thought Jewel, but her brother Handful of Reeds, a loyal supporter of Don Hernán and a bully, encouraged a relationship between them. She was afraid of Handful of Reeds.

On the other side of the table, Lizard sat squashed between Juan and Angry Turkey, a Tlaxcalan, who had rescued Lizard when he jumped with the Quetzal Owl. Now they were firm friends, but it seemed that their friendship went back even further, to when they had shared a canoe. She did not know the whole story. Father Olmedo said it showed how God had saved Lizard for a purpose.

There were so many guests here that few of them could find

seats and some of them walked on the tables, for the Spanish had no manners. Their red drink turned many of them into monsters as the night progressed, and some of them fell down the steps into the street. Everyone shouted at each other. In the corner by the entrance, a group of soldiers gambled and some of them openly fondled the Mexica maids. Four Spanish women were making exhibitions of themselves, encouraged by the noisy claps and taunts of the men. No one seemed to be in charge and everyone spoke freely, even challenging Don Hernán. As for their excruciating table manners, this only added to the general chaos. Even the women were boisterous and the priest, Father Olmedo, joined in, lifting his skirts and tapping his feet in time to the music and drinking copious cups of wine. Her father would never have tolerated such bawdy behaviour. When the Mexica drank on feast days they were never as vulgar as this.

Despite Lizard's presence, Jewel felt utterly alone, abandoned to the coarse noisy Spanish and Mexica lords whom she loathed. Her head swam from the heat and the wine. She was tired by her monthly bleed which had returned. Her clothes felt tight. She wanted to return to her room to be alone, but her brother watched her every move and Don Hernán persisted in his attentions, fingering her arms, whispering in her ear. How old he seemed with his leathery face and lank hair. She had resisted him for two years and it became more difficult every day. He pressed gifts on her, a shawl made of a soft fabric, he called it 'silk', and a woven mat which he said was a 'Turkey rug', which he laid out on her floor, and a necklace of white pearls, which he had hung around her neck, his fingers lingering on her skin like a lover's. These were all gifts she liked. He leant over and filled her cup again, lifting his own and tinkling it against hers.

Handful of Reeds never ceased to remind her of her duty to please Don Hernán to ask for her lands in Tacuba and become a Christian to prove her loyalty to the Spanish. Handful of Reeds, who strutted around in Spanish clothes and rode a horse in Don Hernán's processions, had a new name, Don Pedro Montezuma.

Once when she had shouted that he was nothing more than a Spanish slave, always at his master's beck and call, he had shaken her furiously, tearing her silk skirt, another gift from Don Hernán.

'Whose food do you think you eat?' he shouted. 'Whose house do you live in?'

He sounded so like Wandering Coyote that she had collapsed in a heap on the floor weeping, wondering where Wandering Coyote and Ant Flower were now.

'You can't make me eat,' she told her brother, 'and you can't make me wear Spanish clothes.'

But after two days closeted in her small dark room, when the old terrible hunger returned, when she could have eaten her own flesh, she gave in.

How noisy everyone was, except for Malinalli, who watched her constantly. She was tired of resisting, as she was tired of arguing with Father Olmedo, who was most persuasive. And there was a good reason for resisting the new God. Don Hernán would only sleep with Christian women. Before submitting to Don Hernán, a woman had to submit to his God. Yet it had not helped her that she had successfully resisted both. It had not brought her closer to Falling Eagle, and she was powerless to help her people, now homeless and hungry, treated like slaves in their own city. She felt Don Hernán's fingers stroke the back of her neck where the bodice did not quite fit.

She tried to smile. There was nothing she desired in this wiry manipulative old man but she wanted to see her husband. She knew Falling Eagle was held captive with five councillors in a small storehouse near the temple and, whenever she could, she had taken that route in the hope of catching sight of him. It had been two long years since they had touched or spoken. Two years of resistance that had achieved nothing. It was time to be sensible, as Handful of Reeds reminded her constantly.

The strings started. People jumped up to sing. A noisy group of dancers swirled around her table. She saw Doña María draw Lizard into her rowdy group of dancers. Were all Spanish women as free as Doña María? Would she be as free if she slept with Don Hernán? She felt his hands on her necklace.

'I shall give you diamonds to replace these crystals.'

She did not like the hard brittle stones with no flaws in them, like the stone he wore on his finger. She did not want diamonds but she wanted her husband. She drank some more wine. It altered the mind like the black mushrooms her father imbibed. The alteration was brief but it helped show her what she had to do. If she pleased everyone, she might please herself. Her father had told her that she could separate her tongue and her heart. The price of freedom was to please Don Hernán. She was tired of everything. Only she could help herself. Sometimes at night she heard her father telling her to change, to adapt to a different kind of future. She smiled her most winning smile.

'I have decided to be baptised.'

Don Hernán raised his glass. His face was flushed.

'Lady Jewel has decided to accept the true God.'

Her brother smiled and raised his glass. Everyone congratulated her. Father Olmedo promised her her own prayer book and lessons in Spanish. Doña María promised friendship. Malinalli said nothing.

Jewel returned with her brother to their house in Coyoacan. The wine and her decision had made him oddly exuberant. Yet he was not an exuberant man. Like the other Mexica nobles who strutted around Coyoacan, he was a calculating opportunist who lived in a house whose owner had fled because he supported Falling Eagle.

'You know what to ask for,' he reminded her.

She would ask to see her husband.

'Yes. I will ask for my lands in Tacuba.'

'At last you see sense.'

She sat down in a chair and closed her eyes.

'The priest will come to prepare you tomorrow. And if you were to bear a son . . .'

'Get out!' she screamed. 'Get out!'

'You forget whose house this is.'

'It belongs to a true warrior.'

He hit her. Then he pushed his way through the brocade curtains that replaced the beads and bells over the door. She stayed in the chair all night listening to the howls of the coyotes. She had heard that they feasted on the bodies of Mexica slaves thrown out at night.

'She is very beautiful, your cousin,' said Angry Turkey as they walked home. Lizard agreed. By all accounts Don Hernán was a tireless lover. He did not envy Jewel, although many Mexica women suffered far worse fates.

When he thought of his people homeless, starving, forced into bondage, he felt ashamed of his full stomach. He could never stop gorging himself at these dinners in case it might be his last meal. Never could he forget that terrible hunger or the pleasure of his first meal. Even now, two years later, those memories were still horribly vivid. It surprised him how easily he had slipped into his new life, as if the past had never existed. But it was because of his past that the Spanish made him welcome. He was a cousin of the great Montezuma whom they remembered fondly. There were many of his relations here at the new court, most of whom Lizard despised, especially his brother, the new Woman Snake who had ingratiated himself with Don Hernán. Apart from Angry Turkey and perhaps Juan, he preferred the company of the horses he attended in the stables. He had become quite a horseman.

It was strange too that he did not mourn the old gods. Nor was he in a hurry to embrace the new one. For now, a godless life sufficed despite the blandishments of Father Olmedo, who asked whether Lizard wished to work with horses forever when a brilliant future as a priest and scholar awaited him.

Angry Turkey put his arm through Lizard's.

'Your life will improve if you become a Christian.'

'Is that why you are a Christian?'

Angry Turkey laughed.

'I saw which way the wind was blowing. One god is like another and this one does not demand sacrifice. We Tlaxcalans were fed up being sacrificed to the Mexica gods.'

'You were a novice once.'

'There was no other choice for a poor country boy. I am a realist. The Mexica will never take control again. You must change with the times.'

'And become like those rapacious relatives of mine who crawl to the Spanish.'

'They are realists too. But, if you wish to help your people, as you tell me you do, you will have to become a Christian. You are powerless without their god.'

'I know you are right. I am still living in the old times.'

'You sit up half the night writing about them.'

'Someone has to tell the world about us.'

'Just think. If you learnt to write the Spanish way, you could tell the world about us using their words.'

'That is what Father Olmedo says.'

'Father Olmedo is right.'

In the morning Father Olmedo came to prepare Jewel for baptism. He was a man to whom words came easily. He spoke often and fondly of Don Hernán. He pulled his long skirts together and sat down. His sandals were too small. One big toe hung over the sole. Perhaps that was why he moved so clumsily. This morning he wasted no time on pleasantries. He came straight to the point.

'Don Hernán is not a bad man, although many judge him so.'

He spoke slowly so Jewel could understand. Malinalli stood by his side ready to translate if necessary. Malinalli seemed to be everywhere. How many Malinallis were there?

'He does not force himself on women.' Father Olmedo peered at Jewel. Sometimes he reminded her of the old Woman Snake, although he was much younger.

'I hear they force themselves on him,' she said, staring at Malinalli who sat in on all their conversations – Jewel's Spanish was not perfect.

'He has a wife.'

'I am not seeking marriage.'

274

Father Olmedo did not listen, for his words were in a hurry to escape from his mouth.

'Don Hernán is a man who rewards his friends. You could use your influence to help your people, bring the true God to them. He is generous.'

'He was not so generous during the siege. He massacred my people.'

She remembered Marsh Lily's fouled body. Father Olmedo played with the cross tied around his waist.

'Don Hernán never planned to destroy the Mexica. He admires them.'

'Why then does he destroy women and children? Why does your merciful God permit such slaughter?'

Jewel had learned of the utter destruction of Tlatelolco. No woman was safe. The most beautiful had been taken away. Youths were branded on their cheeks and their mouths with irons. And now these brave warriors worked as errand boys for their captors.

'It was the Tlaxcalans who went on the rampage, not us,' mumbled Father Olmedo defensively.

'That is no excuse.'

Father Olmedo was Don Hernán's personal priest and confessor. He defended him always.

'Look,' he said shortly, 'none of us liked what the Tlaxcalans did. It was impossible to stop them. I know Don Hernán regrets their actions and has asked God's forgiveness, but they wanted their revenge. You Mexica brought this on yourselves, although I pray daily for the women and children. Your husband could have prevented this if he had accepted Don Hernán's many offers of peace.

She said nothing. There was no point in arguing. Father Olmedo would never understand.

'I know how upset you are,' consoled Father Olmedo. 'Think of this as a new beginning.' He patted her hand. 'We should be friends, learn from each other. Don Hernán plans to build a new city here, a city dedicated to the true God. It will not smell of blood and death. It will be fresh and clean, a city of flowers. He has already started. He is using your people to build it. Think of a city belonging to both our people.'

'And what about my husband? Is there room in this city for him?'

Father Olmedo seemed embarrassed.

'I have tried to negotiate on your behalf. I have tried to arrange a visit. But in this respect, Don Hernán has not agreed.'

'He is in good health?'

'All things considered, yes. I am sad to see Falling Eagle a prisoner. I admire him for his courage. If he had surrendered, Don Hernán might have been more merciful.'

'You mean, if Falling Eagle had given him the gold he requests?'

Her rudeness only encouraged Father Olmedo.

'Perhaps you could persuade Falling Eagle.' He leant close. 'Don Hernán is not unreasonable. If you are wise you will learn to work with him, even to like him.'

She wondered if he had said the same words to Malinalli.

'And,' – he rose from his seat – 'if you can tell him where your father's treasure is hidden, you will reap the benefit.'

'As if I would know!' she replied bitterly.

She was desperate to see her husband, to save him if she could. She knew of no hidden gold. There was only one way. First submit to the God, then to the man. She would become a woman of joy. She would use her body to make her own way in life and she would have her own home far away from her brother.

Father Olmedo opened his book. She memorised the responses. They were in another language, a language of dead people which she did not understand. Father Olmedo called it Latin. She wondered whether Nahuatl would become a dead language one day.

She dressed in white and made her way to the chapel with the five women and two men whom Father Olmedo was to baptise on the same day. With Don Hernán as her godfather and Malinalli as her reluctant godmother, she made her promises to the new God. As the holy water washed her old life from her, and her demons were expelled, she smiled, not at the hope of eternal life, but at

276

the prospect of freedom. After the ceremony, Don Hernán presented her with a gold medallion of his goddess. He held out his hand.

'Welcome to the true God, Doña Isobel.'

She had changed her name and she did not like it. She wanted to be Jewel, the favourite daughter of an emperor. But she was Isobel – whore, mistress to a conqueror, soon to betray her husband.

In Don Hernán's house, a handsome building made of red tezontle stone, Jewel was given a small room under the roof. Two maids prepared her. They removed her clothes and bathed her with scented water. Neither spoke nor smiled nor made any gesture of friendship. How often had they prepared other women in this way? She stood mute while they hung a white shift over her shoulders and wove sweet jasmine in her hair. Jasmine, her father's favourite flower. She broke down sobbing.

'It could be worse,' said one of the maids. 'You do not suffer like we do. You will not be raped.'

'I would not object,' said the other. 'It is well known that Don Hernán is a good lover.'

She waggled her hips. How they hate me, thought Jewel. Don Hernán was her only protection now. She heard her father telling her to save herself and save her people. She wanted to save her husband. But tonight she must forget him. She must empty her mind and submit. She prayed quietly to the new God. She felt sure he would listen to a new subject.

Down the stairs, along a corridor she found herself in a large room opening onto a balcony where Don Hernán sat in a tall Spanish chair. Turkey rugs were scattered over the floor. Against the wall was a carved raised bed. The Spanish did not sleep on mats on the floor. On the table beside the bed was a flagon of water, some wine and a new delicacy, sweet spiced plums. Don Hernán smiled and held out his hand.

'Sit here.'

He pulled out another chair. If only he would get on with it, she thought. She wanted to do the deed and return to her little room. How did women of joy behave? Were there any left here in the city? But she smiled as if this were the night she had been waiting for, and took the glass of wine he offered. His hand with its missing fingers lay possessively on her arm. He made no move to undress her. Did Don Hernán have trouble with his *tepuli*? She did not think of Don Hernán as a patient man yet Lizard had told her, with reluctant admiration, how patiently Don Hernán had waited to take the lands of the Mexica. Perhaps his tactics with women were similar. But she was impatient to get the evening over with. She considered whether to make the first move then thought it unwise. She did not know the rules. She did not speak his language well.

Don Hernán poured more wine into her cup. She felt warm and dizzy and confused. He led her to the bed where he undressed her slowly. He did not seem in any hurry. He pulled off his own boots but left the leather pouch which covered his parts.

'Untie me, Isobel,' he said.

She untied the straps and removed the pouch. Then she eased down his trousers. He stood there in his top, with his white parts protruding stoutly. His pouch had not exaggerated. She turned away but he made her look at him. Then he pushed her head down and pressed her face between his legs. He smelt of salt and sweat and horse. He raised her head and shoved her onto the bed. She kept her legs together. As he forced them apart with his fingers, she tried again to think of other things, how it would soon be over. But Don Hernán demonstrated the stamina he had shown in war. She lay there looking at the beams in the ceiling, reflecting on the odd experience of not residing in her own body, as if she were up there on the ceiling looking down upon herself, as if she had eaten sacred mushrooms.

'Isobel!' he whispered as he put his mouth over hers, as if he owned her. But he did own her. He could do what he liked with her. She saw the young Earth Mother, Teteo Inan, flayed, bleeding, sacrificed to save the world. She too sacrificed herself to save Falling Eagle but her sacrifice was tame compared to the Earth Mother's.

She waited until she could hear him snoring, then she wrapped her white skirt between her legs to wipe him away and went to wash. After she had wiped herself clean and washed every bit of him away, she climbed up onto the roof. A full moon hung in the sky. She could just make out the rabbit, the sign of love. Did Falling Eagle still love her?

She heard footsteps. She could tell who it was by his smell.

'Isobel, what are you looking at?'

A naked Don Hernán stood there, looking around as if he expected to find another man.

'The moon. She is the sister of the sun. Every day they fight for control of the world.'

He laughed.

'You are a Christian now. You must forget those superstitions.'

She followed him back to bed. In the morning he woke ready to use her again. This time he took her from behind like a dog. She felt used, dirty, worse than a woman of joy. She ached from the shame of it. She curled up under the bedclothes until the maids arrived to wash her and dress her in the hated clothes. She had the whole morning until her Spanish lessons with Father Olmedo. She was free to please herself. But she felt lonely, without friends or companions. If she stayed inside, she would only weep all day.

She wandered out into the square, admiring the dignified red houses which were being built for the Spanish. She could not believe that no one stopped her. She was free to go where she pleased. She strolled into her father's old gardens at Coyoacan. Her gardens now. He had left them to her.

Here, where some calm remained, Spanish men and women walked hand in hand. Such intimate behaviour shocked her. A Mexica girl never held hands with a man in public. But the Spanish greeted her warmly and some of them knew her name. 'Doña Isobel,' they said deferentially. She liked that. She liked being an emperor's daughter and the Spanish did not hate her father as his own people did. Now she was a Christian and a princess, she was doubly welcome.

She kept to the paths she knew shaded by tall cypress trees. The stone water dog was headless now. A green stone grasshopper crouched in the grass. The lake was still busy with feeding birds. The poinsettia hedges had fallen over, but some of her father's presence lingered. She sat down on a seat and felt the sun on her face. She saw, in the actions of the gardener, her father bending over to inspect his plants. The gardener even looked like him. She tried unsuccessfully to stifle her sobs. The world had ended but she was still here. Her task now was to free Falling Eagle.

In the trees a pair of great-tailed grackle birds argued over territory. Something, probably an armadillo, rustled in the flower beds. The gardener turned and looked at her. Now she saw how thin he was, and when she greeted him the eyes that looked at her with hate were bloodshot and his face was scarred like Lizard's. His fate was worse than hers. She had a room and food. She had clothes. What did it matter how she was used? These were the people she must protect, but for this man she was the spoilt traitor daughter of a despised emperor. Now she noticed how weeds had engulfed her father's favourite dahlia beds and rubbish was scattered everywhere. She picked up her skirts and ran up the path and back to the safety of the perambulating Spanish, enjoying their new possessions. She saw a man watch her approach. He stepped forward. He had an open face and blue eyes. His black hair curled generously on his head. His beard was neat and carefully trimmed.

'Doña Isobel, has something upset you? Let me accompany you home.'

'Who are you?' she asked rudely.

The man bowed courteously. 'Juan Cano at your service, Princess.'

Lizard woke up shaking. Whenever he closed his eyes he saw Marsh Lily sprawled in the mud and heard the screams of women shamed by their captors. He kept his candle burning all night – its quiet steady light comforted him. It was a light, too, that encouraged work for it did not hiss and spit or smell. Father Olmedo, who provided Lizard with candles, had begun to teach him to write like a Spaniard. Spanish writing represented sounds, not symbols, and could convey a whole range of feelings. Not only could it tell the reader everything he wanted to know, but it was quicker to read and write. In Mexica writing you drew a black outline of the symbol of your word – a shield and an arrow for war or a throne under a diadem for a ruler or, for defeat, a burning temple roof with flames and smoke – and then you painstakingly laid the colours in flat washes within the black outlines. This was demanding work and, if done in haste, the washes smudged, escaping beyond their outlines, although this was never the case with Lizard's work.

Ever since the Spanish had ransacked and burnt Montezuma's library, Father Olmedo's interest in the Mexica histories had increased, which was why he was teaching Lizard, even though he had yet to become a Christian. A priest, newly arrived from the coast, had supervised the fires with all the zealousness of a madman. Don Hernán was away on an expedition and not even Father Olmedo could save the books. He had been as upset as Lizard at the loss of such knowledge. He regretted that not all priests were holy. In his own country of Spain terrible evils had been perpetrated; he was too ashamed to mention them. All he could do was to rewrite the books of the Mexica secretly, with Lizard's help. If Lizard could relate the stories, he, Father Olmedo, would write the words in Spanish, and one day they might even recreate the painted books. This was Lizard's dream too. It was the reason he sat up night after night learning to read and write like the Spanish.

He wondered whether the Mexica might, in a few years, have developed a system like the Spanish. A Mexica book was deciphered like a puzzle. You had to search the drawings for clues. Father Olmedo liked puzzles and clues and it was pleasing that he showed such interest in the ways of the Mexica and wanted to keep them alive. But there were many other priests who did not share his feelings. And there was another reason for learning to read and write. If Lizard became a Christian and learnt to read and write like the Spanish, he would be subject to and protected by their laws. He would become their equal. He could use those same laws to defend his people. Don Hernán had trained as a lawyer and used his skill to his advantage. It was no good fighting with bows and arrows. Words were powerful weapons. He could not wait any longer. If the price of this opportunity was the new God, he would accept.

He marvelled that it had taken Jewel so long. She had always been stubborn and it had done her no good. As Angry Turkey reminded him so often, the old times would never return. It was unlikely that Falling Eagle would escape, he was so closely guarded.

Lizard grabbed the candle and paced the room. There was comfort in movement. He walked forwards and backwards, watching the flame dance in his breath. He had not wanted to serve the old gods. He had hoped for escape and now it had come in an unexpected way. He had no status, no future, no country. He was a stable boy who looked after the horses. He knew he had no choice, but why did he still hesitate? Were the old gods still there? He knew that some of their statues had been saved and removed from the city, and that somewhere out there priests still worshipped them.

In the morning he made his way over the causeway to the communal steam baths which had been restored. Every day brought changes. Although the new layout for the city followed that of the old Tenochtitlán, spaces had been allocated for a cathedral, a prison, a palace for Don Hernán, monasteries, a granary, fountains, bridges and causeways, water conduits and sewers. A slaughterhouse was planned to kill the animals the Spanish ate, like the pork which arrived regularly from the coast. It was rumoured that water would be piped separately to each house, although Lizard thought it likely the water would be restricted to the city centre where the Spanish planned to live. The Mexica and the other tribes who had come to build the new city would be forced to live outside in the marshes. The Indian builders who reconstructed this city to Don Hernán's plan now used new building tools, nails, screws, steel knives, carts and barrows on wheels. It made the process of building quicker and easier. Yet so much of value had been lost. With the old rules gone and nothing to replace them but work, the Mexica sank into despair. Men left to their own devices filled the hours with pulque. Now drunkards and thieves roamed the streets. For the Mexica nothing was worse that a godless life without order or meaning.

Lizard observed how carefully the causeway had been repaired, how busy it was with the movements of carts now that wheels had been put into use and more horses had been shipped in. There was so much traffic he had to keep stepping out of the way. Out of habit he peered into the water. The water was clear. What had he expected? The corpses of the many Mexica who killed themselves in despair? Even those who had survived the sickness and the battles and the siege could not sometimes face the prospect of a life of slavery and took their own lives.

This morning he found the streets and the squares in the main city packed. Spanish priests preached from the steps of the temple. One by one people came forward for the holy water. This was another mass conversion. Father Olmedo, who did not approve of coercing people, refused to take part in these ceremonies. These were newly arrived priests, hungry for souls, ignorant of the history of the Mexica. Lizard skirted the Great Square, careful not be sucked into the crowd.

In the street of the Quails, an old man shuffled past. There was something familiar about him. Lizard looked for Wandering Coyote in all the old men he saw. This old man was poor. His feet were bare, his cloak made of cactus fibres.

'Wandering Coyote, is it you?'

A face stared back showing a hole where the nose should be. Pitted skin clung to an empty eye socket.

'Food,' begged the mouth. 'Food, young Lord.'

A Spaniard walked by. He kicked the old man into the mud.

'Lazy beggars all of them!'

Lizard bent to help the beggar. How he hated the Spanish and yet he was their prisoner, without a voice, without rights, unable to save his people.

Don Hernán knew how to pleasure a woman and he liked talking and sometimes he managed both at the same time. He drew Jewel into conversation, correcting her Spanish, asking about her people. His curiosity was as boundless as his energy and sometimes he used her three times in the same night. She knew she was not the only woman he pleasured. There was Malinalli, whose jealousy was so strong she could smell it.

But there was the comfort of freedom, more freedom than she had ever known. Now she had left her brother's home, she could go out when she wanted. She could talk to anyone. She could choose her own clothes. She learned to play dice and gamble and she enjoyed her daily Spanish lessons with Father Olmedo. She knew she could only influence Don Hernán if she spoke his language well. For when Don Hernán tired of her, as he would, she might hold his interest through her tongue, as Malinalli did so successfully. Sometimes she wondered whether Spanish words hovered in the air waiting for tongues to give them birth. She decided not. The words were simply too heavy to fly. She occupied her days and waited patiently for an opportunity to see her husband. She knew she must not appear desperate when she asked Don Hernán's favour. It must be handled lightly and before she fell from grace. So she learned how to please Don Hernán, how to say his name with a slight lisp which charmed him. Now she accompanied him everywhere, sitting next to him at feasts. He gave her more presents – a jade necklace, clothes, silver cups, a silk skirt, ribbons for her hair. At last, after a month, in the sure knowledge of Don Hernán's infatuation and after she had pleasured him in every way known to her, her opportunity came.

'What else can I give you, Isobel?'

She stroked his leathery skin scorched by too much sun. In the moonlight her hands were almost as white as a Spanish woman's. She chose her words carefully. She still struggled with her Spanish.

'There is one thing, Hernán,' she lisped, 'which would please me.'

'Just say it, my dear.'

'I would like to visit Falling Eagle. There are so few of my family left now. Of course, I am no longer his wife, but he is, remember, also my cousin.'

She fondled his 'worm' that nestled quietly between his legs. He had laughed heartily when she told him that the Mexica called that part of a man a 'worm'.

'Did he satisfy you as I do?'

'It was an arranged marriage,' she said quickly. 'A marriage for children not for passion. He did not expect to satisfy me.'

The silence seemed endless.

'I will make the arrangements.'

He smothered her with his body. She turned on her gasps of pleasure. She used to practise these for fun in the old days. And Ant Flower, who knew nothing about men, would judge the levels of ecstasy by the pitch of her voice. How they would laugh! How she missed Ant Flower.

Don Hernán did not forget his promise. Alonso de Grado turned up to accompany Jewel on her visit to Falling Eagle. There was something of the bully in Alonso de Grado and he always eyed her as if prospecting for her jewellery or her person or both. This morning she had dressed in the old clothes, white cotton with plain embroidery. How comfortable they were after the restrictions of Spanish clothes.

Alonso de Grado escorted her along the causeway to Tenochtitlán, carefully avoiding the horses. She noticed that the causeway had been repaired, but the lake was dirty and rubbish floated among the weeds. She had heard that the Spanish let their sewage flow into the lake. She passed through the Serpent Gate, still damaged from cannon shot. She crossed the Great Square to the store house next to the temple, a dank dark cell previously used to store the skins of the flayed and still reeking of them. How nervous she felt, like a bride meeting her husband for the first time. She had taken hours to choose her clothes.

The guard opened the door and let her in. There was no light inside the room and she had to wait for her eyes to accustom themselves. Falling Eagle's voice emerged from the shadows.

'Jewel. At last you have come.'

She forgot Alonso de Grado and threw herself on Falling Eagle, feeling his face, his hair, his mouth, his unwashed body. She seized one of his hands but he cried out in pain and pulled it from her. His hand left blood on her skirt.

'Falling Eagle,' she cried. 'You are ill!'

'Not ill. Only tortured. The Spanish, with whom I hear you are now so familiar, do not spare me in their quest for our gold. They dip my hands in oil and set them alight. Now they burn my feet so I cannot walk, although I am chained, as you can see. I am not the worst here. My companions suffer far worse. I see you do not suffer.'

'But I do suffer, Falling Eagle. You cannot see how I suffer.'

'It does not show. Don Hernán rewards you well. Have you asked yet for your husband's release?'

'I am only here because I had to beg with my body. You have no idea what I have to do.'

'I do not want to know how my wife behaves as a whore.'

She had not expected this.

'How do you expect me to behave?'

He sighed. 'Are you forced to sleep with Don Hernán or do you like the luxuries he gives you?'

'Falling Eagle!' She cried out so loudly that Alonso de Grado looked up from the doorway. She saw now there were other prisoners here in this dank cell. 'I have done this for you. Without this, I would never have seen you. I work now to release you. But it will take time. Don Hernán is no fool. I have to work slowly.'

She did not speak of the nights she lay awake at Don Hernán's side, remembering the past, planning for a future, pleasuring Don Hernán only for the rewards it might bring, the greatest of which was Falling Eagle.

He spoke bitterly. 'You delude yourself, Jewel. Don Hernán wants only our gold. I have thrown it all into the whirlpool. He sends divers to search for it. That is how desperate your lover is. No one can save me now.'

'If Don Hernán is satisfied with the gold he finds, surely he will release you?'

'There is not enough gold even in the lands of the Mexica to satisfy Don Hernán. He will always believe there is more where there is not. And whatever I say he does not believe me. I am a threat to him. As long as I am alive, people will see me as leader of the Mexica. I remind him of the past, of the Mexica who tried and so nearly destroyed him. *So nearly*! How our fates lie in those two words. Your father gave you into Don Hernán's care. I am glad Don Hernán honours his promise. I see your future, Jewel, or has your name changed? You will bear these men children who will give their fathers the right to rule in their name. Despite their blood, these children will be more Spanish than Mexica. You are the link in that chain, Jewel. That is your only importance to Don Hernán and the others, for I have no doubt there are other men who will tempt you.'

'No, Falling Eagle. Do not judge me so harshly. We loved each other once. I will work for your release.'

This time he did not speak so bitterly.

'I am sorry. The past is forgotten. There is only the future. For you, life. For me, who knows?'

She touched him but he shrugged her off.

'You will have to hurry to release me,' he said. 'I hear Don Hernán has other women.'

'He does. He has Malinalli.'

'Ah, so you do not hear what I do. Even in this cell we hear rumours. I hear that Don Hernán has many women in that palace of his in Coyoacan. You and Malinalli are not the only ones. You have the advantage of your birth, and your beauty. Although I hear the others are as beautiful, they cannot match your birth. Many claims will be made through you, Jewel. At least I need not worry about you.'

She began to cry.

'Don't waste your tears.' His voice softened. 'What happened to that young girl I knew who wanted to fight?'

Alonso de Grado grabbed her arm roughly.

'Shall I see you again, Falling Eagle?'

'How should I know? Forget me, Jewel.'

Out in the wounding sunshine, she saw her skirt had been stained with his blood. She did not see Falling Eagle stare as if he could not bear her to leave. She walked across the square, towards the causeway with her head down. She tried not to cry. She did not want to disgrace herself in front of Alonso de Grado, who insisted on walking too close as if to protect her from the Mexica loitering in the streets. Several times she shrugged him off and strode in front. She no longer walked timidly like a Mexica woman. She had learned to walk with the confidence of Doña María. In the middle of the causeway she bumped into Lizard. She was so pleased to see him. They strode together talking without stopping, leaving Alonso de Grado to trail behind.

In the street of the red houses in Coyoacan they reached Don Hernán's house, where Alonso de Grado left them. A small chapel had been furnished in its porch. Next to the chapel, in an open room occupied by Indians, black men, horses and dogs, human and animal smells converged unpleasantly. Jewel crossed herself. She drew Lizard into a corner.

'Falling Eagle spurned me as a Spanish whore.'

'He must understand you have no choice.'

'But you are wrong,' she cried. 'I had some choice. I did not have to accept the new God. I did not have to sleep with Don Hernán.'

'I admire you for resisting him for so long,' said Lizard.

'I tried. But I like the gifts he gives me. I like the comfort and the food. I have been bought. Too easily I have turned into the whore Doña Isobel.'

'You father gave you to Don Hernán,' Lizard consoled her.

He reflected how women, even the daughters of emperors, were given to men as if they were no more than a sack of maize. He left Jewel at the gate to the courtyard and watched her walk slowly through the entrance. She did not look back.

Coyoacan – 1524

Don Hernán was often away from the city exploring the country-side and visiting its mines, but he sent gifts regularly. His latest was a mirror. This mirror was clear, clearer than water. At first Jewel did not want it, which surprised him, for it was silver and very precious. She dared not tell him how she feared to see herself prop-erly, for she still did not believe it when men told her she was beau-tiful. And this mirror did not lie. Mexica mirrors were smokey pathways to other worlds. They showed the soul behind the face. And when at last she found the courage to look into the mirror clearer than water, she saw herself prettier than she had imagined, and she knew this mirror was magic after all, although Don Hernán said it was glass. On its reverse, in finely chased silver, animals and birds frolicked in an extravagant landscape.

She sat in her chair and held the mirror up to her eyes. She could sit without moving and look at her face, which she enjoyed doing, and at the same time see the entrance to her room reflected behind her in the glass. It was wonderful to see in front and behind her at the same time. Now she could monitor who entered and who left the room and she could sit with her back to the street and still spy on the traffic below.

Something moved in the glass as the brocade curtain was pushed aside. A small, dumpy person stood there. This mirror was not supposed to lie. Despite its magic surface, it did not perform magic. And yet a ghost stood there in the doorway. Jewel turned, still holding the mirror. This was no apparition. It ran and clasped Jewel's knees. This was a miracle.

'Ant Flower, you are alive!'

'Just, Lady. I was left for dead. When I came to, I dragged myself back to Wandering Coyote's house but it was occupied by Tlaxcalans. They used me, all of them. They said they had never had a dwarf. Eventually I escaped but there was nowhere to live and no food. What has a dwarf to sell? I would rather die than sell my body. It is not pleasant to be used in such a way and I do not like men. I was given to a Tlaxcalan, who kept me as a slave. And then, just as I was about to throw myself into the lake, a Spaniard found me. He said that Don Hernán was searching for a dwarf. Well, Lady, I asked myself whether Don Hernán too wanted to enjoy a dwarf, and here I am.'

'This is the best gift Don Hernán could give me, apart from my husband.'

Ant Flower took Jewel's hand. 'Lady, I am here to help you. From what I hear Don Hernán respects you. Even in death your father protects you.'

'As I will protect you, Ant Flower.' Jewel picked up the mirror again. 'Look, Ant Flower. This magic mirror shows your face.'

Ant Flower hesitated. She peered slowly into the glass. Then she turned away.

'I do not like what I see. But Lady, I see something else.'

Jewel had told no one. She had concealed her sickness and her expanding waist. Even when Don Hernán commented on her plumpness she said it was the excellent food she now ate. She put her face in her hands.

'I do not want this child.'

'A child might protect you,' soothed Ant Flower. 'If you should bear a son for Don Hernán, a son with the blood of the Spanish and the Mexica, Don Hernán would favour you above all the others. You must not anger him. You need his protection now more than ever, for there are those among your own people who will not look favourably on any son of yours. Perhaps Don Hernán will marry you.'

'He has a wife, although he does not speak of her. A Christian cannot get rid of his wife and he cannot take another. Anyway I do not want him.'

'You need him, Lady.'

'The Tlaxcalans have not improved your tongue, Ant Flower!'

She walked in the gardens every day now with Ant Flower. They would spend hours sitting on the stone seat guarded by its headless water dog. The Emperor Water Dog, Falling Eagle's father, had died before she knew him. This morning, as she sat with Ant Flower, listening to the wind in the cypress trees, the man with the blue eyes stopped and greeted her.

'Princess, I trust you are well.'

Jewel lowered her eyes modestly.

'May I accompany you? It is a beautiful day.'

She could feel Ant Flower's disapproval. But this was a Spanish city now with different rules. She could walk with whoever she wanted. He helped up her from the bench. Did he notice that her waist was larger?

'Tell me about these gardens.'

She led him down the pathways, past the orange and gold marigolds and the double-headed dahlias bred by her father. When they passed a tall plant with broad leaves that tapered like fingers, he put out his hand to touch it. She grabbed him, then shocked by her audacity, let go.

'That is poisonous! The sting is painful, like a wasp's.'

He rubbed his fingers, imagining the pain.

'What is it?'

'The wicked woman plant.'

His eyes twinkled.

'We have beautiful gardens in Spain but we do not have plants like that one. Perhaps you will see our gardens one day.'

Spain! She could cross the ocean in a boat.

'They cannot be as beautiful as my father's gardens,' she said primly. She regretted she had been too familiar. She felt Ant Flower's eyes boring into her back.

'Oh but they are, although the plants are different.'

She stumbled on a stone. He put his arm around her waist to support her.

'Perhaps I could show you the horses, Princess? Perhaps you would like to learn to ride. There are many women in Spain who ride.'

'Ride? Life was full of possibilities, if only she could conquer her fear of those sweating monsters.'

She smiled coquettishly. 'Perhaps one day, Don . . . ?'

'Juan Cano.'

He bowed and left her.

Another godless year had passed and Lizard had become used to his new life. It was not so different from his student days at the House of Tears and, even without a god, it had some meaning. He was desperate to finish the story of his people. He sat up night after night recreating the past, hoping that when he reached the end he could find some meaning for what had happened. Angry Turkey insisted there was no meaning, although Juan said that all meaning lay with the true God.

Lizard walked to the open window. The sun was setting. Despite all that had happened the sun still rose and set as it always had. Now it was the moon's time to shine. The sun had set on the world of the Mexica, leaving the sky to the Spanish moon. Father Olmedo said that the same moon shone over his country. He said that if Lizard became a Christian he could travel to Spain and train as a priest. Lizard knew nothing about Spain, only that it was a long way east and that it was full of schools for priests. Part of him wanted to leave his tragic home behind and discover unknown lands. Already strange animals were arriving in Tenochtitlán – cows, pigs, sheep, goats. And there were new trees – mulberries planted to feed the worms that made the silk that Don Hernán and his women wore. There were olives and something called wheat that grew like grass and was made into bread. He would like to see the land that produced all these wonderful things.

But he really wanted to study Spanish law and use it to defend his people. When he mentioned this to Juan, there had been a shocked silence, as if he, Lizard, were a traitor, learning from friends how to betray them. When Juan suggested he concentrate on the priesthood, Lizard saw the path he would have to take. First become a priest, then study the law. And as a priest, he could help his people now dying from work, hunger and disease. As a lawyer he could use Spanish law to defend them. He had heard that the King of Spain, this distant powerful lord, wished to protect the Indians. But how could the laws of Spain be enforced so far away in the lands of the Mexica, when its conquerors ignored those laws in pursuit of their greed? Sometimes at night Lizard saw visions of Spanish arriving in their thousands, riding on horses, crushing the land, destroying the forests and filling the lake with their waste. He would wake up screaming. Now he saw the path he would have to take.

When he told Father Olmedo his decision, the priest was thrilled. Juan agreed to be Lizard's godfather. As Father Olmedo's wet hands made the signs of the cross on his head, Lizard shut his eyes and prayed to the new God, using the old words. Now his scars would wash away. The terrible images that filled his mind would fade with the Mexica prayers. He whispered the old familiar words.

Here is the heavenly water, the very pure water that washes and cleans your heart and that takes away all stain.

He was born again, cleansed of his sins.

'I baptise you, Don Diego, in the name of our Lord Jesus Christ, in the presence of these witnesses.'

Juan could not contain his pleasure. Lizard looked up at the beams of the chapel as if fearing retaliation from the old gods but only birds nested there now. Had the old gods really been destroyed? Father Olmedo embraced him. Lizard had become Don Diego. It felt different. It felt good. A warmth ran through his veins. This was not the same as serving the old High Priest of Huitzilopochtli, or even Black Dog. This felt real. This God loved him. This God would save his people. Suddenly he had no doubts at all. He wanted everyone to know how he felt.

Don Hernán sent for Jewel three weeks after his return from his latest expedition. He was in a genial mood. His expeditions had yielded new sources of gold and silver. The wheat he had planted in her father's gardens in the hills of Oaxtepec had produced its first grains. He brought her a Spanish puppy with long hair and mournful eyes.

'He will keep you company.' He stared sternly at her. 'This is not a dog you eat.'

The dog wagged its long tail and whined. It would grow into a huge hound like those fighting dogs. She did not want a fighting dog. But she was desperate now to find favour with Don Hernán. There was no one else to protect her.

He still seemed to enjoy her company. He still ran his fingers through her hair, but his interest now seemed more like that of a child than a lover. He would lie with his head on her breast, suckling from her like a child whose mother had weaned him too early. He spoke of a wet nurse who had suckled him as Jewel did, who saved him by praying to San Pedro, for Don Hernán had been a sickly child. Now he prayed daily to San Pedro whose symbol flew on his banners. He spoke, often and nostalgically, of her father Montezuma. He confessed that he had preferred his company to some of his own countrymen's. He stayed the whole night and rose late in the morning as if he could not bear to leave her, even dressing in her room watching her spread out on the bed. She saw how his *tepuli* swelled. She knew how to arouse him.

'I have thought much about your future, Isobel. You need a husband.'

She jumped out of bed. She forgot she was quite naked.

'I do not want a husband.'

She already had a husband, but he did not count. It was not a Christian marriage. He kissed her on the cheek and tied back her hair as Ant Flower did each morning.

'What a fine maid I would make. Now listen. I have found a man who will take care of you and look after your lands in Tacuba.'

'No!' she shouted.

'You have no choice, Isobel. This is not a town for women on their own and you cannot run your estates without help.'

'I can try. You can help me.'

'I shall have much to occupy me. Alonso de Grado asks for you. I have agreed. You will be married tomorrow.'

She faced him boldly.

'I do not like him. He is a bully.'

'Then you will have to learn to like him since he will be your husband.'

'I cannot! I am pregnant.'

He smiled proudly.

'It will make no difference. I will support my child even if he lives in Alonso de Grado's household. And I will still visit. Alonso de Grado will not object to sharing you. So you see, my dear, you will have us both.'

She was a whore, shared by men.

'My mind is made up. I have thought long and hard about your future. Your father gave you into my care. I feel some responsibility for you.'

'Is there someone else I could marry?'

'Someone else? Have you been meeting someone secretly?' He seemed intrigued. 'Believe me, my dear, I know what is best for you.'

At the door he turned and asked what she would like as a wedding gift. She did not know. She did not want a wedding.

'At least I have found your dwarf.'

It was Ant Flower who prepared Jewel for her wedding, who dried her tears and dressed her for the feast. It was Ant Flower who held her head when she had to run out and vomit during the meal. And it was Ant Flower who prepared her for the bridal night, who comforted her after she had been roughly used by a boisterous Don Alonso who cared nothing for the child in her womb. As Ant

Flower dressed Jewel in the morning and bathed her bruises with cold water, she whispered.

'I will pray to the gods of the Mexica for Don Alonso's death.'

'And I will pray to the new God,' said Jewel. 'That way we can be sure that one of them will answer our prayers.'

Jewel was worn out by the attentions of Don Alonso. Fortunately he was often away inspecting her lands in the country, for she had inherited many farms as well as the city of Tacuba. Now she was pregnant, Jewel hankered for the old ways, even for the visits of those boring old relatives. She decided she wanted the child after all. She stopped chewing chicle, fearing it would poison the child's gums. A red silk blouse Don Hernán had given her languished unworn in her chest, for red was an unlucky colour for childbirth. She dared not look at the sky in case the moon should swallow the sun and her child be born harelipped. She worried about the ceremonies. Who would organise the family celebrations and the banquets? Who would make the long speeches to the new parents? Did it matter that there was only one? Was she still under the protection of the old goddess, or had the gods abandoned her? Now she remembered the words of a prayer. *'Down there where Ayopechcatl lives, the jewel is born, a child has come into the world.'* No one would sing it for the Lady Isobel. She grabbed Ant Flower's hand.

'I feel so lonely, Ant Flower, without my mother and my sister, and without the care of a midwife.'

'I am here, Lady. I can be your midwife.'

'No, I would like a midwife who will use the old words. Who else will welcome my child into the world properly?'

Ant Flower sighed. Good midwives were scarce now. She helped Jewel from her bed. Now she slept in a raised bed like the Spanish.

'What if I die?' asked Jewel. 'What if the child dies inside me?'

She saw the midwives brandishing their flint knives ready to cut the child from her. She heard the howling of the mourners as they carried her away. Who would protect her grave for four nights until the magic dispersed? She saw her body carried out in darkness so the warriors could not hack off her limbs, for the flesh of a woman who died in childbirth had magical properties. She felt ill with fear. Or was it different with a Spanish birth? She would ask Doña María.

'I shall find a midwife to massage you,' soothed Ant Flower. She had no idea where she might find one. 'At least she will tell you whether it is a boy or a girl.'

Ant Flower went out reluctantly into the streets of Tlatelolco. She had not been there since the night they had fled. Now the streets were clean, although many of the houses were still ruins. Beggars loitered in the marketplace. There were been no beggars in the old city. The market guardians would never have allowed it.

Each street brought memories. In the street of the Prickly Pear she had been raped, she had forgotten how many times, but she had not died like Marsh Lily. She walked down the street of the Lime Vendors, passing Wandering Coyote's house. The gate hung on its hinges. The courtyard was full of rubbish and dead plants. The bones of the Tlaxcalan killed by Wandering Coyote still lay in a heap by the gate. She peered into the house. She called several times. An old hag emerged from the shadows begging for food. She did not know Wandering Coyote. She had even forgotten her own name.

In the market square, where a church now stood in place of the temple, makeshift stalls offered vegetables, cloth, dogs and flowers. Ant Flower stopped by one stall where a woman steamed tamales.

'I search for a midwife.'

The woman looked shrewdly at Ant Flower.

'Midwives are scarce these days unless you can pay well.'

'Well enough,' replied Ant Flower.

The woman sniffed.

'I know of one nearby but you must pay me first to fetch her. I take anything – food, clothes, cacao beans.'

Ant Flower took a Spanish coin from her skirt.

The woman spat.

'I don't take Spanish stuff.'

'It is gold. It buys anything,' said Ant Flower, putting the coin down on the stall.

The woman sniffed again.

'Very well. Wait here. I will find the midwife.'

She returned with a bent old woman, who eagerly accepted a coin. She followed Ant Flower back to the city. Beggars called out in every street – 'Lady, for the love of the gods . . . Please, Lady.'

Their faces were scarred by disease. Ant Flower gave them money where she could, saddened to see the proud Mexica reduced to such penury. But she felt glad to be called a lady, glad to be clean and wearing decent clothes and sandals on her feet.

The midwife insisted on a proper steam bath. A pregnant woman required hot water and steam for massage. She demanded control of the kitchen.

'This will not work, Lady,' whispered Ant Flower.

But Jewel was determined. They made do with a bowl of hot water. The midwife massaged Jewel's stomach.

'It is a girl, Lady.'

'We want a boy,' insisted Ant Flower.

The midwife stared at them.

'You will need Spanish magic for that. This child is eager to be born. It is a girl but she will have the voice of a man. There should be no problems with this birth but I will bring the *ciuapatli*, the yellow daisy, with me when the time comes to bring on your contractions. And if that does not work, I will make you the opossum-tail drink. It never fails.'

A visitor called unexpectedly the next day. Malinalli on her way to the market, slipped into the small red house in Coyoacan. She sat awkwardly in the large brocade chair in the reception room and waited. Her hair shone. Her skin bloomed. She leapt from the chair when she saw Jewel.

'Doña Isobel. I bring greetings. I am pleased to learn about your child.' She patted her own stomach. 'My own is due about the same time. You see, Doña Isobel, how life treats us like sisters. Don Hernán hopes you will bear him a son. I too would like a son.' She held out her hands. 'Shall we be friends, Doña Isobel? We have much in common.'

'Get out!' shouted Jewel. 'Get out and don't come back!'

She gripped the arms of her chair angrily. Malinalli trembled. She walked to the doorway without looking back.

'That was cruel of you, Lady,' said Ant Flower. 'Doña Marina offers you friendship and you spurn her. You need friends now, Lady, not enemies. Are the Spanish women real friends to you?'

'Leave me alone!'

Jewel curled up in the chair and sobbed. She slipped out the next day and made her way over the causeway to the Sacred Square. She found the room guarded by Spaniards but she smiled sweetly and gave her name and asked to speak to her husband. One of the guards escorted her to the door. She peered through the bars. There was no light, no sound, only the terrible smell of death.

'Falling Eagle,' she whispered. 'It's me, Jewel. It's me.'

No one answered.

'Are they all dead?' she asked the guard.

He took her arm to help her down the broken steps.

'Not all of them. One died yesterday.'

'Which one?'

He shrugged.

'I do not know, Lady. As far as I am concerned, they can all die. Traitors, the lot of them.'

Although he had embraced the new God, Lizard found himself arguing frequently with Juan. Their arguments became increasingly bitter for Juan took every opportunity to criticise the Mexica. He said there were many things of which the Mexica should feel ashamed. Like the sacrifices of people with souls like himself and Lizard. They were not criminals or murderers and did not deserve such terrible deaths. And as for eating human flesh, that was cannibalism.

'We did not eat it for pleasure,' insisted Lizard. 'A warrior always ate something from his captive to imbibe his bravery. You would not understand.'

'I do not.'

'You must understand how the Mexica saw it. The Mexica gods died to give their people life. We, as humans, had to reward our gods with sacrifice. Our gods ate human blood. If we did not feed them, the whole world would die.'

'But you fed them and your world has died.'

Lizard did not agree. The Mexica were not destroyed yet. He thought it would take years to destroy them. They would live on in the air and in the water and in the people's words. They might live on for ever. The Spanish could not stop the thoughts and words of the Mexica.

Juan told him he was obstinate. The Spanish were trying to give the Mexica back their history in the Spanish language, so the whole world could read about them. The Mexica were not the only people in the world. There were French and Portuguese, Arabs and Chinese. If Don Hernán had not found the Mexica, someone else would. And it might even have been worse. Juan admired the Mexica for so many things. When he had first seen the great city of Tenochtitlán he could not believe that such a huge and sophisticated city existed. Some of Don Hernán's men thought it greater than Seville, greater even than Venice which was also built on water, perhaps even greater than the magical city of Constantinople which had been lost to the Turks.

The Mexica were such odd people, in some ways so strong, so resilient, yet everything terrified them. A shooting star, an eclipse of the sun, the cry of a night owl, the presence of a hawk. They lived their lives looking over their shoulders for omens, disappointed when they failed to find them. The Spanish called these things supersititions and did not fear them as the Mexica did. The Lord Montezuma, God rest his soul, was a prisoner of his own mind. A people like the Mexica whose every minute was ordered by trumpets and drums, by festivals and ritual, whose every action was decided by those who governed them, had no control over their own minds.

'You cannot change people's minds overnight!' shouted Lizard angrily.

The Mexica did not usually shout. Words should express themselves without volume. 'We are made up of what our ancestors taught us, of what our gods have given us. Where there is no order there is chaos. You only have to go out there in the street and you will see.' Lizard banged the table. 'You Spanish will never understand. Even if I were to write down all of our stories and myths and history in Spanish, you would not understand. Your rational minds prevent you understanding us. You want to swallow our souls. Why can you not leave us something of ourselves? We did not take everything from the people we conquered. We left them their gods and their souls.'

Juan sighed.

'You sacrificed them!'

'You do not try to understand.'

'One day I hope to understand everything. There is something else I wish to tell you. I plan to train as a priest. I will return to Spain and enter a monastery in Seville. It is beautiful in Seville.'

'No!' cried Lizard, contrite now. 'You are my only friend. I have only Angry Turkey among my own people and I despise most of yours.'

'So you do not despise me?'

Lizard hugged Juan as the Spanish did with each other all the time.

'No, I shall miss you. I shall be lonely.'

'Why don't you come with me? I know you would make a fine priest. You would have to live without women. Have you ever known one?'

'Of course.'

'How many?'

'Only one, but she was special.'

Juan laughed. 'The are all special. I knew a woman in Spain when I was young. I did not enjoy it. The Lord Montezuma offered me a choice of women and I could not accept any of them. I felt more sorrow than desire.' He laughed. 'That's more than the others felt. None of them refused. I can live without that kind of thing. And to be honest, what I have seen here disgusts me.'

Lizard looked through the window where flowers grew again in the courtyard.

'I water those,' said Juan. 'The Lord Montezuma loved his flowers.' He stared at Lizard. 'Come with me to Seville.'

Lizard saw Black Dog hovering on the edge of the temple, his black cloak flapping in the wind, exhorting Lizard to honour the old gods. He heard the whining pleas of the old High Priest of Huitzilopochtli. Conflicting emotions clashed in his mind. Anger, hate, friendship, the stench of congealed blood, the screams of those sent to feed the gods, the greed of the gods, the comfort of the new God.

'There is true power in the words of our God,' continued Juan. 'You and I, Diego, have more power than the rulers we serve, for our power lies in our words. The Mexica will listen to you for you are one of their own. You have this opportunity to bring them the truth.'

'What if they do not want your truth?'

'They will. Everyone welcomes our God. Please come with me. We can travel together.'

Lizard picked up his bark paper and his pens. If he travelled to Spain there would be no time to finish the histories.

'Don't wait too long,' cautioned Juan. 'A boat waits at the coast. It has brought Don Hernán's wife from Cuba. She is on her way now to Tenochtitlán.' He grinned cheekily. 'Don Hernán does not look forward to her arrival. He has had to move all the other women out of his house.'

Everything changed when Doña Catarina arrived. A pale creature who fainted often and demanded much, it was no wonder that Don Hernán had left her behind in the first place. Don Hernán's body-guards carried her along the causeway on their shoulders to the stare of the curious crowds whom Doña Catarina acknowledged like an empress.

She moved into the red house in Coyoacan as Malinalli and the other women moved out. Doña Catarina had no children of her own. Those who knew her said it was not surprising for Don Hernán and his wife shouted in their room well into the night.

Alonso knew all about Doña Catarina. He looked up from the diary he was writing and laughed. Doña Catarina had schemed for Don Hernán and Don Hernán had been gaoled when he refused to marry her.

'Why did he marry her then?' asked Jewel.

'She has powerful friends. Women like that should be left well alone. You will see what she is like. No doubt she will ask for the Emperor's daughter to serve her.'

He returned to his diary. He spent much of his time writing.

Doña Catarina became as demanding as the weather. She developed an appetite for parties and banquets and visits. She paraded like an empress with her retinue of Mexica princesses. There were visits to the Spanish estates outside the city, visits to the Virgin at Cholula, where a Christian church had replaced Quetzalcoatl's shrine. There were canoe trips on the canal and an outing to Oaxtepec to inspect the new wheat fields planted by Don Juan Garrido, a large black man who had been given the farms and orchards belonging to the Lord Montezuma. Although she liked Don Juan, who had once been a slave, it distressed Jewel to see her father's favourite gardens metamorphosed into bright green fields of wheat, a bold invader in a dry land, like the people who had brought it here. And she had to endure Doña Catarina's demands.

'Bring me my shoes, Isobel,' she would say. 'Help me through the grass. Lift my skirt. Hold my hand.' And she would smile with pride, but never with thanks, to show the world how an emperor's daughter served her.

At Oaxtepec the heat was stifling and Doña Catarina fainted in the orchard. It took some time to bring her back from the world of the spirits. But Doña Catarina recovered in time to eat her meal. Doña Catarina enjoyed her food.

'I hope she dies,' Jewel told Ant Flower.

'We will add her to our prayers,' said Ant Flower.

She prayed daily for Alonso's death as she prayed daily for Falling Eagle's life.

On All Saints' Day Don Hernán held a banquet. The air felt like a furnace. So many candles illuminated the room they generated the heat of a thousand braziers. Doña Catarina's face seemed flushed. Her eyes were glassy. She sat next to Don Hernán, her hands clinging possessively to his arms. She wore a gold silk dress, gold necklaces, gold bangles and heavy earrings. Her eyes glittered with jealousy. She sipped her wine and gobbled her food, picking from the plates of fatty pork, red beef and turkey meat. There were goblets of wine, white bread and fruit from the coast. She smiled at the musicians and she enjoyed the display of Mexica dancers and acrobats. She even danced between the courses and seemed in good humour. Then she whispered something to Don Hernán. Whatever she said angered him. He shouted at her which shocked the guests because Don Hernán rarely lost his temper in public. Dona Catarina burst into tears. She lifted her skirts and ran out of the room. Don Hernán ignored her. He swigged his wine. He bid the musicians play louder and then he walked around greeting everyone. When he reached Jewel he kissed her hand and led her onto the dance floor. He patted her stomach fondly. Doña Catarina did not know about the child. And if she did, Doña Catarina's jealousy would be uncontrollable.

Jewel slept restlessly that night. The child kicked. An owl invaded her dreams. Demons threatened her. She heard screaming and the rushing of feet. Torches flickered outside in the street. In the morning she woke to silence. When Ant Flower came to dress her, she trembled with the horror of her news.

'Doña Catarina is dead. They say Don Hernán has killed her!'

After Doña Catarina's hasty funeral, an old man called at the house asking for the Lady Jewel. The servants sent him away but he sat outside the door and refused to budge. The servants reported that the old man smelt. He was poor, he did not wear sandals and his cactus cloak was torn in many places. Out of curiosity, Jewel went down to speak to him. When she saw him huddled on the cobblestones, she knew immediately who it was and rushed to embrace him. She helped him to his feet and ushered him through the front door, past the startled servants.

'It is my turn to help *you* now, even if I have to sell my treasures.'

Wandering Coyote grinned, showing a mouth almost devoid of teeth. He stared at Jewel in admiration. 'I can see you've certainly not lost your treasures.'

She sent for food and clothes. And after Wandering Coyote had eaten, slowly because of his lack of teeth, they sat in the high Spanish chairs and talked. Wandering Coyote was loathe to admit his desperation. He had no living, no food, no home. He had traded openly with the Spanish, selling everything, even his own people as slaves. Now he could no longer compete with the other traders, some of them Spanish and more ruthless than him. He looked down at his bare feet. In the old days he had owned sandals like the Emperor's. That came from being born on the day of Three Water. For a person born on such a day, wealth came and went easily. Like water, it passed away. Now it had dried up.

'I can find you a room here,' enthused Jewel. 'I have more than enough food. I am sure I can find you work with Don Hernán. He sends people to search for the gold and silver mines. You know where they all are.'

Wandering Coyote knew every mine and village in the empire. Even without good sandals and a full stomach, he could still walk to them. If he worked for Don Hernán, he would be able to buy new sandals. Like water, wealth might flow again.

'I have some influence,' boasted Jewel. 'This is my house. I can do what I like. I will tell my husband you are a cousin who has returned from the dead. The Spanish love the Lord Montezuma's family. Here at least we are among friends.'

Coyoacan – 1525

Jewel's child was born in the new year on the day of Eleven Vulture, which promised a long and happy life. The child was in a hurry. She shocked the midwife with her loud voice. She pummelled her mother's breasts in her eagerness to reach the milk.

'She is greedy like her father,' said Ant Flower.

The child had the almond eyes and the long delicate fingers of her grandfather Montezuma. She sprouted a shock of coarse dust-coloured hair, like her father's. If Don Hernán was disappointed not to have a son, he did not show it as he carried the baby proudly through the streets of Coyoacan. He wore new velvet trousers and a cape lined with purple silk and a large medallion of the Virgin made of Mexica gold.

At her baptism the child expelled the Devil with her ferocious lungs, which made Father Olmedo smile. She had for her godfather her cousin Lizard and for godmother Malinalli, whose own child was expected soon. She did not receive the traditional gifts of broom, spindle and work basket, for this child would not cling to her hearth. Nor was her umbilical cord buried in her home, but was thrown out with the rubbish. The child received gifts of gold and silver, a crystal rosary and a painting of the Virgin. But there were no garlands of flowers, no fine speeches, no poems, although chocolate was served with the wine and some guests ended the evening in drunken and melancholic mood. Nor was the child passed around naked for everyone there to welcome into the world. And some were disappointed. Handful of Reeds, sporting velvet and braid like a Spanish noble, whispered as he left.

'Next time, Isobel, make sure it is a boy.'

The child was christened Leonor. But later in the week two Keepers of the Books came secretly to the house to give the child a Mexica name. They called her Precious Greenstone, the name of Jewel's aunt, for it proved most auspicious.

'This one will not give up easily,' said Ant Flower proudly. She loved the child with all the suppressed love of a barren woman. She sang songs from her own people, the Zapotecs on the west coast, and admired the child's toothless smile.

Malinalli's child, born two weeks later, was a boy, christened Martín by his proud father who again donned his velvet and silk and gold and paraded with the child around the streets of Coyoacan. Here was the boy who united two cultures, though he was not royal.

For two months Jewel enjoyed a respite from Alonso's attentions. But then his visits resumed. He did not seem to mind the milk oozing from Jewel's breasts or her tender stomach. He ignored the child. But Leonor collected admirers. Ant Flower guarded her fiercely. Wandering Coyote, when he was at home from his expeditions to the mines, would spend hours amusing her. He would carry Leonor into the gardens and sit on the seat talking to her in Nahuatl, and this proved to be the language of her first words.

'She is a child to whom words come easily,' he pronounced proudly. 'She is a Mexica!'

But Leonor seemed unaware that she linked two cultures, that had she been a boy, she might have inherited the empire of her ancestors. But Ant Flower thought it just as well Jewel's child was a daughter and no threat to the seekers of power.

A month after Easter Alonso sickened suddenly with the sweating fever and took to his bed. The Spanish doctor called daily. Jewel washed Alonso with cloths steeped in ice brought down from the mountains. But, despite their attentions, Alonso died. Who knew which gods had answered their prayers? It was a sin to pray for death. Jewel confessed to Father Olmedo but Ant Flower smiled conspiratorially. The old gods had shown their power.

Don Hernán called a month after Alonso's death. He was in such a hurry that he did not even undress Jewel or untie her hair. He visited regularly again, often staying the night. He was a better lover than Alonso. He liked to please women. Nor did he withdraw his *tepuli* as Alonso did. Perhaps he hoped for a son. But whenever Jewel slept beside him, she could not forget that he might be a murderer. A man who murdered his wife might just as easily murder his mistress. Don Hernán did not behave like a murderer, although he did not waste time mourning and seemed oblivious to the rumours. When Doña Catarina was found, her neck was covered in bruises. Her face had turned blue. She had wet her bed and there were signs of a struggle. No one could verify these rumours for Don Hernán had sealed his wife quickly in her coffin and permitted no one, not even her brother, to see her body.

He certainly did not miss his wife. The women, including Malinalli, moved back into the red house in Coyoacan and life continued much as it had before Doña Catarina's arrival. But whenever Don Hernán nibbled her neck in the throes of passion, Jewel would freeze with fear and dry up so that Don Hernán would ask if there were something wrong with her. She tried desperately to please him. She wanted to see Falling Eagle again.

One morning, after a night when she had managed to relax, Don Hernán informed Jewel that she needed a new husband.

'What do you say, Isobel?'

'Yes,' she whispered. 'I say yes.'

'That is good then. Pedro Gallego is a pleasant man. He is something of a poet. You will like him.'

He noticed her expression.

'You were not thinking of me? I am flattered. I do not plan to marry again. My life at present is uncertain. I plan an expedition to Honduras in search of gold. I will be away for a year. I can offer you nothing. But Pedro Gallego can offer you and the child protection.'

'Why can't I choose my husband this time?'

He was amused.

'Who would you choose?'

'Juan Cano seems a good man.'

'Juan Cano? How do you know him?'

Jewel had continued to meet Juan Cano in the gardens. She felt comfortable with him. They often sat together in the water dog's seat under the morning glory vines. Don Hernán roared with laughter.

'Who would have thought it? The ambitious old dog. He is after your lands.'

'Like all of you! At least he is younger than you! You find fault with him because he is not one of your favourites. You do not like people who do not agree with you.'

Now she was angry with him. He could give her away as a reward to his favourites.

'You pass me around all your friends like a whore,' she told him.

'At least my friends are gentlemen.'

She decided to pray again for Pedro Gallego's death. And this time she would not confess.

Don Hernán explained that Father Olmedo would marry her before he left for the coast. Don Hernán promised to return with gifts. The country to the south was rich in gold, silver and emeralds.

'There is something else,' said Jewel. 'Is my cousin Falling Eagle still alive?'

He seemed in a hurry to leave.

'I am not sure. I think so.'

It was a surprise when Malinalli called a week later during preparations for the wedding. She had never returned since their last meeting. She perched awkwardly in the brocade chair. Her hands played nervously with her red silk skirts. Her long hair was tied back with a matching ribbon. She looked like the goddess María whose image hung on the pendant around her neck. Jewel's dog curled up at her feet.

'You may wonder why I am here?'

'I do.'

Jewel knew she should apologise for her rudeness.

'It was a difficult decision, but I decided you should know what is happening to your husband.'

'Which one?'

'Falling Eagle.'

Jewel felt quite faint and sat down on a stool.

'I am to accompany Don Hernán on his expedition. I shall be his interpreter. I speak Mayan and Nahuatl and Spanish. He cannot do without me,' she said proudly.

Jewel called for some chocolate. It came in silver bowls. Marina sipped hers delicately.

'Don Hernán will take Falling Eagle with us to Honduras. He will travel in chains. Don Hernán does not dare leave Falling Eagle here in Tenochtitlán. He sees him as a threat. You may not know but there have been plots among some of the Mexica nobles.'

Jewel realised she knew nothing of what was going on.

'So Falling Eagle is still alive?'

'He is, although in poor health. I see Don Hernán does not keep you informed.'

Unlike you, thought Jewel. She realised she had not been as clever as she thought.

'Don Hernán hopes Falling Eagle will reveal all the sources of Mexica gold.'

'There is no more!' exclaimed Jewel. She could see that Marina did not believe her. All the Spanish cared about was gold. But she said nothing. She had learnt to guard her tongue.

'I come to offer my help,' said Malinalli.

'How can you help? You have done your best to destroy us.'

Malinalli looked at the floor. She seemed distressed, but you never knew if it was genuine.

'I am the only person who can help you, Lady Jewel. I am sorry for Falling Eagle and I regret what has happened. Yes, I do blame myself. Some of my words have borne bitter fruit. Many haunt me.' She waited for Jewel to speak, but Jewel said nothing.

'I fear that harm could come to Falling Eagle. I suggest that I keep watch for you. I will try to protect him. I still have some influence over Don Hernán. And I would like us to be friends. After all, we have much in common.' She laughed hoarsely. 'Don Hernán is free to marry now.'

Her eyes glittered.

'I do not want him,' lied Jewel.

'But, you see, I do.'

'Then you can have him. Anyway I am to be married again, to Pedro Gallego. You have more freedom than I do. You have not been married off against your will.'

'I would choose Don Hernán. But he does not want me. A man marries for advantage and I have none. I have nothing to offer other than my tongue and my body. Oh Don Hernán will be generous to me. He has already given me your father's gardens in Coyoacan. He will care for our son as he will care for all his children. I will not die in poverty. He is the only man I have ever loved and I have known many. Did you feel like this with Falling Eagle?'

Jewel nodded.

'Then I will try to bring him back. And while I still have influence with Don Hernán I will try to release Falling Eagle from his chains. I know Don Hernán will never free him but at least he could live in better conditions.'

Malinalli rose from her chair. Jewel held out her hand.

'I have misjudged you, Marina, and I apologise.' She called Malinalli by her Spanish name for the first time. 'I should like to see your son. I hear he is a lively child.'

Malinalli smiled. 'He is like his father.'

'Would you like to leave him here while you are away? I will take good care of him.'

Malinalli grabbed Jewel's hands.

'Thank you, thank you, but I cannot bear to be parted from him. He will come with me.'

And with a whoosh of her silk skirts she swept along the corridor through the great wooden doors and out into the street.

When Don Hernán called again and went to sleep with his *tepuli* inside her, Jewel asked gently if she could visit her cousin Falling Eagle. Don Hernán was in a good mood. All the preparations were proceeding well for his expedition. He left the city in good hands. He had dealt satisfactorily with his enemies. He had two healthy children. He gave his agreement amiably.

This time Jewel went alone to visit Falling Eagle. The cell smelt of urine and sickness. Only three prisoners remained, chained to each other. Jewel clutched the locked grille in front of the cell.

'Falling Eagle.'

The words fell from her tongue. How light her language was compared to Spanish. How it floated on the air, searching for tongues. A bundle of rags stirred. Bloodshot eyes stared at her. She dropped her hood so he could see her face more clearly.

'Jewel' he said gently. 'I hear little of you these days.'

'I think of you all the time Falling Eagle, and regret that I have been powerless to save you.'

'We are all powerless.'

He struggled to his feet and shuffled over to the grille, dragging his chains and his companions over the mud floor. He grabbed her hands and kissed her fingers.

'No wonder you have not visited me. I treated you so badly last time. You have sold yourself to survive. I have not sold myself but I barely exist. Don Hernán will drag me to Honduras in his retinue of admirers.' He grimaced. 'At least I will smell the air and see the sky and feel the rain. It cannot be worse than this.'

'He wants you to lead him to the hidden gold of the Mexica. Tell him where it is, Falling Eagle. Let him have it all!'

'There is no more gold. They have melted it all down in blocks and sent it to Spain. They are vulgar men. I am sad to see them use you.'

She did not say that some of them were perfectly acceptable, like Father Olmedo and Juan, that friend of Lizard's. Nor did she mention how she despised traitors like her brother.

'I have Ant Flower and Wandering Coyote living with me.'

He seemed pleased.

'They will care for you, Jewel. Do not forget the old ways. Remember the good ways of your people. Remember their honour, their pride, their fortitude, their stoicism.'

'I have a child.'

'A child?'

'A half-Mexica, half-Spanish child.'

'A boy?'

'A girl.'

'A girl will comfort you. Sing her our songs. Do not let her forget our ways.'

'If only we could enjoy one last night together, have our own child.'

He rubbed her fingers gently.

'The gods do not wish it. They did not wish it before. They did not give us a child then.'

She stroked his face. 'You will come back.'

He hesitated. 'It might be better if I didn't.'

'No!' she shouted loudly. 'No! Do not leave me alone.'

Now she sobbed, hot disgraceful tears. He poked his fingers through the grille and stroked her long unbound hair.

'How shiny your hair is. Someone has found you indigo. Be reasonable, my love. What can you do for me now? Don Hernán will never release me. We must make our own way in life. This is what the gods foretold. We would never have escaped that night on our way to Tepeyac.'

She did not tell Falling Eagle how her mind had been altered by the Spanish, how she even thought like them. She knew they could have escaped to Tepeyac if only they had left at night in small fast canoes and without her father's treasure. But he would not understand. He still thought like a Mexica. How I have changed, she thought. She tried to feel his body but her arm would not extend far enough through the grille.

'Promise me you will come back. Promise.'

He grinned. He had lost some of his teeth and his gums were swollen.

'I shall do my best.'

'Malinalli will look after you. She is called Marina now.'

'Malinalli? I thought you hated her.'

'I have changed my mind. I see now how she is used by Don Hernán as I am used. It is hard being a slave. I never used to think about it.'

'Now our people are slaves in their own land,' he said sadly. 'How we have failed them.'

'You tried!'

'Not enough. Still it is all too late and even if I were to escape on this journey I would never be able to raise a big enough army to expel the Spanish. No, it is our fate, Jewel. And if our story lives on in the memory of our people, we shall be fortunate.'

'There is one thing that might help you,' suggested Jewel. 'If you accept the new God, Don Hernán may treat you better. You will benefit from their laws.'

'You believe that?'

'I have seen how Lizard is treated.'

'He is no threat to them. It makes no difference whether I am a Christian or not.'

'Our Lady might help you.'

'Has she helped you?'

She thought a moment. 'She has given me the strength to endure.'

'Look,' he said, serious now, 'there is something I must tell you. It has been a secret for far too long.'

People were beginning to stare at her pressed up against the grille. If only she could change into a spirit and slip through the grille and disappear into Falling Eagle's flesh. She put her fingers against his lips. Then he spread her hands out in his own.

'How ladylike your fingers are. They no longer tend the garden. Do you remember when I teased you for gardening and how cross you were with me?'

She laughed and cried at the same time. He gripped her hands tightly through the grille.

'You remember that night when we fled from Tlatelolco?'

'How could I forget?'

'I told you I had a secret.'

She nodded.

'Well, I shall tell you now and if it makes you hate me, then say goodbye and never think of me again.'

'I could never hate you.'

'I killed your father. I threw that stone.'

'No!'

'It was me.'

'Did you mean to kill him?'

'I did it to save the Mexica. Unfortunately it did not.'

She wished he had never told her. She wanted to hate him forever but she could not hate any more.

'It cannot be true. It was the gods' wish that he die. They chose you for the deed.'

'I took the decision. Do you forgive me?'

'I cannot forgive you but I cannot hate you.'

She turned and ran away.

'Pray to your Lady for me,' he called.

She sobbed so hard she did not see where she was walking. At the end of the square she tripped over a loose stone. Someone rushed to help her. Juan Cano gave her a handkerchief and escorted her home.

She found Father Olmedo supervising the workmen in his new church. They perched on ladders gilding the angels behind the altar. A carved tree spread its branches towards the heavens.

'It is the tree of life,' said Father Olmedo proudly.

Heads hung between the leaves – saints and prophets and the Mother of God.

Father Olmedo peered down at her.

'What can I do for you, Isobel?'

She tried to be cool, as if nothing mattered. She begged him to persuade Don Hernán to release Falling Eagle. She spoke as if she were asking for an ordinary gift, cotton or sandals or face paint, not the life of a man.

'Do you mind if I sit?'

She saw now how tired he looked. She put her hand on his shoulder.

'Are you all right, Father?'

He smiled wanly.

'I am tired. There are so many things to do. Your country has exhausted me.'

He wiped the beads of sweat from his forehead. She felt tempted to say that her country had not invited him or his god here.

'I know what you will say, Isobel, and you have reason, but it is not for us to question the ways of the Lord.' He sighed. 'I shall do my best, but I fear Don Hernán's mind is quite made up on this subject.'

'There is something else.'

She told him of Falling Eagle's confession. He took her hands gently.

'Falling Eagle did not mean to kill your father. Many threw stones that day. How can he be sure that it was his that struck the Emperor.'

'He says so.'

'He feels guilt. No doubt he threw a stone. Who knows where it went?'

She tried to smile. Father Olmedo always made her feel better.

'Why does Don Hernán refuse to release Falling Eagle?'

'He is a threat,' said Father Olmedo sadly. 'There are thousands of Mexica who would rally to his cause. I know they wait out there.

I have seen them. They pretend to be Christian, but I know that some of them still worship the old gods. I hope you do not.' He glared at her.

'Oh no, Father. I pray every day to the Virgin.'

She crossed herself quickly.

'Good, good. Then with you at least I have succeeded. I hope that you will help bring the word of the true God to all your people. Their situation saddens me. I have struggled to help them. But I see, too, Don Hernán's predicament. He rules here now. He cannot allow any rebellion. The consequences would be terrible for all of us.'

'Worse than what we have already endured?'

'Worse for your people. I do not wish to see them annihilated. I am sad to see so many die of disease and I pray daily for their souls.'

'Why did you ever come here?' asked Jewel bitterly. 'You have destroyed us. Our people did not starve. They did not beg.'

'Some were sacrificed,' pointed out Father Olmedo.

'Not my people,' she replied.

'Others then? Do you not think they suffered or have you not thought about it?'

She had not thought about it. She had not asked questions.

'More die now than ever died on the temples.'

'Maybe, but that does not excuse it.'

He coughed. She saw how thin he was.

'Father, you are ill.'

'No, just tired. I confess I do not look forward to travelling to Honduras. I have tried to persuade Don Hernán against it. And when we are away I know there will be trouble here in the city. Don Hernán has enemies among his own people. There might be fighting. You must be careful. Stay with your husband. He will protect you.'

Now she felt afraid all over again.

'You will try to help Falling Eagle.'

'I will try, Isobel. I always admired him. I promise I will try my best.'

She saw beads of sweat on his forehead. His hands shook when he said goodbye. She hugged him fondly. He felt as if his bones would crack.

It was the last time she ever saw him. He died that night in his bed of the sweating sickness. He was twenty-eight years old.

The expedition left two weeks later. Don Hernán took a retinue of servants, a steward, two toastmasters, a butler, cooks, a chamberlain and a doctor, a surgeon and several pages. He took eight grooms for the horses and two falconers. He took musicians and jugglers, dancers and harpists. He took a priest. He took packhorses to carry his silver cutlery. Four Mexica lords, including Handful of Reeds, accompanied him on horseback. Doña Marina rode at his side on a black horse. As they passed through the streets everyone prostrated themselves. Jewel pushed herself to the front of the crowd and held Leonor up as Don Hernán rode past.

When the slaves approached, linked together in a chain, the crowd fell silent. They stared at Falling Eagle. He walked proudly. Although he limped, he did not stumble like the others. He met the crowd's gaze.

'Save us, Falling Eagle!' shouted an old man.

A group of women knelt in the dust.

'You are our ruler!'

A young woman who ran out and touched Falling Eagle, found herself kicked and beaten by Spanish soldiers.

'Traitors!' screamed the crowd. They surged forward but were held back by guns.

Jewel willed Falling Eagle to look at her. And then just as he went by, he turned his head and saw her. He smiled his cheeky smile and then he was gone.

The blackness came two days after everyone had left. Jewel could not sleep. She sat awake all night thinking of the past and spent all day wondering about the future. She neglected her house and her child. Her father appeared in her dreams.

'Revenge me, Jewel. Falling Eagle is a murderer.'

She covered her ears and screamed. 'Leave me alone.'

Ant Flower and Wandering Coyote would not leave her alone. When Pedro was away, Ant Flower slept in her room and Wandering Coyote, who acted as nursemaid to Leonor, followed her around the house. And then one night she felt Quetzalcoatl's breath and woke to find the shutters flapping in a cold north wind. Some nights Tlaloc wept his tears on the earth and Huitzilopochtli called for revenge. She slipped out of her bed, knelt on the floor and prayed to the new merciful God. And then came the shaking, the shivering. As she fell to the floor she heard the sound of the wind and the water as the earth rushed up to envelop her.

When she recovered she looked at her room with fresh eyes – at the heavy carved furniture and the brocade curtains that shut out the light, at the carpets on the floor and the paintings of the Virgin, at the patterned tiles and the Spanish pottery.

'Take them away!' she screamed.

They thought her mad, but they removed the curtains. They replaced the bed with a simple mat on the floor and the heavy carved chests with a wicker basket. All the pictures of the Virgin went and it their place she hung a Mexica wall covering in bright colours and filled the alcoves with flowers.

They told her she had been ill for six weeks. The priest had given her the last rites. They told her that Juan Cano had enquired daily about her health.

She sat in her garden. Slowly the dreams vanished and in their place she heard her father tell her to live, to help her people, to forgive Falling Eagle. A struggle for power was taking place in the city. Tenochtitlán became a city for the greedy and the ambitious. The first time she had ridden out in her litter she had to cover her nose for the lake smelt like a latrine. The Spanish were not as particular as the Mexica and used its water for their bodily functions. There were no longer three crops a year in the fields and in the floating gardens. But as the population had dropped dramatically, shortage of food was not yet a problem. If the Mexica suffered hunger in their own land it was not because of lack of food but because their rulers did not care whether they lived or died. And many of the workers in the city were people from outside the valley, people who had been conquered by the Mexica.

'Be thankful you have a husband to protect you,' said Ant Flower firmly. 'You will not be forced from your home. You have rights, Lady. You can thank your father for that.'

Jewel knew she was lucky. Pedro did not trouble her much. His love making, now she was better, was a chore she had to endure, but he was often away inspecting her lands. One day, as he was leaving, she asked to ride with him. She had heard that her own people slaved in her fields to give her the wealth that surrounded her. She wanted to see for herself.

'You ride a horse?' He looked at her shiny clothes and her delicate slippers and roared with laughter.

'Doña María does.'

'She has ridden since she was three.'

Sometimes he stayed away longer than expected. Jewel heard rumours of a woman newly arrived from Spain. Some of the Mexica women, married under Christian law, now found themselves cast aside. Jewel feared for her daughter. What if Pedro took her lands and married another woman? What were her rights?

She asked Juan Cano when she slipped out and met him in the gardens, as she often did, for she enjoyed his company. He promised to look into the matter. He said if necessary, he would write to the king in Spain, but with Don Hernán away, there was much corruption and greed in the city. The laws were unenforceable. He regretted how her people suffered. At least Don Hernán had brought some kind of control. He urged her to be careful. He insisted she remain at home.

Don Hernán did not return by Christmas. Jewel went out to Mass in Father Olmedo's new church. Here the golden angels smiled and the saints in the branches hovered protectively over her. But outside in the rubbish-filled streets her people suffered disease and malnutrition. On her way home she saw a beggar boy kicked as he lay in the gutter. She stopped her litter and ran through the mud to help but found herself surrounded by hostile Mexica who pulled at her clothes and taunted her. One of them tugged at her gold necklace. She rushed back to the safety of her litter and made her bearers run so fast over the causeway to Coyoacan that her litter swung from side to side, threatening to eject her into the lake. She had become a stranger in her own country.

She knew it would be a long wait before Don Hernán returned. She must be patient. She wished that Father Olmedo were still alive. She could always talk to him, even of the doubts she now felt. It was strange. The more Lizard spoke of God, the less she desired his god, but she could speak of this to no one.

When Don Hernán did not return in the spring of 1526 his enemies declared him dead. They confiscated his houses and estates and tortured and murdered his relations. They strutted through the streets as if they owned them and sometimes they stopped in front of Jewel's house and measured its size with their hands as if they were plotting to take it, for Don Pedro was seen as Don Hernán's man. And Ant Flower reported how some of the women whose men had accompanied Don Hernán had lost their homes. Many of them starved. They were not married as she was.

'We must shelter them here,' insisted Jewel.

'Don Pedro will not like it.'

'This is my house.'

'He is your husband. He has to be careful. We could take some of them food. That might not be noticed.'

But Don Pedro was so preoccupied that he did not notice how his food bills rose weekly, though he demanded that the carved bed and furniture be brought back and he replaced the brocade curtains. He had never liked the tinkling bells. He gave Jewel a new and larger statue of the Virgin and a special chair for praying.

In July, the old month of the Great Feast of the Lords, Lizard called to say goodbye. He no longer wished to remain in the city.

He was on his way to Vera Cruz to follow his friend Juan to Spain where he would train as a priest. He had grown tall for a Mexica. Without his scars he would be considered handsome. He had something of Woman Snake's wit but with none of his awkwardness.

He brought his precious books which he dared not show to the newly arrived priests. He asked Jewel to protect them for him. In his books he had recreated the old world of the Mexica. As Jewel pored over the black and white drawings with their colour washes, she was drawn back into the world of her childhood when everything seemed so safe and orderly. But, she supposed, the sacrificial victims – for that is how she saw them now – did not share her happy memories. The books helped pass the time and gave her pleasure. It was another link with her father. She asked whether he believed in the Spanish God.

'I believe He has saved me for a purpose,' Lizard told her.

'What about our gods?'

'Superstitions, Jewel. Cruel superstitions.'

'How can you change so quickly?'

'I have thought hard about all these things. I spoke often with Father Olmedo. I do not condone everything the Spanish do here and I shall challenge them when I return well versed in their ways.'

'I wish I could believe like you, Lizard, or should I call you Diego?'

'I have got used to Diego.'

'Until your return then?'

'I will return.'

He embraced her like a Spaniard and told her that if she had any problems while he was away she was to contact Angry Turkey.

'A Tlaxcalan?'

'We are the same in God's eyes,' he replied, his eyes twinkling.

She was sorry to see him go. All the links with the old days were breaking and there were no real friends to replace them. The Spanish ladies who came to drink chocolate and play cards, pretended to enjoy her company and asked about the old days. They cooed over Leonor but they were grateful that their own children were pure-bred and not bastards. And then even the ladies ceased to call and there were no visitors and only Juan Cano stayed loyal, meeting her in her own garden. And then Wandering Coyote reported that Pedro had a new woman, Spanish, greedy for gold and land. He had followed Pedro on his last visit to Jewel's estates where the couple strolled hand in hand, estimating the value of this year's crop.

'She is not as beautiful as you, Lady Jewel,' said Wandering Coyote in an attempt to reassure her.

'But she is Spanish!' she reminded him.

She felt uneasy. What if she should lose all this and her lands? She would no longer be able to help her people. Would she be exiled to a convent? Ant Flower put her arms around her.

'I shall pray for Don Pedro's death.'

'That is a sin, Ant Flower.'

'Not with my gods.'

Don Pedro was a healthy man who showed no signs of sickness. He ate and drank heartily and used her roughly. Jewel knew he wanted her lands and he remained away for months at a time. Her only comfort was her daughter. At night, to settle the child, Jewel would tell her stories of her people, of how the earth was made and how the sun and the moon fought for domination over the world, and how this fight would go on until the very end of time, and how they lived in the fifth and last period which could end at any moment. And sometimes, when Pedro was away, holy men would visit and read the grains in a bowl of water or open their books to study the future. Jewel knew this was superstition but she always prayed afterwards and she knew that God forgave her, as he always did. She wondered whether Don Hernán and Marina and Falling Eagle had all been murdered by barbarians in those festering jungles.

Then, one day, when it was almost Christmas and Leonor was two and a half years old and walking, she heard drums and a servant ran in to announce that Don Hernán had returned.

Coyoacan – 1527

Marina called first. She brought her son Martín, who played in the garden with Leonor. Marina was gaunt and drawn, her skin burnt by the sun. Her eyes seemed swollen from weeping. Her face was covered in bites and sometimes she shivered as if she suffered a fever. She sat down in the chair like someone who had forgotten chairs. She even refused chocolate. She took a dirty lace handkerchief from the pocket in her skirt. She could hardly look Jewel in the face.

'I am sorry, Lady Jewel. I am so sorry.'

She sobbed until the lace handkerchief was saturated and she used her skirt, like one of the women in the villages.

'Falling Eagle is dead?'

'Yes.'

The sun emerged from behind a cloud and pierced the shutters. A shaft of light fell on the red and yellow rug on the floor.

'I shall start at the beginning,' said Marina. 'The journey was terrible. Mosquitoes and flies tormented us. There were snakes and scorpions. We had to hack our way through dense forests. We had to forge many rivers, some of them so fast that several of us drowned within the first month. Hernán took it all so badly. You know how he is, how he likes to be in charge and he will never admit to mistakes. I thought God punished us for our greed.' She crossed herself. 'We suffered hunger, thirst, disease, mutiny. There was nothing we did not suffer. Then we ran out of food and water and we became lost, wandering around in that torpid green hell, following the sun or the stars when we could see them through the foliage. Sometimes we found cities of the dead hidden in that jungle. Their spirits haunted us. The monkeys there scream like dying men and the birds quarrel all the time. Everything there fights with itself, as we did. I visited Falling Eagle every night and sometimes I would find extra food for him. Falling Eagle spoke often of you. He loved you. He was a valiant man. I regret how I have helped destroy the Mexica.'

'It is too late for regrets,' said Jewel. She could forgive Marina. But she could never forgive Hernán.

'I cannot rid myself of them,' continued Marina. 'I hated the Mexica. My mother, who was Mexica, sold me as a slave when I was eleven. I have been used badly by so many men. I hated the Mexica with such bitterness that I felt I could kill you all. Hernán offered me a new life, a new name and a future. Now I hate him almost as much as I hated the Mexica.'

'Hate him. Why?'

'Something changed him in that forest. It was as if demons invaded his mind. He started drinking pulque, anything that made him drunk. You know he always drank sparingly. He mixed water with his wine. This was a different Hernán. His men tried to reason with him but he became violent. Even with me he was violent. I feared he would kill me like he killed his wife.'

'Did he kill his wife?'

'I did not think so at the time. But there, in that forest, I began to wonder. It was as if he hated himself for taking us all there. His temper became terrible. It was when he killed Falling Eagle that the Devil came out in him. He called Falling Eagle a traitor. He hung him from one of those huge silk cotton trees which has its roots in the underworld and its leaves in heaven. It protects all who shelter under it.' She began to cry.

Jewel put her face in her hands. She did not want to hear any more. But Marina continued. These were words she had rehearsed for months and she wanted to use them, if only to clear her own conscience.

'This was no tree of shelter, although we had slept under it. This was a tree of death. The priest confessed Falling Eagle. Had Father Olmedo been with us, things might have been different. He always had a good influence on Don Hernán. I am not sure whether Falling Eagle believed in the true God or whether he confessed to the old gods. There was almost a riot among the men. None of them wanted to kill Falling Eagle. They were so angry with Hernán, I thought they might kill him. Falling Eagle told me he thought of you to the very end, that he flies to the sun to join the warriors, for this hanging could be considered a sacrifice. He died bravely . . .' She hesitated.

'Tell me everything,' insisted Jewel. 'I want to know the truth.'

'Don Hernán hacked off his head and stuck it to that tree. For days we had to look at Falling Eagle's eyes staring at us. The men rebelled. They refused to agree to anything Hernán commanded. Bernal Diaz said he would write it all down in that diary of his so that future generations could read about Hernán's cruelty. Hernán exploded. He tried to burn that diary . . .' Again she hesitated. 'And then, without warning, he ordered me to marry.'

'Who?'

'Juan Jaramillo. He was drunk at the time. He did not know what he was doing. He could neither agree nor refuse. He mumbled the words and the priest married us. And then he returned to his drinking. I am Doña Marina Jaramillo. It is true that I have lands and pos-sessions, without which even Juan Jaramillo would not have married me. He would prefer a Spanish woman. He has told me that. And I am expecting Hernán's child.'

'You are sure it is Hernán's?'

'I knew before I married, yet it will bear Jaramillo's name. Hernán is to return to Spain to marry a young Spanish girl. His father has planned it for him. I am truly sorry about Falling Eagle. I tried my best to protect him.'

'I knew something like this would happen,' said Jewel, 'but I thought it would be disease. I never thought Hernán would kill him.'

'You will see a change in him. He is possessed. He dresses like a monk and he prays all day for forgiveness. He fears hell and damnation.'

She stared out through the window where Wandering Coyote watered the plants in the courtyard.

'I shall have a garden. Even if my husband hates me, I shall find pleasure there.'

Jewel no longer had any tears left in her body. She had cried them all for Falling Eagle at their last meeting. For her, he had died then. But at least he had loved her.

'I, too, am pregnant with my husband's child.'

'How our lives coincide.'

'Then can you forgive me for my rudeness? Can we be friends?'

Malinalli smiled weakly.

'With pleasure, Lady Jewel. I have need of a friend.'

'I am Isobel now.'

'Hernán has given me Chapultepec. I know that was your home when you were young. I did not choose it. He has also given me your gardens at Coyoacan. I have accepted both for my children's sake.'

'They are no longer mine. Are you sure you would not like some chocolate?'

'Yes, I think I will,' said Marina. 'There is something else I should tell you. Before he died Falling Eagle told Hernán that the world would remember him as a hero whereas Hernán would be forgotten, a villain. You can imagine how this angered Hernán. You see, he fears for his reputation.'

Jewel did not reply. She opened the shutters onto the garden where the children were playing. 'See how they are like brother and sister.'

'They are brother and sister,' Marina reminded her.

They both laughed. The chocolate arrived. The two children ran in to claim their share.

Jewel did not recognise the old man in black robes who sat in the chair. His face was haggard. His hair had turned grey. He muttered witlessly.

'I have sinned, Isobel. I have sinned. May the Lord forgive me.'
He held out his prayer book. 'I have prayed day and night for
forgiveness. Do you think our Lord will forgive me? Will he spare
me from hell and damnation?'

She saw that Don Hernán was shivering.

'You are ill?'

'I have a fever. It strikes me from time to time. I still see his
face you know. He hung from that tree and stared at me. He was
a traitor but he did not deserve such a death.'

He hung his head in his hands. She saw that he wore battered
sandals on his feet. His hands were covered in insect bites.

'I shall do penance. I shall fast and wear a hair shirt. I shall
retreat to a monastery until I am forgiven.'

He stood and walked towards the garden.

'I admired your father's gardens. I was sorry we had to destroy
them. One day I will restore them. I regret that I destroyed everything. You know I wanted to take the city intact. It was the most
beautiful city in the world but Falling Eagle put up too good a
fight. Had he surrendered we would have spared the city.'

'You would have killed him then, wouldn't you?'

He looked at her.

'I do not know. Truly I do not know. Part of me admired him
but I had to take the city. My temper was more even then. This
country has changed me. Now it takes its revenge.'

'This country has given you wealth.'

'Nothing counts on the final journey.'

'You could return it to my people.'

He clicked his fingers. His eyes stared vacantly.

'Do you wish to see your daughter? She is like you.'

He smiled weakly. 'Later perhaps. I shall always support her. You
know she will be treated as well as my other children.'

'You only have two.'

He fingered his rosary.

'There will be more when I marry. Did you love him?'

She turned away so he could not see her tears.

'We were cousins who were fond of each other.'

He stood close to her. His breath smelt sour.

'I am sorry. I repent all the time.'

She saw that he was shivering again.

'You need a doctor.'

'He died in that festering jungle along with the others.'

He shuffled to the doorway like an old man. His limp seemed more pronounced.

'You were exquisite, Isobel. When I first saw you with your father, how I wanted you. It is my misfortune to desire many women and love none.'

'Even Marina.'

'Even Marina. I have married her to a Spaniard. It will protect her.'

'And you? What will you do?'

For the first time he seemed enthusiastic.

'I return to Spain to marry a good Christian woman, a noblewoman. I will bring her here to my lands at Cuernavaca. She will be my salvation. Tell me Isobel. Do you think history will remember me kindly?'

'My people will not. You have taken their lives from them. You have taken their city, their culture, their language, their gods.'

'Their gods!' he shouted. 'I have brought them the true God. What better gift is there?'

'They did not ask for it.'

He seemed hurt by her reply.

'You, too, argue with me, Isobel. I am worn out. I have tried my best to sort out this desperate land.'

'It was not desperate until you came here.'

He covered his head with his hood and limped out.

The news reached them in the middle of the night. Don Pedro had fallen from his horse. There was no time to find a confessor. And Flower stood in her nightclothes and grinned.

'We have no protector now,' said Jewel.

'Something will turn up,' said Ant Flower.' At least Don Pedro cannot steal your lands for that other woman of his. Perhaps you could choose your own husband now.'

If only she could. She would choose Falling Eagle.

Pedro's body was brought back into the city for burial. Mercifully there was no sign of the other woman. No one claimed Jewel's lands. No one forced her to marry again.

Some weeks after the funeral Juan Cano called at the house. He brought a letter from the King of Spain. They sat down together in the parlour. Ant Flower fetched chocolate, for Don Juan liked the drinks of the Mexica.

'My condolences, Lady, for the death of your husband.'

He held out the letter.

'I cannot read it.'

'Then, with your permission I will read it to you. You see the King of Spain judges in your favour. Your lands are your own. No one can take them from you.'

'No one?'

'No one.'

She laughed. She jumped up and whirled like a woman of joy, dancing and spinning until her black skirts spread out around her like the petals of one of her father's dahlias. She forgot she was heavy with pregnancy. He laughed too.

'I am pleased to see you so happy, Doña Isobel.'

'How can I thank you?'

'With your company, Lady. With your permission I shall call and we shall take chocolate together. Perhaps I could teach you to read?'

'Yes. Oh yes!' she cried. 'After my child is born.' She held her stomach protectively. 'It is due soon.'

He kissed her hand. Ant Flower showed him out.

'I like Don Juan,' she said when she returned. 'He may be Spanish but I have always liked him.'

'Then you will not pray for his death?'

'Never, Lady. I shall pray for happier times.'

Epilogue

New Spain in the year of our Lord 1551
The Last Will and Testament of Doña Isobel Cano
written in her own hand

In the name of the Father, Son and Holy Ghost, the one and only God who lives and reigns for ever, I write this, my last will and testament. I am forty-seven years old and know I will not live much longer.

I leave all my lands and my farms to my husband, Juan Cano, who has supported me and fought for my rights. I am the only living child of the Lord Montezuma whose death I witnessed when I was fifteen, whose gods I abandoned for the true God. I know my husband will leave my lands to my sons, Pedro, Gonzalo and Juan. I leave my jewels to my daughter, Leonor Cortés. She will also inherit lands from her father, Hernán Cortés. I leave nothing to my two other daughters, Isobel and Catalina, who serve Our Lady in the Convent of the Conception, for they have no need of earthly posses-sions.

I leave a portion to my dwarf, Ant Flower, who outlives me and who has served me faithfully for all these years. I know my husband will take care of her until the Lord sees fit to take her. It is my regret that she remains loyal to the false gods of my people.

I die a true Christian without regret, for I have finally found the true path and therein my happiness. I have had five husbands, three of them Christian men. I have been happy with my fifth and last husband, Juan Cano. It pleases me to know that, with his guidance, I have finally mastered the qualities of decorum, humility and modesty. I have at last become like my mother.

I remember to the day of my death my father Montezuma, God rest his soul, and my husband Falling Eagle, who is still in my heart, although I can no longer see his face. I regret we will never be reunited for he did not find the true God, and I pray for his soul. I pray, too, for the soul of my friend Wandering Coyote, who worshipped no gods and died in my house.

I die with some regrets. Although I have fought for my people and they are now Christian, they remain poor in the land of their ancestors. They are invisible and their voice is not heard. They till the earth and cut the corn, but it is no longer theirs. I have failed to protect them. I pray on my deathbed to the true God to save them and give them back their honour and to spare them from the diseases that ravage them.

Finally I pray for the soul of my friend and sister Marina, who did not live to see her daughter marry or her son Martín become a page to the King of Spain. I pray, too, for the soul of my cousin Diego Lizard, whose painted books I still have here. They record the customs of my people. My husband promises they will never be destroyed. They are a memorial to Lizard who spent much of his life bringing the true God to his people and whose time and place of death will never be known.

I think of my soul as a small bird that will fly to heaven and sip the nectar of paradise. My father called me his little bird.

I confess my sins and I pray to the Lord to forgive me and to receive my soul.

Isobel de Cano, Jewel of Montezuma

Glossary

Ahuehuete trees – *old man of the water*. These magnificent cypress trees are related to the sequoia. Many remain in Chapultepec Park in modern Mexico City, and some are reputed to be over a thousand years old.

Chacmool – *great jaguar paw*. A polychrome, reclining human figure, supported on its elbows, its head turned at an angle of 90 degrees. Its chest supported bowls used as receptacles for human hearts. It was often sited on the top platform of the pyramid in front of the shrines.

Coatlicue – *Snake Skirt*, the old Earth Goddess – was Huitzilopochtli's mother. Among her many children was Huitzilopochtli's sister, Coyolxauhqui, the moon, who competed daily with her brother for domination of the world.

Eagle and Jaguar Knights – these were the top positions in the Aztec military orders. Montezuma's councillors would have belonged to these orders as would Montezuma himself, although such positions could also be earned by prowess in battle. A Jaguar Knight dressed in a tightly fitting suit of jaguar skin with a helmet like a jaguar's head. An Eagle Knight's helmet resembled an eagle's beak.

Huitzilopochtli – *Hummingbird on the Left*, a warrior god, the chief god of the Mexica, brought with them on their migration to central Mexico. Associated with sun, fire and rulers, he needed the 'food of life', human hearts and blood, to strengthen him for his daily fight against darkness.

Patolli – is a game much like a modern board game. The board, a cross within a square, was often carved onto flat stones or plaster floors. In the case of the Mexica, the board was painted onto mats. Counters were made of sticks, beans and bones. Players gambled and sometimes even sold themselves into slavery to pay their debts.

Pulque – an alcoholic drink made from the fermented sap of the agave.

It was drunk mainly at religious festivals. The Aztecs strictly controlled drinking and public drunkenness was often punished by death.

Quetzalcoatl – the Feathered Serpent – a benevolent god from ancient Central America, associated with wind. During the course of his struggle with his rival Tezcatlipoca, the universe was created and destroyed four times (the Mexica believed they were living in the fifth and last cycle of time). In legend, Quetzalcoatl is confused with a king of Tula, Topiltzin, a ruler who banned human sacrifice. In the legend, Quetzalcoatl-Tolpitzin promised to return after his exile in the year One Reed. Patron god of the schools for noble boys, he was an important influence on the rulers of Tenochtitlán.

Tepuli – the word for penis. There are several different ways of spelling this. I have chosen the simplest.

Tezcatlipoca – Smoking Mirror, God of the Night Sky – a powerful ancient Central American god associated with change, conflict and war. He was eternally young and could see the whole world in his obsidian mirror. He could bring life or death as he chose and would sometimes appear on earth in human form. Any sighting of him was a sign of disaster.

Time – The Central American idea of time was cyclical. The Mexica had two calendars, one based on the solar calendar with 365 days. This was divided into eighteen months of twenty days with five nameless or unlucky days at the end of the year. A calendar of 260 days was used for prediction and divination and for religious festivals. Dates repeated themselves every fifty-two years

Tlaloc – He Who Brings the Rain, was the Central American god of rain and lightning. The sculptures depict him with goggle eyes and jaguar teeth. He was believed to live in caves and children were sacrificed to him. He brought life-giving rain but, when angered, retaliated with floods, lightning, snow and frost. An important shrine to Tlaloc existed on top of Mount Tlaloc, the ruins of which still exist today.

336

Select Bibliography

Warwick Bray, *Everyday Life of the Aztecs*, B.T. Batsford, 1968.
C.A. Burland, *Montezuma, Lord of the Aztecs*, Weidenfeld & Nicolson, 1972.
David Carrasco, *City of Sacrifice*, Beacon Press, Boston, 1999.
Maurice Collis, *Cortés and Montezuma*, New Direction Books, New York, 1999.
Nigel Davies, *The Aztecs*, The History Book Club, 1973.
Nigel Davies, *The Ancient Kingdoms of Mexico*, Penguin, 1990.
Bernal Diaz, *The Conquest of New Spain*, Penguin, 1963.
Inga Glendinnen, *Aztecs*, Cambridge University Press, 1991.
Gary Jennings, *Aztec*, Avon Books, 1980 [a novel].
Miguel Léon-Portilla ed., *Broken Spears*, Beacon Press, Boston, 1992.
Miguel Léon-Portilla and Earl Shorris, *In the Language of Kings – An Anthology of Mesoamerican Literature – Pre-Columbian to the Present* W.W. Norton, New York, 2001.
Jon Manchip White, *Cortés and the Downfall of the Aztec Empire*, Hamish Hamilton, 1971.
Mary Miller and Karl Taube, *An Illustrated Dictionary of the Gods and Symbols of Ancient Mexico and the Maya*, Thames & Hudson, 1993.
Laurette Sejourné, *Burning Water: Thought and Religion in Ancient Mexica*, Thames & Hudson, 1957.
Michael E. Smith, *The Aztecs*, Blackwell, 1996.
Jacques Soustelle, *Daily Life of the Aztecs*, Stanford University Press, 1961.
Hugh Thomas, *The Conquest of Mexico*, Pimlico, 1994.
Hugh Thomas, *Who's Who of the Conquistadors*, Cassell, 2000.
Richard F. Townsend, *The Aztecs*, Thames & Hudson, 1992.
Michael Wood, *Conquistadors*, BBC Worldwide, 2000.